DARK MIRROR

A Zee & Rico Mystery: Book 2

Terri Maue

Kenmore, WA

A Camel Press book published by Epicenter Press

Epicenter Press
6524 NE 181st St.
Suite 2
Kenmore, WA 98028

For more information go to:
www.Camelpress.com
www.terrimaue.com

Cover design by Scott Book
Design by Melissa Vail Coffman

Dark Mirror

Library of Congress Control Number: 2025942363

ISBN: 978-1-68492-272-7 (Trade Paper)
ISBN: 978-1-68492-273-4 (eBook)

*To Toni, who opened the door to the authors' world,
and then pushed me through it. Heart of a warrior,
soul of a trickster, mother to so many of us, thank you.*

ACKNOWLEDGMENTS

IT DOESN'T TAKE A VILLAGE TO produce a book; it takes a world, maybe several worlds. Thanks to Toni Pacini and Sin City Writers, who welcomed and encouraged me when I moved to Las Vegas. Thanks to Tonya Todd, my deep critique partner, whose incisive analysis invariably improved my storytelling. Thanks to Gregory Kompes, Paul Atreides, Richard Hendrickson, and all the members of The Writer Workshop, who gave me valuable perspectives and listened to rough drafts and revisions with equal attentiveness and focus.

Thanks to Jennifer McCord at Epicenter Press, whose support gave me free rein to play with my story. Thanks to line editor Nathan Chu, whose insightful questions and comments improved the book in ways I never imagined. And thanks to everyone at Camel Press, including the cover designers, interior designers, and everyone involved in the arcane, mysterious process of turning a Word document into an actual book. My undying gratitude!

Special acknowledgment to my neighbor Brooke, who suggested I check out the pastry at Le Café du Val in Las Vegas. Thanks to Brooke, Zee (and I) delighted in an outstanding apple raisin walnut strudel.

Thanks to my husband Eddie, who brainstorms with me, puts up with my writing obsession, and feeds me delicious incredible food. Thanks to my parents, who valued reading, especially my dad, who gave me my love of the mystery genre. And thanks to you, my readers, who embraced book one of the series with such enthusiasm that I dove into book two with eagerness and joy.

I know there are countless others. I stand on their shoulders, and any sun that shines on my face, shines because of them.

Finally and most of all, I am full of gratitude for the Divine gift of writing, which has enriched my life beyond measure, which I did nothing to deserve, and which I hope I use to bring enjoyment to many people.

CHAPTER 1

A COLD MARCH WIND SLICED THROUGH ZEE Morani's navy pantsuit as she fast-limped toward the Imperial Arms Condominiums and her interview with best-selling author Bette de la Cornne.

Late.

At least she would be if she didn't will her body to move faster.

A rooster crow erupted from her phone. The five-minute warning. Damn.

If the rumors about de la Cornne were true, wet roads and thoughtless drivers—who ought to know how to navigate the rain-slick streets of southwestern Ohio—would not get much sympathy from the notoriously intolerant author. Although surely it wasn't true that she'd once hung up on a reporter who was two minutes late with his scheduled call.

A barb of pain shot through Zee's hip. She shortened her stride. Her tightly-wrapped knee demanded a slower gait, as did the twitching muscles in her lower back, but slowing further was out of the question.

She grimaced. This was what she got for wrestling with a murderer—the price she paid for her *last* high-profile interview.

Remembered dread poked beneath her barely healed ribs. Shoving it aside, she pulled open the door to the building. She didn't have time for dredging through the past. Besides, no way was she going to walk in on another dead body.

Her throat constricted at the image of his wide, horrified eyes, his slashed throat dripping scarlet onto the floor in his office. She hissed through her teeth. That was six months ago. Not here. Not now.

Swallowing a hard knot, she pressed the burnished elevator button. In just a few minutes, she would be interviewing the very much alive Bette de la Cornne. A popular author, one nobody would want to kill, except—

Even a year after its release, her highly controversial book still sparked internet rage.

Selfish bitch

Destroying the foundations of society

Sold her own soul

All anonymous, of course. Zee snorted. People hyped stuff just to get attention. All the more reason not to take them seriously.

Teeth gritted, she glared at the pale green *Up* arrow and resisted the urge to stab it again. She shot a glance toward the stairs, but her stiff knee objected.

A frown creased her lips. She wouldn't be in this predicament if the persnickety author hadn't canceled two earlier appointments. Now, she had only a few hours to meet her deadline. And pack for her weekend at the spa, a task she thought she'd have plenty of time for, except for the cursed traffic problems.

When the elevator doors finally glided open, she all but bolted inside and smacked the second-floor button. *Breathe*, she told herself.

Her hand strayed to her hair. Humidity inspired her mass of curls to explode in all directions. Knowing it made little differ-ence, she patted at it anyway, then grimaced as her jacket bunched around her waist. Maybe this weekend's spa retreat would help her shed a few pounds.

Her phone crowed again. Officially late now, she hoped it wasn't her death knell.

She winced. She hoped it wasn't *anyone's* death knell.

Stop it.

She yanked her thoughts from the ghosts of that other morning. This elevator was empty of other passengers, just as the quiet, tasteful lobby had proffered no staggering murder suspect nor horrified witnesses.

A muted bell announced the end of the car's ascent. Burying her nervousness, Zee exited and traversed a short stretch of thickly carpeted hallway to a door at one end. She paused before the satiny numeral 2. She would project confidence, act as though she'd never heard any of the horror stories about de la Cornne, much less expected to encounter—

Enough!

She tugged the hem of her jacket. Unknotted her stomach. Rapped lightly.

Silence.

What would she do if—

The door swung open to reveal an elegantly coiffed blonde, who though barely chin height to Zee's five-foot-six, filled the space around her with vibrant presence.

Bette de la Cornne.

"Miss Morani. I'm so glad to meet you." No snark. No sarcasm. Bette's southern drawl flowed like honey into Zee's ears. "I'm very much looking forward to talking with you."

Zee covered her relief with a courteous reply. "Thank you for agreeing to the interview."

If Bette noticed any anxiety, she gave no indication. Wrapping Zee's hand in hers, she swept Zee into an elegant, spacious room. "Now you just set up whatever you need, while I get us refreshments from the kitchen." She disappeared through a swinging door, leaving almost visible waves of energy in her wake.

Zee sank into an upholstered chair, dizzied by the warm welcome and slightly stunned to realize she had actually feared to find Bette dead. Swallowing her chagrin, she let her gaze wander the condo, as if by gathering the details, she could ground herself.

Couch and chairs upholstered in sumptuous ivory damask. Two large sunlit windows, framed by pale tapestried drapes with golden ropes and heavy tassels. Gilt-edged mirror above a creamy marble mantel, reflecting an asymmetrical trio of tall gleaming candlesticks. All stylish, sophisticated, and rescued from insufferable chic by the mound of plastic-wrapped, old-time penny candies filling a heavy square dish on the glass-topped coffee table.

"Here we are." Bette set a gold-lacquered tray on the table. "I hope tea is all right. I've had my coffee ration for the day."

Zee laughed, grateful she wouldn't have to politely drink more coffee on top of the three cups she'd already consumed that morning. "We're on the same wave length there."

Bette beamed at her. "I just knew we were sympatico."

Zee returned her smile. She eyed the plate of delicate butter cookies next to the teapot, hoping Bette didn't hear the rumble in her stomach. She shouldn't have skipped breakfast.

To distract her clamoring taste buds, Zee set her phone on the table to record and pulled out her notebook. Her younger colleagues at the newspaper mocked her use of old-fashioned pen and paper, but she could think more clearly when she saw words in front of her.

"Oh, I'm glad to see you take real notes." Bette gestured to the phone. "I don't mind if you record, but there's somethin' comfortin' about seeing a writer, well, write."

Zee restrained a grin. The way this was going, she'd easily get her front-page story, at least in the Entertainment section of the Valerian *Messenger-Tribune*. Her reporter's antennae quivered. If she could build on this rapport, she might even convince Bette to talk for the first time about Marjorie Franklin, the woman who claimed Bette's book ruined her life. That would be a real coup. Bette had refused—

"Now, where would you like to start?"

Bette's question snapped Zee's galloping mind back to the present. She studied the author's relaxed face. No need for the usual ice-breaker questions. "I'd like to dive right in, if that's okay with you."

"Wonderful." Bette's blue eyes twinkled. "I'm truly weary of dreary chit-chat." She leaned toward Zee. "I feel that I already know you, anyway, from your marvelous column. I dearly love it."

Zee sipped tea to cover her pleasure at the compliment. For such a fabulous writer to express appreciation—

The perfectly brewed oolong caught in Zee's throat. She could not let herself be so effortlessly disarmed, or the interview would yield nothing but a puff piece, hardly worthy of space in the paper much less her byline. "Tell me about writing *The Mirror of the Soul*. The story feels very personal."

"I suppose it is." Bette set her porcelain cup in a saucer. "I grew up in a religious household. I was a good Southern girl, so I tried to obey all the rules. But after a few disastrous relationships, way too much drinking, and Lord knows how many sessions of therapy, I discovered I'd been lied to. Religious trauma, they called it. And like all other trauma, it leaves scar tissue. I wasn't weird or weak. I was suffering."

The response was well practiced, but Zee's heart pinched. She met Bette's eyes. "I'm afraid I know all too well how betrayal leaves its mark." As the words left her mouth, her face heated. She didn't usually volunteer such personal information.

Bette reached across the table and patted Zee's hand. "We are so much alike. Has writing been your way of dealing with pain, too?"

Zee gasped. It was as if Bette read her mind. Unsettled, she tried to backpedal, to say something to resurrect her protective wall, but she could think of no answer but the truth. "Now that you say it, yes. After my fiancé cheated on me, I threw myself into my career." She'd built *Z Beats* into a popular syndicated column, even wrote a very successful book culled from its twice-weekly appearances.

Bette sat back, giving Zee space. "As Thomas Carlyle said, 'Adversity is the diamond dust Heaven polishes its jewels with.'"

She averted her eyes, but not before Zee saw the moisture glimmering there.

Zee's journalist's instinct urged her to exploit this opening, but her heart recoiled. To give Bette time to compose herself, she picked up a butter cookie and bit into it, while pretending to consult her notes. Her awakened taste buds sprang into action, demanding she shove the whole delicacy into her mouth. With some effort, she stayed her hand.

Bette's voice, calm and in control, came to her aid. "You might say the book helped me cast out my devils."

A startling admission. And great quote. Zee's pen leapt across the page. Also, a clue where to go next. "Did you mean to stir antagonism toward religion? Was that the point of the novel?"

A bell-like laugh bubbled from Bette. "Oh goodness, not anythin' so lofty. I just wanted to tell a good story."

Zee kept her tone mild. "Many people feel personally attacked."

"That wasn't my intention. I simply wanted to make them think." Bette cocked her head, the light from a floor lamp haloing her hair. "Isn't that what you do with your satire?"

Zee's hackles rose. "But I focus on corporations, bureaucracies; institutions, not people."

Bette's face clouded. Zee held her breath. She hadn't meant to attack. She opened her mouth, but Bette's blue eyes cleared. "Of course." Her voice was soft with compassion. "And you do a wonderful job. What I meant was that you make people think."

Fire crept up Zee's neck. Bette could have taken offense. "I hope they do," Zee conceded. "And thank you. I didn't mean to jump on you."

Chuckling, Bette laid a manicured hand over her heart. "We're two of a kind. We have to be patient with each other."

Warmth spread through Zee's chest. Bette understood her, embraced her as a colleague with a common purpose. Zee smiled at their kinship. She couldn't wait to introduce her to F—

The leap in her heart startled Zee. She was not there to make friends, no matter how the tug in her chest pulled her toward this personable woman. Besides, Bette probably wasn't looking for friendship. She and Marjorie Franklin had been close friends once. Now Franklin hated her.

Although sorry to dump cold water on her fantasy, Zee would keep this relationship strictly business. And if she hoped to broach the topic of Marjorie, she'd better get to it. Her allotted hour was fast elapsing. "Tell me about how you created your characters."

Bette's eyes narrowed. "As in all fiction, my characters are amalgamations of people I've known or read about or heard of or simply imagined."

Another smooth response, but the words snagged on rocks of disappointment. Zee's chest squeezed.

Bette met Zee's eyes over her teacup. "Any resemblance to actual people is . . . unintentional."

Zee shifted uneasily in the comfortable chair. Professionalism demanded she push. She gentled her voice. "I know you've dismissed threats . . ."

Bette flicked a dismissive hand. "Let's not talk about that. Let me give you the inside scoop on how I created that religious fringe group Lilliana joined."

"Religious Refuge." Zee forced enthusiasm into her response. "Those people were fascinating." She'd try later to work the conversation back to Marjorie Franklin.

"It started out in Las Vegas," Bette said.

The tale she spun was fascinating, told with flair, full of astonishing and often humorous anecdotes. Zee knew readers would eat it up. But she'd been close to a much more powerful story. The ache at missing it was almost physical. And yet, she'd seen no opening to broach again the subject of Marjorie.

"Why did you end the book as you did?" Reluctantly, Zee asked her planned final question.

"Life's not so neat. People should ask themselves hard questions. Don't you agree?"

"I do." Zee took in a deep breath. "And that's why I can't end this conversation without asking you about Marjorie Franklin."

Bette leaned forward and selected a butter cookie. Eyes down, she turned it over in her hands. Zee's pulse beat in her ears. An apology pushed against her lips, but she held back. A murmur of traffic filtered through the sunlit windows.

Sighing, Bette met Zee's gaze. "It's such a sad situation. I trust you to tell the story fairly?"

Zee exhaled. "I'll do my best."

"I met Marjorie when she was fifteen." Bette's lips lifted in a small smile. "I thought Lenore, the woman with Marjorie, was her mother. Marjorie was at the age when girls are looking for identity, especially identity very different from their mothers."

A knot hardened in Zee's chest. She had admired her mother, up until her deathbed confession of infidelity.

"We bonded fairly quickly." Bette's voice pulled Zee from her bitter memory. "I was ten years older than Marjorie, and I think she saw me as a kind of cool aunt. Also, Lenore was already descending into her obsession about religious indoctrination."

Zee scribbled furiously on her notepad, her pen quivering with excitement. "Marjorie's behavior seems understandable."

Bette nodded. "She became my shadow. I admit, I enjoyed her company. She had a quick mind, bright, inquisitive."

"How did Lenore take this?"

"She felt rejected, of course. She was furious." Bette crumbled a bit of cookie onto her plate. "Looking back now, I can see that she was hurt, bitter. They fought a lot, probably like most mothers and daughters."

Zee wouldn't know. She couldn't fight with a dead person, though she certainly raged at her mother. But she didn't respond, and thirteen-year-old Zee had been left with an implacable stone in her heart.

"One day, they had a particularly heated argument. Lenore finally threw up her hands and said Marjorie was an adult and she would have to learn to live with her decisions." Bette laid the cookie on her plate and dusted the crumbs from her hands. "After that, Lenore left. Went back east."

"That must have been awful." A modicum of empathy softened Zee's heart. Marjorie had been abandoned too, in a way. "It put *you* in an unfortunate position."

Bette lifted her shoulders in a delicate shrug. "Frankly, it was all so long ago. I believe I agreed with Lenore that Marjorie should make her own decisions. I do generally take that position."

But Marjorie had probably been barely out of her teens. Zee kept her tone neutral. "So, Lenore left, but you and Marjorie remained close." She infused her voice with sympathetic curiosity. "What went wrong?"

Bette nibbled at a corner of her lip. "I—"

A temple bell tolled from Zee's phone. Fontina's ring tone.

Alarm spiked in Zee's gut. Her unfailingly considerate friend would never call when she knew Zee was doing an interview. The phone tolled again. Torn, Zee shot an apologetic look to Bette and picked up her cell. "Excuse me. I'm so sorry."

"Zee-zee, I didn't mean for you to pick up. I just wanted to leave a message. I need to cancel going to the spa."

"Oh, n—" Zee bit back the rest of her reaction. A wave of disappointment had nearly caused her to miss the uneasiness skittering beneath Fontina's usual calm. Adrenaline drove her to her feet. "Are you all right?"

"Everyone's okay. I'll tell you all about it later. I just needed to let you know in case you want to cancel, too."

Zee squashed her regret. Fontina must have a good reason. But damn, with Rico out of town, this had been the perfect chance to celebrate their 30-plus years of friendship. She forced calm acceptance into her reply. "I appreciate that." Fighting a sense of helplessness, she added, "Let me know if you need anything."

"All will be well." Fontina's voice was husky. "Thanks for understanding. See you at yoga Monday morning."

The phone clicked in Zee's ear. She sank back into the sumptuous chair.

"Is everything all right, hon? We can do this another time."

Bette's concern nearly cracked Zee's composure, but she gathered herself. First things first. "Let's keep going." Hand shaking, she sipped her tea, letting its warmth smooth her tangled emotions.

Bette leaned closer. "You sure? I'll listen if you want to talk."

Zee's hesitation crumbled. Though a voice in her head screamed *unprofessional*, she summarized the call. "I'm just unnerved because Fontina is usually so serene about everything," she concluded.

Bette captured Zee eyes. "Trust your friend." Her tone turned wistful. "Friendship is rare and should not be squandered."

Zee winced and looked away. Though softly spoken, Bette's words cut like barbed wire. She wanted this woman as a friend, but she needed to know what happened to poison the relationship between her and Marjorie. Some hidden, treacherous current had torn them apart.

Besides, Marjorie had dominated the news on this story. It was time to tell Bette's side. Was their falling-out a heart-breaking, unexpected price of success? Zee's adrenaline surged. She could weave in the signposts, the warnings that might help other people avoid such a loss, albeit at a much less dramatic scale. Marjorie and Bette were the hook, but her article could serve a greater good, as her dad—

"Darlin.'" Bette's voice startled Zee. "Why don't you tell me what else is bothering you?"

Zee's throat tightened, but she couldn't stop the truth tumbling out. "I don't usually share this—"

Bette held up a manicured hand. "I'm sorry. That was unforgivably intrusive."

"No." Zee inhaled a deep breath. "You're very perceptive. And kind. I was just thinking about the enormous impact your book has had on people. You told a story that touched a nerve. It addressed an important issue in our society. And I'm thinking about how much *I* want to do that."

"You want to write a novel?" To her credit, Bette's voice held no trace of disbelief.

Zee shook her head. "Not that. I'm a journalist. I mean I want to write big stories. To do investigative work. To influence people to think about important issues in a meaningful way."

"I see." Bette leaned back against the couch, steepling her slender fingers. "What's holding you back?"

"My edito—"

"Not outside." Bette's voice sliced like a knife. "Inside."

Blaming Karl had been on the tip of Zee's tongue, but the knee-jerk response died. Zee met Bette's eyes. Under their magnetic force, her frustration spilled out. "I keep second-guessing myself. I like writing satire. Even if I'm not sure it does any good. I enjoy skewering corporate idiocy. It feels good to be the one standing up for the everyday person against feelingless bureaucracy."

"Nothing wrong with that." Bette cocked her head. "What's the other voice in your head saying?"

"That I should push myself out of my comfort zone, use my skills for greater good, do something worthwhile with my talent." Zee humphed. "I sound like one of my dad's lectures. Maybe I just want to stop feeling bad for not meeting his expectations." Especially now that she had no chance to earn his approval.

Bette raised delicately shaped brows. "Guilt is a poor foundation for action. Like building your house on sand." The blue eyes caught Zee again. "Why don't you believe you can do both?"

"It's Karl, the senior editor, who thinks I can't do it." The objection collapsed, falling limp against Zee's ears. Cheeks afire, she broke from Bette's gaze to set her teacup on the coffee table.

Bette chuckled, a cultured throaty drawl. She patted Zee's hand. "Pay no attention to naysayers, darlin'. Even if they seem to be the ones in control."

Zee had told herself that before, but coming from Bette, the statement jolted like a direct transmission of confidence. Zee's spine straightened. "You're right. That's going to be my new mantra."

Smiling beatifically, Bette raised both hands and pronounced. "So shall it be."

Zee high-fived her, wondering what it was about this woman that made every word resonate like indelible truth.

"Seal it with a candy." Bette gestured to the crystal dish.

"Root beer barrels." Zee grinned. "Yum."

In mid-reach, her phone chimed. Two words appeared on the screen. *Bette Dead.*

"What the—" Zee snatched her phone. "Look at this." She stabbed to open the message but lost her grip. The phone smacked face-down against the sharp corner of the candy dish. With a sickening crack, it flipped, and clattered to the table.

"Don't touch it," Bette commanded. "I'll be right back."

Zee's gaze was riveted on the message staring through the shattered screen.

Bette Dead la Cornne, when nothing's left, there's nothing to lose.

Bette's book had stirred a lot of controversy, but this was truly scary. Zee clenched her teeth, cursing anonymous internet posters.

"Here we go." Bette returned with a pair of tongs. Deftly, she gripped the damaged phone and slipped it into a plastic bag. She slid that bag into another one. "Now you can handle it safely."

Zee accepted the swaddled phone. "Did you see what it said?"

Bette shook her head. "It doesn't matter."

"But it's a death threat."

Bette tossed her blonde curls. "It's probably just more blather from Marjorie Franklin." The sparkle in her eyes faded. "I'm sure you've read about her behavior."

Nothing left to lose. Zee shivered, but here was her opening.

"It's nonsense, of course." Bette twisted a glittering pillow tassel around her thumb. "But I'm sick of it. I tried to be sympathetic, but after a year of this kind of stuff . . ." Dropping the pillow, she flicked pearl-lacquered fingernails, a dismissive gesture both graceful and potent. "As we say in the South, that girl's cornbread ain't done in the middle."

Zee forced herself to join Bette's laughter, but uneasiness wormed in her stomach. "Are you sure you shouldn't report it? I mean, are you safe?"

"Perfectly." From a side table, a chorus of notes erupted. Bette sighed. Her voice held a note of melancholy. "I'm afraid we'll have to stop now." As she stretched to silence her alarm, the harsh glare through the window whitened her face, rendering it doll-like, unexpectedly fragile.

Zee sucked in a breath, but as quickly as the image had appeared, it dissipated. Unnerved, she averted her gaze. Her mind said it had been a trick of the light, but her gut told her otherwise.

From the corner of her eye, Zee studied Bette, who had busied herself briskly setting the teacups onto the tray. No signs of distress.

Zee closed her notebook, smothering her disquiet, turning her thoughts to shaping today's story. She was surprised she felt so little regret at losing the chance to delve further into Franklin, but she had a feeling she'd get another chance.

"I need to . . . let you go now." At the falter in Bette's voice, Zee glanced up.

Bette's veneer cracked. Zee saw her isolation, the walls she'd built to protect herself, and what it cost her. Zee spoke before she fully grasped the idea forming in her mind. "Would you like to go to the spa with me this weekend?"

Bette's brows rose. "Why, I'd truly love that." Her face fell. "But I can't."

"Oh. I understand." Of course, Bette would be busy. "It was foolish to ask, but I just thought . . ."

Bette patted Zee's hand, façade fully restored. "It was a lovely suggestion." She met Zee's eyes. "I'm free Tuesday morning. Could we meet? Perhaps at Schreinhardt's?"

Her favorite bakery. Zee warmed all over. "Absolutely."

They hugged at the door. Though much smaller than Zee, Bette's embrace felt almost like a full-body energy massage. Startled, Zee scanned her limbs. No pain anywhere. No aches, no stiffness, no soreness. In fact, no part of her had hurt anywhere for the past hour. For that astonishing space of time, it was as if she'd been sheltered in Bette's invulnerable aura.

A frisson of fear flickered in Zee's consciousness. Such a spell-like effect could be dangerous.

She stifled a snort. No witchcraft involved. Unlike most people, who are usually distracted, their minds on half a dozen other things, Bette gave a person her undivided attention. That was her superpower, to make someone feel completely seen, accepted, and appreciated.

"See you Tuesday." Bette touched the bag with Zee's fractured phone. "That's probably a blessing in disguise."

Maybe, but Zee already felt its absence, the unsettling sense of being disconnected, unreachable.

"You can really get away from everything now." Bette smiled, a sun banishing Zee's shadows. "Trust me. You're not goin' to miss anything important."

CHAPTER 2

On Monday morning, as Zee wheeled into the parking lot of Schreinhardt's bakery, a spear of sun lanced off the white racing stripes on her Mini Cooper's shiny red hood. She grinned. Despite the stinging pain that crawled from her injured shoulder into her neck, very little could detract from the sheer pleasure of driving her small but mighty Mini.

Except possibly the absence of her cell phone. The empty space in her purse ached like a hollow limb. She'd pick up her cell right after breakfast.

As she pushed open the heavy car door, her hip sent a warning twinge across her lower back. Carefully, she levered herself from the driver's seat, but her still tightly wrapped left knee pinched. Even just finding her balance to stand triggered protests from her aggrieved joints.

She leaned against *Po*. Although the name she gave her car referred to the blind Kung Fu master, these days the implied impediment fit her better than it did the Mini. Maybe today's eight a.m. yoga class wasn't such a good idea.

Seven a.m., grumbled a voice in her head. Stupid Daylight Saving Time. Way to ruin a fine spring day. She tipped her face to the sun, banishing her gloomy thoughts.

In a way, she welcomed her various pains. Each pang strengthened her resolve. She was never, ever, getting involved in another murder investigation.

Framed in front of Schreinhardt's front window, Fontina waited, sunlight burnishing her tawny face and skipping among the ebony braids coiled at her crown. "I would have given you a ride," she chided, pulling the door open. "Yoga is more strenuous than it looks."

"So true," said Zee. "But driving's good for me, psychologically as well as physically." She led the way toward the counter, the nutty aroma of fresh-roasted coffee nuzzling her nose, overriding her hip's pleas to slow down.

Fontina kept pace. "Great story about Bette de la Cornne in yesterday's paper."

Zee smiled. "I'm glad you liked it. A Sunday feature is quite a coup." Even though she hadn't been able to include anything about Marjorie Franklin. "I was surprised when Karl approved it."

"I thought you could write about any topic you chose," said Fontina.

"In my column, but if I want any other space in the paper, I need to pry an okay out of Karl. It's frustrating."

Fontina touched Zee's shoulder. "At least this time, you didn't have to get tangled in another death."

"You have a point. And I made a new friend in Bette."

"Hey, good to see you." Zee's barista buddy Miranda poked her head above the counter. Her pale cheeks whitened. "You're hobbling."

Zee mustered a weak grin. "Yoga rehab." She hooked her thumb at Fontina, tall and lissome in her usual form-fitting workout wear. "Her fault."

"Guilty as charged." Fontina chuckled.

Miranda tossed her asymmetrical locks. A patch of hair flashed neon pink, then disappeared among the black folds. "Good for you, Zee." She brightened. "You're lucky today. We have cherry cheese Danish *and* almond horns."

Zee's taste buds leapt at the mention of her favorites, but her recent resolve to improve her diet quashed their excitement. Not much nutrition in glazed, sugar-laden fruit and delicious parchment layers of butter-infused pastry.

She tore her gaze from the gates of gastronomic heaven. A pile of dense, dark mounds on a cake plate looked heartier, and passably tempting. Maybe what glistened on each broad top was chocolate. She pointed. "What are those?"

Miranda scrunched her nose, then covered with a swift smile. "Going healthy, I see."

"That's the plan." Zee crossed her fingers in her coat pocket.

"We call them Turbo-Muffins." Miranda straightened and recited. "Coarse ground whole wheat, bran, oats, flaxseed, raisins, walnuts, bananas, blueberries, apples, sweetened with honey, drizzled with yogurt-carob frosting, and sprinkled with sesame seeds. Energy to get you through your morning." She sucked in a breath and grinned. "Or to recover from it."

"I'll have one," said Fontina. "And chai, please."

"You got it." Miranda raised a pierced brow at Zee.

Zee tried for enthusiasm. During this past weekend at Lotus Spa, her battered body had sung the *Hallelujah Chorus*. And it delivered a clear desire for more of this tender loving care. For herself, and for Rico and their future together. If they had one.

She shook her head to toss aside incipient anxiety. Right now, she needed to subdue her pastry demons. "Same for me." *Maybe it will taste good*, she told her mutinous stomach. "With coffee."

"Coming right up."

Zee swiveled to escape the frosted flaky sirens beckoning from doily islands. Only one of the polished round tables in Schreinhardt's small eating area was occupied. Two women wearing identical maroon jackets huddled together over the Monday morning paper. On each one's back, *The Gray Gladiators* curved in silver script around the image of a bowling ball.

Zee's shoulder throbbed at the thought of lifting that weight, much less hurling it down an alley. Her eyes slid to a peach Danish that sat untouched beside them, and her stomach wailed in protest. How could they not be devouring that flaky pastry cradle of luscious ripe fruit? If she could bowl, she would definitely—

Jerking her gaze from the women and their scandalous negligence, she gestured at a table near the window. "Let's sit in the sun."

"Works for me." Fontina tossed one end of her shawl over her shoulder as she crossed the room.

Zee limped in her wake. She couldn't help but admire her friend's effortless elegance. Maybe it was the shawl, the way those graceful drapes enfolded Fontina's long limbs. And coral too. Such a vibrant color.

Zee glanced at her own tailored black garment. What was she, a nun?

Grateful to reach her destination, she dropped into a chair. Her dissatisfaction probably stemmed from feeling clumsy. And from denying herself a justly deserved, mouth-watering reward.

She angled her seat to block the sight of the torturous culinary temptation. At once, warmth began to soak into her back.

The tightness in her shoulders relaxed. Dark fabric and beaming sunlight were made for each other, melting together like lovers in delicious union. Her mind flew to Rico, his arms enfolding her, the stubbly caress of his ever-present five-o'clock shadow, his scent of leather and juniper. Heat crept up her neck.

Definitely not a nun.

"Holding up okay with Rico out of town?" Fontina's liquid brown eyes, eyes so like Zee's own, twinkled.

Zee blinked, then shook her head. She should have been accustomed to her friend's uncanny perception. From the moment they'd met in first grade, Fontina had read Zee's soul.

"At first, I was a little upset that he wanted a week away from everything." More images flitted past. His rugged physique astride his Harley in the wilds of southern Kentucky, riding and camping with his motorcycle pals.

Away, he claimed, from the *Messenger-Tribune*'s crime beat.

Away, she feared, from her.

After months of trying to keep him in the friend box, she'd finally acknowledged her feelings. Even gave him back the key to her apartment. She thought he reciprocated, but after the *St. Louis Messenger* bought the *Valerian Tribune*, he became distant, distracted. His deep blue eyes lost their playfulness. His tightened lips forgot how to ease into the smile she loved.

Abruptly aware of Fontina's assessing gaze, Zee loosened her shoulders, swallowing her loneliness. "I get it now, why he wanted to get away. Three days unplugged at Lotus Spa really cleared my mind, although I don't understand why I feel so sore after those heavenly massages."

"You survived a vicious attack."

Not to mention a wrestling match with her dad's beloved barrister bookcase, which she refused to relegate to a dusty, neglected storage locker. Zee quirked her mouth. "I should be healed by now."

Fontina ticked off on her fingers. "Broken ribs, bruised kidneys, torn knee ligament, separated shoulder. Trauma like that gets stored deep in the tissues." Her lips curved upward. "Let Rico help when he gets back tomorrow."

Zee nodded, self-conscious in her naked longing.

Miranda grinned as she set cups and plates on the table. "Still dating that super-hot guy? 'Cause if not . . ." She winked.

"Hands off." Zee swatted air, feigning threat to disguise the knee-jerk twinge of envy for the younger woman.

Miranda danced backward. "I'm no danger to you, believe me." She retreated toward the counter, her laugh trailing behind her like the tinkle of bells.

Hoping her heated cheeks didn't betray her, Zee focused on peeling the wrapper from her muffin. Dry clumps separated and dropped to the plate. She tamped her dismay.

"Pretty good," said Fontina. "I like the crunchy texture."

Zee pinched her thumb and finger around a dark shard and

placed it on her skeptical tongue. In seconds, it disintegrated into granules that coated her teeth with grit and sucked all the moisture from her mouth. Gamely, she chewed. A tiny hard pebble yielded a hint of blueberry. Flaxseed clumped and stuck in her molars. And carob-yogurt did not make a *frosting* of any sort. She grabbed her coffee to wash down the mess.

"Not to your liking?"

Zee pushed aside the plate and tried not to ogle the uneaten peach Danish barely a table's breadth away. "Maybe if I added half a stick of butter and nuked it."

Fontina laughed. "Let's talk about something more pleasant then. I want to hear all the inside scoop about your interview with the famous Bette de la Cornne."

Movement caught Zee's eye. She glanced toward the two women still clutching their newspaper. They looked quickly away. Caught trying to eavesdrop. They probably recognized her from the photo that ran with her story.

She returned her attention to Fontina. "Bette was wonderful. I was surprised at how much fun I had, talking with her. I hadn't exactly looked forward to the interview after reading *The Mirror of the Soul*. Such a miserable story."

"I confess I haven't read it." Fontina broke off another bite of depressingly not-chocolate muffin. "Give me the angels-on-a-pin-head version."

"Challenge accepted." Zee twisted in her chair and stared out the window, composing her thoughts. Their game required she encapsulate the plot in a minute or less.

As if magnetized, her gaze skimmed across the rooftops and anchored on the quartet of granite art-deco angels dominating the skyline. Sentinels with their elongated wings arrowing skyward and their granite robes anchored to the corners of the newspaper building's central tower. Under their watchful gaze, she had learned as an intern to pare extraneous information. Assemble the facts. Prioritize the story.

She faced Fontina. "Ready."

"Go." Fontina tapped start on her timer, and Zee began her summary of de la Cornne's best-seller. "When Lilliana is nine, her parents dump her with her grandparents and join a religious cult. Kid gets a strict but loving upbringing and marries a nice guy.

"Then it gets dark. She blames religion for her parents' abandonment and decides she's been brainwashed like them. She falls in with a radical de-programming group and severs ties with her former life. She leaves her marriage, has an abortion, and falls in love with a woman, who rejects her. Alone, addicted, and sick, she goes to a shelter, but refuses to embrace their religious creed. She returns to the streets and dies."

"Uplifting." Fontina raised her tea in a mock toast. "And well done. Thirty points for you."

Zee touched her cup to Fontina's. "I'm sure that puts me ahead."

"Hah."

Zee swallowed a sip in a weak attempt to quiet her complaining stomach. "It blows my mind that the book sold millions. Life is depressing enough. For entertainment, I want a happy ending, even if it isn't," she hooked her fingers into air quotes, "realistic."

"But despite her gloomy novel, Bette won you over?"

"She's amazing, so full of life; she's like an electric current." On cue, a tingle shot up her spine. "I think her writing touches people because, even though her characters create crazy, painful situations, she treats them with respect."

"Yin and yang," said Fontina. "In the depths of darkness, there is still a seed of light."

"That's it. The possibility of change. Even when they refuse to recognize how irrationally they're behaving."

"A kindred spirit." Fontina eyes twinkled. "You've made a career of calling out that kind of absurdity with your column."

Zee crumbled a piece of muffin. "Maybe that's why we connected so easily. I even told Bette about my frustration with Karl, how he kept undermining my dream to move from writing satire in *Z Beats* to more serious journalism."

Fontina raised her brows. "Wow, you *did* bond. Sounds like the start of a good friendship."

"I hope so." Zee toyed with her cup. "Since you couldn't come to the spa with me, I actually invited her to go. But she couldn't make it, so we settled for having tea together tomorrow."

"About the spa." Fontina's usually untroubled face clouded. "I felt torn, Zee-zee. I didn't want to refuse Roshi Patrik's surprise visit, but that meant I had to cancel with you."

"We can always go again." Zee swiped her hand through the air as if to wipe away Fontina's concern. "Thailand is thousands of miles away. It's not every day you have your beloved Zen teacher within a hug's reach."

Fontina shifted her gaze beyond Zee. She fingered the old coin suspended from a delicate chain around her neck. Uncle Ramiz's coin. He'd been the one to tell her about her psychic gift, in a visit from the other side of the grave. It seemed like she was consulting with him now.

Zee leaned toward her. "What is it?"

"A business situation." Fontina's eyes shadowed. "I may need to make a hard decision."

Fear pinched Zee's gut. This must be serious. Fontina had poured her soul into Integrated Life. The weight on her friend's heart hung like a stone around Zee's. "Can I help?"

Fontina's smile was tense. She squeezed Zee's hand. "Let's go back to your interview with Bette."

Reluctant, Zee opted to honor her friend's request. "I had a wonderful time," Zee said, yet in the warmth of the memory, a recollection of the death threat sprouted. Shuddering, she leaned toward Fontina. "Toward the end, somebody posted on a message board: Bette *Dead* la Cornne, when nothing's left, there's nothing to lose."

Fontina raised her brows. "That's alarming."

Chairs scraped. The *Gladiators* got up and hurried toward the door. Miranda called a cheery good-bye.

"It shook me," said Zee. "I grabbed for my phone to show it to Bette, but I got all fumble-fingered and ended up dropping it. My screen shattered."

"Did Bette ever see the message?" asked Fontina.

"No. I told her what it said, but she shrugged it off."

Zee shifted in her chair, seeking relief from a twinge in her hip. "Given what you've been through," said Fontina, "I wouldn't dismiss the danger so easily. The first lesson you learned in self-defense class was . . ."

"Remain aware," they said together.

Fontina gestured toward Zee's plate. "If you're not going to eat that, I'll take it back for Emilio."

A knot in Zee's gut loosened. Whatever the problem was, Fontina and her life- and business-partner were still solid. "He's welcome to it." Zee grimaced.

"I applaud you for trying something different. This was a bust, but you'll find what works for you. Speaking of which." Fontina dug into her purse and set a twist-tied plastic bag of greenish powder on the table. "This is for Candy. After taking care of her this weekend, I agree your plump kitty needs to lose some weight. Sprinkle about a teaspoon of this on her food."

Zee nudged the powder. "I hope this tastes better than what I chose." Her eyes strayed toward the pastry display at the counter, but snagged on the abandoned peach Danish. Rich buttery layers. Succulent fruit filling. And they'd eaten only one bite. A sacrilege to waste such a feat of the baker's art. She squashed her irritation in fists.

As if reading her mind, Miranda began to clear the litter.

"Where are you, Zee?" Fontina tapped her knuckles on the table.

Zee scowled. "In an embarrassing downward spiral of pastry-induced depression."

"Get one if you like. Guilt doesn't make a solid foundation for change." A darkness flitted across Fontina's eyes.

Zee's heart twinged, but she refrained from questioning. Fontina would share when she was ready. "That's what Bette said when I wondered about wasting my life on frivolous writing. But I feel like something is missing."

"What do you think you want?" asked Fontina, fingers straying to Ramiz's coin.

Zee looked again toward the stone angels. "I'd like to be more like Bette." She felt her way through the words. "Take on the significant problems that plague society, but in a way that doesn't use humor to let people off the hook." Her breath caught. She'd never thought of her column as letting people off the hook.

"Humor is a good tool." Fontina's voice called Zee back to the sunlit table. "It can help people see from a different perspective." She laid a hand on Zee's forearm.

Warmth from Fontina's fingers soothed Zee's self-condemnation. She forced cheer into her voice. "I'm looking forward to talking more with Bette tomorrow."

"Oh no." Miranda sat with a thump at the abandoned table. She lifted the newspaper with shaking hands.

A nerve spasmed in Zee's shoulder, sending a tiny branch of lightning across her chest.

"What is it, Miranda?" asked Fontina. "What's wrong?"

"I heard you two talking about Bette de la Cornne." Miranda's voice cracked. She pushed herself to her feet and carried the paper to Zee. "I'm really sorry." She laid the *Messenger-Tribune* on the table, open to a headline in the Entertainment section.

Beloved Valerian Author Found Dead

CHAPTER 3

BETTE WAS DEAD. On Schreinhardt's small round table, amid the remains of their breakfasts, the *Messenger-Tribune* lay like a tombstone. Shaking, Zee pulled the folded newspaper closer. She blinked at the article, but her eyes refused to unscramble the words. She raised stricken eyes to Fontina.

"Let me." Fontina lifted the pages from Zee's unsteady hands.

"I'm really sorry for you to find out this way." Apology colored Miranda's voice.

"It's not your fault." Fontina touched the barista's shoulder. "You were shocked. You simply responded."

The bell over the door jingled. Miranda squared her shoulders and mustered a weak welcome toward the entering patron.

Outside, a vehicle ground its gears. Zee pressed her fingers to her temples. The engine rumbled inside her head, chipping memories loose. Laughing together in Bette's sunny living room, reveling in their new friendship, excitedly planning to have tea . . . tomorrow.

Hot tears stung behind her eyelids. Closing them, she latched onto the calm voice of the new customer ordering coffee, but the carefree normality of it cut like a knife.

The newspaper rustled. "Bette's publicist found her." Fontina drew in a soft breath. "There are unanswered questions about the cause of death. The police are still investigating."

The last words landed with a jolt in Zee's midsection. Six months collapsed in a flood of images. A different death. Another murder investigation. A horrendous vortex of cruelty and deceit, descending into a violent struggle for her life. Fire shot through her shoulder.

She blotted her cheek with the heel of her palm. "They're going to find out she was murdered."

"You don't know that." Fontina closed a slender hand over Zee's. "It's something our minds do, going to our greatest fear. I'll stay with you a while. Emilio can teach my next class."

Warm gratitude swept through Zee, wrapping her like one of Fontina's soft shawls. Through the ups and downs of life, Fontina had always been there. A bulwark, a confidant, a sister of the heart. But right now, Fontina faced her own struggles.

"Would you like me to stay?"

Zee drew back her hand. She cleared unshed tears from her throat. "I appreciate your offer, but I'll be all right. You have obligations of your own." At the uncertainty that shadowed Fontina's face, Zee added, "Maybe we can talk later?"

"Of course." Fontina nodded. "I'm here if you need me."

As always. "I'll call you later."

After she retrieved her phone.

A CHEERFUL YOUNG MAN AT PHONE MEDIC pulled a clear plastic bag from the shelf behind him. "All fixed."

Zee stared hungrily at her trapped phone. The sooner he rang up the sale, the sooner she could dive into her news feed. Where there might be more recent information. Where, irrationally, she might find a contradiction to the cold, hard headline.

He offered a gap-toothed grin. "I suggest a case to help protect it."

"No, thanks." Habitual civility reined in her impatience.

"On sale today." He held the phone beyond her reach. "It's a good bargain."

Zee ground her teeth. He was only doing his job. And a protective cover might have saved her from this mess.

She scanned the accessories display. It mocked grief to choose any of the sparkly bright colors. She grabbed a plain black cover. "I'll take this one."

"Excellent. I'll put it on the phone for you."

Zee stifled a scream. Letting him do the job would take less time than if she argued.

Minutes crawled by while he swaddled her cell in its drab new attire. She forced her antsy feet to keep still. Hours had passed since the morning *Messenger-Tribune* went to press. In all that time, there had to be news.

Finally, satisfaction spread across his face. She reached for the phone, but he kept it, studying it. "You know, this is a fairly new unit. We can give you an extended warranty. That way, if something like this happens again, it won't cost you a thing."

Only innate, bone-deep courtesy kept her from lunging across the counter and snatching the phone from his grasp. "No. Thank. You."

His lips curved in silent empathy. The merest flick of his gaze told her the manager was likely behind the office door, listening to make sure he followed the script. "The repair's guaranteed for thirty days." His voice remained upbeat. "Come back during that time, and I can still give you a great price on the extended warranty."

Zee nodded. She would do that. Some other time.

Interminable seconds dragged while he completed the sale, slipped her phone back into the bag, and stuffed in a flyer. At last, he surrendered the prize into her hands.

She dashed from the store, ignoring her knee's strident warnings. Anxiety sharp in her chest, she threw herself into the driver's seat, ripped open the bag, and stabbed the power button.

The black screen stared at her, reflecting her distorted face, and stayed dark.

"Arghh! You can't be dead!" She resisted the urge to whack the useless object against the dashboard. As if that would knock a few electrons loose and give her the connection she demanded.

Of course, her charger was at home.

She glanced up at the store. She could run back in. Halfway to *Po*'s door handle, she stayed her hand. She could be home by the time she extricated herself from the helpful salesclerk.

Dropping the phone onto the passenger seat, she eyed the radio. Usually, she preferred to use her car time to sift through ideas for her column. Directing a scowl at her dead phone, she twisted the radio knob on. Wasted precious minutes in fruitless scanning, only to reap the same headline offered in the newspaper.

She raked her curls, hoping to dislodge another plan of action. If Rico were in town, she could call him. But he wouldn't be back until tomorrow.

Adrenaline drained. She rubbed her throbbing knee, started the engine, and pointed the car toward home. At least she could take the shortcut from mid-town over the newly completed Cardo Max viaduct. That saved her a good ten minutes of circuitous weaving through overcrowded streets.

Homing in on the tall pillars with their crowns of gleaming laurel leaves, she sped onto the entrance—

And slammed on her brakes.

Apparently, about a thousand other drivers had the same idea. Valerian's newest tribute to all things Roman was subsumed beneath a slow-moving mass of multi-colored metal, taillights blinking like bloodshot eyes.

Fumes fouled the air inside the car as the traffic swallowed her. Hastily, Zee raised the windows. A sledgehammer began working at the back of her skull. She turned off the chattering radio.

Seeking solace, she rested her gaze on the distant forested hills. Against the cloudless blue sky, the stiff, leafless branches blurred into dark brushes. Like Rico's clipped black hair, soft as sable between her fingers.

A knot hardened near her heart. Lately, it seemed he was never here when she needed him.

No, she reprimanded the whining voice. That wasn't fair. Everyone was adjusting to a new reality at the paper. Rico had summed up the atmosphere, referring to the merged publication as the *Mess-Trib*.

The pun had been accompanied by a rare smile. The memory of it loosened the weight in Zee's ribcage. A little. Her relief was short-lived, supplanted by the image of that haunting declaration of Bette's death.

Traffic crawled past another laurel-crowned pillar. Visitors to Valerian, nestled in the pastoral wooded hills of southwestern Ohio, were often shocked to discover the name did not refer to the sleep-inducing herb. For a reason lost to history, the town's founders christened it for a bloodthirsty Roman emperor.

Most days, Zee enjoyed the joke. Today, death was too real.

At last, the viaduct spit her out onto rapidly clearing streets. She lowered the Mini's windows and accelerated, eager to let the spring-fresh air clear the murk from her lungs and the malaise from her mind.

Her plan failed.

Sun-dappled streets and houses rolled past as if they belonged in a different world, a world where Marjorie Franklin hadn't carried out her threat to Bette de la Cornne.

If that's what happened.

She pulled into her space behind the Legate I building. By habit, she glanced toward Alphonse Demetrio's third-floor balcony in Legate III. Recently, he'd fallen and broken his ankle. It pained her to think how long he'd lain on the floor, how much he'd suffered until someone noticed.

She sucked in a sharp breath. How long had Bette been alone before death came for her?

Throat tight, Zee rode the elevator to her third-floor apartment.

A lukewarm meow greeted her. Candy sprawled on the floor,

her fur a striped island of orange and cream in the puddle of golden light leaking through the corner balcony doors.

"Enough with the abandonment guilt." Zee shook her finger at the cat. "Fontina took care of you. And I was only gone for a weekend."

A quiver of anxiety stirred in her chest. She'd gotten home too late last night to do a proper check of her apartment. She eyed the inscrutable cat. "Unless you're apologizing for something."

She scanned the spacious room, the undisturbed drapes framing the french doors to the corner balcony, the unscathed reds and blues of the old Oriental rug, the intact silvery microfiber couch with its vibrant scarlet and jade decorative pillows. Her gaze lingered on the framed photo on the counter. A recent discovery among her dad's possessions, it captured her younger parents with a pre-teen Zee. All smiling, unaware of the cruelties that lay ahead.

She shifted her eyes to Candy, whose face resembled a feline made-you-look smirk. "I do appreciate your restraint in not destroying the place in protest."

Ignoring the lure of the couch, Zee hurried to the bedroom, plugged her cell into the charger, then headed to her office to power up her computer. She chewed her lip while the machine booted with the reluctance of an arthritic octogenarian. Finally, she could stab her newsfeed icon.

Her feed loaded.

She scanned. Scrolled. Refreshed. Scanned again.

Nothing new.

Grinding her teeth, she searched the web. Her efforts yielded a smattering of shocked responses from literary figures. Condolences. A statement from the police. Replicated numerous times. All of which amounted to, "It's premature to draw conclusions."

Premature might mollify her mind. It did nothing to ease the fear growing from a twisted root deep in her gut.

CHAPTER 4

Zee sagged into the nest of her oversized leather office chair. The hollow ache in her heart spread through her body, stirring a chorus of echoes in her muscles and joints. Her stomach clamored for food, but the rest of her wanted the oblivion of sleep.

Unwilling to risk missing an update, she retrieved the charger and plugged it in beside the couch. But instead of heading to the kitchen, she collapsed face down on the cushions. Moments later, a soft furry head worked its way beneath her dangling hand.

She rolled to her side. Candy leapt into the narrow space and snuggled her thick, heavy body against Zee's chest. Warmth loosened the icy fist around Zee's heart. Candy might need to lose weight, but at this moment, she was worth every comforting pound.

"What would I do without you?" Zee rubbed the rounded, soft belly.

Candy turned, wriggled closer. Her soft paws kneaded Zee's midsection, leaching its tension.

Grief draped Zee in a weighted net. Her eyes drifted shut.

Her midsection gurgled.

Candy's head lifted a fraction.

Zee's stomach growled louder, rebelling against the dregs of that miserable Turbo-Muffin.

A tentative paw brushed Zee's face, accompanied by a soft meow. Zee moaned. "Guess it's time for food."

That was a word Candy understood. She jumped to the floor and trotted several steps, then cast a look over her shoulder.

Zee dug Fontina's concoction from her purse and followed Candy into the kitchen. "I have a surprise for you." She filled a bowl with Tuna Delight, mixed in the greenish powder, and set the dish on the floor.

Candy sniffed the contents, circled her bowl, put her nose to it again, then closed her teeth around a nugget. A moment later, she opened her mouth and let the morsel fall to the floor. A grumbling whine escaped.

"It can't be that bad," Zee said, while the memory of the Turbo-Muffin caught in her craw. "You have to lose some weight for your own good. This will help."

Unconvinced, Candy twined herself around Zee's ankles. Zee extricated her foot and nudged Candy toward her food. The furry body deflected from the pressure like a beanbag doorstop, yielding without actually moving.

Zee pushed her toward the Tuna Delight. "Come on, give it another try." Ignoring the narrowed yellow eyes, she turned toward her own belated breakfast.

As she filled the kettle, her gaze fell on *The Mirror of the Soul*. It would probably sell a zillion copies now. She picked up the book and flipped it over. Bette de la Cornne's airbrushed, studio-lit face beamed from the back cover. Artfully curled tendrils of glowing blonde hair; lively blue eyes above smooth tinted cheeks; wide welcoming smile, no artifice needed there.

Zee blinked back tears.

If only Bette had gone with her to the spa. The memory of their good-bye hug wrapped Zee in a bittersweet blanket. Petite Bette had surprised Zee with the fierceness of her embrace, the top of her head brushing Zee's ear, her jasmine scent wreathing them both like a halo.

Across the room, Zee's phone buzzed. Against all odds, she hoped it was Rico.

She seized it. A text sprouted on the screen.

Now we see but darkly. Pernicious mirror.

What the hell? She didn't recognize the number.

Uneasiness stirred in her gut. Her eyes darted back to the book on the counter, *The Mirror of the Soul.*

She clamped her jaws to stem the spiraling fear. It strained credulity that she'd be connected to three violent deaths in less than a year. She could still see the murdered researcher's knife wounds. And before him, the innocent man caught in the drug deal crossfire—a shooting she'd inadvertently triggered.

Her hand strayed to the bullet scar above her elbow. She wrapped her arms across her chest, wincing at the twinge in her injured shoulder.

She didn't have the energy for crackpots right now, but snared by the message, she transferred the phone charger to the kitchen. At the stove, she sparked a blue flame under the kettle, then crossing her fingers that something edible would be forthcoming from her usually sparse shelves, pulled the cupboard door open.

A bagel sat there, gloriously swaddled in its plastic bag.

Quick inspection revealed no patches of gray beard. Grateful, she slid the bagel into the toaster. In the lull while she watched the elements brighten to heat, Bette's death slithered into her thoughts. What if she *had* been murdered?

Cobra-like, the dread rose. Zee clenched her hands into fists. Even if this *was* a murder, she had nothing to do with it. She couldn't have caused it. She wasn't a witness. She hadn't even found the body this time.

Clutching the edge of the counter, she forced herself to breathe in slow, measured counts until the pounding in her chest eased. Emilio's tai chi instruction echoed in her ear: *When your mind wanders, bring it back to your body. Focus on movement. Sensation.*

The toaster disgorged the bagel. She grabbed it like a life preserver.

Slowing her actions to better focus, she gripped the knife, its smooth handle cool in her sweaty palm. She peeled a thin pane of butter from the stick and scratched the knife blade across the bagel's dimpled surface. In a measured stream, she poured hot water over the teabag in her mug, then bathed her face in a cinnamon-orange mist. The clamor in her head subsided.

Her gaze fell on the text. She re-read it, laser-eyed as if by sheer willpower she could divine its meaning. When no revelation manifested, she sent a response.

Who is this?

No answer. Her screen affirmed that the text had been delivered.

Frustrated, she tried again.

What does this mean?

The reply window remained stubbornly blank. She huffed. "If people had something to say, they should just say it."

In response, Candy thwacked the food dish with her paw, scattering green-tinted Tuna Delight across the floor. She fixed Zee with jaundiced eyes and yowled.

"Note to Fontina," Zee said. "Cattitude indicates failure of taste test." She picked up the dish and dumped the contents into the trash. "I can't deprive you today. I need comfort food, too."

Candy rubbed her silken fur alongside Zee's calf while she filled a clean dish with unadulterated Salmon Surprise. Tiny feline teeth fell on the nuggets as soon as the bowl hit the floor.

Zee's gut growled a ravenous reminder. She grabbed her bagel and bit into it. Juicy raisins and a hint of nutmeg. Crusty and chewy. The hearty opposite of the delicate butter cookies Bette served.

The contrast struck like a blow, turning the robust flavors to ashes in her mouth.

She swallowed, crumbs scraping against her throat like gravel. Turbo-Muffin all over again. She washed down the grit with scalding tea, then gasping, splashed water in a glass and downed it.

Mouth still stinging, she snatched the phone and its tether. "I don't know what your game is," she snarled, "but I am not in the mood. Whoever you are, I'm going to find you."

CHAPTER 5

Anger boiling, Zee fired up her computer. Her fingers flew, keying in the texter's phone number. "All right," she implored the emotionless screen, "give me a name." She hit Search.

The computer offered reverse lookup services. She tried one. Two. Three.

No results.

"Damn." She ripped off a chunk of bagel with her teeth. The number probably belonged to a prepaid burner, difficult to trace by mere ordinary citizens. The *Messenger-Tribune* offered better tools, but fat chance she'd get login credentials anytime soon. Merger chaos aside, a syndicated columnist didn't rate in Karl's book.

Not like a certain crime reporter.

Slowing her furious chewing, she grabbed her phone, nearly disconnecting it from its tether beneath the library trestle table that served as her desk. Although Rico wouldn't return until tomorrow, she could leave a message.

On the verge of stabbing the icon, she halted.

He wouldn't call for help. Not yet.

Karl had given her grudging respect after she cracked the researcher's murder last year. "Maybe you're made of sterner stuff than I thought." He had glared at her, his eyes permanently narrowed by skepticism. "Write the story. Prove it."

That article had been a hard-edged piece, without a trace of the irony for which her *Z Beats* column was well known. She'd been proud of it, but Karl criticized it as marred by too much empathy.

She snorted. Empathy was a strength, not a weakness.

Her eyes sought the text again. Steepling her fingers, she leaned back in her office chair. Maybe she could attack this from a different angle.

Pernicious mirror. Who used a word like *pernicious* in a text?

Gnawing on the corner of her lip, she typed in the phrase. A screenful of possibilities popped up. She scanned the listings. Too many, too varied.

The book title might shrink her net.

Adding it revealed that not one entry used the combination.

The smoldering coal in her gut flared. She tore off another chunk of bagel with such ferocity that her twisting torso sparked a sharp pang from her hip. "Sorry." She rubbed the throbbing joint.

Maybe her body was reminding her not to get involved.

"But dammit, I *am* involved," she growled. "Someone wants to drag me into this, and before I quit, I'm going to know why."

She glared at the text.

Now we see but darkly. That felt vaguely Biblical. Religion, another link to Bette's book.

A wave of grief drowned her frustration, pulling her into the murky pool in her mug. She'd lost Bette, lost her smile, her laugh, her encouragement. Lost all the future adventures they might have shared. That was enough to bear without this strange message, impossible to ignore yet offering no direction, no solace.

Maybe she should just report it to the police and be done with it.

A groan escaped her throat. What would the cops do? Probably nothing, except hoot at her.

Closing her eyes against the jiggle of her amber reflection, Zee sipped. Her agitation eased. For now, she'd swallow her failure. Maybe Rico could help solve the riddle when he returned.

She pushed back from her desk, but the evidence of her fruitless efforts pinned her in her chair. Surely, she could learn something useful this morning.

Logic insisted that the pernicious mirror referred to Bette's book. Bette said she and Marjorie had been close friends. That implied they knew each other well.

Cinnamon-orange soured on Zee's tongue. Much as she liked Bette, she wouldn't be the first author to lift too many details from someone else's life to create a dramatic tale.

Zee set the mug on her desk. But a good reporter wouldn't blindly accept that the book actually mirrored Marjorie Franklin's life.

She keyed in Marjorie's name and muttered a curse as her screen filled with entries. She added the book title as a search term. The list narrowed, slightly.

Sucking a breath, she waded in. After the first few items, she learned to avoid book reviews, which offered little relevant information. She also skipped the lurid headlines that titillated but provided shallow substance.

An academic website produced a scholarly exposition of *The Mirror of the Soul* as a dystopian novel. Erudite, but not useful. Likewise for several psychologists who opined on the deleterious effects of sexuality sublimated to spirituality. By the time Zee slogged through a lengthy diatribe against religion in general, she'd consumed most of her bagel, and her tea had gone tepid.

She sagged against her chair. Her spine ached. Her shoulders hurt. Her neck creaked.

Dammit. She'd been hunched in front of her computer like an ancient scribe over an escritoire. Again.

With a grunt, she straightened, then carefully pinched her shoulder blades and lifted her chin toward the ceiling. Her vertebrae released two cracks.

An inquisitive meow floated across the room. Candy abandoned her perch on the futon, trotted to Zee, and leapt into her lap. She kneaded Zee's thighs, then lifted her face close and interrogated her with a yellow-eyed stare.

Zee met her unblinking gaze. "I don't need reading glasses." She slipped her hands beneath her tee shirt and massaged her lower back. "I just need to discipline myself to sit up straight."

Candy twitched her whiskers.

"Don't give me that." Zee arched her back. "But you're right. I do need a break, Candy-pants."

The nickname sent her thoughts to Rico and one steamy afternoon. He'd come up with it when Candy ran into the bedroom, a pair of Zee's red-and-white striped panties clutched in her mouth.

An ache tugged her heart. Lately, the more Rico retreated, the more she wanted to rush headlong into his arms, his heart, his life. That was the naked truth.

She stopped dead. Gently easing Candy aside, she added *true story* to her terms, and hit Search. Three entries down, she found her reward.

Fiction or Truth?

Is Lilliana McClory, doomed protagonist of The Mirror of the Soul, *really Marjorie Franklin? One must wonder why anyone would make this claim, given Lilliana's troubled life, yet Franklin does. What's more, she declares that anyone who knows her would come to the same conclusion. She offered this reporter the following table as evidence.*

Lilliana McClory Fiction	Marjorie Franklin Fact
Parents ran off to join a cult	Parents went to India to live with their guru
Sent to live with religious grandparents	Sent to live with religious grandparents
Parents never returned	20 years pass before parents contact her
Married, divorced	Married, divorced
Drug addiction	Drug addiction
Rejected faith	Rejected faith
Dead	May as well be

The skin prickled on Zee's neck.

Morse code from the brain. The whisper came from Shelby.

Zee stilled her body. She didn't know why her childhood imaginary detective was back, but her nudges during the last murder investigation had proved worthy of attention.

Leaning closer to the computer, Zee peered at the table as if revelation might be hidden in the spaces between the words. She focused on the list of parallels. Obvious though they were, she couldn't see how they could destroy a life. Ruination was Marjorie Franklin's *after*. What was she *before*?

A quick search located Marjorie's professional web page. A smart, stylish woman gazed from the screen. Waves of chestnut hair brushed the shoulders of her apricot silk jacket. Clear hazel eyes, full lips, slightly angular face. A polished malachite triangle lay just below the hollow in her throat.

Marjorie listed her occupation as an investment manager with Hart, Oxford & Sharpe. If Zee had a fortune, she would entrust it to that picture of competence. Prominent names dotted her list of clients: an oil company president, a cosmetics magnate, a philanthropist whose name graced the skilled nursing facility where Zee's dad was living.

Where he was dying.

A pang, sharp as a hot metal spear, shot through Zee's chest. Her eyes flew to her dad's barrister bookcase, shoved against one wall in her office, still crammed with books, papers, and unusual objects: a small crystal ball, a lacquered scarlet box, a pouch of dusty gold cloth. Clues to a mind lost to her forever.

She'd aggravated her injuries, muscling the heavy piece into place. It stood in a temporary location, jutting just inside her door, the best she could do in her weakened state. As it was, her awkward efforts had bent the track for the uppermost glass door, so it no longer closed properly. She winced with guilt at the damage to his treasure, even though he would never know.

She gulped lukewarm tea, repeating her mantra. *Dementia had already taken his mind. His body was merely following.* She forced herself to breathe. There was nothing she could do about her dad.

Marjorie's website drew her eyes, an escape from her helpless brooding. Would it help her understand why Marjorie might kill? If, indeed, Bette was murdered.

Zee clicked to the calendar page. Charity balls, fundraising dinners, trips to the capitol, speaking engagements. The picture of success, but dated nearly two years ago, about the time *The Mirror of the Soul* hit bookstores.

Subsequent months revealed Marjorie's downward spiral. Fewer and fewer events claimed her time. And after last summer, nothing. For ten months, only blank spaces stared off the page.

Marjorie's life had broken off, like an ice sheet giving way beneath its cumulative weight. Only jagged remnants of her once glorious trajectory remained. It was almost physically painful to witness.

Like her dad's decline. Pain wrenched her heart. He'd been a respected university professor, a master of debate, with a memory to challenge an encyclopedia. But his heart attack and stroke a year ago had set off a precipitous chain of events. It was as if the weakened substrate of his phenomenal intellect could no longer fend off the pain of her mother's infidelity. She gritted her teeth. *Dementia had already—*

A motorcycle roar, snipped from a 60s song, jarred Zee's focus. She seized her phone.

"Hey." Rico's deep voice eased the renewed tightness in her neck and shoulders. "I'm back."

Zee swallowed past the lump in her throat. Conversation filtered in the background, the squeak of a chair, a file drawer slamming. "You're at work already?"

"Phone went nuts soon as I got a signal."

She pictured him in his office—the windowless, cramped cubicle he hated but to which he'd been demoted by the merger. All around him swirled the frenzy of a breaking story, but he leaned back in his battered chair, propping a boot on his steel army surplus desk, grabbing a moment to check in with her.

He raised his voice over a surge in the background commotion. "I read your interview. You okay?"

His thoughtfulness cracked Zee's fragile stability, loosing a cascade of silent tears. What she wouldn't give to feel the caress of his deep blue eyes.

"Mostly." Zee swiped her cheek with the heel of her palm. "I suppose you heard about the threat Bette got last Thursday."

"From Marjorie Franklin, yeah."

"I wish Bette had taken it more seriously."

His voice softened. "People blow off web stuff, especially if there's no follow-up."

Bette had blown it off. Zee shuddered.

"Zee?"

"Sorry, I was thinking how right you are."

"Of course, I am."

She smiled at his banter, but his "web stuff" comment brought the morning's enigmatic text to mind. "I got—"

Someone yelled in the background. "On it," Rico called. Then to Zee, "They're bringing her in. See you tonight?" He didn't wait for an answer.

Zee stared at the phone screen. As it darkened, fresh sorrow washed over her.

Marjorie killed Bette. It didn't matter why anymore.

Candy's sandpaper tongue licked a tear on Zee's cheek, offering the ultimate in cat TLC. She hugged the plump, furry body.

In Zee's peripheral vision, the phone with its silent secret prodded her. New irritation surfaced. Why did all the crazies latch onto her?

Despite her despondency, a muffled laugh escaped. Her column advocated for the underdog, the disregarded, the mistreated. Of course, they'd contact her.

But that didn't explain all the damn drama.

She tapped the phone to read the text again, and the voicemail icon snagged her attention. Probably from Rico. The comfort of hearing his voice again drew her to play the message.

Miss Morani, this is Sara Jane Pantonet, Miss de la Cornne's publicist. She asked me to give you contact information for an editor she knows. I have a letter of introduction from her. Please give me a call.

The message had been left on Saturday evening while she was at the spa. Zee stifled a sob. Bette had been alive and well, thinking of her.

Like a riptide, yearning swept through her, pulling her to connect with someone who'd also known Bette, albeit at a much greater depth. She hit the callback icon.

"Miss Morani, so glad to hear from you." Sara Jane's brisk welcome failed to mask underlying weariness.

Her fatigue sparked regret. Sara Jane carried a heavy enough burden. It was selfish to add to it, no matter the invitation. Zee shivered. It was also more than a little ghoulish to pursue her own aims when Sara Jane must be reeling from shock.

With a start, Zee realized the publicist was waiting for a reply. "I'm sor—please know how—I just—" She bit her lip and fell back on a ritual response. "I'm returning your call." She kicked herself. What a cold, self-serving statement.

"Oh, yes." Sara Jane drew in a halting breath. Her misery gouged Zee's conscience.

"I shouldn't have bothered you," Zee said. "Forgive me. We can talk another time."

"No, it's better for me to keep busy, so I don't . . ." Sara Jane's voice cracked.

In the silence, Zee cast about for something to say. "There must be a lot to do." She winced at her lame comment. "I should let you go." *Coward,* accused a voice in her head.

"Wait." Hope laced Sara Jane's tone. "I need to get out of this room. Let me meet with you, give you Be-Bette's letter and the editor's information."

Zee couldn't refuse. To hell with her own discomfort. "That's very kind. Are you sure?"

"Between the police and the press, I have a whole raft of things to take care of this morning, but I'd love to—I *need* to—get away. I'm at the Ambassador. Can we meet at three o'clock at that park up the street?"

"Valerian's Corner. I'll meet you by his statue. You can't miss it."

After ending the call, Zee leaned against her chair and tried to calm the buffeting in her heart. Bette's generosity only sharpened the pangs of grief.

And sparked by Sara Jane's comment, something else nettled her. The police.

Memories knotted her stomach. The last thing she wanted was another bout with law enforcement, another struggle with the weight of official suspicion bearing down on her. But her last investigation had taught her the folly of keeping anything from the police.

And *sterner stuff*, right?

She left the phone on the charger and headed for the shower. Might as well report the text and get it over with.

And given the police force for a city of 150,000 people, what were the odds that Lieutenant Larry Bernstow would be in charge of this case?

CHAPTER 6

WITH EACH STEP TOWARD THE POLICE station, uneasiness coiled more tightly in Zee's stomach. Rico called her distrust of law enforcement, paranoia. He hadn't grown up listening to her dad's impassioned condemnation of police brutality. Race riots, war protests. No amount of logic could loosen the hold of those images.

When she entered the small lobby, her phone sat in her purse like a hand grenade.

At the front desk, Sergeant Jones acknowledged Zee with a small smile. Her kind gesture made slight inroads into Zee's disquiet. Not that the smartly uniformed police officer exuded warmth. She was brisk and efficient, but also not afraid to show her humanity.

Unlike Lieutenant Larry Bernstow.

After Zee explained her errand, the sergeant held out her hand for the phone. "You think this could be connected to the de la Cornne case?" She kept her chiseled face impassive as she read the cryptic text message, then consulted the computer. "Let's see who caught that one."

While Jones tapped the keys, Zee prayed silently to the goddess of bureaucracy. Months ago, Fontina told her about Asphalta, deity of parking spaces. It seemed reasonable to think there must be a divine being in charge of smoothing the tortuous paths of officialdom.

Jones shifted her hazel eyes to Zee. "That's Detective Bernstow's case."

Of course it was.

Zee stifled resentment toward the deaf ears of the unknown goddess. Maybe heavenly favor required sacrifice. The slaughter of a goat. Or the burning of a rules manual.

Poking her head through the inner doorway, Jones gestured toward a corner desk. She raised her voice. "Someone to see you, sir."

As soon as Zee stepped into the room, cacophony battered her: chattering voices, banging file drawers, and squawking chairs, all underscored by the baseline throbbing of electronic machinery and the intermittent buzz of fluorescent lights. She resisted the urge to cover her ears.

Bernstow's gaze locked with hers. A weary scowl swept the neutral expression from his craggy face. "You again." He glanced beyond her as she made her way among the desks. "Where's your reporter partner in crime?"

Zee lifted her chin. "Busy." She fought to keep annoyance from her voice. "And not needed. I'm just doing my civic duty, detective." She proffered her cell. "I thought you might be interested in this."

He grabbed the phone, squinted at the screen, then glared at her. "I don't have time for riddles. What's this about?"

"You're the detective." As soon as she snapped out the words, she wished she could snatch them back. True, the first time they crossed paths was a disaster, but since then, she'd saved an innocent man. Bernstow should give her more credit, but antagonizing him wouldn't serve any purpose.

"Answer the question." He drilled bronze eyes into her.

She sought a way to defuse his annoyance. Sitting might show her desire to be a partner, not a problem; but his jacket lay crumpled on the seat of the visitor's chair. She gestured toward it. "Do you mind?"

He jerked his head, granting resigned permission.

She picked up the garment, draped it over the chair back, and sat down. Modulating her voice to reflect what she hoped was non-confrontational sincerity, she met his stare. "I think it's a reference to Bette de la Cornne's book, *The Mirror of the Soul.* But I don't know what it means."

"And naturally, you have no idea who sent it."

"I tried to find out." Of its own accord, her speech took on a snarky tinge. "I don't have the extensive resources, training, and experience that are the special province of the police." As if on cue, a curse sounded above the clatter of machinery, accompanied by a metallic reverberation. No doubt caused by the application of a shoe to an offending piece of equipment.

Bernstow's hard jaw twitched, but he maintained eye contact. He laid Zee's phone out of reach next to a pile of folders on his desk. "Why you?" He steepled his fingers. "What's your connection this time?"

"Other than interviewing Bette for a story, I have none."

He leaned his bulk against the back of his desk chair, releasing a tortured creak from its springs. "So, like last time, you get a message out of the blue."

Not quite accurate, but Zee gritted her teeth behind a smile. She softened her tone. "I liked Bette, Detective. I want you to get her killer."

"We have." He lurched upright, jabbed a finger at her. "Full confession. Open and shut."

Full confession? The words froze her in her seat. She waited for the elation she expected. Instead, disappointment ribboned through her chest, tying a knot in her throat and descending deep into her stomach.

She swallowed hard as revelation came. She'd hoped this morning's text was pertinent, that by sharing it, she would play some part in avenging her friend's death. Bernstow's statement reduced her morning sleuthing to mere morbid curiosity.

The self-accusation stung her synapses to life. She cocked her head. It wasn't like the hard-nosed detective to volunteer information. "That was fast."

He relaxed his rigid posture, sat back. "Despite what you think, we *are* competent."

His assertive declaration didn't quite conceal his frustration. In a fleeting moment, Zee's perception shifted. Her eyes registered his rumpled beige shirt, its collar wilted and sweat-stained, and his limp mud-brown tie, loosely knotted as though he'd yanked at it more than once already today. Near his scarred knuckles lay a half-eaten breakfast biscuit, a bottle of antacid tablets, and a mug of coffee, congealed cream floating on its oily surface.

His job took a toll. Maybe like her, he simply wanted more respect. Empathy tempered her voice. "I was just surprised it happened so quickly."

"You solve one murder, and you think you're a great detective." He picked up a handful of file folders. "See these? That's just yesterday's crop. I'll—"

He clapped his mouth shut as an officer stopped at the desk. "Captain wants to see you, Lieutenant. It's about that apartment fire. They found a body."

"What the—" Bernstow glared at the young man. "Watch your mouth. There's a civilian right here."

"Sorry, sir." Face reddening, the cop hurried away.

Bernstow flapped the file folders at Zee. "I don't need you barging in to complicate things. I'll take a confession."

Despite her sympathy, her hackles hitched. Mockery crept into her voice. "I didn't want to," she quoted him, "'fail to provide you with pertinent information.'"

He'd practically tattooed that warning on her forehead last time.

A vein throbbed in his reddened neck. "Okay, concerned citizen. You did your civic duty. The Valerian Police Department thanks you."

She stretched toward her cell, but he closed his hand over it. "We're still collecting evidence. Jones'll write you a receipt." A smirk dragged up the corner of his mouth. "Have a nice day."

Zee disciplined her face to show no reaction.

At the desk, Jones didn't hide her sympathy. With a sideways glance at the closed inner door, she leaned toward Zee. "We'll get it back to you soon as we can."

"No problem."

Receipt in hand, Zee pushed through the station doors. The grin she'd restrained broke across her face. Her hand patted her purse, where her new cell drank greedily from a newly purchased portable power supply. Bernstow didn't need to know that she'd expected to relinquish her phone. Give him his petty triumph.

She chuckled. It was easier to handle him than to explain to the curious Phone Medic tech why she needed him to clone her recently repaired phone.

She stopped abruptly. Bernstow *had* been easy.

Doubt wormed in her gut. He'd blurted the news of Marjorie's confession, but he was too experienced to make such a mistake.

On the other hand, he was clearly stressed. The pile of unsolved cases attested to that.

She lifted her face to the brilliant sun. Police stations were dark places, despite illumination bright enough to do brain surgery. Maybe her uneasiness resulted from being trapped in that miasma of misery.

The park across the street beckoned her, a cleansing green oasis. Hoping she had time before her meeting with Sara Jane, she dug out her phone. She flashed on the memory of the Phone Medic tech. Guilt pricked her. Once again, he'd pitched the warranty. She promised to consider it, and she would. Definitely.

She checked the time and set an alarm. Fifteen minutes would have to be enough.

Eying the traffic signal, she hurried toward the crosswalk, but pulled up short at the sharp twinge in her knee. "Damn." Rehab was a drag.

Despite moderating her pace, she was only halfway across when the light changed. Car engines came to life. Sucking in a breath, she pushed to lengthen her stride and gained the entrance just as the first SUV rolled past.

So much for stress relief.

Passing through the gap in the boxwood hedges, she slowed her steps to drink in vibrant colors: slender limbs of redbud sheathed in tiny pink-purple blooms, lazy arcs of butter yellow forsythia blossoms, patches of new grass carpeted in purple and white crocus cups. Balms after months of wintry gray.

Deeper along the bricked serpentine path, laughter and conversation drifted over the boxwood fence. The city's buildings exhaling their inhabitants into the magic of spring.

A turn brought her to a bench bearing a bronze plaque, mottled with age. Inscribed into its patina were immortal words: *Veni Vidi Vici.*

She sank down to rest as a memory curved her lips. Her dad and Fontina's father, Papa Alesandro, engaging in a lively discussion of Shakespeare's *Julius Caesar*. A heart versus head debate. Alesandro said Brutus let his head overrule his heart. Zee's dad argued that the mind must govern, or everything descended into chaos.

Zee's heart pinched. Some things were beyond the mind's rulership. Like love.

Releasing a long, slow breath, she let her fingers trace the worn imprints on the metal. Despite her best attempts to keep her distance when they started dating, Rico had demolished her carefully constructed world. A world that had no place for anything except her career. A world where, for years, intellect had ruled and guarded her broken heart.

He came. He saw. He conquered.

And she would see him tonight.

With a final caress, she left the bench behind.

And yet, the words trailed after her, tugging like toddlers with something to say. She stopped near a bed of spear-like daffodil leaves and let her gaze seek clarity on the horizon. The hulking top floor of the jail intruded on her vision. High forbidding walls, narrow slits that passed for windows. A fortress for failure.

Her mind flew to Marjorie, trapped in a cell.

The toddlers caught up.

Zee had suffered betrayal, her cheating mother, her faithless fiancé. For years, she'd allowed it to strand her from both reason and affection. Had Marjorie Franklin's loss done something similar to her?

Zee had responded by throwing herself into her career. Marjorie's website presented a comparable picture.

Despite herself, Zee felt a twinge of sympathy. Rico had freed her heart. Marjorie had no rescuer.

Unless the anonymous texter was trying to help her.

Zee's reporter's instinct twitched. Maybe Marjorie could shed some light on the mystery. Eagerness quickened her steps. Maybe Marjorie herself sent the text. Or she might know who did. Or have an idea about what it meant. Or—

A rooster crow cut through Zee's thoughts. Her alarm.

Frustration stung her chest like swallowed nettles. Or maybe it was grief that burned, and her curiosity, simply the desire to hang onto her connection with Bette by talking to the last person to see her alive.

Silencing the alarm, Zee blinked back tears. Time to head for her car and her meeting with Sara Jane Pantonet.

Even though moving forward felt like another betrayal.

CHAPTER 7

ZEE BOUNCED *Po* OVER BULKY METAL plates in the street alongside Valerian's Corner. She should have remembered this mess and suggested a different meeting place to Sara Jane. Each bone-jarring rattle made her question—not for the first time—what the semi-permanent obstructions said about the competency of the city's department of public works. Maybe she'd focus on that in her pitch to the editor in Bette's letter of introduction.

She dismissed the idea with a shake of her head. Bette was a worldwide best-seller. She had connections. She knew Zee's dream. She would provide her an avenue to a bigger audience. National, probably. Excitement thrummed in Zee's chest. Maybe she'd even go international. With a big, important story. Let Karl choke on that.

The Mini clanked over a particularly large protrusion. As if the jolting car had cuffed her, Zee snapped out of her fantasy. How could she be salivating at a career boost? She ought to be mourning her friend.

"Thanks, *Po*," she murmured at the dashboard. "You really are like the old master, blind but still seeing better than I do." She swung the Mini into a parking spot, wishing she could corral her ambition as easily.

By midafternoon, Valerian's Corner gurgled with the laughter of children, the yipping of dogs, and the animated conversation of two men playing checkers at a weathered wooden table. Zee approached a tall woman who pored over the inscription below the statue of the Roman ruler. "Sara?"

"Sara *Jane*." She flashed a tentative smile. "You must be Suzanne Morani." The breeze snagged a strand of honey-blonde hair in her gold-rimmed eyeglasses. She tugged it free and offered a surprisingly firm handshake. This woman spent time in a gym. "Your Valerian is quite the namesake. The first time I came here, I thought it referred to the root that made people sleepy."

Zee laughed. "That might have made more sense, here in the bucolic rolling hills. But then, what kind of monuments could we have?"

A grin broke across Sara Jane's face. She gestured toward a bench at the edge of the small plaza surrounding the statue. In a nod to the toga-clad emperor, a carved silvery drape lay across the back and cascaded down one side. "That looks like a nice place to sit. Shall we?"

Zee nodded, marveling at the poise of Bette's publicist. If Zee had discovered her client's bloody body—

The memory ambushed her. She staggered a step, gorge burning in her chest at the image of the last dead body she'd seen. Bloodied corpse sprawled, slashed throat gaping, glistening crimson pools on the carpet.

Her toe caught on the edge of the plaza, and in righting herself, the world came back into balance. Birdsong, sunlight, cool spring air she pulled deeply into her lungs. She was here, now, in the park with Sara Jane, who was, astonishingly, smartly turned out in a tailored, charcoal pantsuit, every polished onyx button in place.

"I appreciate your seeing me." Zee sank beside her on the bench. "How are you?"

Sara Jane lowered her eyes. "Under the circumstances . . ."

Zee revised her assessment. The woman's shoulders were taut beneath her sharply pressed jacket. Her jaw muscles bunched. Her knuckles whitened where she clutched the narrow strap of her purse.

"I'm sorry," Zee said. "We can do this another time."

"No." Sara Jane extended her hand toward Zee but stopped short of touching her. "I'm all right. Bette would want me to do this." She swallowed. "It just feels so unreal. I'll never forget seeing . . ."

"I imagine." Zee's stomach soured again.

Sara Jane twisted a pinkie ring, playing her fingers across its square diamond. "I warned Bette about Marjorie. I told her to get a gun."

Zee flinched. "A gun?"

Sara Jane's head snapped up. Grief fought with anger in her brown eyes. "I could tell she had no intention to stop. But Bette didn't even report the harassment." Her lower lip quivered. "I should have gone to the police. Instead, I called Marjorie's boss, hoping he could reason with her, or give me a clue how to deal with her."

"Did he?"

Sara Jane shook her head. "He seemed as baffled as I."

The trajectory of Marjorie's life struck Zee anew. The same persistence that had built such a glittering career as an investment manager had been diverted into this fruitless, destructive quest.

Pink splotched Sara Jane's cheeks. "I gave the detectives copies of her emails, her texts and voicemails after . . ." She shivered. "If I hadn't waited, Bette might still . . . I'm as responsible as—" Her voice cracked. She fumbled in her purse and drew out a tissue.

To give Sara Jane some privacy, Zee shifted her gaze. On a nearby silver maple tree, two tufted titmice engaged in a spring courtship dance. The little birds always reminded her of butlers, prim in elegant gray jackets over smooth white shirts. Their round black eyes missed nothing, yet gave them the air of disciplined disinterest. Like Sara Jane's façade of self-control. She knew more than she said.

Shunting aside her distaste for probing, Zee turned to the grief-stricken woman. "Why do you think Bette didn't recognize the danger?"

Sara Jane eyed her sharply. "You met Bette. No doubt you felt the power of her charm. She thought she was invincible."

Zee swallowed. Bette made others feel that way too. "What went wrong between Bette and Marjorie? They were close."

"That was before I knew Bette," said Sara Jane. "But charisma has its downside. When the savior doesn't save, love can easily become hate."

A synapse fired in Zee's brain. She spoke slowly, watching Sara Jane's face to gauge her reaction. "That sounds rather Biblical."

Sara Jane barked a harsh laugh. "There are many kinds of messiahs."

It was on Zee's lips to probe further, but another question emerged. "Do you think Lilliana *is* Marjorie?"

Sara Jane pleated the tissue in her fingers, smoothed and re-folded it, then slipped it into her purse.

Zee's brows knit. Surely, she'd already been asked this question and would have a ready answer.

When Sara Jane met Zee's gaze, her eyes reflected cold fire. "Bette did a great deal of research into fringe religious groups. I grant you there are similarities to Marjorie, but many individual stories contributed to the plot of *Through a Mirror Darkly*."

Goosebumps skittered across Zee's skin. "What did you say?"

Sara Jane pinched her brows.

"The book. You called it *Through a Mirror Darkly*."

"Oh." Sara Jane twisted her ring. "That was the original title, but the publisher wanted something more evocative." She chewed the corner of her lip. "I'm not handling this as well as I hoped."

"It's completely—"

Three loud beeps erupted from Sara Jane's purse. She pulled out her phone, studied the screen, and scowled. "So much for a break."

Zee could see Sara Jane reassembling herself, tucking away emotion, fastening her professional mask.

The publicist pressed an envelope into Zee's hand. "Here's the information I promised. Best of luck." Phone already to her ear, she hurried away.

Zee's eyes followed her, while her mind strained to process what she'd just heard. The slip of the title felt big, like a boulder dropped into the stream of Zee's thoughts. She struggled to accommodate it. It seemed to change everything, but she couldn't see how.

Stymied, Zee dropped her gaze to the envelope, the white rectangle lying pregnant in her palm. She traced her finger over the capital Z. Bette had executed it in one long, extravagant stroke that spread over half of the surface. As if to affirm that Zee could claim a bigger space.

A larger audience.

Zee straightened on the bench, pulse picking up a pace. Sara Jane had dodged the question whether Marjorie was Lillianna, instead declaring that Bette researched many fringe religious groups for the book.

Fringe religious groups. The words crackled with promise. Thoughts racing, Zee folded the envelope into her purse. Here was a good feature story to pitch to a new editor—Karl be damned.

She clutched her purse with its precious cargo, research strategies already forming in her mind. Who to interview? Sara Jane's voice replayed, her mention of the book's previous title.

Zee's flesh prickled. The similarity to the text was too much of a coincidence to ignore. She had to chase it down.

Didn't she?

Sure, along with carrying grief over her dad; worrying about Fontina; meeting her column deadline; reporting her column topics to Karl—a weekly obligation since the merger; bracing for Bette's funeral—assuming there'd be one and she'd be invited.

Suddenly weary, she rubbed her wrapped knee, fighting the desire to curl up on the sun-warmed bench and drop into unconsciousness. Her separated shoulder ached with the weight of the day's events. Everything from the shock of Bette's death to that pathetic excuse for a muffin this morning.

What'cha gonna do? Try to grow a third hand? Shelby's way of pointing out that she couldn't and needn't carry the load alone.

Zee's glance grazed the emperor's statue. Though at a different park, the words came back to her.

Veni. Vidi. Vici.

A smile eased across her lips.

Help would be coming to dinner in just a few hours.

CHAPTER 8

T HE WAXING GIBBOUS MOON SLANTED LIGHT through the window in Zee's dining room, silvering the tips of Rico's short black hair. Lunar radiance lit the planes of his cheeks, chiseled the line of his jaw, and highlighted the muscled expanse beneath his snug black t-shirt. Side-by-side beneath the small square table, their denim-clad knees brushed.

The knot in Zee's chest loosened. Disquiet, lingering from the day's events, dissolved.

He nuzzled her neck, the soft bristle of his five-o'clock shadow igniting icy fire over her skin. "Mmm, you smell good."

She shivered with pleasure. The apricot salt scrub from Lotus Spa had been a good idea. "The benefits of being back in civilization."

His eyes met hers, moonglow caught in their blue depths. "I needed a break."

"Things better at work?" She squashed a niggling fear that it was her he needed a break from.

"Let's don't talk about it." He brushed her lips with his.

Electricity short-circuited any further thought. She slipped her hand behind his head, willing him not to break contact. With a soft smile, he accepted her invitation, wrapping his arms around her and pulling her into his lap. He threaded his fingers in her curls.

She gave herself to his kiss, to his protective embrace. Enfolded in his warmth, she forgot her questions. The hard edges forged since reading about Bette's death, melted.

He cradled her. "We better eat while it's hot." He gestured toward the unopened cartons of Chinese take-out, dim shapes in the shadows.

Zee forced her gaze from the moonlit repast. "I'll get the light." She slid from his lap and stumbled over a furry mound.

A disgruntled meow rose from the floor.

"Sorry, Candy." Zee caught her balance, but as soon as she set her foot down, a weight plopped atop her instep. She flicked her ankle, but Candy clung. A claw pricked through Zee's sock.

"Oh no, you don't. These are new." She wriggled her hands beneath the rounded belly and lifted. Candy transformed herself into a blob of orange-and-cream ooze, elongating her thirteen pounds like warm taffy. The sharp point remained stuck.

Behind Zee, Rico chuckled.

"You could help," she tossed over her shoulder.

"Looks like an even match." But as he spoke, his chair scraped back. Avoiding the wriggling hind paws, he knelt and loosened a talon. "Somebody's not happy," he soothed, scratching behind a flattened sideways ear.

"Did Candy actually purr for you?" Zee growled.

He flashed a grin, freed another claw. "Done."

She released the squirming cat. With an aggrieved yowl, Candy leapt to the floor, scampered across the room, and in a quintessentially feline maneuver, simultaneously skidded and turned, coming to rest in a crouch in front of the kitchen island. Yellow eyes gleamed. Her tail thwacked against the hardwood planks.

"Sit a moment." Rico pulled out a chair. Hands on her shoulders, he lowered her to the seat. "Let's make sure you're not hurt."

She swallowed a dismissal. It was wise to check for scratches. Also, her knees seemed to have lost their strength.

Reaching behind her, he flipped the light switch. She inhaled his scent, woody cypress with a hint of leather and Harley. For a moment, she imagined lying in his arms in a forested glade.

He slid her sock downward, breaking the illusion. His warm touch teased prickles. "You shouldn't wear socks on hardwood floors. They're dangerous."

"I massaged body butter on my feet," she murmured, reluctant to divert enough energy to speak. "After my shower."

"Candy's lucky you aren't wearing those spikey red heels." His fingertips, slightly roughened from his week outdoors, traced her ankle and caressed her instep. "Although *I'd* sure like it."

She concentrated on not sliding off the chair.

"No harm done." He patted her leg and sat back on his heels.

An impish impulse seized her vocal cords. "You're not going to kiss it and make it better?"

He smiled. "An ounce of prevention." His lips feathered her instep and continued along her shin. He stopped at the hem of her jeans. "That should do it."

That did it, all right. Goose bumps pebbled her skin.

He lifted her other foot and, sliding his finger along the inside curve, stripped its sock. "For balance."

She leaned back and lost herself in his ministrations. Fontina said every spot on the foot connected to a location in the body. Zee could testify.

"Thank you, doctor." She met his eyes. "Add this to my bill."

He rose and drew her to her feet. "Payment due upon service." He pulled her into a kiss. Deep and lingering.

Wrapped in his embrace, she nestled her head against his chest. "I missed you."

"Missed you, too."

Across the room, a yowl erupted, followed by another tail thwack.

Zee glanced over Rico's shoulder. "I'll deal with you later, Candy."

"You're on your own, cat." Chuckling, he loosened his hold. "I'll go wash my hands and grab a couple of beers."

Zee rubbed prickles from her arms. "Watch yourself. Candy's notoriously fickle."

He headed for the kitchen, dodging Candy's serpentine maneuvers as she tried to twine around his ankles. "What's this green stuff on Candy's food?"

"Fontina's supplement."

"Looks disgusting."

"It's for her own good." Zee gritted her teeth. "She needs to lose weight."

"By starving?" He emerged from behind the island.

"It's only been since this morning. Not even then. I relented and gave her unadulterated food. Whose side are you on?"

He dropped the towel on the counter and raised his hands in surrender.

Ignoring Candy's piteous mews, Zee struck a match to the square brick-red candle on the table.

"Is that new?" Rico returned with two bottles.

"A birthday gift from Fontina."

He cocked his head and narrowed his eyes. "Sure she didn't doctor it?" He flicked his head toward the sulking cat. "She can be devious."

"The candle's fine." Zee stubbed out the match. "And she just wants Candy to be healthy."

He laughed. "You make my point."

Zee punched his arm and settled into her chair, whereupon a furry bulk promptly anchored her foot. Heaving a sigh, she addressed the floor. "You are so stubborn."

"Wonder where she learned that."

She slid the candle his way, exaggerating wide-eyed innocence. "And you are so suspicious."

"Cautious." He played along, waving his hand above the flame as if to waft away suspect vapors. "Goes with the job."

"A reporter's day is never done." Zee opened a carton of shrimp stir fry. "Want me to taste your food?"

"Tempting. Maybe later." He helped himself to orange beef. "But speaking of courting danger, congrats on handling Bernstow. Bet that text made his day."

"Made mine, too." Zee corralled a snow pea and pretended not to notice Rico 'losing' tiny white grains over the side of the table. Nor the soft swish of a tail against her legs. "You have to admit, the text is intriguing."

"'Now we see but darkly,'" he quoted. "Paul to the Corinthians. We can't see like God until we die."

"Scholar of sacred texts." Zee lifted her brows. "This is a side of you I've never seen."

"I grew up Catholic. My mom's doing." A smile crossed his face. "Puerto Ricans are fierce believers."

"Not your dad?"

His good humor faded. "They compromised. Mom got the religion. Dad got the naming rights."

Zee cocked her head. "I thought you told me your dad was German."

"My official name is Richard, but Mom always called me Rico." He drew a pensive chopstick swirl through the rice on his plate. "She wouldn't be happy with me now, a lapsed Catholic."

His melancholy caught Zee off guard. He had never mentioned religion. She'd assumed it was a non-issue. "Fontina would say you're a recovering Catholic, like her."

Except Fontina didn't carry any regret or guilt over her choice. She'd grown up in a big Catholic family. At nine years old, she questioned her parents' beliefs, spurred by a visit from her departed Uncle Ramiz, who urged her to develop her psychic ability. A gift from God, he asserted, not a devil's curse.

Rico twisted toward Zee, rubbed his thumb across her cheek. "No long face." He lifted her chin. "It's not so bad."

The tension in her jaw relaxed. "Fontina says recovery's a twelve-thousand-step program."

"It's an ongoing project." He shrugged, reached for his beer. "All in the past."

She tapped her bottle to his. Subject closed. Best to return the discussion to the text. "So, the message means the police don't see things accurately." She speared a shrimp. "Do they have the wrong person?"

Rico set down his beer and pinned her with his gaze. "Not. Necessarily." He sighed. "Can't you just let it go?"

Zee refused to flinch. "You can't expect me *not* to follow up on this. I'm a professional. What would you do?"

"*Not* jump to conclusions." His cobalt eyes bored into her.

Heat rose in her cheeks. He was right about jumping to unsupported conclusions. It had worked out with the murder six months ago, but that didn't make it a sound strategy.

As if he'd read her thoughts, Rico wrapped her hand in his. "The press hyped your part in the McNeary case. Brings out the crazies."

"You think someone's jerking me around?"

"Lotta nutcases out there."

She laid down her chopsticks and faced him. "I don't want to investigate another death, but I do want to know who sent the text. And why." She gave him a playful punch. "Don't worry. You won't have to keep me out of trouble."

"Good." He captured her fist. "Can't always count on that."

Fear curdled the rice in her stomach, even as her mind scoffed. He was here. He wanted to be with her. She scooted her chair closer and snaked her arm around his waist. Her recently injured shoulder twinged as she snuggled against him. "My body will keep reminding me to stay safe."

"Good," he murmured, breath steamy in her ear.

Her heart thrummed. "No more murder talk." She traced his lips with her index finger. Velvet. Warm. Her fingertip came away with drop of orange sauce. She licked it clean.

Fire smoldered in Rico's eyes. "You have a bit of hoisin there." He cupped her face in his hands. His tongue probed the corner of her lips, gently, carefully, thoroughly.

Her insides liquified. "Mmm. I like your way of cleaning up better than mine."

"Let's hope you continue to be sloppy."

"Oh," she exhaled. "I think you can count on it."

CHAPTER 9

Zee yawned as she woke. Eyes closed, she stretched in her bed, trying to guess the time based on the sunlight illuminating the bedroom. Then, scowling, she tacked on another hour for ridiculous Daylight Saving Time. She caught a whiff of citrus and pulled Rico's abandoned pillow closer, luxuriating in the lingering trace of his presence.

A muted purr escaped the bedclothes, followed by a warm weight settling on Zee's chest. Silky fur brushed her cheek. The citrus scent sharpened. Tangy, orange, undercurrents of . . . Zee's eyes snapped open.

Inches from her face, languorous yellow eyes blinked.

Zee slid from the covers and padded barefoot to the dining table, where tipped cartons of Chinese take-out testified to the cat's crime. "Candy-pants." She whirled to glare at the cat, who sat by the bedroom door, lazily grooming herself. "You know better."

Candy swiped an unconcerned paw across her whiskers and raked it clean. Zee licked her lips, tasting the memory of Rico's tongue, the first domino in the cascade that led the feline to her feast.

Apparently interpreting her action as clemency, Candy paused her ablutions and trotted across the floor. Zee bent and cradled the rumbling bundle. "You've been a bad kitty." A sandpaper tongue scraped her cheek.

Zee sighed. "All right, I forgive you." She stroked behind the soft ears. "Maybe Fontina can design an orange-beef-flavored supplement."

Candy's contented purr roughened toward a growl.

Laughing, Zee released her, then straightened and surveyed the tabletop carnage. It could have been worse. She retrieved a trash can from the kitchen and began to sweep the wreckage into it.

A shame she and Rico hadn't stored the rest of their half-eaten meal. An unregretful smile crept across her lips. She hugged herself, remembering the heat of his embrace. In that shelter, she forgot everything else.

For a while.

His dismissal of the text message irritated her, but his warning not to count on him for rescue, smarted like a cinder in her gut. With more force than necessary, she threw the carton of shrimp stir-fry into the bag. If only she could exile her worries as easily.

As she dislodged a clump of sticky rice from Bette's envelope, her mind turned to yesterday's story idea: religious refugees. Adrenaline zinged in her chest. The decline in church membership was old news, but no one had investigated how modern ex-churchgoers freed themselves from their beliefs. That angle was hers and hers alone.

Gratitude warmed her as she returned to the kitchen. Her parents, full-blown 60s hippies, had spared her religious indoctrination. Their wide-open acceptance of all beliefs freed her from allegiance to any single creed.

Unlike some.

Rico's recovering-Catholic remark flashed through her mind. His firm dismissal. The pain that darkened his face. The memory prompted another problem. She had no idea how to find those would-be liberated souls, or if they would talk to her when she did.

She dumped uneaten greenish Seafood Supreme into the trash, slid the can back under the sink, and paused, struck by the darkness there. If she were honest, a chill void lurked in the midst of her spiritual spaciousness. An unsettling sense of being unmoored, even envious of believers who rested in their safe harbors.

She slammed the cupboard door. Rico wouldn't think those harbors were safe.

"What happens to us when we are too young to defend ourselves, creates the work of our lives," Fontina had told her once. "We come out of childhood with our path to enlightenment,"

"Right now," Zee muttered, suddenly weary of the whole struggle, "I'll settle for my path to breakfast."

While the coffee maker gurgled, she pulled open an upper cupboard. On the shelves, a sparse collection greeted her: twist-tied bag of noodles, bottle of vinegar, jar of Thai paste—a gift from an ex-boyfriend who'd wanted her to be more adventurous in the kitchen.

She scoffed in the direction of the crimson concoction. Radical idea. She didn't cook food. She ate it.

The jar stared back, a challenging red eye. Zee rubbed a thumb along her chin. Her old eating habits needed to change to accommodate her new healthy lifestyle. Did noodles go bad? Could she mix them with Thai paste?

She gulped. That combination was way beyond her comfort zone.

The phrase triggered a frisson of excitement. Sara Jane declared defiantly that Bette had researched many *fringe* groups. Maybe her book contained a useful source. Zee's eager fingers flipped to the acknowledgments. Her eyes flew over the dense print. Her spirits sank.

Nothing.

Empty like her cupboard.

She sagged against the counter. It had been a ridiculous hope, on both fronts. Like food, leads didn't magically appear with no effort.

As she reached to close the cupboard door, a pointed edge peeked from behind the noodles. Pulse quickening despite herself, she swept the bag aside.

Graham crackers!

She grabbed the box and shook it. The contents rattled! She grinned. Sometimes, things just worked.

Encouraged by her good fortune, she cracked open Bette's book for another look at those acknowledgments. Maybe she missed something there, too.

She forced herself to read more slowly, dragging her finger line by line through the long paragraphs. And there it was. *Grateful appreciation to Andrew W. from Believers Anonymous.* Heart pounding, she continued to re-read. A few lines down, she found a list of possible organizations: Center for Religious Liberation, Guerilla Deliverance, 'Canon' Balls.

Spirits buoyed, she snapped the book shut, shook the last three grahams from their package, and carried them with her coffee to her computer.

She started with Believers Anonymous, since it merited special notice, and found it immediately. When she clicked on the site, a garish graphic leapt at her from the screen. She backed instinctively from the blood-red circle, its backslash knifing through the outline of a church. "Whoa, Candy-pants, this is intense."

In Zee's lap, Candy purred, unperturbed.

Gathering her breath, she dove into the description of the group—inspiring, encouraging, boastfully confident in its claims, like any ad. Also strident and jarring. A disquieting chill crawled up her spine. She opened a new window to look for comments on the group.

As she clicked from site to site, her uneasiness spread. The stories were compelling, but often lurid, in the vein of a supermarket tabloid. She would try another source. Then her eyes fell on a post, and all thought of going elsewhere vanished.

CHAPTER 10

Mind racing, Zee stared at the post on her computer screen. Regardless of the theatrical exaggeration in the other comments, she was definitely not done with Believers Anonymous.

"What have I stumbled into?" she asked Candy.

Her cell phone sang a rooster crow, a reminder of her brunch date with Fontina. Glad to shift her focus, Zee bookmarked the last site and headed for the shower.

The steaming water chased some of Zee's shock. Thoroughly warmed, she swaddled herself in comfort clothes: faded jeans, her favorite chili red t-shirt, and a gold Conquerors hoodie.

Outside her door, the benevolent spring sun gilded newly leafed trees and tentative tulip buds. Crisp air rippled through her damp curls, brushing away more of her lingering discomfort. Humming, she slid behind *Po*'s wheel. Light traffic made the drive easy, and Asphalta bestowed her a convenient parking space.

Heart lighter, Zee seated herself at the outdoor terrace table. Moments later, Fontina strode up the sidewalk, sequins sparkling like tiny suns on her lemon-yellow tank top.

They hugged, and Fontina held Zee at arm's length. "You're crackling like a plasma ball. You got something going. Other than with Rico."

"Yes." A flush heated Zee's cheeks. "To both."

Fontina's voice lowered. "You have another mystery, don't you?"

Before Zee could answer, their server arrived, his gangly body swathed in a black apron and green, restaurant-issue t-shirt. "Good morning, ladies. What may I get you?"

Zee smiled up at him. Seth had been awkward and nervous his first week on the job, but the six months since then had infused confidence in his step. "I'll have the chicken salad and iced chai."

"Same here," said Fontina.

"Coming right up."

After Seth departed, Zee tapped her phone to display the text. "This started it."

Fontina scanned the screen. "Sounds Biblical."

"It is, at least the first part. That's from St. Paul. I looked up the reference. It comes at the end of several verses about love, what it is, how it works."

Fontina toyed with the gold filigree dangling from her ear, just visible in the ebony fall of her thick tresses. "Seems straightforward."

"The chapter ends with Paul reassuring the people that it's okay if they don't understand love, because human beings can't see clearly."

"All too true." Fontina's brown eyes darkened.

Zee touched her friend's forearm. "What's troubling you? Is it Teresa?" Zee had been so caught up in her own loss, she'd forgotten about Fontina's young niece. ALS usually progressed slowly, but there were no guarantees.

"No, it's not that." Fontina met Zee's eyes. "She's doing fairly well. Thank you for asking." Her sequined tank top rose and fell. "It's a new development in our plans to expand Integrated Life."

"Something go wrong with the sale of the dry cleaners next door?"

Fontina shook her head. "No problems there." She fingered her earring again. "You remember the monastery where I was on retreat when you and Jeff broke up?"

Zee would never forget. Fontina had flown home when Zee's unfaithful fiancé destroyed her world.

"My teacher there is coming to the States to live. He's looking for a place to set up a meditation center. Part of me wants to offer the new space to him."

"Part of you?"

"A big part. But it's not what Emilio and I planned." Furrows creased Fontina's usually untroubled brow, testifying to the depth of her struggle. She and Emilio had always worked from a shared vision for their holistic living business.

"What does he say?" Zee asked.

"We haven't talked much about it yet. It was a lot to spring on him."

"It's a lot for you, too," said Zee.

Fontina drew in a deep breath. "Right now, there's so much noise in my head I can't think straight." She offered a weak smile. "I need to clean my receiver."

Before Zee could respond, Seth delivered two wide, shallow ceramic bowls. "Here you are, ladies." He set two glasses of chai on the table. "Can I get you anything else?"

"I'm good," said Zee.

"Same here."

Across the table, Fontina picked up her fork. Zee's heart pinched with the desire to help her friend, but for now, Fontina signaled the topic was closed.

Zee turned her attention to her lunch. Her taste buds jumped into overdrive at the sight of the generous scoop of chicken salad. Diagonal slices of celery peeked through the dome, along with crescents of red onion, pale green cucumber sticks, and cheery cherry tomatoes.

Her first bite yielded tender chicken and crunchy vegetables, with just the right touch of mayonnaise. Zee's tongue tingled with the trace of lime. She suppressed a sigh. If Farm Fresh delivered, it would be a lot easier to stick with her new diet.

They ate in silence. From the corner of her eye, Zee noted Fontina unstringing the tension from her body.

"How are you doing since Bette's death?" Fontina asked.

"Up and down. Better than Sara Jane." Zee filled Fontina in on the meeting at Valerian's Corner. "It unnerved me when she used the book's original title," she finished. "I wondered if she sent the text, but I can't see why."

The sun disappeared behind a cloud. Zee shivered in the sudden coolness.

Fontina sipped tea, holding Zee with an inquisitive gaze. "What are you going to do?" She quirked her lips. "Because I know you're going to do something."

Zee speared the last cherry tomato in her bowl. "I caught a break. Bette's book mentioned Believers Anonymous, so I checked it out. You wouldn't believe it." She described the church and the backslash, demonstrating with her fork. "And beneath it, in bold print, it said: *Liberate yourself from the pernicious effects of religion!*"

"Pernicious. Same word as the text." Fontina's brows narrowed. "Makes my skin crawl." She pulled a red grape from the cluster on her plate. "What did you learn about the organization?"

Zee tried to ignore the weight turning her salad heavy. "On the one hand, BA's a deliverance akin to the Second Coming." She grimaced. "Pun intended. A dozen testimonials. Phrases like *smashing the shackles of oppression* and *breaking the stranglehold of religion.* One person said after 52 years, he was finally a spiritual adult."

"Sounds effective, if a bit hagiographic. But surely there were complaints."

Zee nodded. "They used equally adamant, over-the-top terms. Lots of words like *fanatic, crazy, alarming, worse than what I left, just another authority.*"

Fontina raised her brows. "A cult?"

"Several people thought so. But here's what stopped me cold." Zee shuddered at the memory. "There was a diatribe against BA. Someone responded and said her Christian grandparents said her heathen parents were going to hell. Then her parents died in a car crash." The words seemed to burn on her tongue. Zee abandoned the tomato in favor of iced chai.

"Cruel," said Fontina.

"Cruel and familiar." Setting down her glass, Zee pinned Fontina's eyes. "She defended BA's methods, declaring it takes force to dislodge something you learn as a child. And the post was signed Marjorie F."

"You think—"

"Who else could it be?"

Fontina's hand strayed to Uncle Ramiz's coin on its slender gold necklace. Eyes closed, she stroked the worn disk, then traced her fingers along her collarbone.

Zee knew her friend's signs. "What is it?"

"Feels like heavy chains . . . binding Marjorie to BA."

So, both the book and Marjorie were connected to BA. Zee sucked in a breath. "What about the text?"

Fontina seemed to slide her touch along the unseen links. She opened her eyes. "I'm not feeling a clear connection, but there's something there."

Zee felt a ripple in her own energy, as the strands of her inquiry braided.

"You're sparking again," said Fontina.

Excitement lifted Zee's voice. "I have an idea for a great article." She described her plan, concluding with, "There must be recovering Lutherans, Methodists, all kinds of recovering Christians."

"Hindus, Muslims, Buddhists, too, I'm betting," added Fontina.

"Exactly," said Zee. "I plan to pitch the story to the editor Bette knows." She swallowed the sudden lump in her throat. "Knew."

Fontina reached across the small table and laid her hand on Zee's arm. "It's a beautiful way for you to honor your friendship, to continue it in a way."

Zee blinked back tears. Fontina read her heart so well. "I knew Bette only for a short time, and yet . . . I feel so close to her."

"It's one of your gifts," said Fontina. "You create relationships, connections." She patted Zee's arm and sat back. "Sometimes that makes things harder for you."

"You're going to tell me to be kinder to myself right now," said Zee.

"I'm going to offer an alternative to diving into BA. One of my students had a roommate who went to a group called Religious Recovery. Same idea, but a much calmer approach."

Zee's chest eased at the prospect of less emotional intensity. Perhaps she would start with RR. "I'll check into it."

Can you see through all that yellow? Shelby shook a finger at her.

"So," Fontina raised skeptical brows, "you're not investigating Bette's death?"

Zee toyed with her glass. She blew out a breath. "Okay, I confess. The project is real, but I need to know if that text is connected to Bette's death. In fact, that's my next stop."

"Oh?"

"I have a solid lead for my story. That just happens to also possibly connect to Bette's death. I'm going to try to talk to Marjorie Franklin at the jail."

Fontina's eyes widened. "You? Into the haunted halls of justice? Voluntarily?"

"I have to do it." Zee grimaced. "For my story and for the text, Marjorie's my next logical step."

"Sophia help me," Fontina sighed. "I think you're right."

"Goddess of Wisdom. I can use some of that." Zee laughed. "Is there a goddess of crazy?"

Fontina grinned. "Crazy is in the eye of the beholder, Zeezee. From what you've described, a goddess of powerful energy, a wrathful goddess, would be a better ally." She pulled out her phone. "Here's a picture of my favorite. Oya, an African orisha, spirit of wind and storms."

Zee examined the image. A wild-haired woman danced, face painted, brandishing a flaming flail and a lightning-shaped sword. A golden headdress glittered across her dark brow. "She looks fierce."

"She creates destruction to speed transformation."

Zee released a breath, banishing trepidation. With this orisha on her side, she could handle any drama. "Oya is the perfect ally for what I've decided to do tonight."

"Oh?"

Emulating the goddess, Zee lifted her chin. "After I see Marjorie, I'm going to Believers Anonymous."

CHAPTER 11

Zee sped toward the Valerian County Jail. She fully intended to interview Marjorie for her article, but she was also determined to probe for connections between Marjorie, BA, and by extension, to yesterday's enigmatic text.

According to Fontina, heavy chains bound Marjorie to Believers Anonymous. She had to be the author of that defiant defense on the website. It was a short step from *it takes force* to *Bette dead la Cornne*. Despite the afternoon sun, Zee shivered.

She parked *Po* in the shadow of the looming concrete monolith. Her pulse ticked up. Now that she was here, she dreaded entering this bastion of the hammer of the law. A trickle of sweat curled down her spine. She banished it with a deep, purposeful inhalation.

This was nonsense. She was an upstanding citizen. Who was known to the police and not always in a good way. Bernstow's curt dismissal yesterday exemplified their relationship.

She snorted her own dismissal of him.

Straightening her shoulders, she clothed herself in the competent aura of a reporter working a story. A professional, despite her jeans and sweatshirt, who was also on the trail of an enigmatic text, likely connected to the story and to the woman imprisoned behind those forbidding walls.

The jail sat next to the police station and shared the concrete plaza in front. Zee crossed briskly to the outer door designated for jail visitors. She heaved it open, stifling a grunt at the weight and the warning twinge from her shoulder.

At the far end of a garishly lit room, a dough-faced woman sat behind a walled-in partition, fluorescent light flickering off the thin strands of black hair pasted against her skull. She shoved a retractable drawer beneath the thick plexiglass. "Picture ID. Sign the log. Print so I can read it."

Zee cringed at the chewed pen lying on the counter. She wasn't a germophobe, but no way was she touching that coagulated cesspool. She opened her purse and, feeling the woman's eyes like hot coals, slowly withdrew her notebook and unclipped the pen. Sweat beading her forehead, Zee printed her name and Marjorie's, then slid her driver's license with the clipboard into the dented bin. They disappeared behind a rubber flap.

Eyes flicking back and forth, the gatekeeper scrutinized the identification. She pushed the metal drawer back to Zee's side of the counter. "Purse. Cell phone. Keys. Nothing in your pockets."

Zee stowed her license and phone in her bag. "That's everything." She pulled free a couple of tissues. "I have allergies." A lie, but given what she'd already observed, she might need the flimsy protection if she had to touch something. "May I keep at least these?"

The woman grunted assent.

As she pocketed the tissues, Zee cast a wary look at the woman's worn, wrinkled plastic gloves. Those looked like she'd been using them all morning. Or maybe all week. Perhaps she'd change to new ones.

No such luck. As the thin gloves pawed through her belongings, Zee made a note to disinfect everything when she got home.

Or maybe she'd just burn it all and start over.

"Hope you don't need anything in here." Pasty-Hair smirked. "Get it back when you leave."

Zee gritted her teeth. She should have expected this, but in her defense, she'd never visited a jail.

Her face a mask, Zee watched as the woman tore a limp ticket from a damp-looking roll, ripped it in half, and dropped one part with Zee's purse and ID into a smudged plastic bag, which she dumped onto a table behind her. The flap at the back of the drawer squeaked, and the other ticket half appeared.

"Take a seat."

Zee extracted the flaccid paper scrap and joined the silent denizens marking time in a row of hard plastic chairs. Stoop-shouldered or slouched with legs spread, slumped with heads lowered or staring at the dingy walls, no one making eye contact, everyone in their own private netherworld.

To distract her from what might permeate the dun-colored seat, Zee read the list of banned items on a yellowed laminated poster. No explosives, guns, knives, razors, drugs, syringes, or flammable liquids. "I feel safer already," she muttered.

Pasty-Hair shot a lethal glare in her direction. Zee resisted the urge to cower. She fell into stoic silence.

The broken wall clock mocked her with its unchanging face. Or maybe time just moved at a glacial pace here. Her hands itched for her phone, for any tenuous tether to life outside these walls.

After an eon, she heard her name. She joined the other chosen ones, passed through a cave-like metal detector, and shuffled to the elevator. The battered doors creaked open, releasing a gush of fetid air along with the car's occupants. She clamped her teeth, wondering how long she could hold her breath.

The ten allotted passengers crammed into the space, and the doors sealed shut. Within moments, the stink of unwashed bodies and cheap musk cologne smothered the air. Her roiling stomach shot a question to her brain. Why was she enduring this, just to see the woman responsible for Bette's death?

The question answered itself. All other issues aside, Zee had to confront Marjorie, to satisfy herself that the police were right. Then she could grieve in peace.

Through watery eyes, she focused on the stained pant cuffs of the man in front of her. Someone brushed against her shoulder. Her neck prickled. She held still to avoid further contact, or risk confrontation.

A shuddering stop finally heralded deliverance. The doors rasped open, and a wave of frigid air rolled in. Stumbling out, Zee drank it like fresh cool water, unconcerned about the goosebumps on her arms.

A stern-faced officer escorted the group to the visiting room, firearm prominent on his hip. "Take a seat."

She filed past him, perched on the edge of a dented metal stool bolted to the floor, and waited on her side of the barrier. The thick glass—marred by scratches and smears and discolored by time and the smoke of countless cigarettes—wouldn't flatter anyone. Even so, Zee recoiled at the sight of Marjorie Franklin shuffling through the inner door.

Her once attractive figure was reduced to a shapeless lump in a toxic orange jumpsuit. Her chestnut tresses, no longer lustrous as in her website photo, hung in a limp ponytail.

Zee had expected to dislike Marjorie, but the hard edges of her antagonism softened at the sight of the wrecked woman. She could barely hold herself upright. Her head swiveled slowly, as if the effort taxed her endurance.

As inmates hurried toward their visitors, calling greetings, Zee rose from her seat and waved, trying to signal Marjorie. Their eyes met.

Marjorie's brows tightened, but she shambled across the floor and slumped onto the stool. Head lowered, she fingered a clump of hair, stuck it between chapped lips, and sucked on it.

Wishing she'd brought an antiseptic wipe, Zee plucked the tissues from her pocket and lifted the heavy phone receiver. "Hello?"

Marjorie fixed Zee with dull, flat eyes, then closed her hand around her receiver. "Who are you?" Through the wire, her voice was tinny. "What d'you want?"

"Suzanne Morani." The receiver brushed her cheek. Zee stifled a cringe. Starting with the least challenging topic, she offered what she hoped would be a persuasive overture. "Someone sent me a text message. I think it's about you, that the police have gotten something wrong. If that's true, I want to help you."

Zee stifled an impulse to slap her hand over her mouth. What had she just said? This woman killed Bette—and Zee wanted to *help* her? She swallowed astonishment. Her offer was a ploy, but threaded through it was an impetus. She actually did want to help this miserable woman.

Marjorie backed away, screwing her face as though she smelled a stench. "You're one of those religious do-gooders, aren't you." By the time she finished the accusation, she was halfway off the stool and reaching to hang up the phone.

"No." Zee pressed her palm against the partition.

"Hands off the glass." The guard at the door shifted his hand toward his holster.

Zee jerked her fingers from the filthy surface, refocused on Marjorie. "Whoever sent the text believes you're innocent." Okay, not exactly an accurate translation, but it had the desired effect.

Marjorie slid back onto the stool and leaned closer. Red blotches marred her once flawless complexion, and deep circles incised the flesh beneath her eyes. She spat strands of hair from her mouth and glared. "I did it. I don't know why anyone would say other-wise." Message delivered, she crumpled on the seat, as if the paltry cascade of words had drained the life from her.

Instinctively, Zee reached toward the greasy glass, then, feeling the guard's eyes, stopped short. She infused her voice with concern, willing Marjorie's cooperation. "I know you confessed, but the text raises a lot of questions."

Marjorie remained an unresponsive lump. Above the clatter of voices in the room, a woman laughed, too loud, too desperate.

Anxiety pushed Zee to capture Marjorie's eyes. If the woman gathered enough energy to rouse, she might abandon the stool and retreat to her cell. Scrambling for a way to circumvent that, Zee blurted the first thing that came to mind. "Tell me, what happened with Bette?"

The top of the dank head lifted a notch. A monotone string of words ensued. "Nothing to tell. We argued. I shoved her. She fell and hit her head. I knew she was dead, and I ran." Marjorie's fingers found the hunk of chewed hair again. "But somebody saw me, so she won anyway."

Hardly a victory for Bette. Yet, the lifeless recitation melted more of Zee's resentment. "You didn't mean to kill her."

"Doesn't matter. She's still dead." Marjorie folded into herself.

Her desolation squeezed Zee's heart. Having accidentally caused someone's death last summer, she knew the black void that held Marjorie. She leaned as close to the scarred glass as she dared, seeking Marjorie's downcast eyes. "It *does* matter. Your life doesn't have to be over."

No reaction. It was like pleading with a stone, or more accurately, to the rubble left when the stone imploded.

Zee tried again. "It was an accident. Your lawyer should be able to use that for a defense."

Marjorie snorted, but a semblance of animation returned to her voice. "You sound like him. He thinks he can get a deal. I told him not to bother."

Determined, Zee pressed. "Maybe you should listen to him. Don't give up on your life."

Marjorie shifted to the side of the stool. "We done here?" She stuck the sodden strands in her mouth.

"Wait," Zee said. "The text." She couldn't leave without probing for a connection.

Marjorie shrugged, but stopped. "What's it say?"

Zee met the tired hazel eyes. "'Now we see but darkly. Pernicious mirror.'"

Marjorie's face hardened like the jail's concrete walls. "More religious crap."

"What does it mean?"

Marjorie blew the hair from her mouth. "Hell if I know." She twisted the hank around her finger. "Sounds like my Aunt Lenore. Except she's in the business of debunking all that garbage."

Zee's antennae alerted. "The website identified the founder of Believers Anonymous as Lenore Meeris. Is that your aunt?"

Marjorie scrubbed the heel of her hand across her cheek. When she spoke, she seemed to talk to herself. "I thought she cared about me." Her voice dropped so low that Zee nearly missed the addendum. "Instead, she left me to the bitch who ruined my life."

Bette?

The accusation slammed into Zee's chest with the force of a boot heel. She rocked back on the stool. She hadn't given great credence to the idea that Marjorie and the protagonist from *The Mirror of the Soul* could be one and the same. Now it appeared more than plausible.

Head down, Marjorie dropped the phone receiver into its holder. She let her feet fall to the floor and dragged herself toward the inmates' door.

"Wait," Zee called to her retreating back. "Who are you talking about? What do you mean?"

If Marjorie heard through the thick, soiled barrier, she didn't react. Too far gone into the abyss. A guard opened the interior door, and she disappeared into its dark maw.

CHAPTER 12

ZEE SOUGHT REFUGE IN THE STEAMING shower, her second of the day. The filth of the jail clung to her skin. Even worse, the despair of that haunted place stained her soul.

She dug her nails into her scalp as she lathered, her frustrations tangling in her fingers. The lady who cut her hair would be horrified, but this was no time for a gentle approach.

It takes force.

Hot water burned her scalp as she rinsed. She welcomed the pain. Maybe it would cut through her boomeranging emotions.

She went to the jail angry at the woman who killed Bette. She left wanting to help her. Maybe learning that Bette's death was an accident softened her grief. Definitely, the brutality of the whole jail experience sickened her.

She soaped her loofa and scrubbed. From the smirking gatekeeper overseeing the oppressive waiting area to the sneering guard wielding his petty authority in the bleak visitors room—if this was the public face of the justice system, she shuddered to think of the soulless hell behind those locked doors.

Her parents were right about the world of law enforcement. Mindless machinery chewing up soft, vulnerable human beings. Papa Alesandro's words prodded Zee. When she questioned the actions of civil rights protesters who were arrested, he said, "We have to fight when the law is not fair."

Water sluiced away the scum, resurrecting tendrils of energy. *Z Beats* gave her plenty of experience speaking up for the powerless, championing justice and fairness. If Marjorie forbade her lawyer to act, she wielded no such power over Zee.

Anguish ambushed Zee's heart. This new information colored everything about her relationship with Bette. Her sweetness carried a rank tinge now. Like a rotting stone at the heart of a ripe peach.

Her throat tightened. Rico said she was too trusting. Maybe she had been seduced by Southern charm. Fontina encouraged her to trust her instincts, but how could she when they left her so uncertain?

Hemmed in by a cloud of steam, Zee shut off the water and grabbed a towel. Briskly, almost angrily, she whisked it back and forth across her skin. The abrasion woke determination along with her nerve endings.

To find her way through this mess, she needed more information about BA, and she'd get it.

Starting tonight.

UNDER A DUSKY, CLOUD-STREWN SKY, ZEE parked the Mini in the lot alongside the East Valerian Community Center. Anxiety jiggered through her ribcage. She inhaled to calm it. Surely typical Believers Anonymous members wouldn't be as fanatical as the ones who posted on the website.

She blew a breath through pursed lips. She could handle strong emotion. Especially, she smiled, with a wrathful goddess on her side.

Her heartrate slowed as she anchored herself in tonight's goal: learn about this group. Treat the meeting as research for her article. Professional, not personal. Unless she found a link between BA and the text, or between BA and Bette's death, or between BA and Marjorie and the text and the book and Bette's death—Zee slapped her palms over her ears to quiet the yammering voices.

She got out of her car, locked *Po*, and squared her shoulders. In the purpling sky, a pinprick star winked. "First star I see tonight," she whispered.

As she crossed the cracked concrete toward the side door, a gust of wind worried a rip in the taped-up Safe Space poster. A cold drop trickled down Zee's spine. Fontina said Oya's unbridled power sounded like paper tearing. Zee shook off her chill. Oya was on her side.

She climbed the half dozen concrete steps, pulled open the heavy door, and immediately found herself at the rear of a narrow, cavernous room. At the front end, dying fluorescent tubes cast sickly light, jaundicing the lectern and three rows of folding chairs. People clotted in the back half of the space. A pile of pillows and a stack of phone books leaned against a scuffed beige wall.

A small woman with a pinched face detached herself from the cluster and approached. "Hello." She produced a thinly stretched grimace that Zee imagined was meant as a smile. "You're new." With a non-existent chin, eyes like black beads, and cheeks that sloped sharply back from a bulbous pink nose, the woman bore an unnerving resemblance to a ferret.

Zee nodded, her expression frozen.

"Tea, coffee, and snacks over there." The woman pulled up the shapeless sleeve of her sweater and consulted a square watch on a vomit-green plastic band. Not digital, the old-fashioned analog kind, complete with side knob. "The meeting will begin promptly in three minutes." She turned away before Zee could respond.

Taken aback by the brusque greeting, Zee wandered to the abandoned refreshment table. A meager mound of salt-less pretzels slumped in a cardboard bowl next to a desultory heap of shrink-wrapped doughnuts on a paper plate. She stifled a groan. In her jail cell, Marjorie probably ate better than this, and in better lighting.

A stack of papers snagged Zee's attention. *The Four Steps*. She picked one up as the crowd began to push past. Before she could grab a seat, the back row filled.

So much for a quick escape should this all go sideways.

She squeezed through the narrow space next to the wall and, stuffing the paper in her purse, secured the end chair in the second row. The audience consisted of about twenty people, roughly a third of them men. Two gray-haired ladies huddled in the first row, in front of a younger woman fiddling with her phone.

Good idea. As Zee muted her cell, someone plopped down next to her. A young man with a clean-shaven head and a face dominated by angry eyes.

"Kevin." He stuck out a nail-bitten hand. "What brings you to our little club, Miss . . .?"

Zee forced a smile, hoping her face did not betray her mind's scramble for a plausible introduction. "Suzanne." No one but the government used her formal name. She slipped her phone into her purse, buying time to avoid his extended hand and come up with a cover story that didn't involve her writing an article. A sharp thwack from the front of the room saved her from both.

"This meeting will come to order." Ferret-Face rapped the podium again. "We begin with the recitation of the *Four Steps*."

As Zee pulled the paper from her purse, the group members spoke in unison.

"Four Steps to Break Free from the Pernicious Effects of Religious Indoctrination."

She followed along silently as the group broke into a rumbling chorus.

"*1. Unequivocally acknowledge and declare that religion and religious upbringing have exerted a corrosive, corruptive influence on your own life.*"

The voices in the herd grew more vehement.

"*2. Assert that religions are nothing more than the corrupt creations of human beings for their own ends and are rightfully resisted and destroyed.*"

Behind her, participants hurled the phrases like spears.

"*3. Wholeheartedly commit to vigorously resisting all forms of religion and to rooting out, exposing, and destroying the pernicious effects of religious indoctrination."*

The maelstrom intensified. Zee broke into a sweat.

"4. Vigilantly do everything possible to turn others away from the corrosive, corruptive effects of religion and religious brainwashing."

As the last furious syllables died, Zee exhaled a tightly-held breath. Whoever claimed that words would never harm, hadn't heard these people.

A screeching howl pierced her right ear. Zee snapped her head to the side. Face contorted, Kevin threw his head back and wailed at the top of his lungs.

Everywhere in the room, the veneer of civil behavior shattered. The space erupted with shrieks and roars. Even Ferret-Face bellowed.

Zee shrank toward the wall, throat drying. It might not have been wise to come here alone.

Kevin jumped from his seat, arms flailing. Zee ducked. All around her, people scattered from their chairs, screaming, snarling, baying.

A portly man in a three-piece suit flung himself to the floor and began beating his fists against the worn carpet. The two elderly ladies rushed to grab pillows and shove them beneath his thrashing hands, all the while keening over him like he was a lost child.

In the back of the room, three people threw themselves into a stamping dance. Accompanied by guttural growls, they snatched at invisible somethings, stuffed them into their mouths, and chewed them with exaggerated vigor. Then they spat out the ethereal objects and stomped them.

Zee's heart jolted into high gear. Did these people just follow their unleashed fury wherever it led them? She didn't want to wait to find out.

A tiny part of her brain reminded her that she needed interviews. She blew out a negation. No way these people could answer her questions. More likely, they'd grab her by the collar and drag her into participating in—whatever this was. She clutched her purse and half-rose, eying the narrow escape route along the wall.

Maybe she could slip out while they were distracted. She ventured a step.

The stamp-dancers gyrated toward the door. Zee halted. She would never make it past them.

Eyes darting, she searched for another exit.

There.

Blocked by a man in a half-untucked plaid shirt who punched at the unforgiving metal.

Zee sank back into her chair. The website had not overstated. She hoped she'd get out of this to report on it.

Tearing paper sawed at her attention. Ice spliced Zee's shoulder blades.

"Aag-baa-ya-ah!" a woman cried. In the haphazard light, her face darkened. White stripes painted her cheeks. Her arm whipped upward. Strands of fire streamed from her fist. Eyes blazing, she whirled, her long black hair flaying the air. Jewels danced in a glittering golden headdress. "Oy-yah-ee!" She flung her arm toward the floor. A bolt of lightning leapt from her fingertips.

Zee's hand flew to her heart. She blinked furiously, then closed her eyes and gripped the metal frame of the chair. Hard. Cold. Stable.

Real.

Cautiously, she cracked an eyelid.

An ordinary woman's tears streamed down an ordinary face, pale tracks, not paint. Her raised fist held twisted scraps from a phonebook. Across her forehead, only beads of sweat glittered.

Zee stared, trying to comprehend. She couldn't have seen Oya. It must have been the power of suggestion. All around her, the room crackled with collective roused energy. She swallowed against her scratchy throat, her every nerve cell screaming danger.

Inhale. Exhale. Refocus on the goal.

Despite the perspiration soaking her shirt, her hand searched for her phone. This was why she came. If nothing else, she could capture all this in photos. Video would be even better.

A loud crack propelled her to her feet. The phone fell into the darkness of her purse. Her logical mind identified the explosion of a paper bag full of air, but her primitive brain drove her to escape. Fingers closing around the Mini's fob, she prepared to use it a weapon. No matter what she had to battle, it was time to get out of this madness.

But the explosive bang had signaled the end of a crescendo. Kevin's howling died. The ladies' keening faded. As if someone had poured cool water into a boiling pot, the waves of agitation in the room dissipated. The stamp-dancers halted and sank to the floor in spent heaps. The portly man rolled onto his back, his vest rising and falling in rapid breaths. The phonebook gang dropped their volumes and slid down amid the piles of crumpled debris.

Sweat-drenched air clung to Zee's skin and clogged her nose, but curiosity overrode her flight response. She shifted back into her chair.

In slow motion, the formerly frenetic figures roused, rose, and recovered their seats. Some straightened their disheveled clothing. Some finger-combed their hair. Most wiped their faces and eyes.

As he reclaimed his chair, Kevin touched her arm with a sweaty finger. "First time, huh? Someone should've warned you." He grinned, moisture sheening his upper lip. "A lot of us have some rage, so we start with a little catharsis."

"No kidding," Zee murmured. With an effort, she relaxed her face into a smile.

Ferret-Face stood at the front. "We will now repeat the *Four Steps.*"

Zee's shoulders tensed, but the second recitation proceeded much more calmly.

As the words died, the portly man shuffled to his feet. "Today was a hard day for me." His hoarse voice betrayed an effort to withhold tears. "My nephew is getting married, and I had to tell him I wouldn't go to the temple." He bowed his head and covered his eyes with one hand. No one moved or made a sound. "I just can't . . . all the memories . . . my presence feeds the corruption."

He sat with a heavy thump. Several chairs creaked. The plaid-shirted man next to him patted his shoulder.

Zee tried to imagine feeling so outcast. Her Unitarian Universalist parents taught her to accept all faith choices, including none at all. They believed no one source possessed a monopoly on truth and meaning.

She twisted her lips. Their expansive nonjudgment didn't extend to all areas. When she chose to honor truth by writing satire, to honor meaning by pointing out how language was used to cloud it, her dad criticized her calling. *Too easy*, he said. *Too superficial*.

Her stomach knotted. Now she would never get a chance to heal that breach.

One of the stamp-dancers cleared her throat and stood. Exertion or excitement rouged her cheeks. Her skimpy t-shirt clung to her well-toned body.

"I got caught in the trap again." She pushed tangles of dark hair from her face. "Worried about a project at work. What if my boss didn't approve? It's like I always have to be told I'm okay, or I think I'll die or something."

Dashing tears with a quick swipe of her hand, she mustered a smile. "Well, I chewed that one up and spit it out and stomped it lifeless today. I feel better." She sat with a loud exhalation.

Zee found herself nodding in support.

One of the elderly ladies spoke from her chair. "Every day, I struggle to know I'm worth as much as anyone else."

Her voice quivered. "From as far back as I can remember, I wanted to be a boy. Boys, well men, seemed to be in charge of everything. Even God was a man. I hated myself for being a girl for a long time.

"Then I met Danita. It was like I broke out of my cage, I was so happy. I love every day with her, even after all the time we've been together." She worked her jaw. "But I can't get rid of my anger about how I was taught to hate myself. The other day, a guy on the news made a comment that upset me, and I just screamed and yelled at the TV. It feels like a monster takes me over." She tugged at her sleeve and lowered her voice to a whisper. "I'm so sick of this. I want it to stop."

As the testimony continued, tears gathered in Zee's eyes. People spoke of living with guilt, or with fear they couldn't shake, or with intractable struggles over self-worth. They described trouble making decisions, marriage problems, issues with sex. And every one of them laid the difficulty directly at the door of a religion.

Zee's sympathy grew at the litany of pain, but her mind resisted. Their reasoning was too simplistic. Poverty; poor education; sibling rivalry; neglectful, cold, betraying parents. She ticked on mental fingers the many potential causes for lifelong struggles. Beyond that, these people were all running away, refusing to face their own responsibility for their trouble.

A barb stabbed her conscience. She was doing that with Karl, scampering off to an unknown editor, instead of fighting for her right to be heard in her own space.

She straightened in her chair. Karl would get first crack at this story. If he shut her down, she'd go to Bette's editor with a free conscience.

"Anyone else?" Ferret-Face said.

A tall, slender woman rose from the first row and faced the audience. Elegance shone through her disheveled clothing and the sheen of perspiration on her face. With a well-manicured hand, she brushed aside a lock of thick flame-red hair. "Listen up, weak-willed wimps and whiners."

Her crisp voice carried without being raised. She swept her gaze like a searchlight across the attendees. "I have five thousand dollars here. Who wants it?"

CHAPTER 13

Zee swallowed a gasp. In the wake of this brash BA member's offer of five thousand dollars, every slack-jawed face fixed on the flame-haired woman. At the podium, even Ferret-Face gaped.

A rumpled man in the second row raised a swarthy hand halfway, then let it drop.

"Nobody?" the speaker chided. She rested one hand on a slim hip, green eyes sweeping the three rows of folding chairs. "Time's up."

Her spell broke.

The rumpled man stabbed an accusing finger. "You wasn't gonna to give it anyway, Alex." He punctuated the end of his slurred statement with a loud hiccup.

A drunk. Zee pursed her lips, then pulled back from her judgment. She didn't know this man. He could have a medical condition.

"He's right." Another voice piped up, elderly and quivering.

In the meager light of the long, narrow meeting room, mumbles of agreement rose. Alex raised her slender hands, and the rumbling dissolved. "I meant every word."

Beside Zee, Kevin slapped his fist against his palm. Beneath reddening skin, the muscles in his jaw bunched. Probably kicking himself for not jumping at the chance for easy money. He ground his knuckles against his hand.

"You know my story." Alex's emerald eyes gathered the audience. "That sad saga's over. Tomorrow," she raised a triumphant fist, "I'm going to buy a sports car."

Zee clapped. Several faces turned to stare at her. Heat rose in her cheeks.

Kevin canted his head in her direction. "We usually just listen. It avoids judgment." He smiled, his earlier irritation gone. "I wanted to clap, too."

Zee tried to return his friendly gesture, but once again the whipsaw nature of the meeting wrenched her. Like a body blow, the outpouring of rage shocked her. Yet afterward, those same people exposed their wounds with incredible vulnerability. And now this audacious challenge, this dare hurled at them by this confident woman.

Her throat constricted. She would like to be that bold, that unguarded with Rico, but it was hard to surmount the barriers built over decades.

The painful timeline unfolded like a movie. Her mother on her deathbed confessing—*Stefan is not your father*. Zee was too young for such a revelation, and for the anger that followed. Her dad distanced himself from everyone, including her. Friends stopped trying to visit. Even Papa Alesandro. Confused, hurt, bereft, Zee built self-protective walls. Jeff's betrayal laid razor wire atop them.

No wonder she had trust issues.

"See you next week?" Kevin's voice sliced through her memories. People were leaving. She'd missed the end of the meeting.

She nodded to Kevin without thinking, ducking her face, fumbling in her purse for *Po*'s key to hide the rising tears. His chair creaked. Side-eyed, she watched him shrug into a tan jacket and make his way down the row.

She would let the room clear. No point in trying to interview people tonight. Her battered heart wanted only to go home, curl up with Candy, and sip a glass or two of chardonnay. *You can't read a book by licking the page.* Shelby's way of saying emotions, tasty as they were, got in the way of rational thought.

She had hallucinated Oya. That alone proved her compromised state.

A light tap on Zee's shoulder caused her to straighten. She glimpsed red tresses. "Oh. Sorry about the clapping."

"Don't trouble yourself." The tall woman offered her hand. "Alex Welling."

"Zee Morani."

"The reporter who interviewed Bette de la Cornne."

Zee winced. Cover blown.

The line of BA members trickling toward the door paused. Zee felt other glances. She strengthened her voice, but still spoke directly to Alex. "I don't want to cause any problems."

"We're not some freak show," said the woman who had morphed into Oya.

The temperature in the room chilled.

Zee's mind whirred. A part of the truth might allay their fears. She faced the restless cluster and infused her next sentence with neutrality. "The book made me curious about how people coped when they left their religions."

Kevin's angry glare returned. "Why pick on us?"

The eyes upon her multiplied. She resisted the urge to wipe sweat from her brow. "I found you on the internet. The testimonies impressed me." She lifted her shoulders. "I wanted to see for myself."

"Well, you've seen," snapped Lenore. A growl snaked from the back of the crowd.

"So, she investigated," Alex interjected.

Zee cringed at the word.

Alex continued, her voice cool, commanding. "Quit harassing her." She murmured to Zee, "There's more, isn't there?"

"It's not a simple answer."

"I have time."

Zee finger-combed the curls at the nape of her neck, as if the gesture would help untangle her thoughts. Her unexpected ally was canny. Doubtless she had her own purpose for intervening. Still, Zee could turn this to her advantage, redeem this night from a total loss. She slipped her purse strap over her shoulder. "Okay. Could we go somewhere? Grab a coffee, a glass of wine?"

Alex laughed, revealing luminous, perfectly straight teeth. "I know a nice little place. Just a short walk." She flicked her hand toward the BA members. "Go on, the rest of you. Nothing to concern you here."

Lenore muttered. Kevin stared. But the shuffle toward the door resumed.

"Neat trick," Zee said. "I'd like to learn it."

"A girl can't give away all her secrets." Alex arched a sculpted brow. "Not at first, anyway."

CHAPTER 14

Ten minutes after leaving the Community Center, Zee and Alex sat at a softly lit, window-side table in Marlene's Lounge. A jacketed waiter brought glasses of pinot noir, Alex's recommendation.

Zee swirled hers. "I'm curious." And a little stunned. "You offered the BA members five thousand dollars. You must have been confident no one would accept."

Quirking her lips, Alex managed to convey both disappointment and amusement. "I know those people."

Zee cocked her head. "You don't know me."

"A risk I was willing to take." Alex toyed with the stem of her glass. "It would have been refreshing if you had. Our BA stories vary, yet they're depressingly similar. Different curtains, same view."

The phrase tickled Zee's memory, but she couldn't place it.

"We're all brainwashed," Alex continued. "In my case, I learned that my wishes were not God's. Even worse, the very fact that I wanted something constituted proof I shouldn't have it." She lifted one hand, palm up. "Desire," she turned up the other palm, "equals evil."

Zee sucked in a breath. One part of her mind reeled from the twisted cruelty. Another questioned whether this personal revelation was meant to induce a similar disclosure from her. Though tempted, she opted for discretion. "That's seriously warped."

"It's the logic of children convinced that their immortal souls are forfeit unless they deny their desires."

"The money . . ."

"Forces them to see how much they still bought into that nonsense." A corner of Alex's perfectly tinted mouth lifted. "We are all very good at thinking we've conquered our demons, but the body doesn't lie."

Something Fontina would say. Zee's wariness eased. Maybe she could meet Alex halfway. "No one raised a hand, not even me."

"You, I can understand, but them—they couldn't bring themselves to move."

Zee flashed on the image of the rumpled man, his trembling, tentative gesture, followed by hopeless surrender, as if his hand fell off a cliff. She thought again of the manic behavior and Kevin's understatement: *A lot of us have some rage.* The shackles that bound the BA members were invisible, but they were prisoners, as much if not more than Marjorie in her cell.

Alex's voice softened. "I get where they are. But I'm declaring my liberation."

"The car?"

"I've wanted a sports car for years, but wouldn't allow myself to have it."

"And tomorrow, you will." Zee lifted her wine. "To liberation."

They clinked glasses.

Anticipating spicy acidity and delicate fruitiness, Zee brought the pinot noir to her lips. Her first taste, however, swamped her taste buds with strong black cherry. Maybe Alex's expertise didn't extend to wine. Zee swirled the liquid. The bouquet was tempting. Maybe the wine just needed to breathe.

"Your turn," Alex said. "What brought you to BA tonight?"

Zee set her glass on the table. The shock to her palette had startled her into awareness. She perched on a precipice, ready to blurt out everything to her newfound friend. Even the soft jazz floating in the air lulled her. Chastened, Zee reminded herself that

Marlene's had been Alex's choice. Alex, who Zee already knew did nothing without purpose.

And now, Alex was employing one of Zee's own interview techniques: waiting in utter stillness. Even her manicured fingers remained motionless on the wineglass.

Zee mulled how much to share, uncomfortably certain Alex could read her face. No point in dissembling. "I got a text." She recited the message, eyes trained on Alex's face.

No response. Not a muscle twitched.

Frustration furrowed Zee's brow. Alex wasn't even curious? Zee's earlier suspicion roused.

Leaning back, Alex steepled her fingers. Her blood-red nails gleamed in the light. Predator's claws. Zee swallowed her shock. How had she not noticed them earlier?

"What do you think it means?" asked Alex.

Damn. Trapped by her distraction. Zee wished she'd spoken first, but she could still learn from Alex's reaction. She proposed her strongest theory. "Someone wants me to look at the religious connections to Bette's death."

"Ah, tonight was research." The emerald eyes gleamed. "Did you learn anything helpful?"

Alex was quick. And she gave away nothing. Zee dodged a direct answer. "This meeting, was it typical?"

"Some are worse than others." Alex's chuckle emerged from somewhere deep, tinged with personal pain. "How much do you know about Believers Anon?"

"Other than what I learned a couple of hours ago, only what I read on the internet." Zee grabbed the initiative. "I'd like to talk to the woman who led tonight's meeting. Who is she?"

"That's Lenore."

"Ferr—uh—*she's* the founder?" Damn, wrong-footed again. Zee tried to mute the judgment in her reaction. "I thought she'd be warmer."

"Lenore's had a rough time of it recently." Alex eddied the ruddy liquid in her glass. "She was more obsessed about that book than Marjorie."

More obsessed than her niece, who trashed her career, stalked Bette, and apparently caused her death? "How so?"

"Worried about BA's image, of course. And its rocky financial situation, though that's another story." A shadow flickered across Alex's face.

More to learn there. "The movie was a threat." Zee made it a statement.

Alex nodded. "But she couldn't convince Bette to halt the project." She glanced toward the ceiling. "How did Lenore put it? 'That sanctimonious Southern bitch laughed at me. Said no one cared about my piddling little organization.'"

"Blunt." And cruel. Zee tried to reconcile the harsh statement with her memory of Bette's warmth. Sara Jane said Bette had lost patience with Marjorie. Maybe with Lenore, too.

Conscious that silence had fallen, Zee cast about for a way to keep Alex talking. "I don't recall BA in the book." As soon as the words were out, she kicked herself. The book was her stated reason for attending the meeting tonight.

Alex assessed her with a sharp gaze. "The group Lilliana joined after her divorce. To 'cure' people of religious dependence."

"Oh, that." Zee made a note never to try to fool this woman. "I doubt most readers made that connection."

"Marjorie made it for them." Alex shrugged. "But even before then, Lenore kept demanding a public statement, an acknowledgment that there were groups like BA who did good work."

Like Religious Recovery, that Fontina mentioned. Zee would be sure to check it out, for balance in her article. "It doesn't seem like an unreasonable request."

"Perhaps not at first," said Alex. "But I'm afraid Lenore hounded Bette."

The group's furious bellowing echoed in Zee's ears. Ferret-Face encouraged unfettered expression. Maybe it spilled beyond the doors of their meeting room. "Bette's publicist mentioned Marjorie's persistence, but nothing about Lenore."

Alex snorted. "Take whatever Sara *Jane* says with a shaker of salt. She considers herself the guardian at the gate . . . but Bette had that effect on people." Alex lowered glimmering lashes. "And she knew it."

Zee blinked at the rapid mood shift. Her story antennae quivered, but her heart flinched from scraping an obvious—and probably irrelevant—ex-lover's wound. She filed it for later consideration.

Swirling her wine, Zee gave Alex time to recover her composure. When Alex raised her head, Zee returned to her major question. "The text. What do you think it means?"

"Do you suspect Lenore sent it?"

Damn. Alex sidestepped again, but Zee was hitting her stride. "You know her better than I."

Alex shook her head. "Doesn't fit. Lenore favors the straightforward approach. In fact, she confronted Bette the day she died."

"She was there, at Bette's apartment?"

Alex nodded.

"What time?" Zee cringed at the eagerness in her voice and softened it. "Not that it matters. I'm sure Bette's death hit her hard." Zee lowered her eyes. Let Alex feel sympathy, the better to misdirect her.

Cool fingers brushed Zee's hand. "How thoughtless of me. You were with Bette as well, only a few days before she died."

Despite Zee's cover, real tears threatened.

"Don't trouble yourself about Lenore," Alex said. "This is one area where her hard shell serves her well."

In an attempt to regain self-control, Zee shifted her focus to the window. Velvet sky pulled her eyes toward the invisible stars. A benevolent presence, always there, whether she saw them or not. The tightness in her chest eased at the thought of Bette among them, a shining gem hidden from view only by the city lights.

Movement caught her attention. Across the street, a figure skirted a pool of street light. "What the hell?" Zee squinted. "That guy Kevin is watching us." She started from her chair, but Alex raised her hand to bar the way.

"No point in rushing out. He'll be gone before you get to the door."

Zee twisted and scoured the street. No sign. Anger sharpened her voice. "What's he think he's doing?"

"He's probably mad about what happened at the meeting."

"Which part?" Zee snapped.

Alex leaned back in her chair. "Kevin has anger issues in general. I wouldn't worry."

Zee dropped into her seat. "I don't put up with stalking." Alex's calm maddened her. "Is this typical behavior?"

A low, throaty saxophone floated from Alex's purse. She pulled out her phone and glanced at it. "I have to go."

Zee seethed, but didn't want to end the conversation on a negative note. She conjured a weak smile. "Good luck with the car tomorrow. What are you getting?"

Alex's lips curved into a cupid's bow. "Find out at the next meeting." She slid to her feet. "Stay. Finish your wine. As in most things, it takes time for the nuances to reveal themselves." Posture erect, fiery hair glinting in the muted light, she wove her way toward the door.

Zee puffed a sigh, part admiration, part consternation. She gained a lot of new information, but it felt like someone tossed a handful of pebbles in the air and let them fall where they may. She needed time to see how it all connected.

Suspicion sent out a niggling tentacle. That interruption was convenient. Zee looked out the window at the empty street. Alex crossed in front of her view, heading in the direction of the community center.

Zee considered following her, but Alex was too sharp to miss a tail. Of course, there was a perfectly plausible reason for Zee to walk that way; her car was in the community center's lot. She tapped her finger against the wine glass. If she were honest, she remained in Marlene's because she wanted to believe Alex was an ally. Or could become one.

Absently, she sipped the wine. Its earlier sweetness had mellowed, and the liquid slid like silk across her tongue, smoothly rich with undertones of clove, the perfect hint of earthiness. She savored a leisurely swallow.

Alex knew what she was talking about. And not just with respect to viniculture. She'd skillfully deflected Zee's questions, cast doubt on Sara Jane, and directed Zee toward Lenore. Why?

A string of notes floated from her cell. Rico texting.

Drinks at the Sundown Grill?

Zee's heartbeat skipped, but finger poised over her response, she balked. Yesterday, he'd assumed she had no plans when he invited himself for dinner. Tonight, he could wait a minute or two while she finished this excellent wine.

Husky laughter drifted across the room. A couple twined hands at the bar, drawing their heads close.

Zee's throat constricted. Why couldn't she let things be that easy with Rico? She swirled her glass. Light shimmered, gliding across the surface of the wine, changing and morphing. Ever new, moment to moment.

Tension eased from her face. What had Alex said? Change was refreshing.

Zee glanced at the phone. Time to shake things up. And if Rico felt off balance to find the director's shoe on the other foot, so much the better. Smile spreading across her lips, she typed in her acceptance.

CHAPTER 15

Zee angled the Mini into a spot near the Sundown Grill, smiling at the surprise she planned for Rico. Absurdly, she wished she'd worn heels. The sharp, no-nonsense clack would punctuate her message: *Heads up, I am a woman to be reckoned with.*

As he would discover in just a few minutes.

If she could pull it off.

Come to think of it, maybe her soft-soled flats were better. Her sore back and stiff knee would sabotage any confident stride. Also, the last time she wore those scarlet heels, they led a trail of clothing to her bedroom.

Hunger for him surged, threatening to wreck her game. Hurriedly, she pulled herself from the driver's seat. On the sidewalk outside the bar, she slipped into her new Alex persona, letting each soft footfall tamp the tide of desire.

The irony pinched her heart. Earlier in their relationship, he'd been the one who pushed for greater intimacy. She rebelled, the ghosts of former betrayals preventing her from giving him the commitment he wanted. But since her fight with an unhinged killer, she craved a deeper connection. Now *he* hesitated.

A few steps away, light flickered through the Grill's mullioned windows. He was in there, waiting.

She inhaled the crisp evening air, shored her will with Alex's cool confidence, and pulled open the heavy glass door.

Showtime.

Boisterous laughter and chatter rained around her. In contrast to the low-key sophistication of Marlene's, the Grill attracted office workers, girls' night out parties, and exuberant fans after the ballgame. No misty photos of Armstrong and Gillespie on matte-black walls. No tasteful offerings of pâté on water crackers. No imported wines enumerated in elegant script on gilt-edged cards. Instead, amateur pics of local sunsets, a menu that ran to burgers and 'world famous' chili, and a mere three American beers on tap.

The ambience tugged at Zee to abandon her ploy, but then she caught sight of Rico lounging in a booth, the muted light casting a glow on his dark hair and leather jacket. He lifted his beer in greeting. "*Salud*."

Game on.

"*Dinero y amor*." Zee brushed a kiss across his lips.

He trapped her arm. "Money and love?" His eyes crinkled.

"Health, wealth, happiness. It's a traditional toast." Even to her ears, the response sounded too defensive. Aware of his scrutiny, she smiled, loosened his grip, and slid into the bench opposite him.

He tracked her movements, studying her. "You look pleased with yourself."

"I've had an interesting day, but I want to hear your news first."

"What makes you think—"

"I know you." She beckoned with her fingers and a sly grin. "Give."

His chest expanded beneath his snug black t-shirt, and he lifted his hands in surrender. "I want to be your partner."

She rocked back, lungs forgetting how to breathe. Her carefully corralled feelings exploded like feathers from a pillow. Now that the moment was here, she need only speak.

But like trying to snatch bits of eiderdown, her tongue flailed at words that flitted beyond her grasp. It was all she could do to keep her mouth from hanging open.

From a shard of awareness, she caught the mischievous flicker on his lips. A firework burst in her chest and burned her cheeks. How *dare* he—

"What can I get you, miss?"

Saved by the server.

Zee let the words sparking in her throat recede. She glanced at the menu and forced lightness into her voice. "I'm feeling adventurous." She pointed to the menu. "A bowl of your 'famous chili.'"

The waitress cocked an eyebrow. "O-kay." The snigger in her acknowledgment suggested Zee might regret it.

"And a root beer," Zee added.

"Make my beer a real one," said Rico with a wink at the waitress.

Chortling under her breath, she left.

Zee arched her brows at Rico. "You may have taken my greeting too literally. What prompted this . . . proposal?"

He stiffened slightly. "You're stubborn. And unpredictable. So, I figure better to work *with* you than beat my head against . . ." He rubbed his hand across the dark stubble on his chin. "This isn't coming out right."

Perverse pleasure bubbled in Zee's throat at the frustration on his face. Sliding fully into Alex's elegant character, she reclined in slow motion against the back of the booth, shaped her lips into an enigmatic smile, and draped her next words with amusement. "Not usually a problem for you."

She drank in his speechless astonishment. Across the room, someone cheered as a dart hit its target.

Rico rubbed a hand across his stubble. His gears clicked. Gleam effervesced in his eyes. Leaning forward, he lowered his voice to a throaty drawl. "Are you *toying* with me?"

Zee's pulse lurched.

His eyebrows rose, questioning.

She reined in her galloping heartrate. A chess move on his part. Recalibrating her options, she deepened her own tenor. "Would you *like* me to toy with you?"

A flush darkened his cheeks. Smile fading, he retreated with his back to the seat.

In the blue depths of his eyes, uncertainty battled fierce determination. His vulnerability undid her. Time to let him off the hook. "What you get for messing with me."

Relief swept his features. "Well played." He chuckled. "I'm sorry."

"Apology accepted."

He rolled the beer bottle between his palms. "I meant, I want to be your *investigative* partner."

Exhilaration widened her grin. She offered her hand. "Deal." He clasped it to seal the bargain. Despite the chill from his bottle, heat zinged up her arm.

"Here you go." The waitress set Zee's drink and a steaming bowl on the table. "Careful, it's hot." She traded Rico's empty beer for a new one.

Zee stirred the dish, lifted a spoonful and blew on it. Once the waitress was out of earshot, she hooked Rico's gaze. "I'm glad you want to help. That text creeps me out, like I'm being stalked." Goosebumps crawled on her arms. She was, if she read Kevin's skulking correctly.

"Start with this." Rico canted his bottle toward her. "It's not about your friend's death."

Zee stifled a surge of resentment at his confident dismissal. "Why are you so sure?"

"Bernstow's got a witness."

Spoon halfway to her lips, Zee froze. "Who is it? Was it a positive ID?"

"A neighbor. Not a hundred percent, but close enough."

So, her sleuthing really was superfluous. To hide her disappointment, Zee slipped the chili into her mouth. Ripe tomato burst on her tongue. As its sweetness mellowed, nuances unfolded. Smokiness. Peppery spice. Aromatic heat. Nothing to justify that waitress's smirk.

Mid-swallow, the initial mild warmth flared, like kindling catching a spark. Her taste buds sounded the alarm, but too late.

The chain reaction barreled on, unstoppable. Millions of fiery pinpricks exploded against her cheeks, tongue, and the roof of her mouth. As the scorching river streamed down her throat, she grabbed for her drink, flooding even her aching teeth with the cool liquid. "My god," she croaked. "What's in this?"

Rico pushed his beer across the table. "Roll the cold bottle on your forehead."

"What?"

"Trust me."

Desperation for relief overrode all fear of looking silly. She swiped the chilled surface across her skin. The volcanic heat in her sinuses abated. Sweat on her eyelids cooled. Embarrassment forgotten, she rolled the bottle side to side, dampening her forehead all the way to her ears. Ice and fire locked in combat. Gloriously, ice was winning. If only she could move the open bottle between her shoulder blades without spilling it.

Rico slid from his side of the booth, reached for his beer. "Let me."

Even through her shirt, contact with the frigid glass provoked an immediate frosty shock, charging up her neck and driving a spike behind her eyes. She reached back and seized his forearm. "Stop. My head."

He withdrew the bottle and set it on the table. "Put your tongue against the roof of your mouth, high up in back." He leaned close, his breath soft in her ear. "Or I could take care of that for you."

Despite the pounding in her head, she smiled. "I think that may be beyond even your abilities. Besides, I have actual dragon breath."

"I'd make the sacrifice." He nibbled her ear, then gripped her shoulders with powerful hands. Harley hands, she'd called them when they first got together. "This'll help, too."

Her nerves sang as he burrowed his thumbs in long strokes beneath the edges of her shoulder blades. Probing gently with his fingertips along her neck, he chased prickles behind her ears and across her entire scalp. Her headache faded.

"Thank you," she breathed.

He leaned forward and swept his lips across her cheek. "That's what partners are for."

Her pulse surged. Alex's persona had its uses. "Think I'm going to enjoy this partnership thing."

"Me too." Rico settled beside her on the bench.

Zee's thigh burned where the cotton twill of her slacks rested against his denim jeans. She pushed the offending chili aside while she struggled to sort her thoughts. His proposition marked a new dimension in their relationship, but she shouldn't read too much into it, should she?

He'd known how she would react to his word choice. As Alex had with her, he'd teased. Unlike with Alex, she'd turned the tables. Showed herself equal to his challenge.

She twisted toward him "Where were we?"

"Rescuing you from chili."

"My hero." She sipped her drink. Her tongue felt like it had lost a layer of cells. "You were telling me about a witness."

"Add that to the confession. Slam-dunk."

"Marjorie didn't mean to kill her. It was an accident."

He swiveled toward her, face-to-face. "And you know that *how*?"

Annoyance flared at his accusation.

He flashed a hasty smile. "Sherlock?"

Her irritation melted. They were both new to partnership. "I went to see Marjorie in jail."

"Of course you did." His light teasing took away the sting in his words.

While she detailed her interview, his eyebrows danced an emotional ballet, lifting, lowering, knotting, and finally settling.

"I tried to give her a little encouragement," Zee summarized. "Told her she shouldn't give up on her life."

Rico tapped his fingers against his bottle, as if weighing his words. "It worked, but I'm not sure you did her a favor."

"Why?" A warning throbbed behind her eyes. "How can that be bad?"

"She's changed her plea to not guilty."

The pulsing escalated. "What's wrong with that?"

"There's a new gung-ho Assistant D.A. Word is he's going after her, piling on more charges."

Zee's headache exploded. "Because she changed her plea? That's … *extortion*." She stiffened. "It should be involuntary manslaughter."

He brushed a damp curl from her cheek. "You only have her version."

Despite radiating waves of pain, Zee gulped. Just hours ago, she'd lectured herself on the unreliability of her instincts. "You're right."

His mouth twitched but stopped short of a full-on grin.

She appreciated his restraint. And the velvet texture of his lips, still dewed from the cold beer.

"Also, you got a high-profile victim," he said. "Prosecutor can't appear to let her off easy."

Zee bristled. There it was again, feelingless bureaucracy. "Heaven forbid people think he was shirking his duty, no matter the reality."

Rico squeezed her hand. "This kind of case can make or break a career."

"Dammit." Zee smacked her free hand against the table. "Marjorie's a human being, not a pawn in somebody's game of climb-the-professional-ladder."

"I know." Rico's blue eyes caught hers. "I love that about you. You never forget the story is about people."

Zee could drown in his cobalt undertow. As it was, she allowed it to cool her anger. He was only the messenger. Her thoughts returned to her jailhouse visit. "Did your sources shed any light on the text message?"

"Bernstow's chalking it up to crazies."

Maybe she should too, but it irked her, like a burr in her sock. She switched topics. "Speaking of crazies, I went to a Believers Anonymous meeting."

"Of course you did."

She play-punched his arm. "Stop saying that. Do you even know what I'm talking about?"

He made a show of rubbing the alleged sore spot. "Sounds like AA."

"There might be some slight resemblance, but trust me, there are huge differences."

She nursed her soft drink while describing the morning's research, the BA meeting, and her conversation with Alex Welling.

"Bunch of nut jobs." Rico tipped his beer toward her. "The info about the aunt makes no difference."

Zee pursed her lips at his abrupt negation, then checked her exasperation. If he wanted to work together, he would listen to her theory. "I've been thinking. Alex said Lenore went to see Bette that day. What if the witness actually saw *her*? Bette might not have been dead when Marjorie left. What if Lenore came in and . . . finished the job?"

He tapped his fingers on the table, then shook his head. "Sounds thin."

A cramp formed in Zee's neck. She forced her voice to remain calm. "You yourself said the D.A. needs to do his due diligence. Ferret-Face is a detonation waiting to happen. Her motive's as good as Marjorie's, maybe better." She lifted her chin. "My scenario is entirely possible."

"Or you just want it to be."

Zee's jaw tightened. "BA fits the religious overtones of the text.

Someone wanted me to look there."

Rico pinned her with his eyes. "Why?"

"Exactly what I'm asking." Zee scooted away from him, pressed her hands against the bench, and arched her back to ease the resurgent ache in her shoulder blades. "What happened to being my partner?"

"Better I poke holes than Bernstow." He glanced at the chili. "Some mistakes are better made among friends."

Her headache roared back. "You knew?" She bunched her fists, recalling his wink at the waitress. "You're insufferable." She spat the words. "You and she had a good laugh at my expense."

"I saved you, didn't I?" He grinned.

"I wouldn't have needed—you always think—" Unable to finish, she pressed her thumbs to her temples, angry at the tears starting behind her eyes.

Leather creaked as he slid from the booth. "You're tired. It's late. I'll walk you to your car."

She erupted from her seat with such force she cracked her hip against the table. Pain vibrated down her leg and brought tears to her eyes. Half-standing, half-sitting, hanging onto the bench back for balance, she hissed through gritted teeth. "Do. Not. Dismiss. Me."

He reached for her. "Are you—"

She batted his outstretched hand, turned her back. "I'm fine."

A rustle told her he'd dropped money on the table. The staccato clicks that followed said he'd zipped his jacket. His fingers settled on her shoulder, lingered, and withdrew, their whisper filtering into her ears like an empty sigh. His bootsteps faded, the push bar on the exit clanked, and the heavy door thunked shut.

She sank back onto the bench. This would never have happened to Alex.

CHAPTER 16

ZEE PLOPPED IN FRONT OF HER computer the next morning, aware of her five o'clock column deadline but confident she could easily write a thousand words about the idiocy of Daylight Saving Time.

After breakfast.

Feeling virtuous, she leaned back in her chair and enjoyed the first bite of her bacon and egg sandwich. She judged it surprisingly tasty. Fresh rye bread, fluffy eggs, crispy bacon.

She congratulated herself on grocery shopping earlier. Her chilled shelves now boasted cheese, sliced turkey, mayonnaise, lettuce, cranberry juice, green beans, and—in a nod to actually trying to cook—a pound of ground beef. More food than she'd bought at any one time in years. She hoped the refrigerator wouldn't die of shock.

Chuckling, she took another bite. The sandwich had been easy to make, although possibly she overcooked it a bit. The bacon crumbled into brittle shards on her tongue, and she had to chew the egg a little more than she'd like. But the melted cheddar cheese smoothed everything, even the coal of over-spiced chili still smoldering in her gut.

Damn Rico. She shifted in her chair. Her hip stung where she'd cracked it against the bar table, but in truth, her curse had little to do with physical injury.

He was impossible. Supportive one moment, contrary the next. Offering partnership in one breath, then snatching it away. It didn't help that she turned to jelly whenever he kissed her.

Hmmm. She should have bought jelly, or jelly doughnuts.

She grabbed her coffee to wash down the sandwich and drown the enticing image.

Time to get to work. After she met her column obligation, she'd go see Karl. Pitch her fringe-group story.

First, Daylight Saving Time. She'd been storing up wrath on the topic. Now her fingers flew over the keyboard.

Ohio and a number of other states supported efforts to put the country on year-round DST. So far, they had failed. But if the objective was to eliminate the twice-yearly switching of clocks—a goal Zee fully approved—their efforts were completely unnecessary. The Uniform Time Act of 1966 gave any state the power to decide unilaterally to remain on Standard Time.

So, vote for that, she urged, instead of trying to change the federal mandate that created DST. Or was that solution too easy for the convoluted machinations of government?

Aggravation drove her to pound the keys with more emotion than the subject justified, if she was honest. Irritation with Rico had crept back into her thoughts. He shouldn't have criticized her completely reasonable hypothesis. Bernstow's witness only proved Marjorie was there. Someone else could have come later and killed Bette.

But speculation was getting Zee nowhere. Stifling a growl, she wrenched her thoughts back to DST.

Admittedly, change at the state level wasn't easy, but the effort required was akin to re-orienting a little houseboat. Organizing a coast-to-coast campaign was like trying to re-route a lumbering ocean liner.

She ate another bite of sandwich. Cheese and bits of egg stuck to the roof of her mouth. An annoying shred of bacon lodged between her teeth. She gulped coffee to wash it all down.

Her next culinary effort would be better. Unlike the federal government, *she* learned from experience. Not *all* experience, a voice nagged. She'd snapped too hard at Rico last night. He was only trying to help flesh out her theory, to be a good partner. Grinding her teeth, she shoved the judgment aside and refocused.

Congress had tried year-round DST in 1974, in response to the energy crisis. The experiment was supposed to run for two years. Wildly unpopular, it lasted less than one. The vote to kill it was a resounding 383 to 16.

All right. Been there, done that. But that didn't mean people would hate year-round *Standard* Time. What they should hate was this twice-yearly disruption of their sleep and its adverse effects: mood swings, irritability, greater likelihood of accidents, even weight gain. Like the extra pounds she battled.

She choked down another bite of her cooling breakfast sandwich, which was beginning to feel like an adverse effect of its own, though not to the level of a Turbo-Muffin. Yet. Fighting off discouragement, she returned to her keyboard to finish her point.

It was crazy to upend the population with this ridiculous time change.

Just as it was crazy to persist in behavior that yielded negative results. The jailhouse visit yielded no interview for her big story. She'd gotten leads at the BA meeting, but after Alex's brushoff, she wondered who would talk to her. It remained a mystery whether the pseudo-religious text message was connected to Bette's death. And Rico—

Stop! Zee inhaled, sipped deliberately at her lukewarm coffee, eyed the sandwich and decided against it. She turned her attention back to her column, pushing through to her concluding paragraph.

What drove the effort to put the country on year-round daylight time instead of standard time? In a word: commerce. The good old dollar. Longer daylight hours equaled more business transactions. A cold-hearted calculation. Like all bureaucracies.

It was 2019. Time to ditch DST.

Zee typed those last four words for a title and hit Save.

She flopped in her chair, waiting for her usual exhilarating sense of accomplishment. It didn't come. Expelling her frustration proved cathartic, but now that she had brain space, last night's argument roared back into her thoughts.

Rico didn't deserve all the blame. She was quick to take offense, to mount a defense. She raked fingers through her curls, trying to tease out the cause. No one else triggered such an antagonistic response. She never reacted like this to Fon—

A temple bell cut through her thoughts. Fontina's ringtone. A wry smile chased the tension from Zee's lips. She could always count on her friend's impeccable timing.

"Hey, Zee-zee. How'd it go last night?"

Heat flared across Zee's face. Caught obsessing over Rico again. "I—uh . . ." Her tongue tangled.

"Zee?"

Her rational mind asserted itself. Fontina probably meant the BA meeting.

"Something's wrong," Fontina said. "I know that hitch in your voice."

Zee sighed. Most of the time, she appreciated the invisible cord that bound them together. Most of the time. "How about we meet at Schreinhardt's." Get the taste of rubbery egg out of her mouth.

"My schedule's tight. We could meet later at the school. Two o'clock?"

A second chance to make the right choice. "I'll stop at the bakery on the way." She ate some protein earlier. That ought to balance the scales. And she would deserve a treat after squaring off against Karl.

THE CENTRAL COMMON AREA AT THE *Messenger-Tribune* vibrated with terse voices, frenzied keyboards, and slamming drawers. Readying herself to face Karl, Zee threaded her way through an atmosphere so dense it may as well have been the Oxford English Dictionary.

A man, not looking her way, rolled his desk chair across her path. She jumped to avoid him. Wiping a hand across his sweat-sheened face, he muttered something that could have been an apology or a curse.

A few steps farther, Zee skirted a pacing woman growling into a phone. She whirled at Zee, glared, and spun back.

How could anyone think clearly in this dissonance? At least Rico merited one of the cubicles lining the wall. Glancing toward it, she noted his empty chair. Disappointment mixed with relief. She didn't need the distraction.

At the far end of the room, Karl's door gaped open. She hadn't phoned ahead, unwilling to give him an easy way to deny her. Now she hoped he was there.

His office windows gave a view of his massive desk and behind it, the back of his tall chair. Just above the top of the black leather, overhead light caught in a grizzled patch of salt-and-pepper hair.

Anxiety spiked in her gut. She fought it down. She was sleep-deprived, emotionally shaken by BA, and unsteady with Rico. Not to mention dissatisfied with her breakfast. None of that was Karl's fault.

Exhaling to calm her nerves, she tugged the lapels of her jacket and marched to the doorway.

As the noise in the newsroom receded, snatches of his gravelly voice reached her ears. ". . . has to be that . . . yeah."

A silence told her he was on the phone. Remaining where she could listen would be rude, but backing away would leave her loitering outside his door, like a vulture waiting to swoop.

". . . Hahn."

Her head snapped up. What was he saying about Rico? She strained to hear more.

"Got it." He swiveled his chair and laid the phone on his desk. His iron-gray eyes found her. "Morani." He spoke around a well-chewed cylinder of yellow plastic. A pipe stem without a bowl. "What can I do for you?" His tone implied unwillingness to do anything.

She advanced a step. "I have a good story. I want to run it by yo—."

"No."

Anger sharpened her response. "You don't even know what it is."

"I don't have time to play reporter with you."

His phone rang. Zee tensed while he answered, pivoting his chair away from her. She didn't want to eavesdrop, but she wasn't leaving without a fight.

His back to her, she studied his environment. His desk was an island of order. On one side of the broad expanse of polished oak, precisely squared folders stood to attention in three file stands. Beside them lay the separated sections of the morning paper, neatly lined up behind the front page so she could read the headings: Metro, Opinion, Sports, Entertainment. His computer sat on the other side, flanked by a notepad and a pen. The center of his desk held nothing but a banker's lamp with a green shade and a chocolate brown leather mat.

On a side wall hung a photograph of a much younger Karl, posed with a pee-wee baseball team. It was a formal shot, the kids standing in straight rows, staring into the camera. Not smiling. Odd that—

His grunt snapped her reverie. "You still here?"

She took another step toward him. "You need to at least hear my idea. I want to do a follow-up linked to Bette de la Cornne."

He shifted the pipe bit, crackling wetly, to the other side of his mouth. "Crime's got that. Hahn." No wonder Rico always spoke in clipped tones. Karl had no use for extraneous words. Maybe they were too much effort because he never took that disgusting thing out of his mouth.

"That's legal stuff," she countered. "My angle's different." But if she happened to uncover something that affected the case, he couldn't expect her to ignore it.

"Another fluff piece." His teeth continued to grind the mis-shapen plastic.

Zee suppressed a bristle. "A human-interest piece. Broader. That hooks onto the newsworthiness of Bette and her book."

Karl folded his arms across his bulging belly. His nicotine-stained fingertips left damp marks on the rolled-up sleeves of his striped shirt. "One minute. Convince me."

Like angels on a pinhead.

She inhaled. "Bette's book is the story of how a person damaged by her religious upbringing tries and fails to heal her soul. It got me thinking. How do such people recover? Do they ever? I can interview—"

"Okay you got it."

Zee choked on the remainder of her sentence.

He leaned forward, planted his hands on the leather mat.

Zee backed reflexively.

"The Sunday edition. Two thousand words. My inbox, Friday noon."

Two days. Zee blanched. She clamped her lips and yanked her eyebrows down.

A smirk twitched the pipe bit in his fleshy lips. "Take it or leave it."

Zee stepped toward him, pinned his eyes. "I'll take it."

CHAPTER 17

A S USUAL, FONTINA GLOWED, THE PICTURE of vibrant health in an apricot tank top and tights. Zee followed her friend into a small office made spacious by sliding doors opening onto a brick patio. She dropped into a chair and leaned her elbows on the worn round table, a legacy from Fontina's family kitchen. Her fingers sought the faint grooves where pointed pencil tips had pressed hard into lined paper. How many hours they'd spent together there, dissecting their favorite murder mysteries after Zee had invented Shelby.

"Ginger tea?"

"Please." While Fontina busied herself, Zee opened the Schreinhardt's bag and extricated a giant frosted cinnamon bun. She pinched a bit of the crust, but merely crumbled it between her thumb and finger.

"Drachma for your thoughts?" Fontina said.

"I'm not sure they're worth even that much, but okay." Zee launched into a summary of her visit to BA and her subsequent discussion with Alex, finishing with Karl's impossible deadline. She did not mention Rico. That place was too tender to touch.

"What an adventure." Fontina set her mug on the table, laced her fingers, and peered at Zee. "You're hurting, Zee-zee, by more than what happened with Karl and BA."

Zee grimaced. She should know better than to try to hide anything from Fontina. "It's Rico." The story tumbled out across the wreckage of the pastry. "I feel conflicted, angry, sure I've made a fool of myself. Why can't things be simpler between us?"

"Let's do a quick consult with the Tarot." Fontina reached behind her and pulled a deck from the bookshelf. She fanned the rectangular cards across the table, then stirred, mixed, and sifted them, leaving them in a colorful pond in front of Zee. "The energy is awake now. Lay your hands on the cards and formulate a question. Make it as clear as possible."

Zee rested her fingers lightly on the shiny surfaces and tried to quell the racket in her mind. Nothing coalesced. If anything, the mental static worsened.

Her eyes found Fontina's serene face. "I have too many questions: What's the best way forward for my story, pursue BA or go elsewhere for interviews? Should I keep trying to find an explanation for the text? Is Marjorie actually guilty as charged?" A fist squeezed her heart. What should she do about Rico and her?

"What are you feeling in your toes?" said Fontina.

"What?" Zee tore her attention from the tightness in her chest. "What do toes have to do with anything?"

"Just tell me."

"How is this—"

"Your toes." Fontina's tone brooked no argument.

Zee scrunched her face and sighed. "Okay, I feel—"

"Don't speak. Just concentrate." Fontina's voice softened. "Identify the sensations. Be as precise as possible."

Zee zeroed in on her feet. Her toes snuggled warmly against each other inside the soft caress of her wool sock, all held by the firm cradle of her shoe.

"What's your biggest question?" Fontina whispered. "First thing that comes."

Zee blurted, "Rico and me." She snapped her eyes open. "I didn't want to ask that."

"Perhaps not consciously." Sympathy shone in Fontina's deep brown eyes. "But the Tarot has a way of cutting to the heart. The cards will respond to the question you ask, but their answer also often applies to other problems you're trying to solve." She gestured toward the puddle of orange, yellow, and red. "Play with them any way you'd like, but hold the question in your mind and a sincere desire for guidance. That is, if you still want to ask."

Frantic mice skittered in Zee's chest, but now that she'd stated the truth, she needed an answer.

She ran her hands across the cards, pushing them into each other, scattering and gathering them. Sliding her fingers beneath a cluster, she lifted it, then let the cards fall from her palm like rain. One landed face up: a figure encased in armor, fists white-knuckled, face a mask of rage.

"The Knight of Clouds." Fontina rotated the image so Zee could study it.

"Looks bad." Tears pricked behind Zee's eyes. "Is that Rico and me?"

"It's not so much an objective assessment of your relationship as a window into how some aspect of you views it."

A window. Zee's mind snagged on the image. Unsure of the reason, she filed it for later.

"The Tarot shows us facets of ourselves." Fontina stroked slender fingers across the card face. "Clouds is the suit of the mind. This card shows a mind on defense. You already know that about yourself and Rico. A deeper indication, perhaps more useful, is that armor represents an attempt to protect from harm. It masks a buried pain."

Not so buried, based on the ache just beneath Zee's breastbone.

Fontina tapped the card. "The truth is that armoring, while protective, ultimately prevents healing. We can't open to the love we need."

Zee was open, last night notwithstanding. Rico was just impossible. The tea soured on her tongue. "Guess we're doomed."

"The Tarot doesn't say that. The card suggests you love and forgive yourself for whatever you might have done to try to stay safe."

"I love myself." Zee squelched a temptation to stick out her chin.

"You do," agreed Fontina. "But the card suggests you look more deeply. What really prevents you from opening up as much as you'd like?" She stroked Uncle Ramiz's coin on her necklace.

Zee leaned forward.

Fontina's voice softened. "The block might not originate with Rico. That might be only how it manifests."

There was hope then. Zee swallowed the lump in her throat.

Fontina gathered the cards. "How do you feel now?"

"A little stronger, oddly enough. And my toes are very comfortable, thank you."

"A little trick, to get the mind off the merry-go-round." Fontina picked up the Angry Knight. "This card may also offer guidance for your questions about your story, the text, and Bette's death. Perhaps you can look for someone who is seeking forgiveness."

Zee doubted Marjorie, the texter, or anyone in BA felt the need for a pardon. "I'll have to think about that."

"For now, start with yourself."

"For now, I'll start with my job. I'm covering the '60s Fest this afternoon. I planned it for my column, but I can also use it for Karl's Friday deadline. There ought to be a few religious refugees reveling in all those peace-and-love vibes."

Such an atmosphere would also provide balm for her sore heart, Zee hoped. For a few hours at least, she'd be as far away as possible from duplicity, deceit, and death.

CHAPTER 18

A SPEAR OF SUNLIGHT BROKE THROUGH THE cloud cover, splashing a gleam on the admission gate to the Conquerors Coliseum. Inside, Zee scanned a sparse '60s Fest crowd, looking for likely interviewees strolling among real and simulated relics of the time.

She'd been too young to experience the actual decade, but its influence pervaded her childhood and coming of age. Woodstock, the second wave of feminism, those ubiquitous yellow smiley faces, and the triumph and tragedy of Martin Luther King, Jack and Bobby Kennedy, and Malcolm X.

Kent State.

Zee shivered. Fontina's cousin was shot there. He survived. Four others didn't.

She turned away from posters of the civil rights martyrs. She'd learned to stay away from idealism and idealists. They were impractical. Except for Fontina. She'd channeled her parents' New Age ethics into a thriving business, which she and Emilio ran with integrity and heart.

Zee gnawed a corner of her lip. She hoped Fontina would find a workable solution to her teacher's request. Heart versus head, the same *Julius Caesar* debate. Zee had sided with Papa Alesandro, but that was a theoretical discussion. In the real world—

She cut short her meandering thoughts. In the real world, it was time to get to work.

A vintage clothing booth snagged her eye. Nehru jackets and maxi skirts, velvet trousers, textured hosiery, sandals. She approached a man sporting a tie-dyed t-shirt. "Excuse me, sir, could I talk to you for a minute?"

He turned a cherubic face toward her.

She stuck out her hand. "My name is Zee Mor—"

"Oh." His eyes widened. "I know you. You write that column. *Z Beats*. I love that. My favorite part of the paper. Wish you did one every day. You here to do a story? I'd be glad to talk to you. What would you like to know?"

Zee jumped in as he took a breath. "Thanks. Let me get your name first."

"Larry," he said. "And this is Darryl." He elbowed the stocky man next to him. "He's a fan, too, aren't you, Darryl?"

From the depths of his bushy beard, Darryl said something unintelligible.

"He's not much of a talker." Larry grinned. "I make up for both of us."

Zee gestured toward Larry's t-shirt. "Dressing to relive old times?"

Larry heaved a belly laugh. "Can't wear much of the old stuff anymore. Used be a lot thinner." He patted his round paunch. "Fruits of capitalist living. Oh, but back in the day, I cut quite a figure. My favorite outfit was . . ." And he was off.

His garrulous style corralled Zee for the next ten minutes, but by the time she extricated herself, she had a number of funny anecdotes for her column. Also a vivid description of his spiritual search and current status. "I figure God's like a smorgasbord," he said. "Something for everybody, just take what you like."

Larry's good humor infected her. She scanned the crowd, seeking another likely interviewee. Everywhere she looked, she found smiles and laughter. People slapped backs, hugged, linked arms. Camaraderie flowed like the bright sunshine.

Her gaze snagged on a lumpy man in a stiff new ballcap and sharply creased tan windbreaker. Their eyes met. A synapse twitched in Zee's brain. She knew him from somewhere. Before she could coax her memory further, he whirled and darted into a knot of people.

She knit her brows, then shrugged off his odd behavior. Maybe he was skipping work and didn't want to get caught.

At a nearby table, a pony-tailed man dripped colored candles down the sides of a bulbous Chianti bottle. "The fun is in watching the creation happen before your eyes," he told enthralled onlookers. Behind him, stood finished bottles-turned-candleholders and kits for the adventurous to make their own.

Zee chuckled. According to Fontina's father, the Italian word for that straw-wrapped bottle was *fiasco*. An apt description of what could happen to unattended melting candles, Zee could attest.

Her mind a bittersweet amalgamation of sentimental joy and sadness, Zee began to snap photos. Incense tickled her nose. Sandalwood, her mother's favorite. Burning in the bedroom as she lay dying. Carrying forever her mother's whispered confession.

She balled her fists, as if to squeeze the life from the memory. Scanning the crowd, she sought an anchor to the present. A crown of flaming red hair emerged in the shifting sea of grays and browns.

Alex.

Zee's pulse quickened.

The fiery beacon flitted among clusters of caps and scarves, teasing her, hastening her steps. Alex had never answered Zee's question about the text message. And her quick exit after Zee spotted Kevin still felt suspicious.

"Excuse me." A woman pushing twins in a duo-stroller paused in Zee's path. "Do you know where the restrooms are?"

Corralling her urgency, Zee oriented herself. "Just over there." She pointed. "See that? Beyond the booth with the wind chimes."

"Oh, I see them. Thank you so much."

"You're welcome." As the young mother changed direction, Zee returned to searching the crowd. Damn. No red hair in sight. She swiveled slowly, panning her gaze across the thickening throng. Nothing.

Festival-goers pressed in on her, invading her space, stealing the air from her lungs. Or maybe she was unnerved by the unexpected sighting. Beyond the mass of people, an empty sunlit bench beckoned. She worked her way to it and sank down to collect her scattered thoughts and inhale a clean breath.

That person probably wasn't Alex. She would be out enjoying her new car, not strolling around at a nostalgia fest.

The logic persuaded her mind but failed to unknot her gut.

Fontina would say to trust her intuition.

The last time Zee had done that, she'd trapped a killer. And nearly paid with her life.

She pushed the thought aside. The sun-warmed bench spread lethargy through her limbs. She felt herself slipping into a doze. Damn Daylight Saving Time. Every year it got harder for her to adjust.

Needles pricked along the back of her neck. She snapped upright.

Someone was watching her.

She fought the urge to shrink, to pretend she didn't notice. *Face your attacker.* Emilio's instruction from the self-defense class. *Scream. Curse. Draw attention.*

She darted to her feet and spun.

Was that a slight commotion in front of the Pseudo-Psychedelics booth? Zee squinted against the sun. She couldn't be sure. Three women crossed into her line of sight, engaged in animated conversation. A couple of men strolled past in the opposite direction. The five exchanged peace signs.

Zee exhaled, her adrenaline fading. There was no danger here.

A sequence of plucked musical notes drew her attention to a group sitting on a blanket near one of the Coliseum's pillars. She wandered over to them and introduced herself.

"Welcome. Grab a seat." A woman scooched over and patted

the space beside her. Her long gray braid fell forward. She caressed the twisted strands. "We're just sharing memories."

A man whose white monk's fringe trailed along his shoulders tilted his head toward the sky. "It's a beautiful day. Listen to those voices all around us. It's like a symphony."

"A symphony of humanity," said Gray Braid.

The others nodded. The musician strummed his ukelele.

"So, tell me what brings you here today," said Zee.

"Music," said Monk's Fringe.

"Vibes," said the ukelele player.

"Yeah, good vibes," echoed around the blanket.

"The '60s were a great time," said Gray Braid.

The relaxed atmosphere of the little group fed itself into Zee. She took notes as they talked about the mindset in which they'd come of age. Guided by her questions, they shared freely about their spiritual journeys. Ex-Catholic Monk's Fringe went to India and returned as what he described as a Buddhist-enlightened Christian. Gray Braid rebelled against what she called "sterile Zen," and found her home in the joyous rituals of feminist wicca. Ukelele-Man was and remained, as he put it, "a struggling Jew."

With each story, Zee's confidence grew. Karl thought he had given her an impossible deadline. She'd show him.

Uneasiness pricked her exuberance. Now that Karl wanted this story, she had no idea what to write for Bette's editor.

"The thing is . . ." Monk's Fringe said, pulling Zee from her thoughts. "People expect too much from their churches. They're basically organizations run by people, and all people have flaws. So, religions aren't perfect, but they're not completely terrible, either."

"Yeah, I actually get a lot out of the temple services," said Ukelele-Man.

Zee scribbled in her notebook. Although she would lead with the more dramatic tales of struggle, these comments provided useful balance. A satisfied smile spread across her lips. Karl wouldn't be able to claim undue bias as a reason for rejection.

"Would you like a water?" Gray Braid asked.

Zee hadn't noticed how thirsty she'd become. "Thank you. I'd love that."

Monk's Fringe pulled a bottle from a backpack and passed it to Zee. "You hungry?" He produced a paper bag. "We have brownies."

The rich aroma of chocolate rose from the bag. Like the tail wagging the dog, Zee's taste buds nodded her head.

They passed the bag around, helping themselves. When it came to her, she pulled out a thick, coffee-colored square. No frosting, she noted with disappointment. But fewer calories, so she could eat the generously sized treat with less concern for her waistline.

The first bite crumbled across her tongue. A bit dry, but tasting delightfully of cocoa. Too late she realized she might have been in for carob and whole wheat flour. Thank goodness they had avoided that. She lifted the brownie like a toast. "It's delicious."

"My mother's recipe," said Monk's Fringe. He winked. "With a secret ingredient."

"What?" asked Zee, before taking another bite.

He waggled a finger. "Now if I told you, it wouldn't be a secret."

Zee laughed good-naturedly. It wasn't like she'd ever bake these. Between mouthfuls, she continued to ask questions and take notes. After a while, she quit taking notes and just enjoyed their company. Only when the slanting rays of the sun half-blinded her did she realize how much time had passed.

"I need to get going," she said to the group. "I have to cover the concert, and I'm starving, so I'd better get some dinner first."

Gray Braid waved as Zee got to her feet. "Enjoy the show."

Zee left them, a smile on her face. The only thing that would have made this day better would have been sharing it with Rico. Although if the two of them had been sitting on a blanket—she shivered at the thrill that ran through her.

The aroma of crispy fried potatoes drew her toward the food vendors. Suddenly, she was ravenous. So focused was she that she nearly missed the stare. The man in the ballcap. His face wore an unsettling smirk. Irritated, she started toward him, but he ducked into the mass of people.

For a moment, she was tempted to follow the eddy of his hurried passage through the meandering crowd, but her clamoring stomach overrode her curiosity. She was so hungry, she almost stopped to get stringy cheese fondue, but some corner of her brain objected. She passed up astronaut "ice cream" and Swedish meatballs, *de rigueur* at any '60s get-together. Her mouth wanted a burger and fries with a vanilla shake for dessert.

And the heck with her diet. She was glad she'd changed from her suit into loose-fitting drawstring pants. She learned to love that style from her mother, who wore them often and—

Memories clicked. Zee stopped cold and doubled over, laughing. She knew what the secret ingredient in the brownie was. As she straightened, her notebook peeked from her bag. She hoped she could read her writing tomorrow. She hoped the interviews were as good as she thought they were.

Nothing to do about it now.

She nearly ate a ketchup packet while waiting in line, but finally it was her turn to receive a cardboard tray containing glorious sustenance. Resisting mightily the urge to tear open the greasy wrapper, she found an aisle seat in the amphitheater.

She hadn't expected a gourmet delight from a typical festival vendor, but the burger was hot, the dill pickles were sharp, and the mustard was tangy. She devoured it with gusto while around her, fans funneled through the doorways, a multi-colored sea that spilled like a flood across the rows of chairs.

The first band bounded onto the stage as Zee wiped burger juice from her chin. She popped a still-warm french fry into her mouth and prepared to enjoy the familiar guitar riffs. The music rose. She tapped her foot, beating time to the rhythm she remembered. But she was off, slower than the musicians on stage.

She adjusted her tempo. Moments later, she was out of sync again. By the third time, she quit blaming herself for the band's rushed concert. The paltry applause at the conclusion of the set indicated the rest of the crowd agreed with her assessment.

Rico said bands often played faster at live performances, energized by the audience. But bad timing destroyed even the best performance.

Her heartbeat hitched. Last evening's disaster at the Grill could be a textbook case. Their teasing banter had clicked as they played off each other, but then he'd disrupted their rhythm with his skepticism. And she'd let her temper demolish any chance to regain balance. She gulped her shake, hoping the brain freeze would overpower the accusing twinge.

The stage crew had set up for the next performers. This band could have been a clone of the first. Zee grimaced.

To tune them out, she shifted her mind to the other topic that gnawed at her. The text message was meant to draw her attention. Since she couldn't decipher its meaning, she had to figure out who sent it. She could eliminate BA. No one in that group seemed eager for notice.

She dredged a french fry through ketchup. Alex had made a remark about BA's finances. Maybe Zee should follow the money. It had worked last time.

The potatoes had cooled to a mealy texture, but Zee ate every one. Even though they were nearly unpalatable, she couldn't stop. Lost in the gustatory sensations, she didn't note the end of the current band's set. Judging from the lack of enthusiasm in the audience, she hadn't missed much.

She swallowed disappointment with the last of her vanilla shake. The music of the late '80s into the '90s should have been her coming-of-age soundtrack, but her formative years were spent listening to her parents' choices and absorbing their musical values. As a result, disco, punk rock, hip-hop, and rap never appealed to her. She fell out of love with pop music.

Sprightly piano notes catapulted her attention to the stage. A new band played honky-tonk blues with just the right touch of melancholy and hope. Rescued, Zee lost herself in the wailing chords and boogie rhythms, marveling that the young keyboardist had enough life experience to infuse such ache into his voice.

Love found. Love lost. The eternal story. Zee glanced around at the packed auditorium. How many of those rapt faces concealed broken hearts?

The band launched into a rollicking tune. Tension drained from Zee. If the first song asked why people risked love, the second one answered the question. Nothing else opened such fountains of joy, painted the world with rainbows, lifted the feet in weightless dance. That's why people threw themselves again and again into the tiger pit. The stakes that tore the heart asunder also released the magic and wonder.

Too soon the players left the stage.

In the semidarkness, Zee closed her eyes. When they fell out of harmony, lovers could also leave the stage too soon.

Guilt squeezed her chest. She hadn't meant to hurt Rico, last night or six months ago when her dad had a stroke. She'd been overwhelmed. And the specter of Jeff haunted her.

Pressed on all sides, she'd needed space. But she hadn't abandoned the stage, only moved to the wings to catch her breath. She proposed a compromise. They would remain colleagues and friends. Just no longer lovers.

She shook her head. Should have seen the end of that coming. After fighting off a maddened killer, giddy, or pain-addled, she'd broken their rules for one night. Well, two. Three. Okay four, counting a couple of nights ago. She shivered at the delicious memory.

Almost immediately, her joy leaked away in thin trickles. Where did that leave them now? Last night, she'd misread his initial offer of partnership. Her knee-jerk recoil lodged like a knot below her breastbone. Was she actually *not* sure she wanted to marry him?

A high nasal twang reverberated through the amphitheater, pulling her to the present. The newest band's lead singer intoned the opening lines to Bob Dylan's anthem to change, unfortunately, in a poor attempt to mimic the singer's iconic voice.

Zee grimaced, but hope stirred. Censorship, government ineptitude, climate change. One of those might form the basis of an article for Bette's editor. Her sinking spirits told her the answer before she finished formulating the question.

The harsh croaking from the stage flayed her ears.

Time to escape.

She stepped into the aisle and started up the stairs. Off to her left, a pale blur pulled her attention. The man in the windbreaker and ballcap. And this time, her mind furnished identification, if not a name. He was the portly man from BA.

Zee's fists tightened. He was stalking her. She shot a glare at him, and he shrank down in his seat. Doubt pulled Zee up short. He could be just another fan of '60s culture, whose bland clothing just happened to stand out amid the kaleidoscope of vibrant colors. So, why was his vibe so wrong?

Or was her vibe wrong? She giggled quietly. *Vibe* wasn't a word in her normal vocabulary. She might not want to trust her perceptions just now.

A crescendo of drumming burst from the stage, accompanied by the piercing shriek of an electric guitar. All around Zee, people leapt to their feet, swaying and clapping, roaring approval. Resisting the urge to cover her ears, Zee continued her ascent to the exit. She caught sight of the man, clambering across the row, distancing himself.

Her antennae rose. It's not paranoia, they said in the '60s, if they're really after you.

"You're not getting away," Zee muttered. She raced up the steps, overriding protests from her knee, and darted toward the nearest exit. He'd just cleared his row by the time she reached the door.

She ducked outside the amphitheater and positioned herself with several exits in view.

An eternity passed.

Fearing she'd lost him, she scanned the knots of festival-goers. He was not among them. She swung her gaze back toward the doorways and picked up a hurrying figure. No more ballcap, but the windbreaker gave him away.

"Hey, mister!" She pushed through the crowd. "Hey!"

His head jerked, but he didn't turn.

Zee hustled toward him as best she could, strategizing as she closed the distance. She didn't want to accuse him straight out. Well, she did want to. She wanted to wrap her fists in the lapels of that sharply creased new jacket, bang him against a nearby wall, and force him to eject information from his mouth like a verbal equivalent of the Heimlich maneuver.

But then she wouldn't get answers. And now that she recognized him, she wanted answers.

When she got close enough, she snagged his sleeve, and tried to sound friendly. "Do you have a minute? I remember you from the meeting. I'm covering the festival for my column. I'd love to get your comments on the first day."

His eyes threatened to bulge out of their sockets. "Uh, it was fine. Nice to see you again. I need to be going."

He tried to turn away, but Zee held her grip. "You're awfully nervous. Is something wrong? Can I help?"

He ran a hand across his thinning hair. With conscious effort, he stretched his lips into a smile. "I'm meeting somebody. Can't be late." He plucked at his sleeve.

Zee ignored his efforts. She chanced a stab in the dark. "Would that be Alex?"

If anything, his eyeballs popped farther. He shook his head so vigorously Zee worried she'd have to catch the falling orbs. "No, no. What makes you think that?"

Classic move of someone with something to hide. Deny, then turn the question back on the questioner. Zee's patience thinned. "You've been watching me."

"I have not." Bluster.

Zee pushed her face within inches of his. "You have and I want to know why."

He looked around, as if seeking help. His face lit.

Zee resisted a powerful urge to turn to see. Astonished, she watched his transformation. He pulled himself up to his full height, still slightly below Zee's five-foot-six, and stuck out his chin. A picture of defiance, despite his quivering lip and sweating brow. "I don't have to answer to you. Like we told you at the meeting, our lives aren't for your entertainment." He shook free of Zee's grasp.

Anger boiled, but Zee tried a different tactic. "I was just trying to get an objective view of how people cope with the trauma of leaving their religion."

The man laughed, suddenly more at ease. "Lady, there's no such thing as an objective view. You can't be much of a reporter if you think that."

Zee bristled at his insult, but held her temper. If he was no longer afraid, she might yet get some answers.

"Good reporters correct for their biases. Everyone has them." Zee smiled. "Even you."

"Old habits die hard." He met Zee's expression with a smirk. "When a pickpocket meets a saint, he sees only pockets."

Zee's brows lifted. She hadn't expected the man to quote Ram Dass. "An odd reference from one who hates religion."

"It's philosophy," he snapped. "Backed by science." Slapping the ballcap atop his damp scalp, he began to turn.

"One more question. Does this mean anything to you? 'Now we see but darkly.'" She watched his face. "'Pernicious mirror.'" Did he flinch?

"No." He whirled and shoved his way through a cluster of people.

She tried to follow, but banged her shoulder against a beefy man. Pain ribboned across her back. She staggered, and by the time she righted herself, she'd lost him.

Ignoring the staring faces, she found a bench to catch her breath. First Kevin, now him. What was it with BA and spies?

Gradually, the sounds of the festival intruded upon her thoughts. She dragged herself to her feet, and massaging her temples, joined the slow stream of people headed for the parking lot. As she wove her way among the rows of cars, the ghastly music faded into the background, replaced by chuckles, murmurs, and the thunk of closing doors.

She huffed, frustrated. She wasn't sure what she'd learned, only that the mention of Alex made the man nervous. And that someone or something he'd seen had bolstered his courage.

Her scalp prickled as she passed beneath a light pole. Something rustled to her right, near a dark clump of bushes.

She stepped beyond the cone of lamplight and swiveled.

No one there.

Adrenaline filled her mouth with metallic tang. Antennae still trembling, she scanned the patchwork darkness in a slow pivot.

Nothing.

She breathed to ease her pounding pulse. Swept the parking lot. People were leaving the festival, their voices and laughter dancing across the still night air.

For a moment, she let herself imagine she and Rico among them. His strong protective presence, leather-clad arm around her shoulder, deep voice in her ear, scent of cypress and wild orange teasing her nose, her lips. If she hadn't been so thin-skinned, she wouldn't be here alone, fighting off paranoia.

Regret ached in the hollow space in her heart.

She hurried to her car, then loathe to leave the embrace of night, leaned against the Mini's hood and raised her gaze to the stars. Hindus called them Indra's net, a cosmic web in which every jewel reflects every other jewel. Impossible to untangle, impossible to compartmentalize. All or nothing.

And nothing wasn't an option.

CHAPTER 19

Z EE STIRRED IN HER BED, TANGLED in a melancholy gray curtain. Morning rain pinged against her window, needling recollections: her stupid argument with Rico, depressing memories of her parents, her irritating BA stalker. She scrubbed her hands across her face, wishing she could erase the images from her mind. Her '60s Fest interviews offered plenty to write about for Karl and plenty to distract her from pointless, incessant mental flagellation.

She threw back the covers. Might as well get started.

Candy agreed, jumping from the bed with an eager meow. She trotted toward the kitchen, exuding confidence that her ordinary, uncontaminated food would appear in short order.

A motorcycle roared. Rico's ringtone. Zee snatched the phone.

"Got a minute?" he said. Business-like, his tone betrayed no emotional residue.

How could he manage such neutrality after what happened at the Grill? After how they'd left things? Zee fell back against the pillows. "Um, sure."

"Did a quick check on BA's finances. Not good."

His unexpected collaborative move launched a wrestling match in her head. The urge to confront him. The desire to rescue their partnership. Anger. Relief.

Fury boiled her into a sitting position, her fist threatening to crush the phone. He assumed they'd fall back together without so much as an apology. What audacity.

"Zee, you hear me?"

She opened her mouth, but guilt trapped the bubbling acrimony before it reached her lips. She had a share in what went wrong the night before last.

"Yeah. I was thinking." She eased her stranglehold on her cell. "BA is Ferret F—Lenore's whole life. You've just shown that she bears further investigation." And that there might be something to her theory about Bette's death.

"We need more if we want to convince the police."

Two *we*'s in that sentence. A seed of hope budded in her chest. The disputing voices lowered their volume. "Alex said Lenore was terrified the movie would destroy BA."

Rico's chair squeaked. "Not sure bad publicity is lethal."

Zee jerked her head up. The truncated interview at Valerian's Corner replayed. Sara Jane had referred to the rejected book title. They'd been interrupted before Zee could ask about the text message.

"Zee, you there?"

"Sorry. You gave me an idea. I can try to get more information from Bette's publicist."

"Might be good."

His too-quick agreement stirred suspicion he was humoring her. "Aren't you going to interrogate me about what I want to learn from her, *partner*?" Where was the helpful inquisitor now?

A sigh echoed over the line. "Sometimes you probe, see what you find. What connects, what doesn't."

She slapped her hand on the bed, trying to squash her doubt like an irksome bug. Still unsettled, she challenged, "You have any other ideas?"

A pause. Paper rustled.

Uncertainty slithered between her fingers. Was he sifting

through options, trying to decide what would placate her? "Rico?"

"You could talk to Marjorie's parents."

She bunched the blanket in her fist, trying to trap her cynicism. The scene at the Grill reared in her head and sharpened her response. "Haven't the police interviewed them already?"

"Not the point. You talked to Marjorie. The parents haven't."

Zee rocked back, punched to her heart. "They didn't go see her?" If she could brave that jail, they certainly should.

"Word is, she turned her back on them."

Yet, Marjorie had talked to Zee. That gave her a potential advantage, though she shrank from using it. "That's harsh."

His tone matter-of-fact, Rico ticked off the points. "They abandoned her. She ended up living with Aunt Crazy. Who can blame her?"

Blame! Zee's earlier emotions erupted. Did he think everything was fine between them? Surely he didn't expect to end this call ignoring the great flaming elephant in the room. "Rico, what is this?"

"This?"

The words poured out in a torrent. "This phone call. This supposed collaboration. After what happened at the Grill . . ." She inhaled and slowed. "You act like nothing's wrong. We can't ignore everything and move on." She gulped against the knot in her throat. "I can't." To her horror, a sob escaped.

"Zee." His voice caught. "You—I, look, in the newsroom there's a lot of give and take, sharp questioning. Karl, any editor, needs to test an idea, see if it holds up. He'll push you until you come up against a question you can't answer."

How different Karl was from Zee's editor. Penn—never Penelope—Sharp could incise an argument like a laser, but she never destroyed Zee's enthusiasm, or her confidence.

"We call it drill-down honesty." Rico's voice called her back to the present.

"He sure didn't do that with *me* yesterday." Her retort came out combative. Rico's Karl didn't much resemble the one she'd encoun-tered, although, now that she thought about it, that one wasn't probing her story, only setting her up to fail.

"What do you mean?" His voice bristled. "What'd he do?"

Her heart warmed. He was rising to her defense. She lightened her tone. "I guess the *Mess-Trib*'s grapevine is as throttled as every-thing else at the paper. I pitched my fringe-group story to Karl yesterday."

"Shot you down, huh?" Sympathetic.

"He bought it."

Rico hissed an indrawn breath.

"He barely gave me time to explain," she added.

Suspicion colored his question. "What's the catch?"

"He wants it tomorrow, by noon."

"The bas—"

"It's fine. I'll make it work. I got some good stuff at '60s Fest. And I'll get more from Marjorie's parents today." And maybe snag some leads on the text, too.

He growled something unintelligible.

His anger on her behalf moved her to offer rapprochement. "I can't say I'm sorry I avoided the drilling-down. It sounds painful."

"It is." His voice softened. "But you get stronger stories, partner."

Warmth suffused Zee's chest. He was a good collaborator. Better than she deserved.

A plaintive meow issued from the doorway. Candy apparently decided she'd waited long enough for her breakfast. "I'm getting up," Zee admonished her.

"Still in bed?" Rico teased with a salacious lilt. "What're you wearing?"

Zee's Alex persona revved. She dropped her voice, affecting a minx-like growl. "It's red. Skimpy. This weather, it's giving me goose bumps."

"I'll be right o—"

A bellow cut short his reply.

"Gotta go," he sighed.

Zee swallowed her own regretful exhalation. "Quick. I need the address for Marjorie's parents."

"Already texted."

CHAPTER 20

Morning drizzle persisted as Zee threaded the Mini along a narrow, tree-lined street, dodging bicycles and well-used cars parked on both sides. Like so many others, this east side neighborhood suffered from its proximity to Valerian College. Developers had swooped in and subdivided elegant houses into small student apartments with quirky spaces, creaky floors, and questionable plumbing.

As she scanned the crowded curb, she formulated a list of goals: find out if Marjorie's parents knew anything about the text message, learn about their relationships with their daughter and with Lenore, verify as much of Marjorie's life story as possible.

And get another interview for her fringe-group story, a nagging voice reminded her. "Yes, yes," she muttered, then apologized to herself. She had a deadline to meet. And a point to prove.

Her pulse quickened at the sight of a potential spot for her car, but when she drew near, she saw the reason for the gap, the bole of a giant maple that kinked out a foot into the road. "We can do this, *Po*." Several hair-raising maneuvers later, she stepped out, rubbing her throbbing shoulder, and studied the results. No worse than any other vehicle that jutted into the street. At least, she hoped.

Marjorie's parents lived on the ground floor of a three-story Victorian masterpiece. Zee rang their bell, then studied the beveled fanlight above the door, happy that this developer had not stripped that gracious accent from the building before desecrating the interior. A tall, shapely woman, braless in a tight black tank top and leggings, answered the door. A mane of strawberry-blonde hair, streaked with silver, tumbled about her shoulders.

"Shaneah Earthkin?"

The woman's eyes narrowed. "Are you from the media?"

"No. Well yes, but—"

"Go away."

Reflexively, Zee shoved her hand against the door to keep it from slamming. She winced but held her ground. "I don't think your daughter caused Bette's death." The words rushed out. "I need your help to get the police to investigate further."

"We told them everything." The pressure against Zee's hand increased. "They're not interested."

Zee dug in her heels, ignoring the tremor in her knee. She couldn't give up. These thirty seconds scarcely justified her parking ordeal. She stared into Shaneah's stony eyes and said the first thing that came to mind. "I think her aunt's involved."

The force blocking her ebbed. The gap in the entrance widened.

"Let her in, Shawny," a thready male voice said.

As the door eased open, a gaunt man appeared behind Shaneah. The vigor of his thick white hair defied the skeletal face beneath it.

Shaneah retreated half a step. "As you wish."

"You must be Gregory." Zee stuck her hand through the breach. "Nice to meet you both."

She followed them single-file down a narrow passageway and through an archway into the living room.

Given the cramped hallway, Zee expected meanly proportioned rooms, but the room sprawled with generous extravagance. A bay window dominated, flooding the area with light. The misted glass fogged a walled garden outside. It sheltered a small crabapple tree, two green plastic lawn chairs, a tiny wrought iron table, and a cylindrical chime, weathered sepia and charcoal.

A faint, sweet scent lingered in the room. Marijuana? Ohio had recently licensed its first dispensaries for medical use. Zee's synapses stirred. Maybe she could pitch that to Bette's editor, but it lay listless before her mind's eye.

"Please, sit down," said Gregory.

Zee chose one end of an enormous leather sofa. Like the polished wooden rocker beside Gregory's recliner, the gleaming cherrywood tables, even the thick rug underfoot, it bore the marks of use, but it had been well cared for. She sank into the supple embrace of the cushions, running her hand along a butter-smooth arm.

"A gift from my parents," said Gregory. He settled into a matching recliner near the window.

"The redoubtable Doctor and Mrs. Neederson," sneered Shaneah.

Zee's eyes widened at the venom in her voice.

Gregory proffered a sad smile. "Shawny, love, could you make some tea?"

Sunshine broke through the storm clouds on Shaneah's face. "Of course, my Greejie." With fluid grace, she crossed the room and disappeared through the archway.

Zee snuck a glance at Gregory. As Shaneah disappeared, he turned back to her. His eyes were radiant despite his pallor. "She is my true soulmate, the light of my life."

"I can see." Cooed affection aside, Shaneah's outburst left a wake of disturbance in the room. Zee sought a way to ease the tension. "Do you mind if I ask about your last name?"

"Of course not." He leaned back in the chair. Yellow light from a nearby brass floor lamp jaundiced his features. "Our guru, Ram Shantidivananda." Some emotion tightened his face. He closed his eyes and drew in breath. Zee was about to speak when he resumed. "Guru said to seek names to reflect our true essence. We chose Earthkin." His face paled further, as if the walk down the hallway, or memory lane, had sapped his energy.

"Family of Earth," murmured Zee. Her parents would have liked this gentle soul.

Gregory nodded, then wincing, shifted in his chair. "You said Marjorie was innocent."

An interesting word choice, and not what she said. Zee filed the information and attempted to phrase her next request with tact. After all, Lenore was part of this 'family of Earth.' "Tell me more about Marjorie's relationship with her aunt."

A chime drifted through the window glass. Gregory's labored breathing bracketed the bell-like note. "My sister stole Marjorie from us."

A closer relationship than Zee had known and an unexpectedly severe condemnation. "What do you mean?"

Sadness tugged at the long lines of Gregory's cadaverous face. He stretched to pick up a dish of ice cream on a nearby box table. Another Neederman legacy, Zee surmised, admiring the lustrous reddish-brown hue. Gregory spooned a bite into his mouth, then closed his eyes, either savoring the flavor or gathering strength. After a few moments, he refocused on Zee.

"Marjorie was only seven. Shawny and I wanted to take her with us to India, but we could barely afford to go ourselves." His voice gained a bit of strength. "Dad and Mom refused to lend us money. So, we promised to return in a year and asked them to take care of her until we came back."

And, according to Marjorie, one year had turned into twenty.

He replaced the dish on the table and sipped from a glass.

Odd that he asked for tea when he already had a beverage. A ruse to remove Shaneah from the room? If so, skillfully done.

He cleared his throat. "I understand my parents now. But we were devout seekers." His dark eyes shadowed. "Even Jesus told his followers to forsake everything and follow him."

Another spasm contorted his features. Zee moved to rise, but he held up a shaking hand. "This will pass. Today is just . . . particularly difficult." He drew an unsteady breath. "We came home and everyone was gone. My parents died. No one could reach us." His voice cracked. "We couldn't find Marjorie."

Zee's heart squeezed.

"Later Lenore confessed she hid Marjorie. Made sure we wouldn't find her."

"And then your little sister finished the job your parents started." Shaneah's voice sliced through the pensive air. Hands trembling, she set the tea tray on the coffee table. "Bad enough your parents told our little girl we abandoned her and that we're going to Hell. But Lenore, she took her away, raised her around people with no morals, no decency, no soul. And then, when Marjorie rejected her, Lenore just left her out there. Two thousand miles away." Shaneah's voice cracked. "She could have brought Marjorie back to us, but she didn't."

Gregory's quiet tone intervened. "Everyone has karma, love."

His wife rounded on him. "Here's karma for you. I wouldn't be surprised if Lenore contrived to kill the Needersons, so she could get her claws into our daughter."

"Shawny!" Gregory's cry ended in a ragged cough.

Shaneah crossed her palms over her heart and turned toward the window. Her shoulders rose and fell. "I'm sorry, Greejie." She laid her hand on his thin shoulder. "I must speak my truth but without rancor."

He lifted her fingers and kissed them.

Shaneah faced Zee. "I don't know who killed that writer, but it wasn't Marjorie."

Killed. Slip of the tongue? "I'm told her death was an accident."

Anger flushed Shaneah's face. "All the more reason Marjorie shouldn't be in jail."

Gregory shuddered. Shaneah darted a glance at him. His skin looked like chalk.

Zee sensed her window of opportunity closing. "I'd really like to talk to you about a text I received that I think has a bearing on all this."

Gregory made a strangled sound.

As she pulled out her phone, Zee's heart hurt. They'd provided insightful information, and she had given them nothing in return. Before she asked for more, she'd make an offering of her own. "I talked to Marjorie at the jail."

The teapot shook in Shaneah's hand. Gregory craned his neck. "How is she?" he asked.

Now that Zee had opened that door, she wondered what to say that would serve as any kind of recompense. "She's depressed. That's natural, understandable."

"How does she look?" Shaneah's voice quivered.

Zee hid a grimace. She was making things worse. "She's thin." And gray, dead-eyed, destroyed.

Shaneah choked out the words. "Why did she talk to you and not us?"

Now was the time to tell them about the text, but the words stuck in Zee's throat. What would Fontina say? She breathed through her heart. "I'm a stranger. I have no history with her. Sometimes that makes it easier."

"History," Gregory whispered. "It always comes back to that." He reached for his wife and wrapped her cheeks with skeletal fingers. They leaned toward each other until their foreheads touched. "Third eye to third eye to third eye," he murmured.

As their silent embrace lengthened, Zee's spirits sank. She could scarcely bring herself to intrude on such a deeply spiritual moment, but her chance to learn anything further was slipping away. She spoke quietly. "Could I ask you about—"

"No." Shaneah straightened. "I'm not trying to be rude, but you must leave now. I'll walk you to the door." She trailed her fingers along Gregory's arm. "I adore you, Greejie. Guru Ram warned us our soul-bindings would be tested at the seventh tantric stage. There is a block that must be cleared."

At the front door, Shaneah touched Zee's arm. "A warning for you from my heart. That group is a nest of vipers. Don't trust any

of them, even the ones who look harmless. And especially Lenore."
She ushered Zee across the threshold and shut the door.

On the worn wooden porch, Zee tugged her raincoat tighter. The temperature had dropped. Flecks of snow fluttered in the erratic breeze. Disquieted. Like her impressions of this strange couple, they flickered, winked into view, and disappeared.

She shivered, unable to escape a discomfiting feeling.

She'd missed something.

CHAPTER 21

ZEE DESCENDED THE EARTHKINS' FRONT PORCH steps with Shaneah's warning in her ears: Trust no one in BA's "nest of vipers." She shuddered at the image of a seething mass, twitchy and nervous, ready to strike. Brushing an errant snowflake from her eye, she spied her car, and all thoughts of BA were driven aside. A massive SUV had wedged itself into the parking space in front of her.

Muttering, she strode toward her Mini. "How can people be so thoughtless?" A snort vibrated her lips. Gregory had dismissed his wife's justifiable anger as karma. That was the epitome of indifference.

The black behemoth's driver left only a foot of space in front of *Po*'s bumper. As if that weren't dilemma enough, the vehicle stuck out into the street a good six inches beyond Zee's side door. And she still had to dodge the protruding bole of the maple.

Gritting her teeth, she slid into the driver's seat. She backed the car, then wrestled the wheel hard left, inching forward. Then hard right. On the fifth rotation, her bright red hood crept past the great black bumper. She pulled a tissue from the glove box, angled the rearview mirror, and blotted her forehead.

Down the street behind her, a bulky figure exited a parked car. Her pulse jumped. Tan sport coat, brown trousers, sandy hair.

Bernstow.

Too late to hide. She resisted peeling away from her parking space. Maybe he hadn't noticed her. Sweaty hands slick on the steering wheel, she pulled the Mini into the street and drove away.

An incipient headache sprouted behind her eyes, and not just from spotting the lieutenant. She couldn't square Gregory's placid acceptance of his daughter's fate at the hands of his parents, Lenore, or the justice system. At least Shaneah's vitriol was honest, though her parting comment raised Zee's hackles. She shifted through the gears, uneasy, as if her skin itched on the inside.

The feeling spread when she slowed to turn onto her street. Halfway down the block, a ribbon of black smoke snaked into the air. She knit her brows. Not the time of year for burning leaves.

She strained to see the source.

Near her apartment building.

Too near.

"What the hell?"

She accelerated. Ate the distance. Squealed the tires. Wrenched the car to the curb.

The twisting dark scar came from the swath of green space that separated Legate I from Legate III. She launched from the driver's seat, tearing toward her building. "Agh!" With a searing stab, her knee buckled. "Damn!"

Catching her fall on the damp grass, she gasped. At the far end of the landscaped divider, bright orange flamed atop a mound of debris.

She staggered upright. "Help! Fire!"

The combustion flared, eager fingers reaching for twigs on the outskirts. Wind caught an ember and flung it toward a winter-dry hedge.

Tottering, she half-ran, half-speedwalked toward the blaze. Surprised to find her water bottle in her hand, she upended it atop the spreading conflagration. Useless.

"Get them plant pots!" a hoarse voice yelled.

Her eyes lit on the cluttered half-wall that bordered a first-floor patio. She wobbled toward the line of pots as quickly as her screaming knee would allow. "Sorry, Mrs. Huerta," she mumbled toward their absent owner. Hoisting a wide clay vessel still stubbly with the withered stalks of last year's basil, she pushed her legs to the burning heap and dumped the soil. A gray cloud billowed, acrid dust, dirt, and ash.

Orange flickers snaked beneath the edges of the dark mass, feeding on twigs that had escaped suffocation. Eyes stinging, she turned to make another run and nearly collided with a checkered shirt and a bony chest. Spindly arms steadied her. "Mister Demetrio!"

"You stay here. I'll get the pots. We gotta smother this thing."

While the old man sprinted toward Mrs. Huerta's wall, Zee chased cinders with her shoe.

"Here." Returning, he shoved a large pot into Zee's hands. He upended two other containers. Enduring another faceful of airborne debris, Zee dumped hers onto the pile.

The fire died.

Zee gulped air alongside the smoldering tomb. Behind her, Mr. Demetrio coughed and cleared his throat.

A dry stick flared. Legs trembling, she buried it with her shoe, then shoved another glowing twig deeper into the mound.

"Put the big one over the top." The old man's voice told her he'd moved a distance away.

Zee grabbed the former home of the basil stalks and upended it atop the mound of dirt. It made a decent lid. She backed from the sinister sight, coughed, and drew a halting breath.

A bony hand touched her shoulder. "You all right?"

Zee squinted at him through smarting eyes. "I'm okay," she rasped. "Are you?"

"Good enough." He drew out a snowy handkerchief and offered it to her. When she declined, he wiped at his eyes.

"Did you see what happened?"

He scratched his clean-shaven chin. "Can't say for sure. I'm in the kitchen, and I smell something burning. I know it ain't me, so I come out to look. I was gonna call the fire department when you showed, and I figured we could get it out quicker'n they could."

"You're probably right." She took in his smudged cheeks and watery eyes. "But you shouldn't have risked yourself."

He flicked a liver-spotted hand. "It's what neighbors oughtta do. Can't always count on official folks gettin' here in time." A frown creased his face. "You sure you're all right?"

"I'm fine, Mister Demetrio."

"Come on, I told you, call me Alphonse." He cleared his throat again. "I mighta seen the guy who done it."

"The guy?"

"He run into them bushes in the parking lot. Mighta had a gas can." He gestured toward the somber dome of Mrs. Huerta's basil pot. "Can't figure why someone'd go and do a thing like that."

Cold sweat broke out across Zee's back. "Got me." But already suspicion had formed.

"All my life I don't see nothing like this." He shook his head.

Zee's anger flared anew. This sweet, elderly man didn't deserve such a shock. She tried for a light tone. "Criminals aren't the smartest people, Mister—Alphonse."

"True, but that makes 'em even more dangerous." His frown lines deepened.

She sought a way to divert his anxiety. He liked being helpful. Maybe he had useful information. "Can you describe the guy?"

"Youngish. Wearing old jeans and a t-shirt." He sighed. "No way you're gonna find him with that."

She conjured a weak smile. "Guess he was wearing a backward baseball cap, too?"

Her neighbor's eyes brightened. "Yeah, a ballcap, but he's got it on right ways." He worried his chin. "I'm tryin'a think what color his hair is." He scratched his own gray strands and shrugged.

"That's all right," Zee said. "I appreciate the information."

"You callin' the police?"

Zee shook her head, then amended when his face clouded. "I should report it," she said, by way of not actually promising.

His concerned expression eased. "That's a smart girl."

"I'll return these." Zee picked up a pot. "And write a note. I need to buy Mrs. Huerta more potting soil."

"Let me help." He bent, then grimaced, his hand darting to the small of his back.

"I'll do it," Zee said. "You go back to your place." She touched his wrinkled sleeve. "Thank you, Alphonse."

"Age," he muttered. "Ain't for sissies." He raised a leathery finger. "You call the police now."

Zee nodded and waved a farewell. After he reached the door of his building, she gave her attention to the soaked remnants of the fire. Her careful touch confirmed the upended pot was cool, and she lifted the clay cover. An acrid odor stung her nostrils.

She retreated a step, turned her head, and sucked in air, trying to clear her lungs and dampen her re-ignited fear. She shouldn't jump to the conclusion the fire was meant for her. It could have been directed at any of the building's five other apartments.

The ice in her gut argued otherwise.

With her discarded water bottle, she pushed aside a layer of soil, revealing damp, blackened debris. A half burnt piece of paper caught her eye. Squatting, she grasped it between her thumb and finger and carefully prized it free.

Darker shapes hid beneath the smudges and smears. Fearing to cloud them further, she resisted the urge to brush the surface of the paper and instead blew gently across it. Clearer images rewarded her.

Disconnected lines and curves.

Letters.

She lifted the page closer, ignoring the burnt stench and her stinging eyes. Squinting, she made out *Four St p*. More written fragments followed, but she didn't need them.

She knew what the paper said.

CHAPTER 22

Pᴀɪɴ ʟᴀɴᴄɪɴɢ ꜰʀᴏᴍ ʜᴇʀ ᴋɴᴇᴇ, Zᴇᴇ rode the elevator to her third-floor apartment. Her shoulder throbbed from wrestling pots of soil to fight the fire. Her seized lower back telegraphed urgent requests for a heating pad. She groaned. At this rate, her battered body would never heal.

As she stepped from the elevator, her breath caught. A folded paper was jammed between her apartment door and frame.

"What the—" She yanked it loose and opened it.

Next time it won't be your yard.

She mashed the paper into her fist, squashing it before realizing there might have been fingerprints or other evidence. Her minor headache morphed into thundering kettledrums.

Quelling her trembling knees, she opened the door. From the threshold, she scanned the apartment. Everything in place. No sign of an intruder. Candy yawned from her perch on the back of the easy chair.

Exhaling, Zee stepped inside, dropped the note and the half-burnt paper on the coffee table, and collapsed onto her couch. She buried her face in her hands. Someone from Believers Anonymous had set the fire outside her building. *And* had threatened to do more. Her thoughts skittered back to Shaneah's warning, a nest of vipers.

A purring, warm ball wriggled into her lap. Zee burrowed her fingers in Candy's soft fur, as if she could excavate the arsonist's motivation. To scare her away from BA? Or—she shivered violently—from investigating Bette's death?

Sharp rapping on the door roused her.

"Zee-Zee. I'm coming in."

A key clicked in the lock. Moments later, a soft shawl enveloped Zee. Through the lingering trace of smoke and ash, she breathed in cypress and lime.

"I tried to call." Fontina settled beside her. "I sensed flame. You were close."

"You could say that."

"Are you hurt?"

Zee shifted, trying to ease her stiff muscles. "I didn't do my body any favors, trying to put out the fire." Fear and anger scoured her throat as she related the story, concluding with, "Then I find this stuffed in my door." She handed over the crumpled note.

Fontina's face darkened. "Have you called the police?"

"Not yet."

"You need to do it now." Although mild, her tone brooked no argument.

Zee swallowed a hard lump. "I don't know if I can face Bernstow yet."

"Just make the call." Fontina pushed her phone toward Zee. "You can talk to whoever answers." She touched Zee's arm. "You'll feel better."

Under Fontina's vigilant gaze, Zee punched in the number. "I need to report an arson incident," she said. "No, no one's hurt, and the fire's out." She gave her name and address. "I'll be here." Disconnecting, she sagged against the couch. "They're sending someone out." She hugged herself, unable to stop her chattering teeth, despite the feline furnace in her lap.

Fontina wrapped an arm around Zee. "Maybe you should stay somewhere else for a few days. With me and Emilio, or Rico."

For a moment, Zee let herself imagine melting into Rico's strong embrace. Safe in his protection. Despite the warmth that suffused her limbs, she shook her head. "I can't dump anything else on Rico's plate right now." Fury stiffened her spine. "And although I appreciate your offer, I'm not letting some creep drive me out of my home."

"Zee, I don't think you understand." Urgency underlined Fontina's words. "You've said you think Bette was murdered. I don't know if you're right, but if you are, that fire, that note, they could be from the killer."

As if to lend support to Fontina, Candy's head snapped up, ears alert. "I've thought of that." Zee stroked the soft fur, hating the betraying tremor in her hand. "But even as wildly dramatic as BA is, I don't see any of them as murderers."

Fontina pinned Zee with her gaze. "You met them once. And the note isn't necessarily a *death* threat."

Anxiety clawed at Zee's chest at this rare show of alarm. Still, she was determined not to run. She fought to steady her voice. "The police will know what happened. They'll keep an eye out." Even as she said it, she cringed at the idea of law enforcement watching over her.

Fontina's fingers found Uncle Ramiz's coin. She inhaled slowly. "All right," she exhaled. "I wish you had an alarm system."

"I do." Zee tried to smile. "You." When Fontina's brow wrinkled, Zee hastened to add. "I'll be extra careful, believe me." She had survived an attempt on her life during the McNeary investigation, but she was still paying the price. A shudder rippled through her bruised body.

"Let me make tea while we wait." Fontina rose. "And you can tell me what else has happened since you left my office yesterday."

Over green tea and vanilla wafers—the most diet-friendly cookies Zee could find on her recent shopping trip—she described her stalker at '60s Fest and her visit with Marjorie's parents. As she poured out the story, the scattered elements of her frightened psyche reassembled. Strength returned. She'd track down whoever did this. She'd find out why.

"It's a tangled tale," Fontina said when Zee finished. "It strikes me that none of your sources is trustworthy. Marjorie's deeply depressed. BA sounds like a cross between primal scream therapy and AA. Its founder is an angry crusader. Its members slink about, snooping. And the Earthkins are . . . not quite tethered to this reality."

It might have been the comforting sustenance of tea and cookies, or that Fontina, like the shimmering butterflies on her bright yellow tank top, always evoked a feeling of optimism. For whatever reason, Zee's mind cleared.

She set down her vanilla wafer and leaned toward Fontina. "The text pushed me toward BA. It's the key to all this. I'd bet a month's worth of pastries on it."

Fontina raised her brows. "The pseudo-Biblical message, the spying, the fire, the threat—they're all connected to Bette's death? That would be quite a story if it all ties together."

A lightning bolt sizzled across Zee's synapses. This was the story she'd get for Bette's editor. A fitting tribute. A worthy piece of investigative reporting, written from the heart, dedicated to justice for Bette. Her fingers itched for the keyboard, even as her mind scrambled to identify her next steps.

Her phone rang. She jumped.

"Miss Morani." Mr. Demetrio's voice projected pride. "That fire inspector was just here." He cleared his throat. "I apologize. I thought you might not call the police, but you did. Good girl."

Zee's throat tightened. No cop had been to see her yet. Who had just interrogated her neighbor? "Don't worry about that. You were right. I did hesitate." She groped for a way to get more information from him without letting him know she hadn't been interviewed. "You didn't need to call me." She played for time. "But I appreciate it."

"Well, I felt bad, too. I shouldn'a criticized them folks. That was quick work."

An idea emerged in Zee's head. She didn't like to lie to her good-hearted neighbor, but she had nothing better. "I hope he was nicer to you than he was to me."

"He was very patient." He huffed. "Don't know why he couldn't treat you right."

Zee prodded, hopeful. "Maybe you had a different inspector?"

His chin scratching sounded through the phone. "He was an older guy. Name was Quincy, like that TV guy, 'cept he was short and kinda rotund. Nice sharp jacket, though. Said he was in the neighborhood and heard it on the scanner, just came by to get some details."

Zee's stomach lurched. Her '60s Fest stalker. She swallowed bile. "You got a nice one. I'm glad. Don't worry yourself. Mine was just probably overworked."

"Still not right," Mr. Demetrio mumbled. "You let me know if he comes back."

Knowing he wouldn't be satisfied until she agreed and betting it would never happen, Zee promised.

As Zee disconnected, Fontina leaned toward her. "You're white as bread. What's wrong?"

"Someone pretending to be from the fire department just quizzed my neighbor." Zee scrubbed her hands over her face. "It just makes me more determined to get to the bottom of this."

Fontina fingered her gold earring. "Your dedication to the truth is admirable, Zee-zee, but please be careful."

"I will." Zee shuddered, remembering McNeary's murder. The danger not only to her, but also to Rico.

Fontina held Zee's gaze a moment, then reached to pet Candy. "I nearly forgot. I have something for you." She set two small bags of powder, one orange-ish and one brown-ish, on the coffee table. "Let's see if one of these strikes your fancy."

Zee could have sworn those feline eyes shot yellow daggers.

Fontina laid a hand on Zee's arm. "I need to get back. Emilio and I—we set aside some time this afternoon to talk. Will you be okay?"

Zee swallowed. She didn't need to dump anything extra on her friend's plate, either. "I'll be fine. I can handle the cops now."

Fontina's eyes betrayed her continuing concern. Despite her assurances, as they hugged at the door, Zee's heartbeat accelerated to sync with Fontina's. "Call you later," she said.

After Fontina left, Zee busied her hands clearing the coffee table, while her mind sorted through options for her next step. Who could she query about the text? Marjorie had been little—

A rap on the door spiked her adrenaline. She set the rattling tray on the counter and peeked through the peephole. Damn. The police. Just when she was starting to focus.

At least it wasn't Bernstow.

The officer was young, courteous, efficient, and not very encouraging. He recorded her statement, confiscated the note and the burnt paper, and said they'd be in touch if they needed any-thing else.

"You have any ideas who might have done this?" he asked.

Zee pled ignorance. She was a columnist who mocked bureau-cratic and social stupidity. Who would threaten her? A rabid fan of Daylight Saving Time?

The cop admonished her to be on guard and set off.

Once the door clicked behind him, Zee pulled out her phone. The officer's questions had made her realize she lacked basic infor-mation about Bette's death. Such as the time it occurred.

Rico answered his office line on the third ring. "Hahn."

"It's Zee. I have a quick question."

"Not now." In the background, someone shouted.

"I just need—"

"I'm on deadline. Call you back."

Dead air.

Zee stifled the urge to strangle her cell. He could have given her thirty seconds. And he didn't have to snap at her. Like he would be calmly tapping computer keys after finding a fire practically gift-wrapped with his name on it. Not to mention a threat to his life.

She rubbed her collarbone as though she could feel the sting of his dismissal below her skin.

Her gaze flicked to her desk, to the accusing eye of her blank monitor. He was doing his job, just as she should be.

Her stomach tightened. No way she could sit still enough to write.

She detoured to the kitchen, poured a serving of Salmon Delight into a dish, and dusted it with Fontina's latest nutrition supplement. "It's orange, Candy-pants." She pasted on a broad smile. "Just like orange beef." She swore she heard a feline snort as she headed for the shower.

When she rapped on Rico's cubicle wall at the *Messenger-Tribune*, he was on the phone, drumming his fingers against the pockmarked steel of his Army surplus desk. A flash of annoyance furrowed his brow. He jerked a hand toward the guest chair.

Zee tamped her irritation and sat. In the news business, deadlines trumped everything else. She smoothed impatience from her face, crossed her legs, and settled her hands in her lap.

Rico did not look her way. "Right. Got it." He disconnected the call, swiveled to his computer, and typed. After a series of rapid taps, he sat back, scanned the screen, then hit a key. Facing her, he glanced at his watch. "Half an hour. I'd have called. What's the rush?"

Zee shifted in the chair. The fire had driven her to action, but she couldn't tell him about it without triggering an eruption. She promised her skeptical tongue she would confess all later, this weekend for certain, when time didn't pressure them. For now, she infused her voice with conciliation. "I'm sorry I bothered you. I know better when you're on deadline."

His frown eased. "Sorry I snapped at you. Tense around here."

And just like that, they'd both apologized. They were getting better at this partnership thing.

He rolled his chair toward her. "Why are you here?"

"I need some information from my partner," she said. "Bette's time of death." At his raised brows, she hurried to bolster her request. "I should know before I do any more interviews. I can't force anyone to talk, so I have to make the most of my opportunities." She held his gaze and tried not to be distracted by the way the light danced on his thick dark hair.

He squeezed her fingers. Sat back in his chair. "About that. You probably shouldn't be talking to anyone else."

With effort, she held her voice steady. "Why?"

"That update I just sent. Your author didn't die from the fall. The coroner found a second gash in her skull."

Zee's hand flew to her mouth. Bette's death was hard enough to accept as an accident. As murder, it burned her heart like acid. And it was no comfort that her original fear was confirmed. "Do they think Marjorie did it?"

Rico nodded. "Assistant D.A. upped the charge to murder."

"But her confession . . ."

"Wouldn't be the first time a suspect shaded the truth."

Zee replayed the jailhouse interview in her mind. Marjorie had been convincing, precise. Maybe too precise. Zee scraped her hands down her face. "This is going to kill her parents."

"You talked to them." Rico's voice carried his desire to divert Zee. "How'd that go?"

She let herself grasp the lifeline. "They're a strange pair."

"Tell me."

Gratitude bloomed through her chest. Despite the pressure at work, he gave her his time. She swallowed a lump in her throat and summarized her visit.

He steepled his fingers as he listened. When she finished, he shook his head. "They're all religious whack jobs."

Perfect segue. Disentangling herself from shock and grief, Zee leaned toward him. "That's why I'd like a set of experienced eyes tomorrow." Not to mention someone to have her back.

His cobalt stare narrowed.

She kept her voice earnest, her eyes wide, as if by their openness he would not see her deception. "I want your first-hand experience at BA, to balance mine before I write the story for Karl."

Rico seemed to study her. She forced herself to relax. He wasn't Fontina, but he was a keen observer. Finally, his blue eyes sparked with interest. "What's the plan?"

Telegraphing faux concern, she hammered up her reply. "I sense a lot of rage in you because of your catastrophic Catholic upbringing."

A matching ersatz gravity crept across his face. "What time will my planned exorcism start?"

CHAPTER 23

Zee woke with a start. Spasms pierced her shoulder blades. Shot through her neck. Drove spikes into the back of her head. She shifted position, dragging her face across the textured pillow. Blue-white light spattered against her eyelids. She shielded them with a hand and peeked through her fingers. The television.

"Oh, hell." She'd fallen asleep on the couch. Lying on her stomach, neck cricked awkwardly against a decorative pillow, back bent at an odd angle. Groaning, she rolled carefully onto her side.

Except for the flickering television, darkness filled her apartment. She reached for her phone on the coffee table. *Three a.m.*

"Argh." She fell back against the cushions. She'd intended to come home after talking with Rico, make some dinner, then draft her column and the fringe-group article for Karl. But the couch had beckoned, and when she sat down—just for a few minutes—the weight of the last four days fell in on her.

Levering her body, she struggled to sit without setting off more distress flares. Hours in oblivion had brought no rejuvenation. She should go to bed, but with this pain, she'd never fall asleep. And her fringe-group article, due by noon, existed only in scattered notes, without even an outline to guide her.

"Why didn't you wake me?" She addressed Candy, invisible in the dark and probably comfortably snoozing in Zee's bed.

She inhaled to calm the urge to beeline to her computer. After the motorcycle accident last year, Fontina had given her a medicinal bath concoction that worked miracles on Zee's abused body. It was worth trying again. Along with a healthy dose of modern pain medication.

Resolute, she fought to her feet. Though her mind surged like a thoroughbred at the starting gate, her body lumbered like an ox, joints straining as though strapped with hundred-pound weights.

With agonizing slowness, she shed her clothes, wrapped herself in a robe, and filled the tub. At last, with great care, she lowered herself into the steamy water and waited for Fontina's herbs to work their magic.

Relief, when it filtered into her body, was almost painful. Her muscles relaxed. Physical anguish faded. Wafts of lavender and tea tree eased her agitated brain.

Twice, the fragrant warm water startled Zee awake, lapping at her nose. The third time she began to slip under, she reluctantly rose from her healing sanctuary.

Her bedroom clock read 5:20 when she emerged from her bathroom spa, wrapped in a soft robe and feeling halfway human again.

In the dimly lit kitchen, she tripped over Candy's food dish. Based on the nuggets skittering across the floor, Candy had judged the orange supplement no more acceptable than the green one. As if to confirm her conclusion, a sorrowful meow drifted up from Zee's ankles.

"I don't have time for this now," Zee lectured the cat. "But we're not done." She poured Tuna Surprise into a clean dish and turned her attention to her own breakfast.

When she opened the cupboard, the box of vanilla wafers reached for her with aromatic fingers. She stopped her hand mid-stretch. This task called for solid nourishment. Slamming the door on temptation, she toasted a bagel, then sliced off several pieces of cheddar, poured a cup of coffee, and carried it all to her computer.

Only half-tasting what she put into her mouth, she went to work, weaving statistics through the personal stories. But like nettles stuck in her shirt, Bette's death—her *murder*—kept tormenting her.

When she wrote about the allure of Buddhism, Gregory's emaciated face reared before her, then Shaneah's storm-darkened scowl.

Citing hypocrisy as a common cause of religious estrangement raised the bitter voices of BA members, their antics as they exorcised their rage.

Zee's reporter's instinct had latched onto that link to a larger story. BA was a microcosm of a bigger problem: a cultural climate of growing intolerance fueled in part by the rise of the Christian right and in part by the decline of trust in social institutions.

At her keyboard, she huffed in frustration. If she had more time, she could do a better job of this. But at least, like her drug development piece, this story shed light on the current tumult. It made the abstract real, showed how disillusionment could burn like fire in the ordinary-looking guy sitting next to you.

When she typed that line, she shivered.

She pressed on, chronicling the searches of wounded souls, but in every saga, the message with the strange Biblical quotation intruded on her concentration. Like a phantasm, it flitted before her, teasing and promising. It would either reveal Marjorie as the killer or enable Zee to nail the person responsible.

She would solve that riddle.

One bagel, three cups of coffee, and five hours later, she hit Send.

She fist-pumped the air. "Did it, Candy-pants." Exhilaration lifted her from her chair, but halfway to the kitchen, fatigue slammed into her like a fist. Her head ached, her back hurt, her knee throbbed. She couldn't even keep her eyes focused, although that didn't mean she needed glasses. Just sleep.

She steadied herself with a hand on the counter. She had the afternoon to write *Z Beats* before launching tonight's covert operation at BA. She could afford a nap.

A short one to recharge.

In her bed.

After she set her alarm.

CHAPTER 24

THIRTY MINUTES BEFORE THE BA MEETING, Zee turned *Po* onto Septem Decanus, East Seventh Street to anyone but ancient Romans and current inhabitants of Valerian. Her earlier aches were subsumed in the adrenaline-fueled euphoria of meeting Karl's deadline and submitting her column. And a refreshing nap. She was ready to tackle BA.

The community center's stoic, sand-colored face loomed amid the expanse of cracked concrete, deserted except for a derelict Honda Civic near the side door, and Rico's Road King, snugged against the rusting chain link fence. Zee backed *Po* between faded lines a few feet away from the bike.

Rico dismounted and trotted toward her, lean, strong, and confident in the black he wore like armor—tight jeans, taut t-shirt, well-worn leather boots and jacket. Rays from the setting sun brushed gold on his dark hair. He gestured toward the nearly empty space around him. "Looks like we're early enough." Flashing a grin, he slid into the passenger seat.

"I didn't want to miss Lenore." She reached across the console and closed her fingers around his. A shiver passed through her at his physical heat, but even more so at his willingness to help her. "Thank you, partner."

His eyes caught hers, their humor gone. "So, want to tell me what this is really about?" At her hesitation, he pressed. "Your deadline was noon. You don't need my take on BA to balance yours."

Busted. Fire flamed in her cheeks. She pulled free and covered her face with her hands. She had no defense, and she should have known better than to try to deceive him. Yet, here he was. "You agreed to come anyway." Her chest heaved.

He clasped her hands and drew them toward him. Anchoring her in his steadfast gaze, he spoke gently. "How can I help if I don't know the goal? Tell me, why am I here?"

Hot shame burned its way up Zee's throat, triggering tears behind her eyes. "I. Do not. Deserve you."

"Agreed."

A tender smile softened his face. Leaning in, he feathered a kiss across her lips. New fire kindled with old.

"I mean it," she murmured. "Why do you put up with me?"

His chest rose and fell. "Because you're Zee."

She drowned in his deep blue eyes. An ocean of acceptance in those words. He slipped an arm around her shoulders. Despite the console biting into her hip, she leaned into the soft leather of his jacket, inhaled his woodsy scent, tinged as always with motor oil, underscored now with the tang of hot metal.

His Harley had been what drew her to him when they met last year. Well, that and his toned muscled body, thick dark hair, and mesmerizing cobalt eyes. Her first ride on the bike launched a months-long affair, giddy with excitement and passion.

How confident she'd been that, when the time came, she could extricate herself from him. She'd done it with other lovers since Jeff's betrayal had caused her to swear off serious relationships.

How wrong she had been. How wrong she persisted in being.

"So," he broke into her reverie, "wanna tell me the plan?"

Exhaling the memory and the guilt, she straightened to face him. "We want to find out what we can, in particular whether anything or anyone connects to the text. You're going inside, while I waylay Lenore." Tonight, she would either put to rest her doubts about the murder or see her next step.

He rubbed the pad of his thumb across the dark stubble on his chin. "Not letting this go, are you?"

"I need—"

He forestalled her with an upraised palm. "I wouldn't either."

Relief shuddered through Zee's body. Anxiety chased it. "I wish I could go into the meeting with you."

He stroked her hair, fingering the curls along her neck. "Have to figure your cover's blown."

"Definitely." She reached to capture his hand, to break the electricity. "You have to stop that. I can't think."

He grinned. "Good to know."

She kissed his knuckles but trapped his hand in hers. "A few things I want to mention. There's an older guy, might be wearing a three-piece suit." Might have been stalking her. Couldn't mention that. "See what you can learn about him. There's a couple of elderly ladies who want to mother him. They might be chatty."

"Old people, got it."

She hesitated. She needed to mention Alex, but her magnetic, almost hypnotically attractive image sparked a twinge of apprehension. Zee resisted the impulse to physically shake it off. "Look for a woman with fiery red hair. Her name's Alex. If she's there, she'd be worth your time."

Rico raised his brows, then seemed to catch himself and nodded.

Remembering Marlene's, Zee added, "Watch yourself. She strikes me as someone who has her own agenda and is good at getting it."

"Noted."

Zee hurried on, eager to get past the moment. "One other person stood out. A younger man with angry eyes. See what you can find out about him." Like whether he set a fire outside her apartment.

Rico lifted a hand in a mock salute. "Aye, captain." He lowered his fingers and cupped her chin. "Relax. I got this."

She forced a smile.

His eyes sharpened to blue lasers. "Is there something I don't know?"

The urge to tell him about the fire and the threat tugged at her lips. But then he'd never agree to help her tonight.

"No. Yes. My head is spinning with questions." She rubbed her temples, then noted his furrowed brow. "Something bothering *you*?"

The muscles along his jaw bunched. "I can handle myself." He pressed his lips lightly to hers, then moved his mouth to her ear. He deepened his voice to a husky whisper. "Going in now. Can't be seen fraternizing with the enemy." Cradling her face in both hands, he kissed her hard, crushing her against the seat. "That's for luck."

Breathless, body zinging, she barely registered the click as the Mini's door closed behind him. She tracked his leather jacket, a silly grin plastered on her face. The dashing spy on a dangerous mission, walking casually toward his rendezvous.

Maybe too casually. A niggling worry surfaced. He'd brushed off her concern about his religious upbringing, but she'd seen the pain in his eyes. A weight dropped on her heart. She hoped she wasn't sending him into his personal spiritual warzone.

She measured her breathing, four beats in, four beats out. The constriction in her chest eased. Her stomach growled.

Squashing a nascent objection from her conscience, she flipped open the Mini's capacious glove box and withdrew a Schreinhardt's sack. An apple-walnut strudel nestled in its paper folds. "Fruit is good. Nuts have protein," she told her reflection in the rearview mirror. "And I ate a ham sandwich for dinner. *With* lettuce."

She nibbled at one edge, just to taste the pastry itself. Crusty flakes melted on her tongue. Perfect. The luscious fruit peeking from its buttery embrace tempted her to gobble, but she resisted, savoring instead small portions of perfectly baked apples. Firm but juicy, complemented by bits of chopped walnut. As the last fragments faded from her taste buds, she licked parchment thin sugar glaze from her lips. Nirvana.

Her eyes snapped open.

Damn. She'd kick herself if she missed Lenore.

Irritated at her lapse, she scanned the lot, then realized she had no idea what to look for. A handful of vehicles clustered near the door, any one of which could be Lenore's. Her gut squeezed around the illicit pastry.

On sentry duty now, she targeted each entering car. Dusk deepened. One by one, people arrived. But no Lenore.

The digits on her phone clicked toward the hour, while the sugary duplicity on her tongue taunted her. Seven o'clock came and went.

"Well, hell." Zee wadded the paper evidence of her failure and stuffed it back in the glove box. She'd have to wait until after the meeting.

She shifted her eyes to the building. They should be launching into *The Four Steps* about now. Rico might join the din to establish camaraderie. He'd be convincing, a dark raging presence in a weathered leather jacket, black tee, worn jeans, and scuffed boots. Her pulse quickened at the image, replaced by the fear she had sought to calm. His performance would be showmanship only, a strategy to create trust.

But uneasiness nagged at her. She hoped he could keep his emotions in check.

Muffled screeches and thuds filtered into the lot. That would be the catharsis stage of the meeting. Rico would probably participate. His powerful hands could easily tear sheaves of pages from a phonebook. Heat flushed her cheeks. She would like to see that.

Surely, she could sneak a peek inside the room. They'd all be too busy to notice her. And she should check that he was coping with all that roiling rage.

Before she could talk herself out of it, she opened the car door. Adrenaline quickened her steps, but at the bottom of the steps, she hesitated. Other people didn't matter so much, but Rico might see her. She had to trust him.

Besides, the noise had died inside. She'd missed her chance.

Disheartened, she turned back toward the Mini. Her hand was halfway to the door handle when she remembered the testimonies. Anxiety burned behind her rib cage. She'd sent him in there alone. That wasn't right. To hell with whether anyone recognized her.

She spun, driven by urgency, and sprinted as best she could.

As she headed up the steps, someone burst through the exit.

Zee crashed into her.

Staggering, she reached to seize the other person. Her hands closed around thin arms. She pulled a woman upright as the door slammed shut behind them. "Lenore!"

Tears glistened on the gray cheeks. "What? You!" Lenore's face tightened.

Zee sucked in a breath. "I'm sorry. Are you all right?"

Lenore brushed at her misshapen sweater. "Leave me alone." She pushed past Zee.

"Wait, can we talk?" Zee stopped herself from grabbing Lenore's shoulder.

"I have nothing to say to you."

"Please." Zee called to her retreating back. "I need your help."

On the last step, Lenore twisted toward Zee. "I know what you want." Weariness replaced some of the anger in her voice.

Zee descended to meet her. "I'm not here as a reporter. Someone from BA threatened me."

Lenore jerked as if jabbed. She reached a hand to the railing. "What do you mean?"

Zee glanced around. No telling when people might interrupt them. "Can we talk in my car?"

The fight drained from Lenore's frail frame.

"Just a few minutes, I promise." She gestured toward the Mini. "It's right here."

"If we must . . ." A long sigh escaped Lenore's sunken chest.

Zee steered Lenore toward *Po*, wishing she'd parked closer. Lenore twitched when they passed the battered Honda, but let Zee continue to shepherd her. Once Zee settled Lenore into the car, she hustled to the driver's seat.

"I do not encourage violence," Lenore said, as Zee slipped in. "But rage is real." Defiance glinted in her watery gray eyes. "Some people have a difficult time controlling it."

Zee squared to her. "Someone set a fire in my front yard and left a threatening note on my door. That wasn't rage against religion."

Color drained from Lenore's already pasty face. When she spoke, the words seemed forced from her throat. "How do you know it was someone from my group?"

Zee described the fragment. "I'm betting they wanted me to find that flyer. Who'd set a fire to get my attention?"

The small woman shook her head, stiffened her spine. "I do not judge people, only institutions."

Not exactly an answer. "So you don't know."

"No."

"No suspicions?"

"No." Lenore clamped her colorless lips.

Zee bit her tongue. It was worth a try, but she hadn't expected a confession. Time to go for her primary purpose. "I also got a text that hinted Marjorie didn't kill Bette. It contained a Bible reference. Can you shed any light on that?"

"What would I want with a Bible?" Lenore wrapped her sweater more tightly across her chest.

"I don't know," said Zee. "But the text refers to Bette's book and uses the very unusual term *pernicious*. Feels like there's a connection to BA there."

"That damn book," Lenore snarled. "Nothing but trouble."

"And you have no idea—"

"I don't know anything about a text!" Lenore's vehemence startled Zee. "If I have something to say, I say it." She reached toward the door handle. "Is that all you wanted?"

But Zee had seen an opening to elicit more information on a different question. Softening her voice, she scrambled to exploit it. "I appreciate your honesty. I prefer the straightforward approach myself." *Unless it's with Rico*, her mind reproached.

Lenore hesitated.

Zee leaned toward her. "I understand that you went to see Bette on the day she died."

"That . . . bitch Sara Jane tell you that? Don't believe everything she says."

"I'll keep that in mind." Another warning about the publicist. "What I'm after right now is timing. When did you go to see Bette?"

"I don't know. Around two." To Zee's astonishment, Lenore crumpled. Her faded brown sweater collapsed like a worn paper bag that could no longer hold its shape. "I knocked and the door opened a bit. I went in and . . . she was already dead."

Zee felt the blood drain from her face. She stared at Lenore across the Mini's console. "You sure?"

Hunched in the passenger seat, Lenore grunted. "She was lying on the floor. Not moving. I saw the blood . . . I was scared to go any farther." She swallowed noisily. "I left."

Accusation flew from Zee's lips. "Didn't you call 9-1-1?" Bette might have still been alive.

Lenore plucked at her shapeless sweater. "I know a dead person when I see one. I couldn't do her any good . . . and I might do myself a lot of harm."

Her misery thickened the air in the Mini. Night closed around the feeble lighting in the community center parking lot, deepening the gloom. Zee glanced toward the door to the community center, but no one else had emerged from the BA meeting. Making an effort to soften her voice, she turned back to Lenore. "What harm were you afraid of?"

Lenore stared at her. "They would think I did it. Because of the book and the movie."

They might not be wrong. Studying Lenore's defiant glare, Zee saw Believers Anonymous in a different light. A crusader against an oppressive cabal, Lenore fought with as much vigor as anyone who'd ever taken on evil.

Zee gentled her voice further. "You have to tell the police."

"But Marjorie." A sob shook Lenore's bony frame. "Marjorie confessed."

There were holes in that confession, but now was not the time to mention them. "The police need all the pieces. I do too. That fire tells me someone wants me to investigate."

Lenore dug a tissue from her pocket. She wiped her face. "It does seem that way."

Relieved that Lenore no longer protested, Zee pressed. "Did you see anyone when you went to Bette's apartment?"

"No." Lenore cracked off the word. Brittle.

Zee quashed a scowl, kept her tone mild. "Think back. Take your time. Start when you arrived at the building."

Lenore wadded the tissue in her lap, but said nothing.

"How did you get there that day?"

"I drove," Lenore snapped. "Stop badgering me."

Zee lifted her palms, placating. "Your recollections could be helpful." At Lenore's silence, Zee continued. "You drove your car. Where did you park?"

Lenore's chest rose and fell in a long-suffering sigh. "I parked a block away. I was glad it wasn't raining. I don't see how this is helping."

"It's good. Keep going."

"Then I just walked to the building." She pursed her lips. "Like I said, I didn't see anyone."

"No one on the sidewalk? Or leaving through the doors?" Zee bit her lip. Slowed her speech. "Take a moment and look around. See everything again."

Lenore sucked in a breath and blew it out. "There's no one outside." She furrowed her brows. "But inside—"

A rap on the window cracked across the words. Zee flinched. Lenore clamped her mouth shut.

Zee twisted toward the driver's side. In the dim light, Alex's red hair glinted. Zee lowered the window an inch.

"Missed you inside." Alex gave a sly smile. "Let me guess. Didn't want to wallow in drama, but couldn't pass up my new car?"

"No doubt the car," rasped Lenore, her voice dripping bitterness. Tight-faced, she shoved open the Mini's door and scrambled free.

Zee grabbed for her. "Lenore—"

Only the retreating back of a wrinkled brown sweater met Zee's entreaty.

"Didn't mean to scare her off." Alex's cool emerald eyes held a hint of mockery.

Yet, that was exactly what had happened.

CHAPTER 25

ZEE RESISTED THE URGE TO BANG her fists against the Mini's dashboard. Damn Alex. She had interrupted just as Lenore was on the verge of recalling something from the day Bette died. And just so the arrogant redhead could show off her car.

With effort, Zee smoothed the frustration from her brow. She could use this opportunity to quiz Alex further about the text, or to find out if she knew what Kevin was up to with his spying, or to explore Lenore's surprisingly bitter reaction to seeing Alex rapping on *Po*'s window. "All right." She met Alex's calm green gaze. "Let's see your statement of independence."

"Come feast your eyes." With a toss of her fiery waves, Alex strode off.

Zee slid out. She followed, hurried and breathless as she tried to match Alex's long strides. At once, she recognized the new purchase. Even in the paltry lighting, the Corvette convertible gleamed. Top down, crimson body, with a cream-colored leather interior.

How had she missed it when Alex arrived? The taste of traitorous pastry crumbs answered.

Zee managed an appreciative laugh as she circled the broad expanse of shining hood. "Nice choice."

"Get in." Alex opened the passenger door and patted the seat back. "Enjoy the new car smell."

Zee swung into the seat. Or that was her intention. Instead, her hips sank. And sank. Her hand snatched at the door frame. How far down did this go? Just as she lost her balance, she thumped gracelessly against the leather. Heat rose in her cheeks. "I thought the Mini rode low."

"Mini Coopers are certainly larger than they look." Alex slipped behind the wheel. "But the 'Vette is more spacious."

Maybe that was fine for a six-foot-tall person with long legs, but Zee felt like a four-year-old sitting in big sister's chair. In the half-reclined seat, her eyes barely cleared the lower edge of the window. The dashboard receded a mile away.

Nonetheless, the touch of buttery leather charmed her, and she reclined into its embrace. Like a sly lover, it eased tension from her back. Her jaw unclenched, releasing unnoticed strain that had accumulated during the conversation with Lenore. Her shoulders dropped.

Alex started the engine.

Zee bolted upright. She'd been a hair's breadth from falling asleep. Hoping Alex hadn't noticed, she hid her burning cheeks in a search for the seat adjuster.

"Listen to her purr," Alex said over the sultry growl.

"Smooth," Zee managed. Her fingers found several small oblong controls along the padded side. She pushed one, and the seat glided forward. Quickly, she stopped the motion.

Wheels screeched. Zee snapped her head up in time to see the old Honda Civic tear across the lot and out the exit.

"Lenore's miffed." Alex switched off the engine. "She doesn't like it when she thinks I've found someone new."

But Lenore's fury could be directed at herself for what she'd just admitted.

"Don't worry." Alex flashed a conspiratorial grin. "She's not a threat."

"How can you say that?" Zee blurted. "She might have killed Bette de la Cornne."

Alex cradled the key fob in her palm. With her thumb, she traced the embossed checkered flag. Silently, Zee berated her careless tongue. Alex took time to think before she spoke, a more useful trait Zee should emulate.

"That's a rather large leap," Alex said. "The police have their culprit."

"I . . . there are questions."

"But then," Alex mused, "Lenore had history with Bette."

"Oh?" Zee struggled to sit upright on the tilted seat, wanting a better look at the woman's face. She pushed down with her thumb on the front part of a switch. The forward edge of her seat lowered. She reversed it.

Alex glanced toward the exit. "Lenore does not take breakups kindly. She wouldn't, however, resort to violence."

Unless one counted driving like a madwoman. Zee tried to make her voice casual. "Why do you say that?"

A small sigh escaped Alex's coral lips. "Lenore is an amazing woman. She's given many people the courage and clarity to break out of their religious conditioning." She faced Zee, green eyes glistening. "That's where her passion truly lies. It's why her partners end up leaving." She dropped her gaze. "I tried to tell her. I didn't want her to end up all alone."

Zee averted her eyes from Alex's vulnerability. She'd underestimated Lenore's power to inspire devotion. Like Bette. Two powerful personalities. No wonder they clashed. The question was: did their devoted followers?

"Liberation from trauma can create fanaticism." Alex's voice pulled Zee from her contemplation. "People become attached to someone they believe saved them." She fixed Zee with a sober stare. "If you're truly looking for someone other than Marjorie Franklin, you might investigate Lenore's more rabid fans."

Zee struggled to project simple curiosity. "Such as?"

"Kevin would be a start. He was an emotional cripple when he first arrived."

Zee's back ached from the effort to sit upright. Abandoning subtlety, she slid her fingers past the rocker switch and found another set of small controls. She pushed one up. The sides of the seat began to snuggle against her thighs. Hurriedly, she halted them.

"Slide higher," said Alex. "Grab the big lever."

Zee's hand closed around the long handle. How had she missed it? She pulled. The seat back sprang forward, nearly catapulting her into the dash.

Alex laughed, a dusky chuckle. "Do I make you nervous?" She reached across the space between them. "Don't worry. I don't bite." She patted Zee's knee. "Unless that's what you like."

Heat boiled up Zee's neck and flooded her cheeks. She was an idiot. She swallowed against her dry throat.

"Hey, there you are." Rico jogged toward them. He focused his gaze on Alex. "I wondered where you went."

Zee's fingers scrabbled and found the door release.

Rico whistled as he came abreast. "Nice ride."

Zee glanced back at Alex. Her emerald gaze lingered on Rico. "I'd give you a ride any day." She drew a breath through parted lips.

Rico raised his brows.

Zee choked. Her admiration for Alex only went so far. Hauling herself from the leather-lined lair, she resolved to project relaxed confidence. "Thanks for letting me enjoy the new car smell."

"I enjoyed your enjoyment." Alex's eyes crinkled.

Zee sketched a wave. Her body strung with tension, she set off at a brisk hobble toward the Mini. Rico stayed behind, presumably to take his leave as soon as possible. Zee hoped.

As she unlocked *Po*, her phone roared with Rico's ringtone.

"Debrief at your place," he said.

Zee stuffed her concern into a tight package beneath her ribcage. "Okay. Take a different route. Someone could be following me."

"Got it, chief." He clicked off.

As she pulled from her parking spot, a few raindrops plopped against her windshield. Zee slowed and took pleasure in seeing Alex busy raising the top. Would serve her right to get rained-on.

Zee drove home while her mind and her heart argued. She had no reason to doubt Rico. But Alex was so damnably charismatic. Heat climbed Zee's neck when she replayed the teasing conversation in the luxurious 'Vette. And Alex hadn't missed a beat, switching on the charm for Rico.

Zee pursed her lips. Rico had been different since he returned from the camping trip. Her stomach twisted, entangled in fear. She couldn't lay it all on the newspaper merger, could she?

She reached no resolution by the time she pulled into the lot behind Legate I. Rico's bike already stood in a visitor space, collecting droplets from the continuing light rain. He trotted to the Mini, opened the door, and let himself in.

She squelched disappointment that he chose not to go up to her apartment.

"Gotta make this quick," he said. "Jake gave me a heads-up. Something's brewing."

His damn job. She pushed away the urge to run her fingers through his damp hair. So nice after a shower—

"Did you talk to Lenore?"

Zee fumbled. She needed time to regroup. "You first. What did you learn?"

He rubbed knuckles along the dark stubble on his jaw. "The theatrics put me off. But the stories . . . impressed me."

Guilt prickled Zee's skin.

He turned toward her, eyes serious. "You joked that I'm a recovering Catholic. I am, but I resent it."

Zee's heart sank. She'd brought this on him. "I wish I could say I understand. Fontina's family was Catholic, but she's either shrugged it off or maybe never believed it in the first place."

"Lucky her."

Silence filled the car. In brief sidelong glances, she searched

Rico's face for clues, for a way to respond to his pain. The engine ticked as it cooled, a counterpoint to the drizzling rain.

"I shouldn't have sent you in there," Zee murmured.

Rico cleared his throat, facing her. "I'm not like them. They blame religion, like there's no other factor."

"I thought that too." The tightness in Zee's chest eased. "To paraphrase my dad, if the only tool you have is an exorcism, everything looks like a demon."

Rico's chuckle dissipated the tension. "Good one."

Zee grabbed the chance to redirect the conversation. "So, did you learn anything?"

"Open to question. That bald-headed guy boasted that Alex wasn't the only one who could do something dramatic. Said he'd sent a message that the group wouldn't be messed with."

Zee lassoed the yelp that wanted to rise. She kept her voice calm, curious. "What did he do?"

"Hinted it was violent. Then all hell broke loose." Rico ran a hand through his hair.

Zee bit her lip to keep from joining him. "Sounds crazy." She wished she'd ignored her hesitation and snuck into the meeting. "Didn't Lenore try to stop it? Give him a chance to explain?"

"She handed Alex the meeting and dragged the guy to the back of the room. Looked like she wanted to throw him out, but he wouldn't leave. She slapped him, then she left."

Even as she reeled in shock at Lenore's violence, a voice barbed in the back of her head. Rico knew Alex's name, but not the guy who caused the pandemonium. She smothered a jealous twinge. "Lenore slapped him? I wouldn't have expected that from her."

"My take too."

"What happened then?"

"Not much," he said. "A few more stories. I stayed, tried to talk to a few people. Not a friendly bunch."

Alex was friendly enough, Zee would bet.

"My turn," Rico's voice diverted her thoughts. "What did *you* learn?" He grinned. "Or based on the scene in the 'Vette, should I ask? Never seen you exit a hot car so fast."

Zee feigned a punch, but he caught her fist in his hand. Electricity shot up her arm and wrapped around her chest. She tried to ignore it. He'd been looking for Alex, not her. Pulling her hand free, she shot back. "You were stepping pretty lively, too."

"Coming to your rescue. Car gave me good cover."

Zee's face burned. He'd admired the 'Vette to show he had a reason to be there that didn't involve finding, or even knowing, Zee. When would she learn to trust him?

When she learned *not* to trust people like Alex.

"You find out anything from Lenore?" His voice derailed her self-criticism.

She caught his blue eyes, as a shower pattered on the roof. "There's a lot of emotional entanglements in that crowd. It feels practically incestuous." She filled him in, ending with Lenore's startling revelation.

"Two o'clock narrows the time of death," he said.

"Did you get info on that?"

"Between noon and four." The rain intensified, running in rivulets down the windows. "I gotta say I don't like Lenore for the murder. Despite what she did at the meeting."

"She obviously can be provoked, but to kill?" Zee shook her head. "She showed genuine horror at . . . the murder." Zee flushed. She'd nearly mentioned the fire. She smothered the impulse to tell him. "Wish I knew who the guy was, the one she got so mad at."

"His name's Kevin."

Kevin confessed. Zee covered her shock by grabbing her water bottle.

"I got a card." Rico dug into his pocket. "Saw it on the table." He passed the wrinkled rectangle to her.

Zee kicked herself. She had been too distracted by the horrible pretzels and doughnuts to notice an opportunity like that. Foiled by food. Again.

Rain pounded against the car. Leaning across the center console, he pulled her close. She laid her head on his leather-clad shoulder, breathing deeply of the moisture-sharpened spice in his juniper scent.

Her breathing slowed, meshed with his. Murder, oppression, resentment, all the stupidity of humankind lay outside the cocoon of his arms.

He wound the tips of his fingers among her curls. "I love how your hair rebels against rain. Wild, untamed." He kissed the top of her head and lifted her chin.

A flicker of lightning illumined his face. It could have been a trick of the light, but his blue eyes seemed to shine wetly.

"I won't lie," he murmured, so softly against the tumult of the downpour that Zee held her breath to hear him better. "Those people touched me." Another flash lit his cobalt gaze. "They can't see how to get what they want from life."

"What do you want from life?" She surprised herself by asking.

He answered without words.

CHAPTER 26

AS NIGHT SETTLED AROUND HER, ZEE lay in bed, the rain a susurration against the window. But instead of soothing her, its gentle hiss conjured snakes, slithering from the snarled nest of BA. She tried to bury the uneasiness by focusing on her body, still tingling with Rico's caresses. On her lips, where the taste of his kiss still lingered.

Lulled by rain, cat-warmth, and his lingering scent, at last she fell into a restless sleep. Like a fog-shrouded thornbush, snatches of Kevin snagged the currents of her dreams. His angry eyes. His rage. She woke with a start, tangled in sun-streaked bedclothes. Inchoate images loitered at the edge of her consciousness, leaving her unsettled, lonely, and fearful.

The morning light usually chased night's specters, but this stark daylight only delineated more clearly the menace in the fire, the threat on her door, and the reality of Bette's murder.

Zee clenched fistfuls of blanket. She wanted to nail this story. She just didn't want to die trying.

The tail bone's connected to the brain bone. A Shelby-ism from her detective's folksy period. When you're stuck in your head, get up and *do* something.

Kevin's cowardice fueled her anger, burning through her anxiety. She threw back the covers, shucking her uneasiness along with the blanket. "Time for action, Candy-pants, after I feed my brain, and you."

Yellow eyes narrowed.

Recalling the rejected orange supplement, Zee stroked behind the silky ears. "We have a new flavor today. You'll like this one."

Candy stared at Zee, then stretched and flexed her paws, spreading her toes wide and extending needle-sharp claws. A not-so-subtle warning, which Zee decided not to take as an omen.

In the kitchen, she scooped canned Tuna Supreme into Candy's bowl, hoping the moist food would make Fontina's experiment #3 more palatable. Blocking Candy's view, she stirred in a sprinkle of brownish powder. She hummed a cheerful tune as she placed the dish on Candy's mat and turned away. If she didn't watch, she couldn't get the blame, right?

Her own mouth watered as she toasted a sesame-seed bagel and tried not to notice the silence from the vicinity of Candy's dish. "It's for your own good," she said over her shoulder.

She carried her breakfast to the balcony to drink in the rain-washed morning. Last night's storm had bejeweled the trees in the green space between buildings. Myriads of tiny droplets clung to the limbs and tiny budding leaves.

Her eyes strayed to the blackened splotch from the fire. A guilty twinge wriggled through her chest. Despite her promise to herself, she hadn't told Rico.

A motorcycle roared from her phone. She jumped, sloshing coffee over her hand.

"Hey," Rico said when she answered. "Gotta leave town. Probably 'til Monday."

She stifled a disappointed groan. Weekend assignments seemed to occur more frequently since the merger. "Where's Karl sending you this time?"

"Chicago."

Zee gulped. Home of the corporate office of Allied Communications Media, the conglomerate that owned the *St.*

Louis Messenger, now the *Valerian Messenger-Tribune*. Fear spiked in her heart. Rumor had it that reporters summoned there got reassigned, or fired. "Cold there in March," she managed to say, then kicked herself. He'd just returned from a camping trip; weather wasn't a problem.

"I'll live." His chuckle sounded forced. "Don't get into trouble while I'm gone," he teased.

Appreciating his effort to lighten the mood, she tried to match his tone. "I'll do my best."

After he disconnected, her eyes strayed to the bagel. "I'll always have you." She bit into the chewy crust. Even sparsely buttered—a reluctant concession to her fitness goal—nothing satisfied like a hearty doughnut-shaped treat from Nachman Brothers.

Well, except for an actual doughnut. Or a cherry-cheese Danish. Or an almond horn. Or a croissant with brie and apricot jam . . .

A chime floated from the table beside her lounge chair, a text rescuing Zee from the pastry spiral of death.

Our foolishness is his wisdom. Look.

From the same number as the previous text. The bagel congealed in her stomach. "Dammit." She stared at the offending phone, tempted to hurl it over the balcony railing and watch it self-destruct on the burnt patch below. "Just dammit."

Candy poked a wary head through the doorway.

"Who's sending me these messages?" Zee queried the slitted eyes. "What do they want from me?"

In answer, Candy sidled up to her knee, crawled into her lap, and began to lick buttery crumbs from Zee's fingers. Priorities.

Zee let her breathing slow. The text didn't change her course of action; in fact, it reinforced her plan. Gently, she dislodged the furry body, gathered her breakfast, and headed for her office.

Halfway across the living room, doubt sprouted. She should report the second text to Bernstow. "Argh!" That meant having her phone cloned again.

Shelby poked her in the ribs.

Right. Bernstow could wait. He hadn't put much credence in the first text. And he probably wasn't in on a Saturday, anyway.

She resumed course, but a voice nagged. She could report the text to anyone who answered. In fact, that might be better.

No. She would not be dissuaded right now. She shook her head as if to throw aside the argument.

A sharp crack jolted her hip. Pain streaked down her leg. "Damn." She staggered, balancing phone, coffee, and bagel, watching helpless as her dad's barrister bookcase shuddered. In the topmost shelf, the crystal ball jumped the red box and rolled across a pile of papers toward the poorly secured glass cover. Her hands full, Zee sucked in air. The frame held; the glass remained intact.

Heart pounding, Zee hobbled toward her desk. She'd repair the cover this weekend. The bag with the parts already sat on her kitchen counter. Sinking into her oversized leather chair, she aimed the promise at the bookcase, and her dad.

While the throbbing in her hip subsided, she powered up her computer. Back to her original task. Within fifteen minutes, she had Kevin's place of employment. She narrowed her eyes at the hairless bland face on the monitor. Come Monday, the firebug defender of BA was going to have an interesting visit.

But that was two days away. Shelby's directive wasn't satisfied by a quarter-hour's internet search and the promise of future action.

Zee sifted through ideas. She could track down Alex, but her cheeks burned an emphatic negation to that idea. Not until Zee regained her footing would she confront that wily, unpredictable adversary. She could talk to the Earthkins about the new text, but they'd probably provide no more help than they had with the first one. She could call Sara Jane, follow up their conversation at Valerian's Corner. That one appealed to her, but Zee shied from intruding on Bette's grieving, overwhelmed publicist.

Her phone rang. Another number she didn't recognize. Teeth gritted, she answered.

"Zee," a brisk voice, "it's Marian, Entertainment editor at the *Messenger-Tribune*."

Why was she calling? "What can I do for you?"

"Great job on the fringe religious groups story."

That article wasn't for the Entertainment section. It was supposed to be Metro front page. "Thanks." Zee swallowed acid. Damn Karl—again.

"Giving you a courtesy call. We might have to hold it for the Wednesday supplement. Just wanted to alert you. That's al—"

Before she could end the conversation, Zee interjected. "What's going on?"

To her credit, Marian's sigh was barely audible. "The production team for the movie based on *The Mirror of the Soul* is coming into town."

Zee's spirits lifted. If the production was moving forward, tension might mount at BA, and someone else might act or let something slip. The timing of the new text might even be relevant. "Are they making an announcement?"

"Don't know yet. Could just be here for the funeral."

Zee's heart lurched. "When's that?" And why didn't she know? Bette was her friend.

"Tuesday. Listen, I've got to run."

"Can you let me know if you hear anything about the movie?"

A dry laugh. "You reporters. Once you get your hooks into a story, you think it's your private preserve." Another chuckle. "Tell you what, I'll tell Philo to give you a heads-up."

Philo came with the merger. Sporting spikey neon purple hair, a zipper-festooned leather pantsuit, and chunky buckled boots, the snarky reporter tromped in on that first day and commandeered the desk formerly occupied by Zee's friend Jessica. Smirk-faced, Philo swept heavily mascaraed eyes around the newsroom. Zee could almost see her cataloging who was important and who wasn't. Zee didn't make the cut.

She swallowed her animosity. "Let her know I'm just looking

for background . . . for *Z Beats*." She wouldn't scoop the twit. "A column about making movies from books." Which was actually not a bad idea. And it gave her a legitimate reason to poke around.

"Works for me. Gotta run." Marian disconnected.

Zee wouldn't expect much from Philo. And now she suspected Sara Jane would be wrapped up with the movie production team. Maybe the publicist would appreciate a break, a chance to unwind a bit. Not that the conversation would necessarily be relaxing.

Zee nibbled her lip, discomfited by her floundering. She wanted this story, for herself, for Bette, for Marjorie. A good reporter—even one with a conscience—could gather information with skill and compassion.

Before she could hesitate further, Zee called Sara Jane's cell. Unsurprisingly, she was asked to leave a message.

As she hung up, another idea presented itself. She didn't need Philo. If anyone knew—and would be willing to share—what was happening with the movie, it would be Victor. She tapped in a number.

"Victor here. Leave a message."

Extraordinary simplicity from the loquacious virtuoso who covered the arts scene. Zee left a short request.

Her burst of energy faded.

Thwarted at every turn, she sank back against her chair, drank cooled coffee, and rubbed the dull ache in her hip. Okay, if she couldn't move her investigation forward, she'd work on next week's column to get ahead of her deadline. That would free time on Monday to deal with Kevin. And she had a good idea for a topic, stupid label warnings.

She had already snapped a shot of one while buying parts for the bookcase. A piece of paper taped across the front of a portable propane heater: *Remove before use.* No kidding.

But first, she'd report the text.

As she reached for the phone, it rang. Hope spiked her heart-rate. Half a second later, she squelched disappointment. Not Rico's motorcycle tone. She grabbed the insistent cell. Maybe Sara Jane was calling back.

Zee's gut lurched at the caller ID.

Leehammer Pavilion.

"Ms. Morani," the clinical voice on the other end said. "Your father has taken a turn for the worse."

Her heart fell to her shoes. "I'll be right there."

CHAPTER 27

DWARFED IN THE BIG HOSPITAL BED, Stefan Morani looked like a child. A very ill child. His eyes were closed. Shallow breaths barely moved his rib cage. He had a DNR, so at least his face was not distorted by a breathing tube.

Zee dropped her purse to the visitor's chair and used both hands to grip the bedrails. Her dad's skin looked waxy, stretched over his bony structure. "Is he in pain?" she asked the attendant.

The young man's soft gaze met Zee's. "We're keeping him comfortable."

"Do you know," Zee forced the words from her parched throat. "Do you have any idea, how long he has?"

"That's always hard to say. People rally." He laid a gentle hand on Zee's shoulder. "It's good you're here." His eyes seemed to search her face. "If there's anything you want to tell him . . ."

She nodded her understanding.

He dropped his hand. "Press the call button if you need us."

Blinking back tears, Zee gazed at the small form on the bed. After all this time, it came down to this. This pinprick moment. All the pain and hurt, all the anger and disappointment, all the struggle of a lifetime— irrelevant. Her dad had done his best, and if it wasn't perfect, that just made him human. Like her.

She heard his laugh in her memory. His strong, confident voice asserting his position, outlining his argument. She was seven years old again, sitting on the floor in awe of him. He'd rummage in his beloved barrister bookcase, pull out the book he needed, turn to the page he wanted, extend it as proof, often to Papa Alesandro.

Zee's tears spilled. She made no effort to stop them.

He would have told her the secret of her paternity if he had been able. Some hills are just too hard to climb. Remorse washed through her. She could have been more forgiving.

Marjorie flashed through her thoughts. A great deal of misery probably could have been avoided if she had forgiven her parents.

Zee shook her head, clearing the questions from her mind. Marjorie wasn't her concern. She reached across the rumpled sheet to grasp her dad's hand. Skeletal, the skin barely covering the bones.

His eyelids fluttered.

"Dad." Zee leaned close. "It's me. I'm here."

A sliver of eyelid lifted.

"It's okay," Zee said. And then because there wasn't anything else to say, she choked out, "I love you."

His grip tensed on her hand. Her nose dripped, but she refused to pull free.

She loved him. She should have used that bridge years ago. The ground truth that might have saved them.

A question knotted her vocal cords. Did Rico know how she felt? The answer lay in the very fact that she had to ask. She brushed her sleeve against her wet cheek. It was time to be clear, to find out what spurred the draw-near, push-away dance in which they seemed to be locked.

With a sigh, she bent forward and touched her forehead to her dad's. His skin was clammy. The hospice nurse told her that as he approached the end, his body would burn itself up.

Her heart cried that it wasn't possible for him to leave her. Her mind reminded her that he would. She had to face the facts. His death would hurt, but it would happen.

He was so small now, so far gone already.

She was too far away.

To hold him, to make up for all the lost hugs, she crawled onto the bed beside him. Inching closer, she snuggled her head against his bony shoulder.

Life was ebbing from him. His breath no longer lifted even half his chest. It was all that was required now. She imagined that terminus creeping upward, to his collarbone, to his throat, to only his mouth. Then that final exhalation.

He shifted position. She raised up on an elbow. "I'm here, Dad. Everything is okay."

His eyes opened. His gaze found her. A thread of voice worked loose from his lips. "Bread . . . box."

Breadbox? "Dad, what did you say?"

But he was spent. Eyes closed, he sank back against the pillow.

Zee shunted aside her question. It didn't matter now.

She laid her head next to his and willed him to feel her presence, to know that he was not alone. "I'll walk with you," she whispered. "All the way."

A CRACK OF THUNDER STARTLED ZEE TO wakefulness. A string of ominous crackles unwound left to right, rending the world overhead. Leehammer Pavilion shuddered in its wake. Strobed by lightning, the bird feeder outside his window arced in wild swings.

Beneath the bedclothes, her dad lay unmoving. Zee jolted upright, her heart pounding. She scanned his silent form, dread crawling up from her gut to lodge at the back of her mouth.

There.

The slight rise of his chest.

Still with her.

She sagged against the mattress.

A gale rattled the window. Rain battered the glass, blurring the bird feeder behind a sheet of water. Zee sobbed quietly. Unable to scream and rage at her impending loss, she borrowed the voice of the storm to do it for her.

The lights in Leehammer Pavilion flickered.

Zee sat, swinging her legs over the edge of the bed. Although rationally she knew the facility would have backup power, fear clawed at her. As if in the darkness, her dad might slip away unnoticed.

A distant siren wailed.

The lights went out.

Zee's breath caught.

Another flicker, then pale, sickly yellow dispersed the darkness.

A young man in scrubs poked his head through the door. "Everything okay in here, miss?"

"He's fine," Zee said.

"We have plenty of backup power. Don't worry."

He was gone before she could thank him.

Easing down next to her dad, she resumed her vigil. Her hand rested lightly atop his chest, tracking the tremulous tide of his breath. Like him, the dimly lit building seemed barely alive.

Gradually, the storm faded. Outside, the day brightened. Inside, normal lighting returned.

A temple bell sounded from Zee's phone.

"Zee-zee, are you okay?" Fontina's voice carried concern. "I sense something's happened."

"It's my dad." Zee's voice wobbled.

"Want me to—?"

"Yes." Zee forced down the lump in her throat. "Please."

"Be right there."

As Zee disconnected, a smear of red drew her eye to the bird-feeder. A cardinal balanced on a dripping perch, his crimson plumage glinting in the resurgent sunlight. On a nearby branch, a duller-hued female companion paced.

The male selected a seed and flew to land beside her. He leaned close and placed the tiny kernel inside her beak. After she accepted it, he flew back to the feeder and chose another morsel.

Tension eased from Zee's limbs. The dance might be pure courtship instinct for survival of the species, but it warmed her heart. At the same time, a pang of longing squeezed. She'd once pushed Rico away because she was overwhelmed with caring for her dad. Now she wished more than ever that he was here with her.

Other birds joined the courting cardinals. A blue-and-white striped nuthatch perched upside down on the tree trunk, awaiting its turn at the feeder. Two black-capped chickadees flitted to and fro, dodging between rufus-brushed brown house wrens.

Zee swallowed tears. Burgeoning life outside, full of promise and hope, while inside, worn and weary, the cycle neared its close.

She turned at the click of the door opening. Tears filled her eyes. "Thank you for coming."

"Of course." Fontina enveloped Zee in a soft cotton embrace. "How is he?"

"He doesn't have long." She clung to her tall friend, suddenly too weak to stand on her own. In silent communion, Fontina held her until Zee's ragged inhalations slowed. Their breathing synchronized.

Fontina's deep brown eyes met Zee's. "Do you think he'd mind if I touch him?"

"I'm sure it's all right." Zee swallowed salty tears. "We're family."

As she spoke, gratitude welled in Zee's chest for the rich decades of their friendship. Shortly after they met in first grade, Fontina's father had declared Zee an honorary daughter. Zee, the only child of intellectual parents, had been delighted to join Fontina's eight rambunctious siblings and to call him, at his insistence, Papa Alesandro.

But more than the transformation of her lonely external life, in Fontina, Zee found a sister of the heart, one whose soul resonated with Zee's, like notes of the same chord.

In the softly lit room, her figurative sister stepped to the bedside. She laid a slender hand on the motionless forehead and bent toward Zee's dad, murmuring words that fell below the threshold of Zee's comprehension. Peaceful repose spread across his face. His breathing deepened.

"How did you do that?" Zee whispered.

Fontina lifted her hand and turned to Zee. "Uncle Ramiz has many gifts."

Zee blinked back more tears. "Did he tell you to call me?"

"In a way," said Fontina. "His picture in my office fell over."

From the bed, Zee's dad blew out a puff of air. It could have been a weak chortle.

"Did he tell you . . ."

Fontina touched Zee's forearm. "Your dad's death is approaching, but it is not as close as you fear."

Zee's knees sagged with relief, but she brought herself up short. "Is he in pain? Is there anything I can do?"

"No pain," said Fontina. "And you're doing all you can right now. Although," she knit her brows, "do you know anything about a shiny red box?"

Numbly, Zee shook her head. "Why?"

"I saw an image."

Zee massaged her temples. "I'm too exhausted to take on another mystery. My brain feels like an aching fist."

Fontina cocked her head. "When did you last eat?"

"I can't leave him." Zee flinched under her scrutiny.

"I understand. But he has time. You both have time." Fontina's fingers sought the old coin on its chain. She pursed her lips, as if reluctant to speak, then sighed. "I have to say, there's a very strong sense that for someone else, time is running out."

Zee's stomach twisted. "You don't know who? You *would* tell me, right?"

"Yes, I would." Fontina straightened. "The important thing right now is to get you some food." She raised her palm to forestall Zee's incipient protest. "Stay here. I'll go to Farm Fresh."

Zee squeezed her friend's hands in appreciation.

After Fontina left, Zee sank into the recliner near the window.

Fear scraped at her heart. Was Rico's time short? Hers? Theirs?

Wrapping her arms across her chest, she rocked in the chair. Bette had already been taken from her. She couldn't bear another loss so soon.

She raked fingers through her curls, trying to shake loose the dread. If only Uncle Ramiz would talk to her. Closing her eyes, she pictured the photo as clearly as possible, sharpening the details as if by the power of her visualization, she could summon his presence.

He smiled at her from the picture frame, a swarthy man with a thick dark mustache, eyes that twinkled behind round John Lennon glasses, and curly hair spilling from under an oft-worn, soft flat cap. After his death, he'd told Fontina where to look in that cap to find the coin she now wore around her neck.

The room grew warm around Zee, but Uncle Ramiz had no message for her. Instead, her brain sprouted speculations. Perhaps Fontina's intuition pointed to Marjorie. But she no longer despaired of life. Of course, if she wasn't the murderer, someone else could be in danger. Like Lenore, who'd been at Bette's apartment.

Zee's eyes snapped open. In the Earthkins' apartment, there had been a highly polished, cherrywood box table by Gregory's recliner. Was that what Fontina saw?

A snuffle pulled her eyes to the bedclothes. She swatted away thoughts of the case. It would still be there later. For now, she would spend her time with her dad.

A tear rolled down her cheek. No matter how long the life, no one is ever ready for it to end.

The weight of what she faced dragged down her eyelids.

She started at a gentle shake. "Miss? Miss?"

Zee jerked awake. "What? Is Dad okay?"

The young man in scrubs smiled. "He's rallied. They do sometimes." He gestured toward a carton on the table. "Your friend brought you some food. I think you could take it home. Get a good night's sleep. We'll call you if anything changes."

Zee forced her unsteady feet to the bed. Her dad's chest rose and fell in regular rhythm. She brushed the white hair from his forehead, put her lips to the cool, dry skin. "I'll be back, Dad." Her throat constricted. "Don't go anywhere without me."

CHAPTER 28

THE WORKWEEK DAWNED CLEAR AND SUNNY, the remnants of storm clouds receding to a thin dark streak along the eastern horizon. In defiance of the beneficent weather, Zee's own storm continued to brew.

A phone call this morning had confirmed that her dad remained stable, but that relative reprieve only sharpened her displeasure with Karl. He'd run her thought-provoking fringe group story on Sunday, consigned to the Entertainment section.

She would deal with him later.

Now weaving her way through late morning traffic, she channeled her energy toward the upcoming interrogation of Kevin. He was an arsonist—she needed to remember that. He'd been friendly at the meeting. He also howled like a raging beast when released from the confines of civility. Zee shuddered at a stoplight, wondering which Kevin she would see today.

It didn't matter. She stomped the gas. He wasn't getting away from her until she knew why he set the fire, why he left the threat on her door.

She inhaled cool air to dampen her anger and slow down. Ahead lay the newly installed Ovid Circulus, what locals called the Ovid Circus. The roundabout theoretically saved money and improved traffic flow, and maybe it would, when Americans learned that it didn't function as a four-way stop; vehicles already in the circle had the right of way.

As she waited for an opening, the driver on her left barged in front of an oncoming SUV. Zee cringed, bracing for the crunch of metal. None came. The SUV's horn blared. The offending driver honked back.

Zee snorted. The Ovid Circus. Not a bad idea for a column.

She parked the Mini between two eyeball-searing white lines in the newly resurfaced lot of the West Valerian Office Plaza. Kevin's workplace, the corporate offices of the First Community Bank, stood four proud stories tall among the stern gray buildings.

Time to enter the arena.

Zee smoothed the lapels of her pin-striped navy jacket, checked the crease on the matching trousers, and rubbed her thumb over her mother's opal ring. Girded for battle, she stepped from *Po*.

And was mugged by a suffocating blanket of humidity. She groaned silently. Her dewed scalp heralded a rebellious explosion of her curls. So much for a professional appearance.

Many a rat gets caught in a trap he didn't see 'til he heard the snap.

Zee chuckled at Shelby's rhymed advice. Let Kevin underestimate her, if he dared. Squaring her shoulders, she strode toward the building, albeit at a measured pace.

The bank's glass door opened easily at her push, exhaling chilled breath from an enormous atrium. A two-story circular fountain half a football field away dominated the tile and glass cavern. Between it and the doors, a young woman perched behind a high desk cocooned in thick glass. She leaned toward a gap in her enclosure. "May I help you?"

Zee pitched her voice toward the narrow opening. "Yes, thank you. I'm here to meet Kevin Freswidden."

"I'll call him for you." She favored Zee with a practiced upward tilt of her lips. "May I give him your name?"

"It's Zee. I'm taking him to lunch."

The receptionist's smile grew a fraction wider. Zee felt the sweep of blue-green eyes, cataloguing details. Kevin would be the subject of much speculation by the time he returned to the office.

Zee's cheeks warmed. Good grief, she was old enough to be his . . . older sister. She shifted her attention to the fountain. The burble of water slid into her ears, a soothing white noise. The knot in her chest loosened.

"He says he's very busy today." The receptionist's voice cut through the peaceful interlude. "He's sorry."

Zee kept her voice pleasantly professional. "Remind him it's about a legal matter with the landscaping on my lawn."

The young woman's penciled brows drew together, but she picked up the phone and relayed the message. A moment later, she addressed Zee. "He'll be right down."

Zee turned to hide her grin. Twenty feet away, an enormous gray leather ottoman offered backless seating and a clear view of the elevators. She settled on the ultra-firm edge. She'd caught Kevin by surprise, as she'd hoped. Now she had to strike a balance. If angry, he could blurt out something useful. If defensive, he might clam up.

The fountain's sonic bombardment began to grate on her nerves. She refocused on her goal. Kevin set the fire. She needed to use that as a lever to learn whether there was a connection between BA and that mysterious text. Maybe Kevin sent it. Or knew who did. Maybe it was Lenore. That could be why Ferret-Face slapped him at the meeting.

Like an audible tide, the fountain's constant whoosh and babble beat at her ears. How did anyone think with that racket?

She struggled to shut it out, but the sound swelled, a living thing, filling her head: dishwasher level, vacuum cleaner, garbage disposal. It was well on its way to lawn mower volume when across the lobby, a set of embossed brass elevator doors opened. Kevin strode out, his face glacial.

CHAPTER 29

The ice in Kevin Freswidden's glare could have chilled a meat locker. Zee rose to meet him as he crossed the lobby of the First Community Bank.

"What are you doing here?" he said between clenched teeth.

She wrapped her arm through his. "Taking you to lunch." She tightened her grip. "Unless you want to make a scene."

Kevin stared at her, veins bulging in his neck. "I'm not going anywhere with you."

Zee lowered her voice. "We're going to chat in a nice quiet restaurant, or I'll have you charged with arson."

"You can't—"

"I have a witness." She steered him toward the door.

He pried her fingers loose. "All right, we can talk. But I'm not leaving."

Zee flicked her eyes toward the receptionist in her aerie. "She's already got enough to gossip about, don't you think?"

To his credit, he did not turn to look. Gracelessly, he shoved open the door.

First goal achieved. He was out of his office. Zee hoped it wasn't a mistake to be alone in the car with him. "Over here." She gestured toward the Mini.

"I can't fit in that," he grumbled. "Why can't we take my jeep?"

Seriously? She reached for his arm. "You'll find my car is bigger than it looks."

He shrugged away from her touch, slouched toward the Mini, and with an air of resignation, folded his frame into the passenger seat.

Zee relaxed a fraction. He would be more likely to provide information if he didn't see her as an adversary. She'd also be safer. "Geez," she faced him from the driver's seat, "how does that receptionist not go insane, listening to that racket all day?"

He cracked an unexpected smile. "Who says she's not?" His grin faded, guard in place again. How quickly he could switch gears. "Where are you taking me?"

"Cactus Cantina." Where Carlos, bartender, waiter, occasional cook, and proprietor, would have her back.

"What if I don't like the food?"

Zee side-eyed him. "You're worried about *that*?"

He shrank into himself and chewed his lip.

Good, he shouldn't get too comfortable.

Ten minutes later, Zee pushed open the door to the small Mexican restaurant.

"Hola, Zee." Carlos waved from behind the bar. He was a sweet, gentle man, but she hoped Kevin saw only his imposing six-foot frame, massive arms, and barrel chest.

"Hola, Carlos."

He gestured toward the far wall. "Conference corner?"

She nodded.

"What to drink?"

"Iced tea for me." Zee looked a question at Kevin.

"Whatever kind of beer you have in this place," he mumbled.

"Give him that one." She pointed to the first beer on the chalkboard list. When he didn't object, she shepherded him to her chosen meeting place.

Zee took the seat against the wall, forcing Kevin to slide onto the smooth wooden bench opposite. Where he couldn't see anything going on behind him. Where he couldn't see Carlos, keeping a watchful eye.

Kevin worried a nail, eyes darting everywhere but her. She let him stew until Carlos brought their drinks, salsa, and a basket of delectable corn chips.

"What to eat today?" Carlos smiled widely. "Beef enchilada is very good."

"I'll have that," said Zee.

Kevin spoke through gritted teeth. "I don't want anything."

"Suit yourself," Zee said.

The picture of patient attentiveness, Carlos waited.

Kevin huffed. "Gimme a taco."

With a twitch of his thick brows, Carlos turned toward the kitchen. Zee would have about ten minutes before he delivered their food.

Kevin's cell buzzed. He pulled it from its holster.

"Ignore that," said Zee.

"It might be work."

"Is it?"

He didn't answer. Under her glower, he swallowed the rest of his objection and set the phone on the table. Face-up.

Zee's eyes strayed to the basket of crisp, golden corn chips. Her stomach whimpered. She tore her gaze away. Hard to interrogate with a mouthful of crunchy, salt-encrusted heaven. She skewered Kevin. "Let's get to it. Why did you set the fire?"

He studied the beer bottle. Except for the sweat sheening his brow, he looked like any other office worker, in pressed tan slacks and a blue polo shirt discreetly embroidered with the First Community Bank logo on the left breast. A vanilla façade she couldn't trust.

Vanilla. Zee's mouth watered. Julio's Panadería next door made the best cream rolls in the city. Rich, smooth vanilla custard filling, her favorite chock full of chewy coconut shreds, all wrapped in a lightly sweet sugar crust. She'd get one after lunch, eat it later with—

Stop.

She stifled a snort and sucked tea through her straw, flooding her insubordinate taste buds and nearly precipitating an icy headache.

What was Kevin doing in all this silence? Concocting a story? Gauging how much he could shade the truth? She held her impatience while Carlos seated a group of young men in a far booth, then pinned Kevin with her eyes. "Answer me."

Decision apparently made, he leaned against the lacquered cactus shapes forming the back of the bench. His chin jutted. "I set the fire so you'd leave Believers Anonymous alone."

As she had thought. A clumsy attempt. "Why were you worried?"

He spoke with confidence, accusing. "I heard you talking to Alex. Figured you were going to ridicule us like everyone else."

Zee squelched a denial. Sixty-seven newspapers carried *Z Beats* twice weekly, precisely for its witty, biting satire. Her mind did a quick tap dance, searching for a way to defuse his defenses. "That wasn't my intention. I know someone who's struggling with leftover religious indoctrination. I thought BA might be useful to him."

She winced inwardly as the words left her lips, hoping he wouldn't connect her to the new guy in the leather jacket. Quickly she added, "Don't you think the fire was excessive?"

Kevin scowled. "We're fighting for our lives right now with that cursed book. And the movie that's coming." He rubbed his bottle in wet rings on the glass tabletop, smearing them across a carved scene of colorfully costumed, dancing Mexicans.

His cell buzzed again. He flicked his eyes toward it, then covered it with his hand. Zee got only a glance, not enough to read the caller ID. The last time someone's phone buzzed to interrupt her, she was with Alex. And Kevin had been across the street, spying.

She put steel in her voice. "Your plan backfired. It only made me more curious." As he should have known, dealing with a reporter.

She drilled her gaze into him. "You're smarter than that. Want to go for the truth this time?"

He picked at the label on the bottle. "Okay, so it wasn't the most brilliant thing I've ever done."

She granted him that, noting he didn't provide a different answer to the question.

"But I meant it when I said we're fighting for our lives."

"Because of *The Mirror of the Soul*?" Across the room, the young men cheered the arrival of their drinks and chips. Zee stopped her hand from automatically reaching for a tantalizing triangle of toasted corn. Refocused. Time was slipping away. "Maybe I'm thick-headed here. Help me understand how Bette's book threatens BA."

"Ask Alex. I bet that—" He bit his lip and averted his eyes.

"What?"

"Nothing. Forget it." He tipped his bottle and drank. By the time he set it down, he'd refastened his mask of sincerity. "The thing that gets me, the thing that gets most of us, is how hard this is on Lenore."

His voice softened when he uttered the founder's name. An unexpected level of intimacy. Or a diversion.

He leaned across the cheery Mexican scene. "All she's ever done is try to help people. Bad enough she had her own horrendous brainwashing, but she volunteers to live everyone else's pain while they're working through it."

There was honesty there, but he'd also provided a lot of information without much prodding. Offered it as easily as if he'd rehearsed it.

She filed her reservations. This might be a crack she could exploit, a way to learn more about this *nest of vipers*, as Shaneah put it. Zee infused her voice with sympathy. "I admit, the people who spoke at the meeting really affected me. I could hear their suffering."

Kevin let his head drop. In the bright overhead light, perspiration dotted his bald scalp. "Lenore's a saint. Not by the canon, but in the true meaning of the word."

An odd reference, *by the canon*. She spoke quietly. "What's your story?"

"Me?" He lifted his gaze. "I wanted to be a priest, if you can believe that. I even went to seminary. But I got disillusioned with the petty displays of power, the unquestioning obedience, the whole kissing-the-ring thing."

The corners of his mouth tugged downward, but the crestfallen expression did not reach his eyes.

The eye don't lie. Shelby never let grammar get in the way of a pithy piece of advice.

Lenore had slapped him. For breaking an ironclad rule. For disobedience. His devotion to her didn't jive with his seminary tale.

"Seems twisted to me," Zee said.

"Twisted, yeah." Something glimmered in the depth of his eyes. Embarrassment. Or grief. Something he wanted to hide. She had a shortening window in which to find out.

"Is that seminary still operating?"

"Don't know, don't care." His answer came too fast.

"What's the name?"

His face shuttered. "I don't remember."

She raised her brows, telegraphing disbelief. "Your cherished dream, destroyed, and you don't remember?"

With a flick of his hand, he brushed off her comment. His phone buzzed. He grabbed it, challenging her. "Look, I'm sorry I upset you. I admitted what I did. We done now?"

"Not yet."

He stared daggers at her.

She saw her opening. "Someone sending you texts?"

He jerked the phone out of reach.

"Maybe you sent *me* a text." She fixed him with a stare, boring through his defenses. "Maybe you tried to warn me off with a text—"

"No—"

"And when that didn't work, you escalated—"

His voice rose. "I don't know what you're—"

"And set a fire in my yard to scare me."

He half-rose, yelling. "I said I was sorry." Faces in the other booth turned. If Kevin saw, he ignored it. He slammed his fists on the table. "What do you want from me?"

In the kitchen, dishes clattered. "Settle down," Zee said. "All I want is the truth."

Teeth clamped, he resumed his seat. He lowered his voice, measuring his words. "I didn't send you anything." In his face, the desire to end the conversation warred with curiosity. And some other emotion. His chest heaved. "I told you the truth. Whatever else happened, I've got nothing to do with it."

Zee released a strangled breath. "Okay, I believe you." Not completely, but before Carlos brought lunch, she had another thread she hoped to tug on. "It's clear you care about Lenore."

He nodded, his dark eyes wary.

"Your devotion to her is commendable. She's made a big difference in your life." She sipped tea as his breathing slowed. "I think your real motivation for the fire was to convince me to leave Lenore alone."

"They're the same thing." Kevin resumed decimating the label on his empty bottle.

"I wonder. Why are you so worried about her?"

The remaining color drained from his cheeks. "I'm not."

"Maybe you know something. From what I'm learning, I'm not sure Marjorie Franklin is guilty."

If possible, his face paled further. "Is that why you came to the meeting?" The next question seemed torn from his throat. "Do you think Lenore did it?"

Alex had called him a basket case when he joined BA. His wounds were still raw. "Do you?"

"No." His voice carried no conviction.

Zee softened her tone. "I don't suspect her." Not a totally honest statement, but she needed to keep him talking.

He wiped his palms down his face and rocked back. "That's a, a great relief." He straightened. "But if it's not the Franklin woman or Lenore, then who is it?"

Zee wished she had a clue. She wished she understood the clues she had. Not that she would confess that to him. She cloaked her next question in collegial sincerity. "Who do *you* think?"

Whatever fractured in Kevin had fused together again. He reached toward the basket of chips. "No idea. I wish you good luck finding out."

Too dismissive. He thought he was off the hook. She chose her words carefully. "I'll leave that to the police."

He jerked in his seat, gripped the edge of the table.

Good. She had him off balance again. She played her frosted glass in the moisture atop the scene of whirling dancers. "Why did you stop yourself earlier, about Alex?"

"It doesn't matter."

Zee trapped his eyes. "I think it does."

He grabbed a chip. Massacred it in his fist. Zee had the distinct impression he wished he could crush her in the same way. "Something going on between Alex and Lenore?"

He snorted. "Not anymore." He snapped shut his jaw and looked away.

"So there was something." Zee leaned toward him. "What?"

"It doesn't have anything to do with—"

"I'll decide that."

He flattened against the bench. "I swear . . ." He buckled under her glare. "She and Lenore were a hot item, but Alex supposedly dumped her."

"Why?"

"She said Lenore has one love, Believers Anonymous."

Their stories agreed. Didn't mean they were true. Zee sat back. "You don't believe her?"

He shrugged and plucked another chip from the basket. If he destroyed that one, she'd throttle him. Her mouth, her tongue, her stomach clamored for salvation, but she couldn't waste a precious moment on tangy salsa and crisply fried golden corn. She yanked her eyes from the basket, refocused on Kevin's face. "What makes you think Alex is lying."

"Word from the sisters Swithenstein—" He stopped at Zee's quizzical look. "The two ladies who fawn all over Harold PQ, the old dude who falls on the floor all the time."

Harold PQ, who'd stalked her at '60s Fest. She was beginning to appreciate Shaneah's description of BA.

"Beef enchilada. And taco." Carlos set plates in front of them.

Every taste bud in Zee's arsenal fired, obliterating her frustration with Carlos' interruption. She planted her hands on the bench to keep from launching them toward the glorious apparition in front of her.

"More tea, Zee?"

She nodded, afraid to open her mouth lest saliva dribble down her chin.

"Another beer?"

Kevin grimaced. "Gimme a dark ale if you got a decent one."

"We got something." Carlos flicked a glance at Zee. "Enjoy."

"Absolutely I will," Zee said. And without delay. She'd return to the subject of Alex later. The oblong plate barely contained the rolled corn tortilla, glistening in a coat of thick chili sauce and crowned with a substantial portion of shredded cheese.

With a glance at Kevin, Zee cut into the enchilada, dredged a forkful of tender beef through dollops of sour cream and guacamole, and scooped it into her mouth. She suppressed a groan at the sweet-hot explosion of peppers, chilis, and cumin, perfectly balanced with tangy sour cream and cool avocado. When she swallowed, a hint of lime and cilantro lingered on her tongue.

Three hefty bites later, Carlos returned with their drinks. "Good?"

Zee nodded, mumbling agreement through another mouthful.

Carlos' culinary artistry taxed Zee's concentration, but she managed to keep a surreptitious eye on Kevin. Petulant, he resisted at first, but then devoured the taco. His phone buzzed once, but he merely glanced at it and kept eating.

Gloriously sated, Zee pushed aside her empty plate. Kevin sipped his ale. His face had regained color. His hazel eyes had lost their darkness.

"Carlos is a good cook," said Zee. "You should treat him better."

Kevin picked at the label on his new bottle. "Sorry. I'm not usually this rude."

Satisfied Kevin had calmed, Zee returned to the earlier thread of questioning. "You were telling me about the sisters and Alex."

He knit his brows, or rather, where his brows should be. For the first time, Zee noticed his total lack of hair. Not a strand on his forearms. No eyebrows or eyelashes. Alopecia? That might explain a lot about his defensiveness. Ingrained from childhood.

"Alex breaking up with Lenore," she prompted.

His face tightened. "That's her story, but the sisters say they walked in on Alex in the ladies' room one night. She was pitching a fit, throwing stuff, carrying on about 'why that crazy woman just won't listen.'"

Zee considered a moment. That loss of self-control didn't fit her picture of Alex, but many people who try to keep a tight rein on their emotions explode when their willpower fails. "What would Alex gain by killing Bette?"

"Payback. Maybe she thought Lenore would be blamed. And she would have, if that other woman hadn't confessed."

Rejected love. And a woman used to getting what she wanted. The pieces fit, but created a more perplexing issue. "How could Alex orchestrate that? She wasn't there that day."

"Wrong," Kevin snarled. "The bitch sure was."

Zee recoiled. The fury in his words could have scorched the paper Mexican flags draped overhead.

She trod carefully. "How do you know?"

"I saw her." He hurled the indictment like a spear.

Zee had an odd sense that Kevin had seized the interview for his own purpose. Very well, she'd follow his lead. "How did that happen?"

"I was outside, walking toward the building, and she came flying out the door. She took off in the other direction."

What was he doing there? "How'd she seem?"

"Mad as a swatted hornet."

Zee slapped at a hornet once. Stupid move. "What did you do?"

"Nothing. I went home."

Fat chance. Zee raised her brows. "Why were you there?"

He shrugged. "It was dumb. I was going to try to convince her at least to say that the group in her book wasn't BA, hell, maybe even to get her to say something good about us."

Zee let her voice drip skepticism. "So, you witness Alex in a violently agitated state, rushing away. You know about her past with Bette. And you don't wonder what happened? You don't go up to see her?"

Kevin's jaw bunched. "I thought about it, but . . ."

Impatience boiled in Zee's chest. In the time they'd been in the restaurant, Kevin had whipsawed: angry, vulnerable, deceitful, sincere. A chameleon, he adapted whatever camouflage would serve his preservation. She'd had enough. "But what?"

"I didn't want to get involved. I went home." He wadded his napkin into a damp ball.

Sure he did. The tension in his body screamed denial. An idea struck her. "You saw someone else." She said it as a hard fact.

His eyes darted, left, right, up, down, anywhere but her.

"Lenore," she said. Another fact.

The color drained from his face.

"When?" Zee pressed.

He mashed his arms across his chest. "You said you didn't believe Lenore did it."

"True, but you need to tell me everything. Or blame yourself when an innocent person goes to prison."

His mouth twisted. "It's not my—"

"It is." She slapped her palm against the glass tabletop. "You saw Lenore. After Alex?"

He threw out his hands. "Ever consider a career as a black ops interrogator?"

She hid a smile at the compliment, a last-ditch attempt at misdirection. "Flattery won't work."

"'Course not. Different badge, same sneer."

Zee's antennae twitched, but he continued before she could draw breath.

"Guessing I saw Alex a few minutes later. And before you ask, she was all upset too. Honestly, I figured they had another lovers' quarrel."

"Lenore and Alex?"

"Them. Or Lenore and Bette. Or Alex and Bette. Or all three of them."

Zee gulped. Forget snakes, BA was a for-cryin'-out-loud soap opera.

Kevin deflated against the lacquered bench, letting his bald head thunk against the glossy green row of cacti. "I decided it wasn't a good idea to try to talk to Miss de la Cornne right then. I left."

No wonder he worried that Lenore had killed Bette. He'd made a lot of assumptions, but they were reasonable. "What time did you see Alex?"

"Not sure." He gnawed his lip. "Around one, I guess."

One? Lenore had been there about two. "You sure?"

"Yeah." He huffed. "I just reset the clock in my car, and it's a pain."

Stifling her own frustration, Zee switched gears. She leaned across the tableau of happy Mexican dancers. "Did you see anyone else?"

"No." He rubbed the back of his neck and darted his eyes toward his phone. She could taste his desperation for it to rescue him. "What time is it? I need to get back."

Her brain felt as full as her belly. She had a lot to sort through, enough for the present. "Okay." She fixed him with a stern stare. "We're done. For now."

CHAPTER 30

After Zee dropped off a disgruntled Kevin at First Community Bank, she turned the Mini toward home. The tension from her interrogation ebbed, leaving in its wake an ache behind her eyes. Her temples throbbed under the weight of information overload, multiple griefs, and sleep deprivation.

And on top of that, she'd forgotten to get her coconut cream rolls.

Heavy traffic forced her stop at the Ovid Circulus, waiting as one car after another grabbed a place in the swirling nexus. Arriving, departing; arriving, departing. A continuous stream passing through.

Zee's headache grew. Ovid's Circus was like Bette's apartment last Sunday afternoon. Marjorie, Lenore, Kevin, Alex. If she knew the order, she might be able to figure out who really killed Bette.

She saw an opening and mashed the gas. If Marjorie's account was true, she didn't kill Bette. Zee couldn't quite slot Kevin into that role either, despite his volatile behavior. And her gut told her Lenore wasn't the killer.

That left Alex.

Gliding smoothly into her exit, Zee recalled the way Alex had toyed with her in the sleek Corvette. Manipulated her. Steered her toward Kevin.

But Alex's scheme was impossibly convoluted. Kill Bette, pin it on Lenore, then hope that Lenore turned to her for support? Zee couldn't see it.

As they often did when she searched for clarity, her eyes sought the *Tribune*'s angelic sentries. She twisted her lips. The stone guardians would always belong to her hometown paper. The *Messenger* had not earned the right to claim them, simply by moving in.

Some things weren't for sale.

A shiver crawled beneath the collar of her pin-striped jacket. More of Shelby's Morse code. Bette had written the book. Had she simply appropriated Marjorie's story and put her stamp on it?

The angels offered no answer.

Suddenly, Zee wanted a pastry. She deserved a treat, diet be damned. She pulled a U-turn at a stoplight and headed for Julio's.

The lot was crowded, lunch business at Cactus Cantina in full swing. Zee parked *Po* in what had to be the farthest spot from the door, next to an old green pickup. Hoping Julio wasn't sold out, she hurried as best she could across the lot.

As she neared the entrance to Cactus Cantina, the door swung open. A woman emerged. Unable to sidestep in time, Zee collided with her. She caught a glimpse of figure-hugging red tights and tank top. A tumble of strawberry-blonde hair.

"Shaneah!" Zee faltered on her feet.

Shaneah grabbed her shoulder, steadying her.

"What are you doing here?" Zee grimaced. The question sounded like an accusation. There were any number of good reasons for Shaneah to be there. Yet Zee's whole body vibrated with suspicion.

Cautious eyes assessed Zee. "Ms. Morani, are you all right?"

Feigning shakiness, Zee stepped clear of the door. As she hoped, Shaneah remained with her. "I—yes. Sorry, I couldn't stop in time." Zee gestured toward her wrapped knee, invisible beneath her pant leg. "Knee injury."

"That's all right." Shaneah's voice was cool. "If you are okay, I need to be going." She gestured with a carryout bag. "I must get this home."

"Of course. It's such a coincidence that I should run into you." Unless she was following Zee. Or Kevin. Zee needed to keep her talking until she got her wits about her. "How are you? How's Gregory?"

Shaneah appeared to deliberately tamp impatience, as if she didn't want to be rude. Or she had something to hide under a veil of normalcy. "I'm as well as I can be. All is perfection. And Gregory . . . is also perfection." She turned away. "This is for him. It's his favorite."

Perfectly plausible, but it clunked like a dull cowbell. The Earthkins lived all the way across town. Surely, there were good Mexican restaurants closer.

Shaneah had begun to walk away. Zee hurried to catch up. "I want to say I'm sorry if I upset him."

Shaneah whirled. Zee nearly crashed into her again. "Are you following me?"

"No. I—" Zee decided the best strategy was abject contrition. "I'm sorry. I guess I still feel bad about causing him and you so much distress."

A softness spread through Shaneah's body. Her voice lost its gruffness. "You didn't know about his condition. His cancer has gotten much worse. Not long ago, he was going places on his own, but now . . ." She bit her quivering lip. "Marjorie's arrest has devastated him. Some days, it seems half of him is already in the next world. Still, sometimes for an hour or two, it's as if he isn't even ill." She clutched the bag to her chest like a barrier. "And I run out for a cheese and bean tortilla."

Zee schooled her face to neutrality. "I'm glad he's having a good day." She couldn't square gaunt Gregory with one of Carlos' huge portions. Like she couldn't square Shaneah's description of his radical swings in health.

But this line of inquiry was getting her nowhere. Now that Shaneah had relaxed, maybe Zee could find out what she'd failed to learn in her earlier visit.

"I really need to get this home." Shaneah turned away again.

"I'll walk with you." Zee matched her stride, ignoring twinges from her knee and an ominous popping in her hip. "If I could ask you a quick question—"

"Now?" Shaneah's voice had taken on a shrill undertone.

Zee pushed on. "I never got an answer about the text. In fact, I never got to tell you what it said."

They reached the old green pickup. Shaneah rested a manicured hand on the door handle. "I don't know anything about a text." She pulled the door open.

Without thinking, Zee launched another question. "What do you know about Kevin, from the BA group?"

Shaneah's mouth twisted. "He's a pathological liar."

"That's a strong accusation." Though believable, from Zee's perspective.

Shaneah set the bag on the seat and straightened. "You've been talking to him? Did he tell you that sob story about wanting to be a priest and then leaving the seminary because of the hypocrisy?"

Zee gave herself a mental fist-bump. She knew he'd lied. "That's not true?"

"He just worked in the office. He got busted for running a con." She laughed sourly. "Milking donations from unsuspecting pious fools. He's doing it again at BA."

Anger burned in Zee's throat. Kevin was worse than she thought, that lying, sneaking—

Mid-condemnation, she caught herself. Shaneah's accusation might not be true. Zee's gaze strayed to the bag on the seat. Shaneah's hurry to get home had vanished. Now she was volunteering a great deal of information. Zee cocked her head. "How do you know all this?"

Before Zee's eyes, Shaneah shapeshifted. Her body became sinuous, her eyes blade sharp, her mouth the hungry rictus of a predator. Like Candy stalking the cardinal outside the balcony door, but infinitely more sinister. A hunting panther. "You think I wouldn't find out as much as I could about the woman who stole my daughter? And her adoring disciples?" She leveled a hard look at Zee. "She might be Gregory's sister, but her soul is alien from his."

The denunciation jolted something loose in Zee's memory, the thing she'd missed. If only she could grab it. "I understand why you hate Lenore," she said, as Shaneah slid into the driver's seat. "But I thought she was against violence."

Shaneah barked a sharp laugh. The truck's engine coughed to life. "Look her up in the county arrest records. Go back about five years. Lenore might be against violence, but she's certainly capable of it."

Zee backed against *Po*.

"I warned you," Shaneah said. "Take care, Ms. Morani."

The truck trundled out of the lot. Zee ran fingers through her hair, trying to fit these new pieces of information into what she already knew. But they clanked like the truck's misaligned gears. And she didn't know if she could ever make them mesh.

CHAPTER 31

ZEE TRUDGED UP THE STAIRS TO her apartment. Everything she'd learned from Kevin and Shaneah clumped in her brain, like a slab of the sticky clay that lined the Great Miami River. She didn't know how she would ever pull it apart or even begin to understand how the pieces actually fit together. And yet, she had to do it, for her own peace of mind, for the new career she hoped to launch, and for Bette, to whom she'd vowed justice.

As she opened her door, a temple bell tolled from her purse. She scrambled inside, dumped the bag of coconut rolls on the counter, and snagged her cell before it went to voicemail. "Hey, Font—"

"Zee-zee, do you have a few minutes sometime today?" Fontina's words tumbled through the phone. "I need a listening ear."

Zee's chest constricted at the distress in her friend's voice. "Of course. When do you want to meet?"

"Farm Fresh around four?"

"I'll be there."

Zee fought a wave of uneasiness as she disconnected. Fontina was her rock, a steady presence amid the turmoil of Zee's life. She flinched at her selfishness. Some friend she was, that her concern flew so quickly to the effect on her own life.

Don't hate yourself for being human, Shelby said.

Zee drew in a deep breath. Exhaled. The sharp edges of guilt eased. She would be there when Fontina asked, like a good friend.

From her perch atop the living room easy chair, Candy meowed. Zee crinkled her lips. "You like me now, but tomorrow, it's back to dry food."

Yellow eyes narrowed.

"It's my fault, Candy-pants." Zee ran her hand along the cat's plump furry side. "I let you get into bad habits. I let both of us." Over this past weekend, mind consumed by her dad's alarming turn and heart gnawed by Rico's absence, Zee had no energy to continue to fight feline food wars. Candy got wet food, doctored with supplement #3, but long-term, that wasn't healthy.

Zee glanced at the pastry bag on the counter. She would exercise discipline there, as a good example, to strengthen her moral high ground. Instead of self-indulgence, she would focus on dissecting her new information about the murder.

Another meow from Candy.

"Argh, you're right." She stroked the orange-and-cream head. "Today's column first."

She steeped ginger tea while changing from her pin-striped suit into jeans and a tee shirt. As she dressed, eagerness grew to attack her chosen topic: ludicrous product warning labels.

Don't let your child play with this chain saw. This food you just microwaved for five minutes will be hot. Don't take this drug if you're allergic to it.

Strange that corporations went to such great lengths to warn consumers of the obvious. It was organizations like BA—much more stealthily dangerous—that should carry warnings.

Shaking her head to toss aside the distraction, she put fingers to the keyboard. The words flowed in a torrent, line after incisive line, flushing her with pleasure. Her dad thought satire unworthy of her talents. She disagreed. People needed to see an absurdity they'd been caught up in, so they could free themselves from it.

Maybe Fontina was right about the usefulness of *Z Beats*.

Her phone emitted a rooster crow. Three-thirty.

The words for her column still leapt onto the screen. Five more minutes. This piece was practically writing itself. *Handle with care, this knife is sharp.* Isn't that why we buy it?

Zee pulled up short, staying her flying fingers. Perhaps the warning intended to remind users there was danger beneath the colorful cardboard sheath. Unwary consumers, eager to examine their new acquisition, might not exercise appropriate caution.

She should add that acknowledgment.

Don't hurt yourself for being human.

Her thoughts flew to Rico. To the tug-of-war between her yearning for him and her fear of what that might mean. Relationships were like sheathed knives. Wisdom said proceed with caution, but the blade remained useless if it stayed hidden. At some point, people needed to confront what could hurt them.

Her phone crowed again.

She swallowed hard. Maybe Fontina wrestled with that dichotomy, too.

Zee snatched another few minutes to credit the opposing view, liking the balance it gave to the column. But the easy precision of her earlier word choices eluded her.

Another rooster crow sounded. If she didn't leave now, she'd be late. *Later*, she amended.

She saved the document with the final paragraph unfinished. Sketching a wave to Candy, she shrugged into a hoodie, grabbed her purse, and headed for the door.

Gray light greeted her. Capricious Midwestern weather; sunny all morning, now overcast in the late afternoon and starting to drizzle. Overriding her mind's objections, she declined to run back upstairs to get her raincoat.

A decision she regretted halfway to Farm Fresh.

The skies opened, releasing a pummeling downpour. Lightning speared her eyeballs, sparking a headache. Thunder reverberated, exacerbating it. Nearing Farm Fresh, she searched in vain for a parking space. Where was Asphalta now?

Hiding in the wind-whipped deluge, apparently.

Zee snugged *Po* into a barely legal space a block away. Rain washed in waves down her windshield.

Damn. Nothing to do but make a run for it. She grabbed an umbrella from the back seat. Under its ineffectual shelter, she speed-walked as best she could toward the restaurant.

Cold puddles splashed her ankles, soaking through her sneakers. Within moments, the rain drenched her jeans from the knees down. At the front door, she wrestled the wind to close the umbrella, while a waterlogged buffeting saturated her remaining semi-dry parts. Dripping everywhere, she pushed open the restaurant door.

Bright light revealed tables crowded with patrons. Great, an audience for her drowned Lady of the Lake impression. She sloshed her way to Fontina and plopped into a squeaky metal chair.

"What on earth?" Fontina darted from her seat, pulling a sunny yellow shawl from around her shoulders. "Where's your raincoat?"

"Keeping my closet dry." Zee peeled off her sopping hoodie. She willed her teeth not to chatter as Fontina wrapped her in woven cotton. "I'll be okay. I just need a hot drink."

Fontina clucked. "You could have texted me. I would have waited until the rain let up."

"I was already late, got caught up in writing." Zee glanced toward the large windows. As if to taunt her, only a fine mist fell now. A chilly rivulet snaked from her earlobe along her neck. Shivering, she grabbed a corner of the shawl to trap the trickle.

"Miss Zee." The server's voice startled her. "Can I bring you a towel or something?" Seth's young face creased with concern.

Zee attempted a reassuring smile. "I'm fine." She peeled the damp curls from her cheeks and tried to ignore the heavy, cold denim stuck to her ankles. "Hot chocolate, please. Dark."

"Please bring her order as quickly as you can, Seth," Fontina said.

"Sure thing. Something for you?"

Fontina's slender fingers twisted around themselves. "Hot chai, please."

As he departed, Zee wiped a dripping waterslide from her cheek. Anxiety stirred in her midsection. "I can see something's really bothering you. What did you want to talk about?"

Fontina looked away.

Fear jabbed Zee's spine. "Are you okay?"

Fontina untangled her fingers. "It's my teacher." One hand rose to toy with her filigree earring.

Zee mopped her brow. "What's going on?"

Golden light from the overhead fixture caught in Fontina's brown eyes. "My heart leaps at the thought of being so close to him again."

A shiver crawled down Zee's neck that had nothing to do with the droplets seeping down her collar. Before she could stop herself, she blurted, "Were you two lovers?" If so, his presence could certainly cause a problem for Emilio.

Fontina laughed, shaking her head. "Oh no, nothing like that. Patrik has impeccable integrity. He's just the kindest, gentlest man I've ever known." She leaned toward Zee, the light in her eyes suffusing her face. "And those words are completely inadequate to describe how deeply he opened my heart and soul."

Uneasiness quivered along Zee's shoulder blades, despite Fontina's radiance. Or maybe because of it. Images of BA imposed themselves, the adulation expressed on the website, Kevin's cult-like adoration. She pushed them aside. This was Fontina, her wise, grounded friend. "What's the problem?"

Dropping her gaze, Fontina stroked Uncle Ramiz's coin at her throat. "I'm torn. I deeply desire to be close to Patrik once more, but I don't know if it's the right move for Integrated Life."

"Here you go, one dark hot chocolate." Seth set a steaming mug in front of Zee. He laid a pile of thick napkins next to it. "In case you change your mind."

Zee smiled, plucked one from the stack, and blotted her neck. "You're smarter than I am, Seth."

Color spread in his cheeks. Nodding, he hurried off.

Steam from the chocolate rose toward Zee's face. Inhaling its delectable warmth, she cradled the cup with both hands and touched the rim to her lips. Bittersweet fire filled her mouth, slid down her throat, and melted the freezing pool of ice in her gut. She clutched the mug, trying to stifle a reactionary shudder that threatened to spill the saving brew. "Have you talked more with Emilio?"

Fontina worried the earring. "We're not on the same page yet. He wants to support me, but he's also pragmatic about the business. He's worked hard to make it a success."

"You both have." Comfort fought with disquiet in Zee's chest. "Is there something I can do? Help you make a list of pros and cons?"

"I've tried, but maybe you can help me see what I'm missing."

That would be a switch. "You first. Tell me what you've already thought of."

Fontina held out her left hand, palm up. "Using the space for massage therapy and acupuncture treatments provides needed revenue. By comparison, I don't know how much income the business would receive from a meditation center."

"Okay, that's an important consideration."

Fontina flipped up her right palm. "However, Patrik has enriched my life beyond measure. I feel like I should support him."

Zee cupped her damp chin on her knuckles. "I see the dilemma. But aren't these two different things, not really comparable?"

A sigh escaped Fontina's lips. "You're right. One is a debt of contractual honor to Emilio and the business we've built. The other is a soul debt that I have a chance to repay."

Zee's mind flashed on her dad, nearing the end of his life. If there were such things as soul debts, she hoped he'd paid his. Like barbs in her heart, the years of confusion, hurt, and isolation after he distanced himself still shackled her.

She scrubbed a napkin across her forehead to clear her thoughts and refocus on Fontina's troubled face. "Not sure that's a fair comparison. Don't you have a soul debt to Emilio, too?"

"You're right." Tears shone in Fontina's eyes. "And maybe to all the people who benefit from Integrated Life. What happens to them if we can't financially sustain the business? And yet . . ." She tugged at her earring.

Zee's heart pinched. "Is there a way to offer both the meditation center and the other services you planned?"

Fontina blinked droplets from her lashes. "It's not a big space . . . and I wanted to offer it all to Patrik . . ."

All or nothing. Was that the only choice? "Maybe you can find a compromise." Zee tried a small smile. "Isn't there a goddess you can consult?"

"Well, let's see." The lines in Fontina's face eased. She ticked on her fingers. "There's Caerus, Greek goddess of opportunity. Maia, Roman goddess of growth. Lakshmi, Hindu goddess of wealth and good fortune."

"If it were me, I'd ask them all."

Fontina shook her head, struggle once again deepening the furrows in her brow. "Too many cooks." She pinched her earlobe with such force that it reddened. "This is terrible. I can't even figure out who to ask for help."

Helplessness colored Zee's voice. "I wish I had an idea."

"Hot chai." Seth set Fontina's cup before her. "Enjoy."

Fontina wrapped her hands around the drink. She took a long swallow, then met Zee's eyes. "Talking about this did help."

As they quietly sipped, Zee winged a silent plea to any deity who might be listening. She felt the energy shift.

"Enough about my dilemma." Fontina cradled her cup. "How is your dad?"

Trusting in divine providence, Zee set aside her friend's troubles. "He's holding his own." Her chest tightened. "This is so hard. He's close to death. I feel like I should drop everything and stay with him." She scraped fingers through her wet curls. "But I don't want to. I mean, I do, but I'm involved—" She gulped hot chocolate, hoping it would free the words. "I can't just stop . . . and we have all this history. But that doesn't feel so important now."

Fontina laid a warm hand on Zee's arm. "The veil is thinning, and not just between life and death, but also between the two of you."

"You mean he knows . . . how I feel?" A stricture around Zee's heart eased. "Oh, I hope that's true." She inhaled a shaky breath. "Not that I doubt you."

Fontina gaze softened. "In this world of duality, hope and fear always exist together. But the Buddha says hope is stronger."

The weight in Zee's chest lifted. "You always know just what to say to help me feel better."

"I might say the same thing about you." Over the rim of her cup, Fontina's eyes regained a spark. "You ready to tell me how your non-investigation is going?"

Relief washed through Zee, tinged with guilt at her eagerness to change the topic. "I'm more confused than ever," she admitted. "Everybody and his brother was at Bette's apartment that day. I got another anonymous, quasi-religious text. Kevin's a liar and a con—."

Fontina held up a hand. "Take a breath, Zee-zee. Then start at the beginning."

Zee obliged, pouring out the story over a second cup of hot chocolate. "And now," she concluded, "I find out that Lenore is not as anti-violence as I thought."

Fontina steepled her fingers. "What a tangled mess."

"Almost as convoluted as Bette's book."

"I finished reading it last night," Fontina said. "Such a sad story. I'm not sure which was the bigger problem for Lilliana, religion or sexuality."

Zee crossed her legs and flinched at the rush of frigid air across her sodden sneakers. "It's a toss-up, I'd say. Her problems start when her parents abandon her to join a cult, but her lover's rejection is what tips Lilliana into drug abuse, and ultimately destroys her life."

"Another abandonment," said Fontina.

"Another betrayal." The word cut Zee's tongue as it escaped. What wreckage it left in its wake. Victims struggling to find their way through the rubble, stumbling, blinded. Sympathy welled in Zee. "Everyone in this case is lost somehow. And someone thought that murdering Bette would help them find their way."

A shiver prickled across her scalp. Morse code? Reporter's antennae? There was truth there, if she could see it.

She met Fontina's eyes. "I keep coming back to those texts. *Pernicious mirror. Look.*" Her voice strengthened. "When I figure out what the texts mean, I'll know who killed Bette."

CHAPTER 32

Z EE LINGERED IN THE SHOWER, LETTING the steaming spray cleanse her skin, clammy from her rain-soaked clothing. She wished it could sluice her mind clear.

Talking with Fontina had stirred up questions and frustration, like mud in water. Her weary body demanded she shut down her roiling thoughts for a while. Rest, then she might be able to think straight.

The water cooled. She turned it off and toweled dry, despondency spiraling.

The texts were the key to solving the murder, but she was no closer to divining their meaning than she had been two days ago when the second one landed on her phone. In fact, she was no closer than she'd been a week ago when she received the first one. If she didn't crack the code soon, justice would be lost for Bette. So would the chance for a story she hoped would launch her new career.

Her failures dragged at her limbs like iron chains. Wrapped in her robe, she fell onto her bed, eyes closing before her head hit the pillow.

In the kitchen, her phone rang. She bolted upright. Not a tone she recognized. If this was another text . . .

Dread burgeoning, she hurried toward the insistent summons. It could also be Leehammer, calling about her dad. That would be bad news. They never called with anything good. She snatched the phone from the counter in time to see the message flash: Identified Spam.

She snarled at the screen. Heartless scammers, calling at six in the evening when people are worn out from the day.

Trembling, she sank onto a barstool. Her pulse pounded in her ears. She really ought to get dressed and go see her dad. There was still time before visiting hours ended.

Exhaustion broke over her like a tidal wave, threatening tears. Nausea turned in her stomach. She tried to rouse the energy to move, but her body revolted.

She'd pushed herself too hard, too long. It wasn't even safe for her to drive. Fragile as an eggshell, her control would crack at the slightest provocation.

At least she could call. She punched in the number.

"There's been no change," a kind voice on the other end said. "He's resting comfortably."

The sympathetic reassurance sapped the last of Zee's resistance. The couch was closer than her bed. Succumbing to its call, she dragged herself across the room, and the moment she stretched out, unconsciousness claimed her.

She woke to a tickle on her cheek. A sweet fragrance drifted past her nose.

"Hey, sleepy."

The deep voice pulled her eyes open. Her unfocused gaze drifted across thick black hair, cobalt eyes, a dark-shadowed cheek. "Rico!" Had he not been holding a bouquet of roses, she would have thrown her arms around him.

She propped herself on an elbow and inhaled the rich scent, feathered with his citrus and leather. Skirting the deep red petals, her fingertips brushed the stubble along his jaw. "This is a nice surprise. What's the occasion?"

"Six months, six roses."

Warmth blossomed in her chest. He'd been keeping count. "They're beautiful."

He laid the bouquet on the coffee table, then wrapped her in a fierce kiss. Electricity sparked, yet even as her tongue explored his, the murder intruded. Annoyed, she broke contact before she intended.

He raised his brows.

"I have new information." The words spilled before she could stop them. "I'm sure it's important."

He rested a finger on her lips. "Just for tonight, let's leave it."

Zee kissed his fingertip. "I don't know if I can. I'm angry all over again."

"All the more reason." He captured her face in his hands.

The tension that had crept onto her brow melted.

"You know I'm right." He flashed a grin. "Dinner at that new steakhouse?"

As if that smile and the tug on her heart weren't disarming enough, Zee's taste buds and stomach demanded surrender. "Give me five minutes."

"Race you." He gestured toward a garment bag draped over the chair. "I need to change, too."

Her pulse skipped. She loved his usual fitted leather jacket, taut t-shirt, and tight jeans, but her mouth dried at the mental image of him in a well-cut suit. To cover the fire in her cheeks, she picked up the flowers and inhaled the heady scent. "Would you put these in water?"

"Playing for extra time, I see." His blue eyes sparkled.

"It's only fair. You already have your clothes. I have to choose yet." She swung her legs over the side of the couch. Her ankle met a furry body, which erupted in a yowl. She glanced at Rico. "Would you feed Candy-pants, too?"

"Of course." He helped Zee to her feet. "I'll still be ready before you."

Especially if she didn't stop picturing him in formal wear. Maybe she could even the playing field. She leaned close and nipped his ear. "Anticipation is half the fun."

His low growl weakened her spine. He pulled her to him, laid a gunpowder trail of kisses along her neck. "Yes," he breathed in her ear. "It is."

The room wobbled when he released her. "Candy, uh, give her some Tuna Delight. Sprinkle a bit of that brownish powder on it. Put in some of the greenish stuff, too."

"Your wish is my command." He sketched a bow.

She had to get out of this room. On unsteady feet, she made her way to the bathroom. She splashed her face, letting the cold water shock her into sensibility. Why did she ever doubt her importance to him?

An ice shard pricked in her chest. He'd just returned from corporate headquarters in St. Louis. Maybe he brought the roses to soften bad news. What would she do if—

Just stop.

She narrowed her eyes at her reflection in the mirror. He bought her flowers. He was taking her to dinner. He kissed . . . like that. For tonight, it was enough.

As she applied mascara, she decided not to race to get ready. Better to make him wait, and then stun him with a look that made him glad for his patience. Her favorite clingy black dress, silk stockings, and those scarlet heels he liked.

D'ÉLITE VIANDE WAS BUSTLING YET SUBDUED. Jacketed waiters held trays aloft as they glided among tables. Glassware and gowns sparkled in the diffracted light from beaded chandeliers. Perched on a padded barstool, black silk shawl draped around her bare shoulders, Zee sipped cabernet and drank in Rico's crisp gray shirt, silver tie, and smartly tailored black jacket.

"This is lovely," she said.

His smile reached all the way to his deep blue eyes. "I hear the food's good too."

A nearby phone chimed, the same tone as Zee's for an incoming text. She grimaced at the unwelcome reminder.

The sommelier appeared promptly with a bottle of St. Emilion pinot noir. Zee's heart fluttered at Rico's choice, a beautiful Bordeaux from a renowned French winery. He intended this six-month anniversary to be a celebration indeed. The fidgeting in her rib cage amplified.

She tamped it by attending to her wine, fragrantly aromatic, smooth on her tongue, kissing her palate with a hint of ripe berries. "This is wonderful."

Rico touched his glass to hers. "For six wonderful months."

Her breath hitched. He was building to something. "How was your trip to Chicago?" If it was bad news from corporate, she wanted it out of the way early.

"Frustrating." He swirled his wine. "Chasing a lead on a fraud story."

Not a summons to headquarters, after all. The frigid coil below Zee's breastbone unwound. "Sorry."

He shrugged. "It might still pan out, but let's not talk about work."

He turned the conversation to other things, a concert he thought they'd enjoy, her rehab progress, food adventures with Candy. Zee relaxed. It was just a pleasant evening, nothing more. No earth-shaking revelation lurked behind the softness lingering in his deep blue eyes, the smile continually playing across his lips, the flush of color tinting his dark cheeks.

A young server brought their salads. After he departed, Rico raised his glass, pinning her with his gaze. "You look beautiful."

Like a flash of lightning, she saw it all. The wine, the roses, the nice restaurant, his insistence on focusing on this evening together. How thickheaded could she be?

He meant to propose.

Her blood roared in her ears. She wasn't ready. She replayed his teasing a week ago. *I want to be your partner.* A trial run? She hadn't thought so. As through a veil, she saw his lips parting, clocked the inhalation as he leaned toward her.

She had to stop him. "Shaneah wants me to believe that everyone else is lying except her." She gulped wine.

With exaggerated deliberateness, Rico laid down his salad fork. "You are obsessed."

She cursed herself as the sparkle of the evening dimmed. Anxiety drained into a sour pool in her stomach. Had she deflected his purpose? Or—her gut twisted—misread him entirely? "I can't help it."

Sighing, he sat back in his chair. "Five minutes. Tell me about your liars."

Relief flooded, obscuring the jagged rocks of her self-doubt. The words tumbled out: Kevin's story, Shaneah's revelation, Fontina's insight.

While she poured out her thoughts, Rico rested his chin on his knuckles and studied her. Certain the gears were turning in his head, she hurried her recitation. Her final words faded into the murmur of conversation around them, the laughter, the clink of cutlery.

"Feel better?" He picked up his fork and speared a cucumber slice.

"Yes, I do." Now she was a liar, too. "What did you put together that I haven't seen?"

He swallowed, reached for his water glass, and sipped. "This isn't how I wanted to spend the evening."

Zee's heart fell. "I'm sorry. Forget it." She stabbed at a cherry tomato. It leapt from her plate and skittered across the table.

Rico trapped it before it landed in his lap. "I'm going to answer you, and then we're going to drop this. First, a few years ago, Lenore was charged with domestic violence."

Zee choked on her wine. "That's what Shaneah referred to."

He nodded. "And Kevin is managing the finances for BA and some of the group members. He's why I went to Chicago."

"He's running a con," blurted Zee. "That's why he set the fire, not to steer me away from Lenore, but to scare me away from *him*."

Rico's fork slipped. "What fire?"

Zee froze.

"What fire!"

A waiter nearby turned his head. Rico motioned him away.

Zee struggled to keep her voice calm. "Kevin set a little fire in my yard. When I confronted him, he said he wanted to protect Lenore."

Thunder darkened Rico's face. "When were you going to tell me? Damn it, Zee, we're partners." He reached for her. "More than that."

"I just learned who did it." She dodged his hand, pushing aside the inconvenient fact that the fire happened last week. But the lie singed her tongue.

She swallowed more wine, bristling at his stony stare. His fault she didn't tell him earlier tonight. He wouldn't let her talk.

A lousy excuse. Acid burned in her stomach, scorching any further ability to bear her shifting internal ground. "I'd share everything, but I'm just so confused."

"Why?" His voice held hurt.

"You tease me about wanting to be my partner, then you shut me out. You go away for days, you come back and you're preoccupied. Then you show up with roses and you kiss me like . . ." Her throat closed. Tears prickled behind her eyes. The flaw was hers, not his. She moved to stand, but he captured her hand with his, stopping her.

"Zee, I don't mean—that is, I don't want—" His grip tightened. His chest rose and fell, rose again.

Walls were falling.

His voice when he spoke was soft, strung through with risk and helpless surrender. "Zee, I love you. I just—half the time, I don't know what to do."

He loved her. The room wavered around her, the glittering chandeliers blurring as if the space had been swamped by water. A tide of emotion trapped her tongue. She wrestled a breath into her lungs, drove it deep down into the place where fear lodged like an implacable stone. Through teary eyes, she met his cobalt gaze. "Rico," her voice cracked, "I love you t—"

In a blur, he slipped around the table, pulled her to her feet, and smothered her lips with his. She melted into his embrace, tightened her arms around him. The rock in the pit of her stomach fractured.

He kissed a trail of electric pulses down her neck. She stroked his muscled back, pulling him against her, wishing in that moment nothing more than to rip off his tailored jacket, tear loose the buttons on his shirt, and rake her nails across his skin until the fire in their bodies exploded.

But not now. In her peripheral vision, their waiter approached, bearing two wafting platters.

Sizzling every bit as much as those steaks, Zee pried herself from Rico. The waiter served them, studiously avoiding eye contact. Zee stifled a chuckle.

After he left, she studied the man across the table from her. In the muted light, his silver tie glowed, a perfect knot crowned by the dark line of his jaw and the soft, inviting crease of his lips.

Had he meant to propose?

If he asked now, there'd be no holding back.

She sipped the seductive liquid in her glass. His eyes told her *not tonight*. Maybe in the future. But in this perfect moment, nothing more was needed. Their silent communion filled her, crowding out everything but the reality of their presence with, for, and in each other.

The immensity of what she'd done dizzied her. She'd actually said it. She loved him. Her tongue feasted on those words. And he loved her. Whatever lay ahead, this moment anchored them. A unity. A singularity. One, facing the world.

"Dessert?" he asked.

Somehow her plate was empty. She shook her head, then cocked it, teasing. "Not here."

A gleam shone in the depths of his eyes.

She stroked his fingers. "I have a treat at home."

His smoldering gaze stoked an answering flame deep inside her. "Mmm." He deepened his voice to a growl. "Can't wait."

Later, as she licked vanilla coconut custard from his lips, his neck, and his chest, she had to acknowledge there was something to be said for delayed gratification: Julio's pastry had never tasted better.

CHAPTER 33

ON TUESDAY MORNING, ST. STEPHEN'S OVERFLOWED with well-wishers. Zee gritted her teeth. She disliked being around public displays of grief, but she needed to say goodbye to Bette.

Dodging the milling media outside, she skirted the back wall of the church and wedged herself into the end of a polished pew. Her feet refused to join the slow stream of people moving up the central aisle to pass before the closed casket. She couldn't bear to look at it when she'd made so little progress in her investigation.

Her thoughts wandered to her dad's coffin. How hard it would be to gaze upon that. She pushed away the idea. Focusing on the pastoral music floating from the overhead choir loft, she breathed to loosen the knot in her chest.

From this vantage, the crowd resembled a restless wave of heads and shoulders. Despite her heartache, Zee scanned, searching for someone who gloated or looked inordinately pleased. Her suspects were probably not in attendance, but criminals were known to enjoy witnessing the aftermath of their grisly deed.

No one jumped out at her. She also didn't see anyone from BA. No Sara Jane, either. That was surprising.

Her gaze fell on a large screen projecting a video collage. Mostly publicity pictures, Bette at book signings, receiving awards, posing with celebrities. Zee cringed at the impersonal nature of it.

Nowhere did she see the Bette she'd met, the funny, encouraging, generous woman.

Her throat tightened. Maybe coming to this memorial was a bad idea. She glanced at the people now clustered along the walls. Escape might prove difficult if she didn't want to cause a disruption. Whispering a prayer for stamina, she thought again of her dad's funeral. There would be no running away from that.

The semi-gothic architecture pressed in on Zee, narrow stained-glass windows, pointed arched ceiling, intricate stone tracery crawling everywhere. All dominated by an elongated cross depicting the eternally suffering, dying-for-our-sins Christ. The carved and painted crucifix hung over the sanctuary like a monstrous Sword of Damocles.

Zee shrank beneath the Savior's tortured all-knowing gaze. The dark pain in Rico's eyes flashed before her. What would it do to an impressionable boy's spirit to endure such scrutiny, week after week, year after year? The words on BA's website came back to her: *it takes force to dislodge something you learn as a child.*

Her temper bristled. The force didn't need to be violent. Love had gradually crumbled her walls. True, she had resisted at the restaurant, a terrified last-ditch attempt to cling to the illusory safety of non-commitment. But it had been too late. Perhaps she had cried enough tears—or banged her head against the bricks long enough—to dissolve the mortar. A pleasant warmth filled her chest. His declaration last night, and hers, nestled in her heart.

The soft background music faded, and the ensuing silence drew her attention to Bette's mahogany casket. Bette's photograph, the same one that graced the back cover of *The Mirror of the Soul,* smiled beatifically from the center of an enormous floral wreath. Zee blinked back tears.

A man in an expensive suit mounted the pulpit and began to speak. He looked polished to perfection, like a producer from Central Casting. His words drifted in and out of Zee's hearing. "I knew her for . . . terrific writer . . . miss her . . . like family . . ."

Grief spiraled in Zee's chest. Soon she would be arranging her dad's final tribute. Nothing so grand as this. At least, she hoped not. His instructions were stuffed away somewhere. She really should find them. Preferably, before she needed them.

Anxiety clenched in her midsection. Where had he put them? She stared at the static in her mind, panic synapses firing. She couldn't lose his last wishes.

Her brain offered suggestions. Closet. Attic. Bookcase. Bookcase—that had to be it. He kept everything important in that barrister bookcase. Maybe they were in that lacquered scarlet box.

Urgency to rush home and check nearly propelled her to her feet. She gripped the pew's armrest, pulling in a deep, calming breath. There was no hurry. Incense trickled into her nose, along with the sweat of several hundred bodies.

A woman was singing now. Some mournful hymn. The notes landed like weights in Zee's ears.

Someone behind her sneezed, spraying the hairs on the back of her neck. She cringed at the thought of infected droplets merging with the moisture already in residence there.

In her cramped space, she twisted to extract a tissue from her purse. Her gaze fell on a statue of the church's namesake, a serene, beardless St. Stephen. Two large stones sat on his shoulders, symbolizing the manner of his martyrdom: stoned for heresy.

Zee shuddered. A blow from a heavy object killed Bette. Someone had judged her guilty of sacrilege. She swallowed bile. So many people had done monstrous things in the thrall of religious fervor.

Acid stinging her throat, Zee scrambled from her seat. The whole memorial suddenly seemed unbearably gruesome. Lowering her eyes to avoid the stares from standing mourners, she hurried from the church.

Bette would understand, as she had understood Zee's desire to be more than a clever columnist. Rather than sitting in a cloying monument to violent death and trying not to vomit, Zee would honor her lost friend by finding her murderer.

Outside, she drew in deep draughts of cool air and prayed fervently that her dad didn't want a memorial in a church.

A desire to see him seized her.

Speed-walking toward the Mini, she tried to calm the twinges of alarm. All those reminders of mortality had simply made her paranoid. Or, a voice countered, this feeling could be a premonition. Her dad's condition could turn quickly.

She'd parked along with several other vehicles half in the grass along the driveway. As she reached *Po*, she felt rather than saw the approach of a tall, elegantly dressed man. She swiveled at the glimpse of magenta silk. "Victor."

"How fortunate our paths should cross at this moment." He lifted the fedora from his thick silver hair in greeting and resettled it.

"Yes." Zee struggled to hide her impatience. Of all the people to run into, it had to be the loquacious arts reporter. "You covering this for the paper?"

He nodded. "Interviewing the producer after. But as you and I have encountered each other, I thought you might like to know that your recent tantalizing inquiry has yielded several tasty tidbits."

Half of Zee's heart tugged her toward Leehammer Pavilion. The other half wanted Victor's information. It might lead her closer to Bette's murderer. Perhaps it would take only a few minutes. "What can you tell me?"

"I perceive your haste to depart. Allow me to summarize. You no doubt know that dreadful movie has been put on hiatus, most likely until after the trial, and there is no certainty that it will ever be removed from that status, although tragedy has a way of sharpening the rapacious public's appetite, so I should not be surprised if we do see the film, execrable as it will be, once a suitable time for a show of grief has passed."

Glad she was getting the abridged version, Zee resisted the impulse to make the hand-circling gesture for 'move it along.'

"What I found most intriguing . . ." Victor inclined his head as though about to share a secret, "was what people were saying about Madame de la Cornne's publicist, the formidable Sara Jane Pantonet."

Why did everyone look like they'd swallowed a lemon when they said the woman's name? "Oh?"

"Let us just say she was persona non grata among the dramatis personae, or at the risk of being pedantic but more accurate, among the *effectrix et rectores*."

Heat from the morning sun seeped through Zee's charcoal blazer. Her knee complained, the effect of standing too long in heels. A colony of ants had mobilized in her chest, urging her to get to her dad. Stifling irritation, she cocked her head in a question.

Victor permitted himself a pleased smile. "Producers and directors."

"Ah." Zee granted him his moment. "What happened?"

"The producer told me he'd demanded Madame de la Cornne terminate Miss Pantonet."

Zee's eyes widened. "On what grounds?"

"I believe he called her, 'a pushy, entitled, arrogant little bitch.'"

Startled at the forceful condemnation, Zee glanced around. They were alone, the media still clustered around the church entrance. She shifted her weight to ease the growing ache in her knee.

"Did Bette actually do it?" That might be why she hadn't seen the publicist today.

"Alas, I do not have the answer to your question." He paused and flipped the magenta strip of silk over his shoulder. "However, what I did discover as I followed the labyrinthine paths in search of understanding, was how the famous author of an anti-religion book and the not-so-famous founder of an anti-religion cult became entangled." Victor arched one sculpted brow. "They met in that quintessential city of sin, Las Vegas."

Despite the fact that she already knew this, a shiver frosted the sweat on Zee's neck. Sinful. Wicked. Some might say, *pernicious*. But if Vegas was the mirror in the text, she couldn't puzzle out what that meant. Maybe there was a clue in the rest of Victor's report. If only he would hurry so she could get to her dad. "Go on, please."

"Your Lenore Meeris fled to Vegas after her parents' death. Having been betrayed by a putatively God-fearing but lecherous husband, she met Madame de la Cornne at a group called Religious Rescue." Victor stroked his clean-shaven chin. "Apparently, the mecca of debauchery is home to quite a few recovering souls of all kinds. Perhaps those who are sick must immerse themselves entirely in their chosen poison before they can gain enough impetus to claw their way back to health."

"So that's how it all started." Zee reached for the Mini's door handle. "Thank you for uncovering this."

Victor held up a manicured hand. "A moment. We have arrived only at the penultimate revelation." He gestured with a sweep. "If you will permit me."

Releasing the door handle, Zee nodded. "Please, but could you make it quick?"

"Of course. To be brief, the excesses of the desert city appealed. Drugs, bars, clubs."

He really *was* giving her the short version now. She should have asked him sooner.

Victor wrinkled his aquiline nose. "It would all be banally familiar, but for the testimony that during many an altered-state hour, Miss Meeris bared her soul to Madame de la Cornne, expounding on her struggles, her abhorrence of religion, and her conviction that only the power of fury could break the chains of oppression."

A shudder crawled across Zee's shoulder blades. "Based on what you've said, the book could just as easily be about Lenore's life as Marjorie's." Which gave Lenore, or someone devoted to her, a powerful motive. "Were Lenore and Bette lovers?"

"Unclear," Victor said. "Also irrelevant, one might argue. That sort of fanaticism could overwhelm the hardiest of souls. For whatever reason, their association fractured." His cultured voice was apologetic. "I fear I have not eased your dilemma."

Despite the heat, she leaned against the Mini. "You've given me a lot to think about. I appreciate your help."

He favored her with a sympathetic smile. "This quagmire has elicited volatile emotions. The arts are a business as well as a passion. The combination can be frightfully dramatic." He tipped his hat, and without a hint that he was aware of the irony, turned and strode away.

Zee slid behind *Po*'s wheel. Firing up the engine, she grappled with the picture of Lenore and Bette living the wild life in Las Vegas. Horror tightened her stomach. Marjorie had absorbed it all, growing up untethered to conventional morality, getting crushed in the process, then rising from the ashes to create a successful life. Only to have it implode.

What had Bette said of her? "'Cornbread not done in the middle.'"

Whose fault was that? Zee wanted to scream.

She slammed the car in gear, wishing for all the world she could send *Po* flying out into the countryside beyond the city. She needed the wind to whip her breathless, to drive the stale air from her lungs and smash the churning miasma in her mind.

A selfish wish. Anxiety about her dad reared, so powerful that her limbs trembled as she turned *Po* toward Leehammer Pavilion.

CHAPTER 34

Zee sped toward Leehammer Pavilion, her uneasiness growing. At a traffic light, she checked her phone. No messages. Yet she was unable to quell her rising concern. A terrifying image rose to taunt her, the staff covering her dad's face with the sheet. She choked back a cry.

Tires squealing, she pulled into the lot, parked *Po* haphazardly beneath a sprawling maple.

"Oh, Miss Morani. I'm so glad you're here," the nurse at the registration desk said. "We were just about to call you."

All the air left the room.

"Your father has experienced a decline."

Not her *father*. Zee bit back the churlish, knee-jerk reaction. He was the only dad she had. And he was still alive. Chewing her lip, she hurried down the corridor. She'd never forgive herself if she was too late.

At the door to his room, she caught her breath. He was so much smaller than the last time she'd seen him. He seemed to be disappearing before her eyes.

His face was gray above the pale blue blanket. She stared at his bloodless lips, his motionless eyelids, his still chest. Her heart cracked.

He inhaled. A sudden gasp.

She held her breath, bent closer. A thread of air trickled from his mouth.

An eternity passed. He inhaled again.

She dragged a chair to the bedside and sank into it. "I'm here, Dad." She brushed a wisp of white hair from his ear. "I'm sorry I'm late."

He pulled in another breath. Agonizingly slow. And then another. Laboring.

She laid her head beside his. Time to let him go. "Dad," she whispered, "you don't need to stay. I'll be all right."

Tears gathering, Zee closed her eyes. Next to her, the fragile rhythm of her dad's life continued to pulse. Ever so slowly, his respirations stabilized, lulling her. Exhausted, she slid into sleep.

Ghosts dance around her in a ring.

Her mother.

Trailing scarves. They fade into bloodstains.

Fontina's brother Paulo. Young, laughing. Then wailing.

Bette, jasmine scented. Turning to corruption.

The dance grows crowded. Kevin joins in. Alex appears, then Lenore, Shaneah, Gregory. They taunt her. Whisper.

She can't understand them.

Abruptly, they scatter. A signpost is there. A circle of flowers. An arrow pointing upward.

Zee's eyes flew open.

Her dad's breathing had deepened. His flesh had lost its gray pallor.

She rubbed goosebumps from her arms, relieved that the upward arrow hadn't meant he'd gone to heaven.

Not that it had to signify anything, but she and Fontina had interpreted so many dreams together that Zee defaulted to looking for meaning. And when a dream hit as hard as this one—almost like a physical blow—it usually wanted her attention.

Of course, her reaction could have stemmed from her fear that she'd lost her dad while she slept. She'd let down her guard, abandoned her post, failed in her promise to be with him.

She gazed at her dad's peaceful face. Or it could be that the dream had a message for her. Without realizing, she began to analyze it.

The arrow gave a sense of movement. It looked like a street sign, the kind that pointed to something ahead. She wished she had understood the whispers. All she had for a clue was a ring of flowers. Like the wreath on Bette's casket.

If she had to go somewhere, please let it not be back to the church.

Staring at her dad in peaceful repose, she remembered Fontina's trick at the Tarot reading. "Okay," she breathed. Closing her eyes, she concentrated on the sensations in her toes. Stiff leather wrapped them, squashing them together, pressing them against the hard soles of her dress shoes. Her poorly healed toe, broken years ago, throbbed hotly. Pulsing.

Go where? She shot the question into the ether.

North.

What? She stifled a snort. The entire city was north of Leehammer Pavilion. Her home, the jail, Kevin's workplace, Bette's apartment—her meandering thoughts snagged. That was it. That's where she was meant to go.

Her mind objected. There was nothing to find at Bette's place.

When your heart barks, listen. Shelby elbowed Zee from the chair.

Zee capitulated. She had no better idea. Bending, she kissed her sleeping dad and grabbed her purse.

CHAPTER 35

The elevator that served Imperial Court Condominiums glided silently toward the second floor. As she had during the entire drive from Leehammer Pavilion, Zee searched for inspiration. The dream urged her to go to Bette's apartment, but when the polished oak doors whispered open, she still had no idea what she was supposed to find.

The sight of the familiar hallway hit Zee like a punch in the gut. Recoiling from Bette's door, she turned toward the only other residence on the floor.

A shiver wracked her body.

Surrounding the peephole hung a Happy Easter wreath of blue robin eggs, baby chicks—and artificial spring flowers.

Zee swallowed hard as information clicked. Bernstow had a witness who claimed to see Marjorie Franklin leave Bette's apartment. This neighbor had to be that person. Silencing the voice that argued otherwise, Zee stood in front of the tiny aperture and rang the bell.

Silence for a few moments. Then a quavering, high-pitched voice, "Just a minute please."

A series of thumps on the other side of the wall grew louder. The door cracked open, caught by the safety chain, and a wrinkled face peered up at her. "Yes?"

"Good morning, ma'am. My name is Suzanne Morani. I wonder if I could talk with you a few moments."

The parchment brow furrowed. "Are you with the police? The officer who took my statement said they probably wouldn't need me, since that other woman confessed."

Zee floundered a moment, then decided her dark, tailored blazer must be why the woman thought she was a police officer. She declined to correct the erroneous assumption, another deception on her conscience. "I just have a couple of questions."

The gap in the doorway narrowed. "My eyesight isn't what it used to be. I told the young policeman." She flattened her lips. "And that nosy reporter."

Zee's remorse dissolved. Scrupulous honesty would have resulted in the door slammed in her face. Besides, she wasn't here to get a story. Not solely. "I'm just tying up loose ends. May I come in, just for a minute or two?"

The door shut with a thunk.

Damn. Now what? Zee stared at the Easter wreath, as if she might discover another idea among the eggs, chicks, and petals.

On the other side of the decoration, a chain rattled loose. The door opened. "All right." The woman waved her inside. "Come on in."

Hiding her relief, Zee entered. Into an explosion of flowers: blue and pink floral upholstered couch, loveseat, and chair; white doilies blooming on polished end tables; cream draperies sprouting tiny blue forget-me-nots; a floral swag across the top of the picture window.

"Flowers are evidence of the presence of angels," the woman said as she closed the door.

Regrettably, angels didn't require real flowers. A cloud of artificial scent swarmed over Zee. She swore the saccharine molecules were collecting on her skin, weighting her pores. Eyes stinging, she forced her feet forward.

With the aid of her cane, a stout affair painted with yellow daisies, the woman lowered herself into the chair. "Please sit."

Zee chose the loveseat. Closer to the door, where perhaps a filament of fresh air lingered. Too late she spied the air freshener plugged in nearby. To give her brain time to recover from the olfactory onslaught, she gestured to a photo of a young man smiling in an ivory frame crowned with a sculpted peach hibiscus. "Your son?"

The woman beamed. "Grandson. He's a darling, Arthur is. Comes every Tuesday to take me shopping and to the beauty parlor."

Today. Another reason to make this visit quick. "Thank you for seeing me, Mrs. . . .?" Resisting the urge to press her fingers to her throbbing temples, Zee pretended to consult her phone.

"Branson," the woman supplied. "AnniElla Branson." A smile curved her rose lips. "It's from a Polish name that means angel."

Zee tapped her phone as if affirming her notes. "Yes, thank you." As she lifted her eyes, she glimpsed another 'freshener' plugged in on the far wall. She'd heard that elderly people sometimes lost much of their sense of smell. She tried to moderate her disapproval. The apartment's cotton-candy miasma wasn't intended to nauseate, just provide pleasure to its occupant.

"How can I help you?"

AnniElla's voice jarred Zee from her thoughts. "I know you've already given a description of the person you saw, but sometimes other details come to mind after a few days. Maybe we could begin with you telling me why you noticed them."

AnniElla's papery cheeks pinked. "There was an awful commotion. I was knitting, and I heard it over the TV. I got worried, but then everything quieted down, so I went back to my show."

Zee leaned toward her, across a coffee table festooned with ceramic hummingbirds drinking from trumpet throated morning glories. The perfume attack spiked. Had AnniElla dripped faux nectar into those hollows? Zee stifled a cough. "Go on, please."

AnniElla twisted a ring on her knobby finger. "I couldn't settle down. I just kept feeling like I should check on Miss de la Cornne. But I don't like to pry." The lines on her face deepened. "Maybe if . . ." AnniElla lifted a heavily veined hand to her mouth.

"You couldn't know." Zee's own guilt pricked as she tried to soothe the elderly woman's distress.

AnniElla sighed. "Finally, I went to look through the peephole. I couldn't see anything, and I was debating whether to go over there, when a man came through Miss de la Cornne's door."

A man. Zee gritted her teeth. That liar Kevin.

"He seemed quite calm," said AnniElla. "So I thought whatever happened, everything was all right." Tears shone in her eyes. "I liked Miss de la Cornne. She was always very pleasant to me."

Zee forced aside her own sadness. "You sure it was a man? What did he look like?"

"Well, that view through that tiny peephole isn't very good, you know. I couldn't see his face. He had his head down, and all I could see was the hat."

"What was he wearing?"

AnniElla scrunched her eyes, as if it would help her focus her memory. "One of those coats that come to just above the knees. I want to say a light-ish brown, but I'm not sure. I think he had a white scarf around his neck."

"Did you see his hair?"

"I don't recall. The light wasn't good." AnniElla's shoulders drooped. "I'm sorry. I wish I could tell you more."

Zee checked her non-existent notes again, grateful she didn't actually need to read through her smarting eyes. "Do you recall what time you saw him?"

AnniElla's gaze strayed toward the rose-bordered rug. "Well, mid-afternoon, as I told the other officer."

Too general to be much help. "Can you be more precise?"

"Let's see ..." Gray brows pinched. "That was a Sunday. So, I would be watching a movie in the afternoon. Popular Playhouse, the show's called." She twisted the ring again. "I don't recall the name of the movie, but you can look that up, right? It's on channel five."

"Yes." Zee nodded what she hoped was encouragement. "It

would help to narrow the time frame if you could tell me how much of the movie you had seen when you heard the disruption."

"Now let me think . . ." AnniElla leaned back in her chair and laced her fingers.

On the mantel, slender gold shafts ticked across a sunflower clock face. How much longer before Arthur arrived? More to the point, how much longer could Zee's lungs scavenge breathable air? Her gaze picked out two more scent plug-ins. There was probably one in every electrical outlet in the place.

"They do some previews first," said AnniElla, "and all the commercials at least for the first half of the movie. That way, the movie isn't interrupted once it starts. I like that."

Zee bit her impatient tongue. Let the witness follow the thread of memory.

"Then there's a sort of intermission break halfway through." AnniElla nodded her head as if confirming the memory to herself. "It was a little after that. I hadn't finished my tea and cookies."

An additional sliver of information, bought at a tortuous price. "Did you tell all this to the police earlier?" As soon as Zee asked the question, she realized that, as a supposed member of law enforcement, she probably ought to know this already. She held her breath.

"They didn't ask about the movie."

Zee tried to exhale discreetly. "That's all right. This is very useful."

AnniElla sighed. "Miss de la Cornne was a sweet woman. I'll miss her. I hope someone nice takes that apartment."

The dead were gone. The concerns of the living continued.

Zee's sinuses screamed for relief. She should leave anyway, before the grandson arrived. Better to avoid any questions from him. "Thank you for your time." She offered her hand. "Enjoy your grandson. I can see myself out."

"Thank you, dear." AnniElla plucked a silken spray of violets from a vase on the end table. "Please, take this. Angels will guard and guide you." She pressed the sweet-smelling blossoms into Zee's hand.

Zee managed what she hoped was a smile of gratitude.

On the other side of the door, Zee sagged against the wall. Great draughts of clear air scoured her lungs. How did AnniElla live in all that? Zee was sure any number of her brain cells had died from lack of oxygen in the short time she was in there.

The elevator bell chimed, jolting her. That could be Arthur.

She ducked through the fire door and descended the stairs, mind synthesizing what she'd learned. AnniElla's account didn't match the others. The action was different. Marjorie and Lenore admitted they ran. Kevin described Alex as fleeing. AnniElla's person was calm when he left.

The biggest discrepancy was her gender identification, but she could be wrong, based on the poor visibility. On the other hand, she could be right. And the only man Zee knew for sure was there that day was Kevin, who had already lied. But then, so had Lenore, and Marjorie, and Alex. And Harold PQ.

Frustration burned an acid hole in Zee's chest. Her hands ached to grab someone, anyone, and shake them until their lies fell away like desiccated leaves.

As she exited the building, a stiff breeze whipped her rising anger, stripping any remnants of caution.

BA met tonight.

Come hell, high water, or raging African orishas, Zee would get answers.

CHAPTER 36

AMID SPORADIC BURSTS OF RAIN, ZEE escaped Imperial Court Condominiums. As she drove toward home, drops peppered her face through the partially opened window. A sacrifice she was prepared to make in exchange for rescuing her sinuses from AnniElla's uber-perfumed haven.

With every mile, the pounding in Zee's head eased, although her mind continued to batter itself against the inconsistencies in the timeline of Bette's death. AnniElla provided a clue in her details about the movie she watched. It should be simple to find out when Popular Playhouse aired. Zee hoped it would clarify the conflicting accounts of Lenore, Alex, and Kevin.

Zee checked the time on her dashboard. *5:45.* She had time to do some research before girding herself for battle at BA.

And battle it would be. Her chest tightened. "I won't leave until I have answers," she vowed to the rearview mirror.

Ahead, a traffic light wavered, a red smear in the rivulets trickling down the windshield. Zee's foot faltered on the gas. A hollow weakness spread through her midsection. Not fear. Hunger. She'd eaten nothing since a handful of almonds this morning before leaving for Bette's memorial.

Once recognized, deprivation roared.

Her mind ran through the possibilities for quick sustenance. A carryout from *Ming's* appealed, but the restaurant was too far. A brief stop at Farm Fresh, then. Whole wheat bun, crunchy sprouts, GMO-free chicken breast. That would be good. But instead of the expected approval, her taste buds produced the image of a juicy hamburger. Huge, thick, slathered with mayo, a big old-fashioned—

Her face softened. Last year, a young man who worked at the Big Ol' Burger diner had rescued her from a murder-weapon dumpster-dive. Maybe he still worked there. She could get dinner and thank him at the same time. And she was already halfway there.

Re-energized, she sped through town.

As she pulled into the diner's parking lot, a picture of the establishment's signature sandwich greeted her from the window. A thick slab of ground beef, resting on vibrant green lettuce and dew-kissed red tomato. A golden corner of melted cheese peeked from beneath a flour-dusted bun.

She twitched her lips. How do food advertisers get away with such outright fabrication? That could be a good idea for a column.

She doubted anyone had ever eaten a burger that looked remotely like that one.

Not that it mattered now. Her ravenous stomach would eagerly accept whatever appeared on the plate.

Wishing she knew her dumpster-rescuer's name, Zee pushed open the door, then chuckled at her luck. A placard on the wall displayed his proud photo above a notice. Manager on Duty, Tristan Robertson.

A cheerful young woman led Zee to a high-backed, red-vinyl-upholstered booth and presented a laminated menu. "Can I get you something to drink?"

"Cola," Zee answered. Always good for cutting the grease.

As the waitress disappeared, Zee took in her surroundings: a chrome-edged counter fronted by a row of shiny, red cushioned stools; black-and-white checkerboard floor tile; booths like hers flanking three walls. Classic diner décor that augured well for decent food.

Her server arrived, balancing a tray on the flat of one hand with practiced ease. She presented Zee's cola in a bell-shaped soda glass complete with a shining stainless-steel holder. Classic 1950s-era, two-piece serve-ware. Another encouraging sign.

As the waitress flipped her order pad, Zee let her eyes slide past salads and grilled chicken. Facing off against BA required high-octane fuel. "I'll have the Big Ol' Burger hearty meal."

"Hey, is it you?" a voice called. Tristan hurried toward her. He'd traded his brown polyester uniform for a white button-down shirt.

"It's me." Zee grinned. "The dumpster queen."

Above his big black glasses, his brows crawled to his hairline. "You look great. What a change . . ." His cheeks colored.

Zee read his attempt to compliment without insulting her. When last he'd seen her, she'd been filthy and reeking of garbage. She decided to rescue him. "I wasn't exactly at my best then. But I clean up well."

Relief spread across his face. He pushed his glasses up on his nose and turned to the waitress. "Her meal's on me, Lucy."

"Oh, you don't need to feed me." Zee reached for her purse.

"Manager perk." His chest expanded.

"Sure thing." Lucy fluttered her eyelashes at him.

Tristan's blush deepened. Poor guy . . . or slick move on his part. As Lucy left, Zee gestured toward his name badge. "Manager."

"A month ago today."

"Congratulations."

He shrugged thin shoulders. "Different hat, same fryer."

Zee knit her brows. "Why do I keep hearing variations on that phrase?"

Tristan laughed. "It's a meme now, from that book, *The Mirror of the Soul.*"

A shiver crawled across Zee's shoulder blades.

He cocked his head, a question in his eyes. "Hey, you okay?"

"Just hungry." Zee forced a smile.

"You came to the right place." Half-turned, he sketched an awkward wave. "Really nice to see you."

Smiling, Zee unwrapped the straw. In her peripheral vision, Lucy swept past, delivering two bowls of chili to a corner booth. The spicy aroma sent Zee's mouth into high alert, triggering prophecies of imminent demise from her starving stomach.

Zee paused. Guzzling down the sweet, ice-cold cola would mollify her gut's complaints but also spoil her appetite. After one long swallow, she clamped her lips, lectured herself on discipline, and pulled out her phone. A quick search revealed that Popular Playhouse ran on Sunday, from 1:30-4 p.m.

Zee rewarded herself with another sip, then excavated a notebook from her purse. Down the side of one page, she listed the times from 1:30-4, in half-hour increments. She estimated the intermission AnniElla mentioned would have taken place at about 2:45. She slotted that in.

A thought flitted past. AnniElla had given her information that Bernstow might not have. She should call him.

Not yet. She shoved the idea aside. First, she'd try to understand how everything fit together. Then she would have something concrete to share.

Tapping her fingers on the laminated tabletop, she scoured her memory. Kevin said he saw Alex and Lenore leave Bette's building around 1 p.m. He wasn't completely trustworthy, but that didn't mean he lied about everything. Reluctantly, Zee added 1 p.m. to her outline, then recalled that the coroner had given the time of death as between noon and 4 p.m. She inked in noon.

Lenore said she had gotten there around two o'clock. Based on Kevin's account, Zee put both Alex and Lenore in the one o'clock and two o'clock slots. With no idea how to reconcile this impossibility, she set it aside.

A meaty aroma rode in on the sizzle from the kitchen, activating a wave of mouth-watering anticipation. *Soon*, Zee promised her taste buds. She swallowed more cola to mollify them. They were not fooled.

Gritting her teeth, she returned to the sketch of her timeline. AnniElla heard raised voices before the intermission. That could have been about 2:30, but according to Lenore, Bette was already dead at two. Zee worried her lip. AnniElla could have heard Lenore and Alex, but that meant Lenore either had to stick around with a corpse for half an hour, or come back later, at exactly the same time as Alex arrived. Improbable at best.

But say that's what happened. Then what? They screamed at each other over Bette's body? Zee couldn't picture it, but these were two volatile women.

The more logical answer was that someone else had been to Bette's apartment, the man AnniElla saw through the peephole. That had to have been Kevin. Zee calculated that, based on the time of intermission and AnniElla's partially consumed tea and cookies, that unidentified person would have left around 3:15. But if Kevin had been outside the building at one, why would he return so much later?

Zee pressed fingers to her temples. The scenarios were more tangled than the pile of crispy golden onion strings two tables down.

The tempting heap trapped her gaze. She should have ordered them instead of the fries. But then she'd have onion breath. Which might work in her favor at the BA meeting. She pictured herself, blasting malodorous fumes inches from Kevin's face, or Alex's, or Lenore's.

With effort, she pulled her eyes away, only to have them land on the large, round clock on the wall. Her order had better arrive soon.

While she was grilling Lenore, Kevin, and Alex, she'd also get some other answers. Like the truth about Lenore's relationship with Marjorie, Bette, and *The Mirror of the Soul*. Like why Alex spied, and what Kevin was up to. And she'd nail down whether and how any of it connected to the text messages.

As she scribbled, acid burned in her gut, an assault stronger than mere hunger.

She stopped her pen.

Don't run. Investigate pain. Fontina's instruction, when she helped Zee recover from her battle with McNeary's murderer. Zee laced her fingers in her lap and inhaled a slow, deep breath.

Kitchen sounds and conversation faded. Zee concentrated on the fiery sensation in her midsection, waiting like a patient hunter, stalking its prey.

Her eyes snapped open.

She'd overlooked Harold PQ. The stalker. The spy.

She added his name to her list, her fury driving the penpoint deep into the paper. Smarmy little man. He wouldn't get away from her this time.

Her stomach rumbled. Where was her food? If her meal looked anything like the one with the onion strings, it would be a crime to have to rush through it. She had enough frustration with BA without adding indigestion.

She grabbed her phone and grimaced at the home screen time display. Forty minutes before seven. Still time, barely.

"Here you go. Big Ol' Burger meal."

Saved before her head exploded.

The oval platter Lucy set before Zee groaned under a burger so thick and piled with accompaniments that it needed an eight-inch toothpick to hold it all together. Zee shoved her notebook aside and smiled her appreciation.

The mountainous burger actually resembled the photo.

She bit into a spear of eye-watering kosher dill pickle. The garlicky assault on her tongue deprived her of breath for a moment, but engineered the perfect setup for a bite of ground beef. Juicy, meaty, with just the right amount of creamy mayo.

She'd have to tell Rico about this place. Better still, surprise him with it. Easy joy swept through her. Their lives would be filled now with these shared simple pleasures. How much the three words she'd managed to finally say—and mean—had freed her.

Another mouthful brought velvety cheddar, crunchy lettuce,

and a sweet onion tang. Sustenance—almost spiritual—flooded her, grounding her, cooling her ire. She banked the coals. She'd need the energy later.

"Can I get you anything?" Lucy returned with the ritual question. Zee shook her head, her mouth too full of golden, crispy-skinned potato wedges for any other response.

She checked the time on her cell. Less than she'd like, but she'd be okay. She picked up her pen, then realized the futility. This enormous burger required both hands.

Maybe she could at least cogitate and every so often, wipe the juice from her fingers and make a note.

The curved slice of onion peeking from beneath the bun seemed to smile indulgently, as if it knew her taste buds would override any attempt at strategic thinking.

Lowering the pen like a flag, she surrendered.

CHAPTER 37

A TWINGE OF REMORSE PRICKING HER CONSCIENCE, Zee slipped behind the steering wheel. She shouldn't have lingered over that Big Ol' Burger meal. Now she had only ten minutes until the BA meeting began.

She'd make it if she pushed the speed limit, but even as her foot goosed the accelerator, her taste buds mocked her guilt. With that massive marvel of meat, she really had no choice. Even now, the seductive scent of fried potatoes wafting from the take-home sack tempted her.

At a red light, she grabbed the bag and shoved it onto the back seat. Enough distraction. From this moment on, she refused to be sidetracked. Before she left the BA meeting, she would know who was at Bette's, when, and why; how all these people connected to each other; and whether any of it was linked to those damn texts.

She leapt forward when the light changed, already picturing herself cornering Alex, Kevin, Lenore, and Harold PQ. As she rounded a corner, *Po* skidded on the wet pavement. She jerked her foot from the gas. The liars would be there, but she'd learn nothing if she didn't arrive in one piece.

With a minute to spare, she turned into the parking lot. A dozen cars sat in the misting, meager light, none of them a shiny red

Corvette. Strike one for her plan. Gritting her teeth, she searched for Kevin's jeep. Irritation flared. Strike two.

She slammed *Po*'s door and stomped toward the side entrance. Halfway there, her gaze fell on Lenore's battered Civic. Zee bunched her fists. The game wasn't over yet.

At the top of the steps, she paused and inhaled slowly to calm her racing pulse. On her second breath, a buzz of conversation reached her ears. And laughter.

Odd for a BA meeting.

She pulled open the door and entered a party in full swing. Roughly twenty people chattered in clusters in the back half of the long, narrow room. The elderly Swithenstein sisters frolicked in a circle around a dazed-looking Harold PQ. Lenore ladled red punch from a large plastic bowl next to a partially devoured cake.

Cake? Punch? *Frolicking?*

Zee ventured a few steps inside the door. A tall, fit woman in jeans and a tight sweater strode toward her, the Oya stomp-dancer. "This is a private party."

Unfazed, Zee parried, "Why the celebration?"

A swarthy man in a rumpled suit sidled next to Zee. "The movie's cancelled."

"Postponed," the woman snipped.

He laughed, sharp whiskey billowing on his breath.

Zee recalled him from her first meeting. He'd been in his cups then too.

"Good enough." He spread his arms wide. "And everyone's invited to party with us."

With a huff, faux Oya turned away.

The man tried to sling his arm around Zee's shoulders. She ducked, then hoped she wouldn't have to prop him up. Wobbling dangerously, he produced a silver flask. "A little something to punch up the punch." He guffawed at his own cleverness and tipped the flask into his mouth.

Seizing her the chance, Zee escaped across the room. To her

relief, the man did not follow. His drunken bonhomie faded into the general hubbub.

She scoured the crowd. Definitely no vibrant red tresses. Frustration tightened her eyes. She scanned more slowly. No bald-headed Kevin, either. And Lenore had disappeared from the refreshment table.

Damn. Jaw tight, Zee swept the room for other opportunities.

Near the pillow pile, Harold extricated himself from the sisters. Not Zee's first choice, but his behavior at '60s Fest still rankled. Beelining to intercept, she blocked his path, then cut him from the others like a weakened calf.

Trapped near a wall, he swallowed hard. "Wha-what do you want?"

She stared into his bulging brown eyes. "I want to know why you were spying on me."

He glanced left and right, then tried to slide sideways.

She choked off his path. "Answer me."

"I wasn't stalking, nothing like that." His Adam's apple bobbed against his damp shirt collar. "I'm not a creep."

She pushed her face within inches of his. "You *are* a creep."

"Okay, okay." He mashed himself against the wall. "Alex made me do it. I don't know why. She just wanted to know where you went."

Zee scowled at him while she digested this information. "How long were you watching me?"

"Just a day or two, a week maybe."

"Which is it?"

He shrank beneath her glower. "A week."

So, it started right after her first BA meeting.

His lower lip quivered. "I'm sorry."

Zee pinned him with her gaze while she sensed the room around her. No one approached. To forestall interruption, she relaxed the set of her shoulders. She lowered her voice, but maintained its menace. "Alex must have given you a reason. Spit it out, and maybe I won't report you."

In the scant space that separated them, he snaked an arm upward to wipe the sweat from his brow. "Look, I don't know . . . I figured she liked you and . . . just wanted to know more about you."

"She doesn't strike me as afraid to ask her own questions." As she said it, Zee recalled Shaneah's warning not to trust anyone. Particularly Alex.

Harold flicked a nervous tongue across his lip. "Alex can be . . . persuasive."

Zee allowed her mouth to curl into a sneer. "You?" It was cruel to let him see her opinion. She didn't care.

The exophthalmic eyes above his flaming cheeks threatened to roll out of their sockets. He exhaled in a rush of cloying cake breath. "No. Nothing like that."

"What then? No, never mind. I don't want to know."

"She paid me." He managed to inject a hint of defiance in his voice. "It's hard living on a pension. And after what Kevin did—" He dipped his head.

"What?"

"I don't want to talk about it."

"Too bad. You don't have the right to remain silent."

He shook his head. "It's private. Nothing you need to know."

Zee grabbed his limp tie. "I'll decide what I need to—"

"What's going on here?" One of the Swithenstein sisters interposed an arm between Zee and Harold. Gray eyes, barely Zee's shoulder height, glowered at her. "Here now, what are you doing to Harold?" Without waiting for an answer, the elderly woman swiveled to him. "Are you all right?" She clasped claw-like fingers around his flaccid bicep. "Come on. She has no right to upset you."

With his free hand, Harold made a pathetic attempt to smooth his tie. "I'm not proud of myself." His voice quavered, pleading to Zee. "I'll never bother you—or anyone—like that again, I swear. Please don't make trouble for me."

"You made your own trouble."

As if bolstered by his champion, belligerence sparked in his eyes. "Alex likes to play with people, don't you know that?"

His rescuer tugged at him. "Come on, Harold." With a parting glare, he let her lead him away.

Zee leaned against the wall, heat creeping into her face. She knew all too well how Alex played with people, but it stung to have that flung at her by this mealy-mouthed man.

Anger kick-started her brain. A manipulator like Alex collected knowledge, squirreling it away until an opportune time. What did she have on Harold? Or for that matter, on Kevin, or Lenore, or even Bette? The questions gathered like crows on Zee's brow.

Maybe Bette knew something about Alex, something that fiery redhead would kill to hide. She was audacious and hot-headed enough to do it, and according to Kevin, she was there at the right time. But Lenore's story contradicted that. Zee's eyes swept the room. None of her primary suspects was here. Once again, she was stymied.

An ache throbbed in her jaw. Drawing in a deep breath, she loosened it. Tying herself in knots would not produce results.

Her gaze fell on the Swithenstein sisters, both now fussing over Harold. He slumped in a folding chair, while one sister mopped his brow with a flowered handkerchief. The other patted his back like she was soothing a baby.

Zee pursed her lips. She should have forced her advantage with Harold, squeezed more from him. By indulging in petty revenge, she'd lost the chance to get any other information. Not that she thought he knew much.

She considered whether she might learn anything from Harold's two elderly nannies. Frustration pounded like a fist against her rib-cage. She'd come here tonight, determined to get answers. She had to ask *someone* her questions.

Harold's rescuer continued to comfort him, but the other sister detached from the trio and headed toward the refreshment table. Zee shoved aside her misgivings and moved in her direction.

The one piece of information she'd gleaned from Harold confirmed that Kevin had cost him financially. Perhaps she could use that as a starting point.

The sister was helping herself to coffee from a bitter-smelling urn when Zee came abreast. "Strong," Zee said. She grimaced. Insult the refreshments. Great icebreaker.

The old lady shot her a wary glance.

Zee coated her voice with apologetic friendliness. "I'm sorry if I upset you. I had some private business to take care of with Harold. That's dealt with now."

Behind smudged lenses, narrowed eyes studied her.

Zee made a show of glancing around. "I wonder where Kevin is."

No response.

She tried again. "I wanted to talk to him. Or Lenore."

The sister dispensed opaque black liquid into a second cup. "Why?"

Finally, a reply. "I heard BA might be in financial trouble. Harold said something that made me think Kevin was involved."

Withered lip curling, the sister faced her. "He's a snake."

Zee's eyes smarted from the coffee fumes, but she held her ground. "Do you think that's why Kevin went to see Bette de la Cornne the day she died?"

"I didn't know he did."

"Did you know Alex did?"

A shake of the head.

"Lenore?"

"No."

Dead end.

"Having a nice little chat?" An angry voice snapped Zee's attention. The Oya dancer advanced upon her, eyes afire. "I heard you were conducting interrogations."

Across the room, Harold's rescuer stared, arms folded across her chest. Her sister glared at Zee, suspicion darkening her face.

"Interrogations? What exactly are you doing here?" Without waiting for an answer, she grabbed the coffees and stalked away.

"I think it's time for you to go." Oya reached for Zee but stopped short of touching her.

Zee scanned the room. Still no Alex, Kevin, or Lenore. Only poisonous eyes wherever she looked. Except for the drunken man bobbing in her direction. As he neared, Oya stepped into his path. "Get out of the way. She's leaving." She elbowed him aside.

Zee caught him before he fell. "Hey," she addressed Oya, "that was rude."

He brushed at his rumpled suit jacket. "S'okay."

Zee whirled to face the woman. "I thought you people in BA were all about understanding each other's struggles."

"I know him better than you do."

The man wiped a hand across his damp face. "My cousin." He gave Oya a weak smile. She huffed and strode off. Facing her retreating figure, he executed a dangerously unbalanced bow. "She's gotta put up with me. Blood's thicker than water."

A neuron in Zee's brain perked, stretched—

"And whiskey's thicker than everything." Belching, the man held out his flask to Zee.

The neuron curled back into its crevice.

Zee stifled a scream. The noise in the room stabbed at her ears. Saccharine sweetness drifted from the punch, soured by the rank breath of too many overexcited voices.

She needed to get out of this place. Think. Coax that connection. This night can't have been all for nothing.

Sucking shallow breaths, she pushed her way to the door.

CHAPTER 38

O UTSIDE THE COMMUNITY CENTER, THE NIGHT was blessedly cool. Traffic hummed in the distance, a river of sound. Zee wished it would carry away the BA-induced cacophony in her head, clear the way for that tantalizing twitch in her brain to reappear.

"Blood is thicker than water," her inebriated companion had said.

Zee tried to let her mind rest on the statement without spinning meanings from it. She closed her eyes. Her curls ruffled in a gust of moisture-laden air, a warmish caress, but undergird with an ominous chill. Wind from the north. It presaged rain, or worse if the temperature dropped low enough.

Zee shivered but kept her focus, visualizing the words in her mind. They began to drift apart. Something like vapor spiraled from the spaces between them. She breathed gently, coaxing.

Clank-thunk-clank!

The vision shattered, bits of meaning scampering like frightened animals. Zee's eyes snapped open. Out on the street, a semi rattled past.

She groaned. Chalk up another failure for this night.

Leaning against the corroded handrail, she summed up her inability to narrow her list of suspects. Means. No help there; she didn't know what the weapon was, much less who had access to it.

Opportunity. Contradictions in her sketched-out timeline made any conclusions unreliable and actually added a person, AnniElla's unknown man. As for motive, everyone who went to Bette's had a reason to want her dead. Lenore, to save BA's reputation; Alex, to exact revenge from an ex-lover; Kevin, to keep his scam going.

Lined up like this, Marjorie still had the strongest motive—despair at her ruined life. Doubt gnawed at Zee. Occam's razor said the simplest answer was usually the right one.

She stared up at the inky sky. Through the scattered clouds, she picked out the Seven Sisters. Some astrologers said they symbolized coping with sorrow. Another place where Zee fell short.

Shame pricked her for abandoning Bette's memorial for this fruitless quest. She had no murderer to unmask. And no big story.

She should have toughed it out in the church.

But then she wouldn't have talked with Victor and learned about Sara Jane.

Her eyes widened. Bette's ex-publicist could be a viable suspect. She'd lost her job, suffered damage to her reputation and maybe future employment prospects, and been banished from her charismatic employer's presence. AnniElla's description was vague enough that she could have misidentified the gender of the person she saw through the peephole.

Zee huffed. She needed to face reality. All her mental machinations were nothing more than speculation, as diaphanous as her misty breath. The cold metal railing bit into her palms. Cocking her head sideways, she murmured, "Help me, Shelby."

From the shadows emerged a tired voice. "Find what you were looking for?"

Zee whirled.

Lenore's weary figure stepped into the meager light, shoulders slumped beneath a thin sweater.

"I was actually looking for you." Zee softened her voice at Lenore's defeated posture. "I'm surprised you're not celebrating with the others."

Lenore wrapped her sweater more tightly across her chest, as if to draw structural support from the threadbare fabric. "I'm not much in the mood."

Zee raised her brows. "Isn't cancelling the movie a victory for BA?"

"This might come as a shock to you, but sometimes success is scarier than failure." Lenore turned to stare out at the parking lot. "You think it will be snatched away, because it often was. I don't expect you to understand."

Distrust, another legacy of betrayal. "I'd like to understand."

A sigh shuddered through Lenore's thin frame. She gestured toward the door. Laughter and chatter filtered from behind it. "Listen to them in there. They're children, happy for the moment—and I'm glad. But tomorrow, the weight will come crashing down on them again. And they don't know, they don't know how long . . ." She covered her face with bony hands.

As if stepping into Lenore's mind, Zee saw through the beleaguered founder's eyes, the aging woman trapped between two mirrors, staring at a multitude of defeated faces replicated into infinity. All born from that first treachery that cleaved her soul. "It's been a long struggle for you."

Lenore jerked as though stung by Zee's words. "I don't need your pity." Whirling, the wilted woman vanished, replaced by an angry defender. "What are you doing here? Thought to pick at our carcasses like a vulture?"

The rebuke smarted. "It's not like that. I've actually come to care about BA, about you, about what you're trying to do."

As she spoke, Zee felt the truth of the words. She disliked Lenore's methods, but her goal was admirable, healthy even. And in that moment, Zee's heart knew another truth: Lenore was not her enemy.

It was time to make her an ally, if she could.

Zee faced the furious warrior and drew in a deep breath. "I think it's time I was honest with you, about why I'm here."

Lenore's lips thinned. A spark of triumph flickered in her eyes. "That would be a refreshing change."

Zee's cheeks heated. Although she hadn't exactly lied, she'd hidden her deeper purpose. She had no right to debate Lenore's judgment. A chilly breeze sent shivers across her shoulders. "Could we go somewhere to talk? That is, unless you want to stay at the meeting."

Lenore glanced toward the party, then back at Zee. "Let me tell someone I'm leaving." She disappeared through the door.

Her original purpose reborn, Zee breathed to ease the tightness in her chest. She could be close to finally getting answers, if she played it right. She raked fingers through her curls, as if that would help her chart a useful path in the coming conversation. But the tangled spirals had staged their usual humidity-induced rebellion. Clarity eluded her.

The door clicked open. Excited voices escaped.

"Let's go," said Lenore.

Zee blurted the first thing that came to mind. "Is Marlene's okay?"

"I'll meet you there." Lenore already fingered her keys.

During the three-block drive to the elegant bar, Zee tried to formulate a plan. She'd tell Lenore the truth from the beginning. Beyond that step, her mind wouldn't go. She parked *Po* and hurried through the rapidly chilling night to the welcome lights of the bar.

Inside, the same soft jazz floated above murmured conversations. The same seminal celebrities posed in artful portraits. The same gilt-edged menu offered that seductive pinot noir. Zee slapped the scripted wine list on the polished ebony table. Not today.

After a prompt server took their orders, Lenore folded her hands on the tabletop. She pinned her eyes on Zee. "Well?"

"Before I tell you why I was at BA, I need to ask you a question." Zee winced inwardly. She hadn't intended to begin the rapprochement by denying Lenore a response.

The sagging jaw clenched, but Lenore nodded.

"Did you send me a cryptic text?"

Lenore snapped her head back, narrowing her eyes. "What? No. Why the hell would you ask me that?" She pushed up from her chair.

Zee put out a hand to stop her. "A text is why I'm at BA."

Lenore sat down, but strain tightened her face.

"I got a strange text the day after Bette died." Zee offered her phone.

Lenore studied the screen, then handed it back. "That's cryptic, all right. I didn't send it." She relaxed a fraction. "How did that get you to BA?"

"It sounded like someone wanted me to investigate Bette's death because Marjorie didn't kill her. The mention of a mirror and the quasi-religious wording made me think of the book. A little digging—especially finding the unusual word *pernicious* so prominent on your website—brought me to BA, wondering if there was a connection."

Twenty years washed from Lenore's wrinkled face. "So, you've been sniffing around, trying to prove my Marjorie's innocent."

My Marjorie. Zee filed that response. And *innocent*, that was the word Gregory had used, though it was far from accurate.

"Do you think you can help?" Lenore's voice lifted. "I don't know what I can tell you, but ask."

Zee's tight chest loosened. This was going well.

Perhaps too well. Caution reined in her optimism. She hid it, striving to project trust. "Tell me exactly what happened the day you went to Bette's. We were talking in my car, but Alex interrupted us."

Lenore grimaced. No fan of the malachite-eyed manipulator.

Zee pressed on. "If you don't mind, would you start again? What time did you go to the apartment? What did you do? When did you leave? Who else did you see?" She bit her tongue to stop firing questions.

Lenore stared downward, rubbing a knobby thumb across the back of her hand. Her lips moved, as if she were talking to herself.

Zee leaned closer, trying to screen out the clink of glassware and the buzz of voices. Low laughter surfed the soulful notes of a saxophone. Zee's synapses quivered. She glanced around.

"I left my apartment around one-thirty."

Zee snapped her attention back to Lenore.

"I got to her place about twenty minutes later. I was agitated, so I made myself sit in the car 'til I calmed down. I'm guessing I went up around two o'clock. The door was ajar. I pushed it open. She was dead."

Same story as last time. Zee clamped her teeth so hard they hurt. Kevin must be lying.

"Chardonnay." The server set Zee's glass on the table. She slid a pot and a cup in front of Lenore. "Decaf Earl Gray."

While Lenore dunked her teabag, Zee sipped her wine. Smooth, buttery, slightly oaky, hints of pear. The frustrated tightness in her throat eased. "Did you check for a pulse?"

Lenore squeezed the lemon with such force her knuckles whitened. "No. I told you, I just ran."

She was lying. It was blazoned in her flushed cheeks.

Blood, thicker than water.

Zee's mind raced. Could Lenore have killed Bette to avenge 'her' Marjorie? Zee had only Lenore's word that Bette was dead when she got there.

Leaning across the small table, Zee trapped the watery gray eyes. "I'm having trouble believing that of you. You didn't call 9-1-1?"

Lenore shook her head, but there was no assertion in the gesture.

"You're telling me," Zee sharpened her voice, "you left a woman on the floor who might have still been alive?"

Lenore shrank against the seat.

Zee dialed back the aggression in her tone, offering sympathetic disbelief. "That's not you. You care about people, even people you don't like."

Lenore's chin quivered.

Zee pressed. "You cared about Bette, even if Marjorie did replace you in her affection."

Lenore choked. "What? You think we were lovers? Oh God, I'd laugh if I could." Anger strengthened her voice. "Marjorie fell under Bette's spell. I didn't like it. I didn't like Bette's lifestyle. I didn't like her power over Marjorie. But would that child listen to me?" She snorted. "Eighteen-year-olds don't listen to anyone."

Zee winced inwardly at her mistaken assumption. Even worse, she'd let Lenore escape the precipice. Time to change the line of attack.

"Did you know that Bette didn't die from the fall? There was a second blow to her head. That was the fatal one."

Blood drained from Lenore's face. She swayed as if she'd been struck.

Steeling her heart, Zee hammered. "Do you realize that if you had stayed, not only would you have helped her, you might have prevented her killer from murdering her."

"Or she might have murdered me too!"

She?

Zee would come back to that. For now, her adversary had cracked. Zee pressed her advantage. "It's time you told me the truth, Lenore. What really happened?"

The small woman curled into herself. Her narrow chest rose and fell.

A long minute passed. The saxophone changed tunes. Zee held her gaze steadily on Lenore. If she didn't cave, Zee was out of ammunition.

"Okay," Lenore exhaled. "I went in, but I didn't see her, so I called out. She came into the living room. She had a towel or something wrapped around her head. We argued. I lost my temper. I called her a few names. I stormed out."

Zee scrambled to integrate this new information. Bette was alive—not dead—at two o'clock. It didn't solve much, but in Zee's mind, a logjam began to break apart.

"I shouldn't have lied," Lenore murmured.

Zee stripped her voice of accusation. "Why did you?"

"I heard there was a witness who saw Marjorie." Lenore dashed a hand across her cheek. "I thought if I said Bette was already dead when I got there, it would prove Marjorie couldn't have done it."

Zee leaned against the back of her chair. "You told that story to the police?"

"I did, but they didn't believe me, probably because I'm her aunt."

Or they had evidence to the contrary. Zee swallowed wine to soothe her exasperation.

Lenore's jagged sigh sawed the air. "If you had my experience with authority . . ." She grabbed her teacup like a life preserver, lifted it to her lips.

Zee sipped more wine, regrouping. In their truncated earlier conversation, Lenore had seemed on the verge of disclosing who else was in the building that day. "A few minutes ago, you said 'she' might have murdered you, too. Who did you see?"

Lenore spat her answer. "Alex."

Zee definitely needed to track her down. As if in mockery, a throaty chuckle drifted across the room. Zee scanned the room, cursing the muted light. Half a dozen possibilities, or wishful thinking. Zee returned her attention to Lenore. "When did you see her?"

"After I left. She was coming out of the elevator."

"Did you speak to her?"

Lenore shook her head. "She just rushed past me."

Zee resisted the urge to dig her fingers into her scalp. Kevin said he saw Alex and Lenore around one. It strained credulity to think they were both there earlier and returned later, to run into each other again. This timeline was like a bridge built from two different origin points. Each one got to the middle, but they didn't meet. "I have to ask, are you sure about the time?"

"I looked at my watch." As if to demonstrate, Lenore lifted her raveled sleeve to display the vomit-green strap.

Zee's hand, on its way to massage her temples, shot out and grabbed Lenore's wrist. "This watch?"

Lenore pulled free. "It's the only one I have."

"Did you set it forward for Daylight Saving Time?"

"Of course, I did." Lenore huffed. "Why are you—"

"On Saturday night, or Sunday morning?"

"No, it's a nuisance. I always forget until I'm late for—" The gray eyes widened.

"That's it. You were at Bette's around three o'clock, not two." A wave of relief swept through Zee. AnniElla *could* have heard Lenore and Alex. And Kevin, Zee would bet, had set his car clock back instead of forward. That would account for the discrepancy in his timeline.

Bottom line: Bette was alive at three, hurt but alive.

"You know what this means?" Lenore's voice broke. "Marjorie isn't responsible for her death, and all this time, I . . . I . . ." Tears welled and spilled down her withered cheeks. "Alex was there after me. She could have done it."

Zee winced. Lenore assumed Marjorie caused Bette's first injury, not the second. The reverse could be true. And although AnniElla said the person she saw was a man, her description was vague enough to fit a debilitated woman.

Zee wanted to throw up her hands and scream. Maybe the police actually had the right person.

She felt Lenore's expectant eyes on her. "Alex is a possibility," she conceded, "but why would she do it?"

"You're the clever one," said Lenore.

Zee rested fingers below her chin. "I'm wondering if there's a romantic angle. I heard that when you two split up, Alex didn't take it well."

Lenore's cheeks pinked. "Alex doesn't deal well with what she thinks of as rejection."

"She seemed okay when I met her."

Scorn laced Lenore's laugh. "She moves fast. Needs to show she's over it. I'm sure she's found someone new."

Some*one* or some*thing*. "Maybe Alex decided on a car this time."

"Not because of me," said Lenore. "We parted ways ages ago."

Bette then? Zee played out the scenario. If Bette dumped Alex, and in a fury, Alex killed her, she could buy a flashy new car to, what? Give herself a sort of alibi, a fit to her pattern? That sequence felt more stretched than a bungee cord.

"I'm not making any assumptions." Zee gulped wine to help curtail her speculation, but her mind rebounded, pursuing the same thought line. Maybe, Sara Jane, the teary-eyed publicist, wanted to be closer to Bette than a merely professional relationship suggested. Maybe "the guardian at the gate" somehow got between Alex and Bette. Would a rejected Alex kill Bette to hurt Sara Jane?

Zee bit her lip hard. She could be building another bridge that ended in thin air.

Lenore set her cup on the saucer with a clink, jarring Zee from her thoughts. "The important thing is, Marjorie didn't kill that woman." She clenched her fists. "But of course the police are happy to blame her." She leaned toward Zee. "Can you talk to them?"

Zee pictured Bernstow's eye-roll response to her conjecture, but she couldn't douse the hope burning in Lenore's gaze. "I can try." She could at least run all this by Rico, get his reaction and maybe some ideas about how to proceed. Warmth blossomed around her heart. It was good to be working together again.

Lenore sagged against the backrest, as if she felt the thinness of Zee's promise. Over the drooping shoulders, Zee spotted two women across the room. Her stomach jolted. She'd know that flaming hair anywhere.

The other woman made her way toward the door. She passed beneath a muted pendant lamp, and Zee recoiled at a second slam in the gut. She'd last seen that tall, shapely figure in the parking lot outside Cactus Cantina, admitting to employing a spy.

CHAPTER 39

B y force of will, Zee anchored her feet beneath the table at Marlene's. One eye remained on Alex at the bar. The other tracked Shaneah, who crossed the room toward the door. Up and down Zee's arms, goosebumps fought with sweat.

"Are you all right?" Lenore had raised a weary gaze from her tea. "You look like you've seen a ghost."

Not a ghost, a chilling realization. Shaneah had a spy inside BA. Harold was too clumsy, but Alex—Zee's skin crawled. Two vipers who subcontracted their dirty work.

"Miss Morani?" Lenore's voice quavered.

"I'm okay," Zee said. "Just thought of something I need to do." Storm across the room and confront Alex. Plant her face an inch from that cool green gaze. Let spittle punctuate her demands for the truth. But first, she needed to end this conversation with the exhausted woman across from her.

"I know you can't promise anything," Lenore said.

For a moment, Zee was lost. Then, she remembered. Lenore was still thinking about Zee's promise to talk to the police about Alex.

Stomach sinking, Zee catalogued everything she needed to tell Bernstow: AnniElla's timeline, Bette's mysterious late visitor, Kevin's fiscal shenanigans. She swallowed a sigh.

Lenore pushed her cup aside. "I'm suddenly very tired. It's been like this since they arrested Marjorie. One moment I'm full of energy, the next . . ."

"Are you okay to drive home?" Zee forced herself to make the offer. "I can give you a lift." She held her breath and crossed her fingers under the table.

Lenore shook her head. "I don't live far." She pushed herself to her feet, wobbled, and grasped the chair.

"Let me walk you to your car." The moment the words were out, Zee wished she could retract them. She wanted to ambush Alex, but that chance would be lost if her quarry spotted her. On the other hand, Lenore looked perilously exhausted.

"I would appreciate that," said Lenore. "Normally, I'd decline, but I'm a bit unsteady on my feet."

Zee left a twenty for the bill. She curbed her eyes from the bar's magnetic pull as she shepherded the old woman out the door.

The night mist had thickened to an icy fog. Mother Nature sending a reminder that she wasn't done with winter yet. Zee tugged up the collar of her blazer, trying to shield her neck. The chill crept in anyway.

She schooled her feet to careful progress, but her mind rabbited. She wanted to know what Alex and Shaneah had been talking about. Why Alex had sent Harold PQ spying? But most of all, what happened when Alex went to Bette's that day? If Alex spotted her leaving Marlene's with Lenore, all would be lost. The manipulator par excellence could at this moment be slipping out a rear exit, slithering through Zee's fingers.

After an eon, Zee and Lenore reached the decrepit Civic. Murmuring thanks, the old woman settled behind the wheel. Zee forced herself to wait while the engine coughed to life and the Civic pulled into the street. Then she hurried back into Marlene's.

She hustled through the tables toward the bar, craning her neck until she finally had a clear sightline. Her gaze raked the barstools. No redhead. Damn.

Alex might have gone to the restroom, a hopeful inner voice offered. Jaw tight, Zee wove through knots of people toward the Ladies sign.

She forced herself not to thrust the door open. It swung smoothly at her touch, and she stepped into the brightly lit, rose-and-cream-tiled interior. A large mirror, several sinks, half a dozen stalls—all empty, but one. Zee positioned herself near the door. No way was Alex going to escape.

The stall door opened. A short blonde emerged.

Zee stifled a growl, yanked at the door, and rushed back into the main room. Several heads turned in her direction. Smoothing the tension from her face, she slowed her steps to pass the bar. Unabashedly, she searched the occupants.

Useless. Her prey had escaped.

Back outside, she scanned the parked cars. Under the vapor-shrouded light from the street lamps, no shiny red 'Vette material-ized. Zee stifled a face palm. She should have checked for Alex's car earlier, but she was distracted with Lenore. She buried a frustrated hand in her rapidly dampening hair.

The wind flung icy drops against her cheeks. She should get home before the weather worsened, but the fire in her belly demanded action. She was not going home empty-handed. If she couldn't corner Alex, she'd go after Shaneah.

Po's tires slid sideways when Zee pulled from her parking place. She sucked in a breath. Black ice could form in this weather. Many a vehicle met its end on treacherous patches masquerading as water. She flexed her fingers to relax them and pointed the car toward the Earthkins' apartment.

Road spray blurred the windshield. Zee flipped on the wip-ers. To their metronome, her mind bounced among questions. Did Alex spy because she was part of Kevin's fraud? No, that cool Machiavelli didn't get her hands dirty. Maybe she actually cared about BA and its members. Zee snorted. More likely, the schemer was busy snaring people into her web for her own purposes.

Slush thrown by a passing car all-but-obliterated Zee's view of the road. Mother of—! She slammed the wiper lever.

It was crazy to be out on a night like this.

But she was halfway to her destination.

Which was all the way across town from her home.

And the weather wasn't getting any better.

Stupid dressed up as brave is still stupid.

"Be quiet," Zee muttered to Shelby's voice.

She notched down the wiper speed and focused on the road. The rain lessened as she approached the eastern side of Valerian, and her thoughts turned to Shaneah.

Keeping tabs on the people who 'stole' Marjorie could be a strong enough reason to spy. But if Shaneah had discovered Kevin's scheme . . . For the first time, Zee considered the cost of Gregory's medication. His high-minded spirituality might object to ill-gotten gains, but his wife might suffer fewer qualms.

Motion ahead sliced through Zee's musings. Some distance in front of her, a camouflage SUV slewed sideways in slow motion. It must have hit ice. Zee slowed, horror seizing her breath as its over-sized tires carried the SUV toward oncoming traffic.

White-knuckled, she edged *Po* toward the curb. Safer there. She hoped. Better than trusting she could get past the chaos ahead.

The camo-painted vehicle fishtailed. Crossed the double-yellow line into oncoming headlights. Zee's chest spasmed.

Tires squealed, a terrified shriek that scraped along Zee's nerves. An approaching car swerved wide. Dove to the side of the road and halted.

Zee's breath hitched. The SUV skidded, screeched, careened, a wild animal. Suddenly, it made a sharp turn.

Directly at her.

Fear jammed a fist into her solar plexus. She had to move, but even as her foot jerked toward the gas, she knew it was too late.

She thought to squeeze her eyes shut but couldn't.

A green-tan blur rocketed past.

In her rearview mirror, the SUV bounced like a billiard ball against the guardrail behind her, whipped back across the road, and banged to a halt. It sat rumbling, its front end buried in a pile of trash bags.

Behind her, the big door opened. Deep bass thundered as the driver swung himself down to the street. Hunched in his fleece jacket, he circled his vehicle. Apparently satisfied he could continue, he got back inside. The low throbbing muted.

Zee swallowed a dry lump in her throat, rubbed her temples.

The driver's window retracted, renewing the assault. A flare lit his face, and a plume of cigarette smoke floated into the icy mist. The engine growled, and the monster pulled back onto the street, crossed to Zee's side, and drove past.

Zee's hammering heart crawled down from her throat. She wiped damp palms on her blazer. No more speculating on motives. And forget strategizing. She had to concentrate on getting safely to her destination, or her investigation might end up in a ditch.

UNDER THE YELLOW GLOW OF PSEUDO-GASLIGHTS, the Earthkins' crooked street glimmered like a treacherous river. Wary of complicated maneuvers on the suspect surface, Zee grabbed the first parking spot she saw.

Despite the freezing drizzle snaking down her neck, she had to choose her steps with care on the cracked sidewalk. She slipped and slid past the row of dignified converted Victorian houses, shoes squeaking, curls stuck to her brow, a sartorial mess.

A bedraggled beggar, how unwelcome she'd be among these once fastidiously groomed painted ladies. She imagined their drooping eaves telegraphing disapproval, a sagging porch rail frowning. On the faces of the next two houses, partially lowered shades censuring her like haughty, lidded eyes.

Zee chuckled at her fantasy. If they knew her purpose, they'd damn her no matter her appearance. Those grande dames of old would have had nothing to do with murder.

She hurried as safely as the weather and her protesting knee allowed. By the time she huddled beneath the beveled fanlight above the Earthkins' front door, she had to clamp her jaw to keep her teeth from chattering. Shivering, she rapped. No answer. The wind slapped the damp hems of her trousers against her ankles.

She knocked again. Surely, Gregory was home. But he might be unable to come to the door. Cold seeped through the scant protection of her shoes, the same heels she'd worn all day. She shifted her weight from one foot to the other. She might scream into the frost if she had come all this way—

The door swung open. "Oh, hello." A warm smile lit Gregory's cadaverous face. "Thought Shaneah forgot her keys again. Please come in. Nasty night out."

Zee stepped quickly across the threshold. As she followed Gregory down the narrow hallway, she couldn't help but notice his shuffle was steadier than the last time she'd seen him.

In the living room, a corner fireplace boasted a brisk blaze. Gregory gestured to a coat tree near the archway. "You're welcome to hang that over there."

Grateful, Zee shucked her dripping blazer. She started to hang it next to a fawn three-quarter length coat, then moved it to the opposite hook. No sense in getting such a nice garment all wet.

The fire drew her with warm fingers. Barely suppressing sigh, she sank onto the soft leather couch.

Icy pellets clinked against the window, now shrouded with heavy emerald drapes. Cautiously, Gregory lowered himself onto the edge of his chair. He indicated the pot on the table. "May I offer you tea? Rose hips. Good for the immune system."

The pair of cups told Zee he'd made this for Shaneah. Courtesy said she should decline. Her quaking body overruled polite pretense. "Please."

Gregory poured, a slight quiver in his skeletal hand.

"You look well." Zee couldn't keep the surprise from her voice.

"I have my moments." He passed her the cup. "Shawny will be

pleased." His pale brow furrowed. "If it lasts until she gets home."

Zee winced. She knew from her dad the ebb and flow of terminal illness, ever lengthening stretches of absence, ever shrinking moments of presence. Angry as she was, she still hoped Shaneah would arrive in time to enjoy this one.

She studied Gregory as he poured his own tea. Perhaps she could take advantage of his alertness. Her throat tightened. If she caused him too much stress, she might deprive Shaneah of precious moments in his company.

Hesitation to dampen his good spirits rose with the fragrant steam, but she pushed aside her anxiety. She'd damn near risked her life to get here. She could make the most of the opportunity, while staying watchful for any flagging of his energy.

He smiled an uncertain invitation. "What brings you to our humble home on such a dismal night?" Something trembled beneath his words.

Zee's stomach sank. He was hoping she brought good news. "I wanted to talk to Shaneah." Knowing that she'd already fractured his serenity, Zee tried to convey non-threatening curiosity. "I think she's having me followed."

Gregory's hand jerked, sloshing his tea. He set down the cup and wiped his fingers on a napkin. "I'm sorry."

The skin on Zee's neck prickled. "It's not your fault. I just wonder what she wants with me."

He shook his head. Some of the light faded from his face. "Truly, I don't know."

"She never said anything to you?" Zee cringed. She hadn't meant to badger him.

"Not specifically." He folded the napkin with careful precision. "But consider . . . Marjorie is big news, then a reporter shows up at Believers Anon. It's not too hard to draw a line between those two things." He sucked in a breath, as if so many words had tried his stamina.

Zee swallowed embarrassment with her tea. She wanted to deny her scheme, but the lie wouldn't slip past her lips. "So, she hopes to learn something new from me."

He pinned her with his eyes.

Zee blinked to cover her shock. His sclerae were so darkly yellowed they obliterated his irises.

"You have a reputation for digging." There was that hope again.

Zee squelched a grimace. Her investigative efforts thus far had yielded paltry results. "Did she send me texts?"

He inhaled another raspy breath. "She didn't say anything to me."

"But she might not have told you." Zee recalled Shaneah's bitterness toward Lenore. "Even the most loving couples don't always see eye to eye."

"She is headstrong." He cleared his throat. The harsh scrape came from deep inside his chest. It sounded like a shovel dragging over broken rocks. "But she is entitled to her own way."

"As are we all." Unless her own way leads to death for someone else.

A grimace contorted his features. He drew in air as if to speak, then exhaled. He licked his dry lips. Inhaled again. Swallowed.

Zee winced. He was holding himself together by the barest of strings. She should leave, let him recover himself.

"What did they say?" His voice quaked. As if he dreaded her answer. "The texts?"

She had to answer. She pulled out her phone and read the first one.

He shook his head weakly. "She'd never quote the Bible."

That denial came too quickly. "That's just the first part," Zee said. "What about the pernicious mirror?"

A tremor shook his body. Zee's insides quivered in response, like a tuning fork homing in. "That means something to you."

"Guru Ram." He dropped his head, dragged fingers through his mass of white hair, and absently let his open palm come to rest over his heart. Sweat sheened his pasty face. "We cannot directly see ourselves. We need mirrors, but . . ." He coughed and sagged against the chair.

She started to rise, but he continued. "We have to work . . . to make them clear." His jaundiced eyes bored into her, as if imploring her to understand.

Zee decided to ponder philosophy later. He looked as though he might collapse, but her tuning fork clamored. She spoke gently. "It's too much of a coincidence. I'd lay odds the text refers to both BA and *The Mirror of the Soul*."

An indecipherable emotion flitted across his skeletal face. His wheezing grew more pronounced. Zee rose from the couch. Staying here, continuing to question him, wasn't fair to Shaneah. Maybe if he had a chance to rest—

"What if it does?"

His croak slashed through her thoughts. She forced herself to respond. "Then it's a message that's led me to one conclusion: Marjorie is not the murderer."

A shudder wracked his body. "You know that?" he cried.

"I feel certain—"

"Then she'll be released." The statement came out on an explosion of breath.

Zee softened her voice. "I was going to say I feel certain she is not, but the police don't care what I think. It might be different if they had another suspect, but they don't."

"How about his sister?" Shaneah swept into the room in a swirl of chilly air and stared at Zee through frosted lashes. "That is, if I may take part in this conversation."

"My perfect sister." Acrimony soured Gregory's voice.

Their accusations stung Zee's newfound soft spot for Lenore. Without thinking, she sprang to her defense. "Lenore may be many things you don't like, but she's not a killer."

"She murdered . . . in the only way . . . that counts." Gregory grimaced, as if each word tore out a piece of his own soul. "Killed her spirit." He slumped.

Murder of the spirit. The thought was an ice pick to the heart.

Fontina's face leapt into Zee's awareness. Zee's hatred would know no bounds if someone murdered her dearest friend's beautiful spirit.

Shaneah crossed to him. Sinking to her knees, she took his hand and crooned. "It's all right, Greejie. Don't upset yourself." She began to sing, soft syllables that washed the strain from his face. After some moments, his ragged breathing lapsed into a gentle susurration.

Rising, Shaneah turned toward Zee. Her voice was a vicious whisper. "What are you doing here?"

Zee's questions seemed trivial in the face of their tragedy. "I didn't come here to talk about Lenore. I came to discuss you and Alex." As she spoke, her anger returned. "What were you doing at Marlene's today? Getting a report? Or giving one?"

A bitter laugh erupted from Shaneah's lips. "Not everything is about you."

"I didn't say—"

Shaneah charged across the room. "I don't have anything to say to you." She tossed Zee's blazer at her and backed her through the archway. "Go."

Under Shaneah's furious glare, Zee shrugged into her coat. The tall woman blocked the living room entry, legs wide, arms crossed, apparently intent on ensuring Zee left. Aggravation spurring her, Zee resolved to wrest something useful from Shaneah. "You implied Lenore could be the killer," she challenged the angry face. "But for my money, Alex Welling is a better bet."

Shaneah snorted.

Zee's tuning fork vibrated.

Shaneah advanced on Zee, forcing her down the hallway toward the front door.

"What do you know?" Zee pleaded. "Tell me. I'm trying to help Marjorie."

"You're just after a story." Shaneah's voice was sharp, but her accusation lacked conviction.

"I'm after justice." Zee debated what to tell Shaneah, wondered how much she already knew. She needed to say something quickly. Shaneah's armor was reassembling. "There were other people at Bette's apartment that day, and from what I've learned, they all had motives."

Shaneah pushed strands of silver-streaked strawberry-blonde away from her face. "You're actually on to something?" Hope flickered in her eyes. They were green in the dim hallway, a gentle hue, like tender shoots of grass.

Zee pressed. "Help me to help Marjorie."

Shaneah's gaze flicked toward the living room. "It's nothing concrete, but you ought to look at Sara Jane Pantonet."

"Why? What did Alex—"

Wet hacking commandeered Shaneah's attention. She thrust her arm toward the door. "Show yourself out." Her voice hardened. "And please, do not return."

She turned on her heel and disappeared down the hall.

"What's wrong?" Rico covered her hand with his.

She couldn't—didn't want to—lie. "I got another text message."

He frowned. "A threat?"

"No."

Warning edged his tone. "Then let's talk about it later."

But once the gate had opened, Zee couldn't shut it. "Can I at least tell you about Shaneah? I'm starting to think she's a good suspect."

Rico withdrew his hand, set his scotch on the bar harder than necessary. The man sitting next to him glanced his way, then returned his attention to his companion.

"Not now. We'll sort it out later."

Zee toyed with her glass, tracing rings on the polished bar. "It makes my brain hurt, trying to figure it all out."

"I know it's hard, but that's why you should let it go." Rico clasped her shoulders, turning her toward him.

Zee conjured a smile. "It's confusing, you know. Everyone seems to be lying." She laughed. "Gee, suspects lying, who'd have thought?"

"Exactly." His warm palms cradled her face, awakening a shiver in her spine. "So, think about this instead, because it's the truth."

In the thrall of his velvet lips, the clamor in her head dissolved. Breathless, she rested against his shoulder, letting their shared heat torch the last tendrils of anxiety. When she opened her eyes, she caught the man on the next stool twisting away. Laughter lifted like a butterfly from her throat. "Truth is good."

The maître d' appeared to shepherd them to their table. Captured in the warm circle of Rico's arm, Zee couldn't help but notice the admiring glances from other diners as he escorted her through the restaurant. The radiance in his eyes bathed her in light. Surely, her heart emanated visible waves of happiness.

They ordered wine from an impressive list and filets from the simple menu. "Signs of a good steakhouse," Rico said.

Was he glowing or was it a trick of the glittering facets in the chandelier overhead? A tiny tremor jittered in her chest.

CHAPTER 40

Z EE DROVE WHITE-KNUCKLED THROUGH NIGHTTIME CURTAINS of falling ice. She'd gained useful information from Gregory, but guilt over his decline knotted in her gut.

Crystals plinked against the windshield. The wipers swept them into slushy piles that slowly massed in the corners. *Po*'s tires skidded, then grabbed, then skidded again, a nerve-wracking danse macabre through the glistering streets. Zee tightened her grip on the wheel. She didn't regret her decision to brave the elements, but she would be glad when she reached the safety of home.

Her mind turned to Gregory's comment about mirrors. It seemed impossible that it didn't connect—

A dark shape darted into the street.

Zee tapped the brakes.

Po skated.

Zee swallowed sickening helplessness.

Just as the tires found purchase, a dog scrambled past her headlights.

She resisted the urge to curse the poor creature, wishing instead that it would find some warm, dry place to spend the night.

At last, she eased *Po* into the Legate I parking lot. She shut off the engine and sank against the driver's seat, letting the taut cords in her body unwind. If there was a goddess who kept people safe on treacherous roads, Zee owed her.

The ice shower lessened. Zee grabbed the chance to escape into the building.

When she opened her apartment door, a feline guided missile barreled into her ankles. "I'm glad to see you too, Candy-pants." She bent to stroke the cat's head.

Snarling, Candy swiped at the bag of Big Ol' Burger fried potatoes.

Zee jerked the bag beyond the assault and stepped toward the kitchen. She toed the cat dish, a nearly empty ceramic island surrounded by a scattered archipelago of greenish-brownish lumps. "This has to stop, Candy-pants."

Tail snapping like a whip, Candy stalked back and forth. Without warning, she hurled herself at the carryout bag.

"Hey! What do you think you're doing?"

The bag broke open. Candy leapt after an escaped potato.

"Oh no, you don't." Zee bent to snatch the wedge, then jerked her hand away from a razor-sharp talon. "What's wrong with you?"

Candy hissed through bared teeth. The aggression shocked Zee to stillness. This wasn't her usually lovable cat. Rigid posture. Lowered brows. Slitted yellow eyes. A front paw quivering aloft, ready to strike again. This wasn't even her cat's usual *unhappy* behavior.

The realization slapped her in the face. "Oh, Candy-pants, you must be starving." Guilt swamped Zee. Her obsession with Bette's death had blinded her to Candy's desperation. She should know better from her own experience. Grimacing, she recalled the disagreeable sensation of deep hunger before she went to Big Ol' Burger. Candy had probably been feeling that way for days.

Leaving Candy to munch on her prize, Zee retrieved the bag, tossed it into the garbage, and poured a fresh dish of Seafood Supreme. "I'm sorry, Candy. Aunt Fontina and I will figure out a new approach, one that's kinder to you."

Fontina! Zee hadn't shared her big news with her dearest friend! She glanced at the wall clock. 9:45, not too late to call. She tapped the icon.

"Hi, Zee-zee. What's up?"

"Lots of stuff, but first things first." Zee inhaled a trembling breath at the magnitude of what she was about to share. "Last night, Rico said he loved me and—I said it back."

Fontina's gasp sailed down the line. "Oh, Zee-zee, I'm so happy for you! Tell me all about it."

As Zee unfolded the scene, every cell in her body sang, even the injured ones. There was no pain she could not endure with Rico's heart joined to hers. She pulled a bottle of chardonnay from the refrigerator, poured a glass, and settled on the couch.

"I lift my cup of tea to your joy," Fontina said.

Zee tapped her wine glass against the phone. The chardonnay tasted like ambrosia, suffused with their shared happiness.

"You said 'first things,'" Fontina said. "Is there more good news?"

The shadow of Zee's conversation with the Earthkins encroached on her buoyant spirits. Reluctantly, she shifted focus. "Nothing at the Rico level, but do you have a minute?"

"As many as you need."

Zee's heart warmed. Fontina never failed. "I saw Marjorie's parents tonight, and I feel unsettled. Like something important happened, which I noticed at the time but then forgot." As she recounted her visit, the sense that she'd missed something strengthened.

"Hmm."

Zee wished she could see Fontina's face. "I know that *hmm.* What are you thinking?"

"I caught a spike, but let me ask you first. As you were telling this to me, was there any part of the story that triggered a stronger reaction than others?"

The image of Gregory leapt to Zee's mind. "Yes. Gregory's big turnaround. He was getting weaker and weaker, coughing, sweating. Then all of a sudden, he had a burst of energy. It was such a huge change that it startled me. I wondered where all that energy came from."

"Do you know?"

Zee inhaled a sad breath. "He thought I said the police didn't think Marjorie was the killer. His relief was massive, like a tidal wave. So strong it filled the room. I remember now that I thought it was over the top, but then he said that Marjorie would be released. I hated to be the one to destroy his optimism."

Candy jumped into Zee's lap, smelling of fried potato and satisfaction. She stretched, then commenced licking her paws and cleaning her whiskers. Zee stroked the soft, warm fur. It was good to be friends with her cat again.

"Does that scene help you see what you're looking for?" Fontina asked.

Zee rubbed Candy's ear. "I feel like it's still vague, shadowy. You have any ideas?"

"I sense that it's there but off to the side." Fontina's brisk tone pulled Zee from incipient disappointment. "Let's keep going. What happened next?"

"Gregory was crushed. Bitter. Then Shaneah came in, and they both attacked Lenore." Zee's tuning fork rang in her ears. She bolted upright, startling Candy from her lap. "They know something they haven't shared with the police. Something they don't want to share."

"Do you have any idea what it is?"

Ice pellets plinked like barbs against the balcony doors. "No, but I can taste that I'm right." Zee slumped on the couch. "This is maddening." She reached for her wine.

"I sense that you are getting nearer." Fontina's voice was pensive. "What happened next?"

"She threw me out." Zee gritted her teeth at the memory. "Guess I can't blame her. Gregory was feeling okay when I got there, and I wore him out, so that he was practically comatose by the time Shaneah got home. And I didn't even get to talk to her about what she and Alex were doing at Marlene's. That's why I was at her house in the first place."

A thread of eagerness laced Fontina's words. "Didn't you talk to her at all?"

"I did, come to think of it, as she was escorting me down the hallway. I pleaded with her to let me help Marjorie, and she softened a little. And then told me to look into Sara Jane." Zee squinted, as if sharpening her focus. "That's the second time Sara Jane came up today. Victor told me this morning that she'd been fired."

"Twice. You might want to pay attention."

"You know, my day seems to have come full circle." Zee's pulse skipped. Another circle, like the one on Bette's casket and the one on AnniElla's door. "It started and ended with Sara Jane Pantenot."

Zee could picture Fontina stroking Uncle Ramiz's coin. "Are the Earthkins connected in some way to Sara Jane?"

"Not that I know of—" Zee drew in a quick breath. "Maybe that's what Shaneah and Alex were talking about at the bar. When I tried to ask Shaneah, she cut me off." Zee sucked a quick breath. "I have to talk to Sara Jane, before she leaves town."

"I think that's a good idea."

Silence fell. Zee stared into the golden liquid in her glass, as if she might see confirmation that she'd found the elusive detail. Candy crept back into her lap.

"Do you feel complete on this?" Fontina said softly.

A restless filament wriggled in Zee's chest. She swallowed wine to soothe it. "There might be more, but I know what to do next, and maybe that's all I needed."

"It's progress." Fontina's voice caught. "I'm glad I could help you find clarity."

Zee's heart swelled. Fontina was always so generous with her time, her wisdom, her insight. It was easy to forget that she had problems, too. "Are you any closer to deciding what to do about your teacher?"

"The fog is clearing, but I can't see the way yet."

Weight sagged in Zee's heart. "Can I help you?"

"Actually, you have. While we were talking, I felt a telltale lift regarding my own question."

"Do you want to talk about it?"

A soft, appreciative chuckle caressed Zee's ear. "Not now. I need to get to bed."

Zee wished she could reach through space to hug her friend. "Sleep well. We can talk tomorrow."

The ice storm raged outside. In her cozy living room, gratitude welled in Zee. So much love filled her life. Her beautiful sister of the heart, her contented purring cat, her handsome beloved Rico. Enfolded in these, the truest source of strength, no threat could touch her, no obstacle could defy her success.

CHAPTER 41

ZEE WOKE TO LOUD BANGING. HEART thumping, she jumped from her bed. Pain stabbed from her knee to her hip. "Just a minute," she yelled, grabbing at the mattress to keep from falling.

The doorbell assaulted her ears, followed by more hammering. Each thud drove a spike behind her eyes. "Hold on, dammit!"

Tying her robe, she limped as quickly as possible toward the front door. The bombardment continued. At this rate, it would wake the whole building. Fear spiked below her heart. Maybe there was reason to wake up everyone. A fire?

She sucked a breath, remembering the threat on her door. A fierce tremor rattled her body. She grabbed for the knob, but pulled up to peer through the peephole.

Alarm ratcheted her heartrate for a different reason. She knew that face.

Her fingers fumbled at the deadbolt. The bell blasted again. Finally, she jerked the door open, wobbling from the effort.

A furious hulk filled the doorway. Tan-brick sport coat, unbuttoned, drooping over a wrinkled beige shirt and loosely knotted brown tie. Craggy face, hard bronze eyes, sandy hair that looked like it had yet to see a comb this morning.

Lieutenant Bernstow.

Zee fought not to shrink from his glare. He must know she had information she hadn't shared with him.

Or, there was something else in the grim set of his mouth.

Zee's knees weakened. Rico. Something had hap—.

"Mind if I come in?" Bernstow was halfway through the door when he snarled the question.

She backed a step, nearly tripping over Candy. "Why are you here?" She hated the tremor in her voice.

"To give you a friendly warning."

Relief spread like cool water in her chest. In its wake, a wave of anger.

"Excuse me." She turned toward the kitchen, biting her tongue. If this visit was friendly, she'd hate to see what he considered hostile.

Bernstow dogged her steps. Propping his elbows on the counter, he cracked his knuckles the way fighters do, one hand dominating the other "What were you doing at Mrs. Branson's apartment yesterday?"

So, he did know what she'd been up to. She gulped water to buy time. "I'm working on a story."

"Yeah, what about?"

Zee said the first thing that came to mind. "About why people leave their religion." Her stomach lurched. She hoped Bernstow hadn't read Sunday's paper.

He leaned toward her. His breath smelled like old coffee. "That why you visited Ms. Franklin in jail? Why you went to her parents' house last week?"

Zee backed inadvertently from the onslaught. "Yes." Mostly true.

"Because," he pushed his grizzled face closer, "I have the strongest impression that you are involving yourself in my investigation."

Guilty heat consumed her cheeks, even as she protested. "I have every right to follow a story. It's not my fault if it happens to overlap with—"

The storm that broke across Bernstow's enraged face was enough to kill the rest of her objection. He jabbed a finger toward her. "I'd better not see you. I'd better not find out you're talking to witnesses. I'd better not notice any form of your presence anywhere near this case. Got it?"

Without waiting for an answer, he turned on his heel and strode toward the door. He yanked it open and stomped out, not bothering to close it.

Drawing a shaky breath, Zee finger-combed the bed-mussed curls from her forehead. "Ever think I might have been able to help you?" she muttered to the sound of his retreating footsteps.

She crossed her living room and bolted the door. If he was going to treat her like a criminal, he didn't deserve her help.

But Bette did. And Marjorie too. Zee sagged against the wall. If she was more forthcoming with the police, her own story might benefit as well.

A tall order. Bernstow had just slapped up a brick wall.

As she trudged toward the kitchen, her gaze fell on *The Mirror of the Soul*, still resting on the countertop. Sara Jane had called the book by its original name, which closely paraphrased most of the first text. She'd dismissed the slip as unimportant. That unfinished business itched like a burr in Zee's scalp.

Remembering last night's conversation with Fontina, Zee let her irritation hold sway. Bernstow could wait until she had another talk with Sara Jane. And that could wait until Zee had breakfast.

Her hand froze midway to the coffeemaker. Sara Jane had been fired. She'd been absent from the memorial yesterday. She might at this moment be on her way out of town.

Zee grabbed her phone.

"Ambassador Hotel," a polished voice said.

"I'd like to know if one of your guests has checked out. I was supposed to meet her, but I overslept." Zee poured sincerity into her spontaneous lie. "I just want her to know that I'm on my way."

She held her breath.

"What is the guest's name?"

Quietly, Zee exhaled, and gave Sara Jane's name.

"Oh."

A world of disdain in that syllable. Zee had the distinct impression that hotel rules be damned, the desk clerk would tell her anything she asked.

"She's here." By his tone, she couldn't leave soon enough. "Checkout is at eleven."

Zee glanced toward the wall clock. Just after nine. Later than she'd like, thanks to Daylight Saving Time. "Great. If she asks, tell her I'm on my way." She disconnected before the clerk could ask her name.

While she dressed, Zee wolfed down half a bagel, chasing it with gulps of coffee. Hoping she wouldn't regret her actions or the time it took to take them, she headed out the door.

In typical Midwestern fashion, the sun had warmed last night's icy coating, festooning trees and shrubbery with diamond droplets. Flanked by the jeweled landscape, Zee wound *Po* through the streets. Her chest tightened. Sara Jane would not be a cooperative interview, but one way or another Zee would learn what she needed.

She stopped for an elderly man, making his way through a crosswalk. The biggest unanswered question in this whole case was who AnniElla saw at about 3:15 on the day Bette died. For now, Sara Jane was Zee's best suspect.

A shiver crawled up her back. She could be confronting a killer. As she parked *Po*, she vowed to find a public place for their talk. Shoulders set, she hurried toward the glass lobby doors.

Half a dozen steps across the tiled floor brought her to the registration desk, a chest-high, ersatz wood counter bracketed by artificial ficus trees. "I called earlier," she addressed the clerk. "I'm looking for Sara Jane Pantonet."

He looked down his thin nose. "She *should* be checking out."

"Would you ring her room?"

"With pleasure, Miss . . . ?"

Zee supplied her name. "Tell her I have exciting news to share," she added, hoping to forestall any reluctance on Sara Jane's part.

The man's boney fingers punched in numbers. Seconds ticked past. The clerk's face registered impatience. "She's not answering." He made it sound as though Sara Jane chose to ignore him.

Dread crawled in Zee's stomach. If this were a movie—

She stifled a scowl. Maybe Sara Jane was in the shower.

The hum of a well-oiled mechanism pulled Zee's attention to the elevators. Sara Jane stepped through the parting doors, purse slung over one black-jacketed shoulder. She dragged a massive roller bag behind her, atop which balanced a computer case.

"Ah, Miss Pantonet, you have a visitor." The clerk drenched his voice in faux friendliness.

"I don't have time—oh, you." Sara Jane smoothed the frown from her face as she dropped the room key on the counter. "Email the receipt," she snapped. "And call me a cab."

"Heading home?" Zee came abreast.

"New York." Sara Jane tossed her hair. "Look, if the editor didn't work out, there's nothing more I can do."

"It's not about the editor," Zee said. "I have a couple of questions. Won't take a minute."

Sara Jane flattened her lips. "I don't have a minute. I need to get to the airport." She whirled toward the counter. "Is my taxi here?"

"I'll drive you." Zee hoped she wouldn't regret the offer.

Sara Jane eyed her as though she were a venomous snake.

"The taxi will be twenty minutes, Miss," the clerk replied. The edges of his mouth twitched upward.

"We can talk on the way." Zee crossed to the glass doors and waited while they slid open.

With a huff, Sara Jane lifted her head and strode through. "I hope you have a reasonably comfortable car."

Zee bit back a snarl. It could be a long half hour to passenger drop-off.

Wordlessly, Sara Jane thrust her luggage into the Mini's trunk, yanked open the door, and took possession of the passenger seat. Her hands gripped the computer case across her chest like a shield.

Gone was the friendly persona at Valerian's Corner. Zee turned *Po* toward the freeway, musing how to pierce the defenses of the woman sitting next to her. Empathy seemed the best choice. "A shame how things turned out, I mean, with the movie."

Sara Jane's gold-framed eyeglasses remained locked in place. She faced forward as if by force of will she could shut out Zee's words.

Zee merged into traffic, tried again. "Any chance of resurrecting it?"

Silence.

The Mini wobbled in the wind stream as Zee changed lanes to pass a semi. Her passenger's grip tightened on the computer case. Suppressing a grin, Zee accelerated and whipped back in front of the big truck. Maybe a bit of aggression would shake loose a response. "I love this car," she said. "Do you drive?"

Honey-blonde hair turned a fraction of an inch in Zee's direction. The voice dripped ice. "Are these your questions?"

Small talk over. Time for the direct approach. "Did you send me a text about seeing through a mirror darkly?"

Sara Jane's head snapped toward Zee. "What? No. Why on earth would I do something like that?"

"Because you're the only one who's mentioned that title for Bette's book. That can't be a coincidence. What I can't figure out is why you would text me."

"There is no *why* because I didn't."

Zee pulled into the passing lane to skirt a motorcycle, took pleasure in Sara Jane's clenched jaw. *Keep her off balance.* "Who else knew about the other title?"

"How would I know? The publisher, the editor, anyone who did research." She cut her narrowed eyes at Zee. "You."

Zee shrank from the acid in Sara Jane's tone. Or maybe from yet another dead end. Unless Sara Jane was lying, which she might be doing if she was the murderer.

Zee dropped behind a limo in the exit lane. The luxurious car gave her an idea. "Guess you're going to miss the perks of being a best-selling author's publicist, but at least you're spared the public knowledge that she sacked you."

Sara Jane exploded. "Not true." Spittle flew from her pink lips. "Vicious rumors."

Zee kept her voice cool. "I heard from a trusted source who never makes mistakes."

The tall frame slumped, then jerked upright. "I told her Marjorie was doing drugs again. She was more dangerous than ever. I brought Bette a gun, but she wouldn't take it. Said she'd sooner fire me than a gun." Her defiance melted. She swiped a hand across her cheek. "She didn't mean it."

Zee pounced on the opening. "A harsh thing to say to someone so devoted to her."

Sara Jane reddened. "She inspired devotion. She made you believe in yourself. You wouldn't understand."

Zee recalled her own experience with Bette, wrapped in that aura of confident invincibility. For a moment, Bette's loss slammed her heart like a brick. She murmured almost to herself, "So, to lose that, to be rejected—"

"She didn't reject me," Sara Jane snapped. "She was stolen from me."

Zee forced herself to the present. A puzzle piece hovered close to its place. She had to keep Sara Jane talking. "You found her." She hid her urgency behind empathy. "That had to be difficult."

Sara Jane released her hold on the computer case and fished a tissue from her pocket. "You can't imagine. I'll never forget the sight. All that blood."

Guard down. Zee's thoughts leapt ahead. Sara Jane had discovered the body hours after Bette died. Now was the best opportunity to find out if she had been at the apartment earlier, as well.

"What a terrible sight," Zee said. "Maybe in time, it will be eased by better memories?" She brightened her voice, as if she hoped to help Sara Jane replace the image right then and there. "When's the last time you saw Bette, you know, before . . .?"

"Just earlier that Sunday. That's what makes it so unreal."

A frisson of triumph zinged through Zee. She slowed, diverting into the airport lane for departures. "I guess that was before everybody else showed up."

Sara Jane blotted her cheeks. "I was there when Marjorie barged in and started wheedling. I left, but that's how I knew, when I came back later, that she killed Bette."

How convenient for Sara Jane. Yet her grief seemed real. She could be telling the truth.

Sara Jane's voice rose. "If only Bette had taken the gun. I'm never going to forgive myself."

Anger was supplanting the publicist's grief. Quickly, Zee pressed. "You sound so sure, but did you know Bette died from a second blow to the head?"

Sara Jane made a choking sound. "Why are you telling me all this? Why are you interrogating me?"

Zee pulled to the curb marked for passenger drop-off. "Because I'm wondering who else might have wanted to kill Bette." She shut off the engine and faced Sara Jane. "Did you?"

Sara Jane's face purpled. "That's a hell of a question to ask me." She yanked open the door and stomped toward the back of the car.

Zee met her, opened the trunk. "So answer it."

Sara Jane wrestled free her suitcase, hoisted her computer bag atop it, and started to turn away.

"Answer it." Zee moved to block her.

Sara Jane halted. Her face had smoothed into a cold mask. Skewering Zee with ice-chip eyes, she lowered her voice and spoke slowly, each word deliberate. "I'll tell you something: that book—and that movie if it ever happens—neither was worth murder."

With that, she turned on her heel and dragged her suitcase toward the airport entrance.

Zee watched her go. Her last suspect. Her last hope. She had nowhere else to go, nothing else to pursue.

Yet, she felt strangely light. Maybe because the struggle was over.

Or maybe because, somehow, she had all the pieces she needed.

CHAPTER 42

Zee pulled the Mini back into airport traffic. Hope wriggled beneath her breastbone. She might have all she needed to solve Bette's murder now. The thought lifted her spirits, but by the time she stopped at the first traffic light, doubt dragged them down. She had already tried every which way to make sense of the pieces.

Fontina would prescribe tea. Not the right remedy this time. Although the soporific effect often worked to collect Zee's thoughts, in her bones, Zee craved action.

She headed for the freeway. A drive, fast and manic, that would clear her head.

Speeding up the entrance ramp, she strove to banish her failure with Sara Jane. She had been so sure AnniElla's timeline was the key, that it would prove Sara Jane the murderer. It was suspicious that she had not answered when asked point blank if she killed Bette, but any chance to wring a confession from her was gone. And somehow Zee believed her when she said the book wasn't worth killing over.

She merged into the stream of vehicles, struck for a moment at how blithely everyone, including her, traveled at breakneck speeds, with nothing to keep them safe except painted lines. What an act of faith to take such a deadly risk.

Of course, spurred by their own interests and faults, drivers weren't always trustworthy. Like her suspects. Kevin, Lenore, Alex, all could have lied about when they were at Bette's. The problem was that it defied belief that their timelines would so precisely dovetail.

She huffed. This wasn't getting her anywhere. She couldn't think her way through this.

Lowering the Mini's windows, she tried to lose herself in the glorious day. Brilliant sun honeyed the rooftops of Valerian. She admired the gilded, fairytale-like spire of St. Stephens, the glass-crowned atrium of the public library, the rooftop garden of the Hotel St. Dierdre.

But Helios's magic failed, perhaps because of the dark clouds smearing the horizon. Instead of freeing her mind, the cityscape tangled it in memories of McNeary's murder.

Her gaze fell on the stone angels, standing vigil atop the *Mess-Trib* building. She sighed. Solving this puzzle was like trying to fly with granite wings.

What're you lugging all those rocks around for? Shelby's voice sounded in her ear.

"I'd drop them if I could," Zee snapped aloud.

It was a cruel paradox, she'd complained once to Fontina, the more a person tried to let go of something, the harder it was. "Newton's Third Law," her friend had responded. "For every action, there is an equal and opposite reaction. What you push away, pushes back."

An iron band tightened around Zee's chest. Cars, trucks, tractor-trailers crowded her, stealing the oxygen from inside the Mini. The chaos of machinery smothered her: grinding engines, blaring horns, hissing tires. The urge to escape hurled itself against her ribcage.

She needed to fly into the wind, to let it blast from her brain the snarl of lies, the sinkhole of selfish decisions, all the detritus of her disappointing investigation. Whipping the steering wheel north, she fled into the outskirts of Valerian, into what always renewed her, nature.

Ignoring caution, she opened the throttle on an empty country road. Windows down, sliding through the gears, the Mini soared along the blacktop ribbon. Cool wind lashed her face. A yellow sign flashed past, a warning to watch for deer. She ignored it, demanding release, and lost herself in the gale cleansing her ears. Her eyes teared, but she pushed, feeding gas until the tires barely skimmed the road.

Finally spent, she pulled to the edge of the road. Breathing hard, she checked the car's gauges and, satisfied that her reckless handling had done no harm, shut off the engine.

She'd come to rest atop the crest of a low rise. Naked trees bounded a dark, newly plowed field. Cattle grazed on the flank of a hill. She leaned her head back, eyes closed, and filled her lungs with deliciously clean air.

The soundscape trickled into her ears: the muted clicking of branches not yet softened with foliage, a dog barking in the distance, the breath of moist wind across *Po*'s hood, but most of all, silence.

She opened the door and stepped out to walk along the side of the deserted stretch and let the tranquility soak into her pores.

Up ahead, a sunlit boulder offered the perfect place to sit and be still in this space of stillness. Finding toeholds on the serrated sides, she climbed into its smooth lap. She let her eyes go unfocused. Breathed.

At the edges of her mind, thoughts tried to spring up like tiny blades of grass. She paid no attention to them. They wilted.

She had no interest in thinking, just resting in the protective arms of nature. The next best embrace to Rico's.

Warmth spread through her chest. If he were here now, he'd stroke her hair and tell her she'd done her best. He'd say, "You can't win all the time." He'd understand that she'd wanted to re-create her success with McNeary.

She could see it now with amazing clarity. Frightening as it had been at times, solving the researcher's murder had been exhilarating. She'd been energized, convinced she had contributed to justice in an important way. She'd felt—respected.

In a flash, she saw the deeper meaning. Respect had always been important to her, and betrayal was the ultimate disrespect. So, she fought against it, for herself and for others. Defying Bernstow, confronting bureaucratic idiocy and callousness, it was worthy work.

Some part of her psyche, long lost and exiled, returned home.

A tear leaked down her cheek. The weight of decades fell from her heart.

Shelby patted her back. *'Bout time, sister.* Zee could almost see her twenty-something self smile.

A cacophony of caws cracked her eyes open in time to see a flock of crows boil up from the trees and into the sky. She sighed. Even here, murder followed her.

Different curtains, same view.

She bolted upright.

Marjorie, Lenore, Shaneah, Alex, Kevin, Sara Jane: different circumstances, same conclusion. In their eyes, in varying ways, Bette was the problem. And in every case, her death was the solution.

Zee conducted her investigation based on that belief and her own relationship with Bette. She too had been drawn in by her personality.

What if she was looking at this wrong?

She gripped the rough edges of the boulder, grounding herself while her thoughts sparked and crackled like a Jacob's Ladder.

Forget different curtains, same view. She was looking at Bette's murder through an entirely different window.

Her mind strained toward a conclusion, but she forced herself to leash her eagerness. Wind pestered the trees while she tested the insight, twisted it, turned it sideways. With every pass, the sickness in her heart grew. The theory remained convincing. Not perfect, but every nerve cell in her body told her it was true.

If she shifted the motive away from the desire to eliminate Bette, she got an entirely different story.

Icy fingers grabbed her spine. Wrested her from her perch.

Apologizing to her abused knee, she hurried to the car. Her mind chattered resistance. She refused to listen.

Bernstow wasn't going to do what had to be done. Not in time. If she was right, she had to act now.

CHAPTER 43

ZEE DROVE DOWN THE FREEWAY LIKE a woman possessed. Despite the gaps in her theory, she knew she was right. Yet when she angled the Mini into a spot on the narrow, crooked street, her confidence faltered. She'd been sure before in this case, and wrong.

She glanced at the sky, half-eaten now by swollen clouds, and clenched her fists. For Marjorie's sake, she had to try to force a confession. She pulled up the recording app on her phone and slipped the cell into her pocket, ready to press the button.

At the heavy wooden door, she squared her shoulders and knocked.

No response.

Her eyes searched the beveled fanlight for a reflected sign of movement.

None came.

She rapped again. Harder.

A wail, terrible enough to cleave the world, erupted from inside.

Zee grabbed the handle. Fear coppery in her mouth, she shoved against the door. It creaked open. "Shaneah? Gregory? Are you okay?"

High keening rode on a windy draft from the depths of the house. Zee's hesitancy vanished. On flying feet, she ran down the narrow hallway and into the large living room.

She skidded to a stop.

Gregory lay motionless in his recliner by the window. Shaneah knelt next to him, her cheek resting on his knees. His skeletal hand lay atop her tangle of red-blonde tresses. She whimpered.

Zee's heart sank. She was too late.

A chorus of aches from her mad dash moaned through her body. She chewed her lip, unable to decide what to do. To speak seemed an unconscionable intrusion, but she couldn't just leave, not with Marjorie's fate at stake. She cleared her throat as softly as she could. "Shaneah, I'm sorry." She tensed for a volatile response.

It was Gregory who answered, voice rough and rusted. "I knew . . . you would come."

Shaneah lifted her head. "Oh, Greejie, I thought I'd never hear—" She choked a sob.

Relief swept through Zee. "Should I call an ambulance?"

"No." Gregory twitched his mass of white hair, negating.

Shaneah straightened. Her voice was weary. "Why are you here?" She flicked a hand toward Zee. "Go away."

Gregory coughed, a gravelly wet sound, and touched his wife's arm. "I need . . . her."

"She should go, Greejie. It's wrong for her to be here."

"No, love." His gossamer words disintegrated almost before they left his mouth. "It is finished."

Zee shivered. Another Biblical reference. If she had recognized his familiarity with scripture, she might have seen the truth more quickly.

"I must . . . tell . . . witness." The syllables were strung like frayed prayer flags along the thread of his voice. His fevered eyes found Zee's.

Shaneah bracketed her husband's face in her hands, blocking his gaze. "Greejie, tell *me*."

Zee held her breath.

Gregory inhaled, triggering a spasm of coughs. His face purpled. Air wheezed in his throat.

"Here." Shaneah guided a glass of water to his lips.

After three attempts, he managed a small swallow. Then a whispered croak, "I'm sorry." His eyes found Zee. "Help me . . . tell."

Zee winced. The words she meant to say would pierce Shaneah's already wounded heart. Zee pictured Marjorie in the jail. To save her, to bring justice, Zee would do this. "Gregory, I know Marjorie is not responsible for Bette's death. I—"

Shaneah erupted from her place on the floor. "This is *not* the time. Leave us alone, so he can pass in peace."

Behind Shaneah's back, Gregory reached for her. His scrawny arm fell short. He sagged into the chair, eyes closed, unmoving.

Zee stood her ground. "Listen to me, please. You have to, if you want to save Marjorie." She swallowed the knot in her throat. "Gregory killed Bette."

Fury swamped Shaneah's face. "You're insane. Greejie isn't a *killer*. And he wouldn't put Marjorie in danger. He loves her."

"He does." Zee hoped her agreement would blunt the force of Shaneah's anger. "But he let his love for her get distorted by your guru."

"No!" Shaneah crossed the room in two strides. "Guru Ram is nothing but love." She snatched at Zee's arm.

Zee sidestepped. Wrong choice, criticizing their teacher. "I'm sorry. Let's just say that, for whatever reason, Gregory got confused."

Shaneah lowered her voice to a snarl. "First you accuse Greejie, now Guru Ram." She flung her arm toward the door. "Get out."

Zee shot a glance toward Gregory. No sign of life on his flaccid face, but his bony chest still rose and fell. She hoped he could hear her. All he would need to do was confirm she was right.

"Leave us alone." Tears glistened on Shaneah's cheeks. She turned back toward her husband.

Zee had to buy time until he regained consciousness. Backpedaling to a safer distance, she held her hands up, placating. "He wanted me here. You heard him."

Shaneah smoothed Gregory's hair from his forehead. "He's delirious. Why would he want you?"

"Because I know what happened the day Bette died. He's too weak to explain now, but he knows I will." It would have to be the most persuasive story she'd ever told.

Shaneah faced her, lips compressed to a flat line. "For his sake, I'll listen."

With a prayer to whatever goddess opened people's minds, Zee unspooled her theory, stating it as fact. "I finally understand the real reason for Bette's death."

"It was that book," spat Shaneah. "It destroyed Marjorie. She lost her mind."

Not quite the response she expected, but Zee pounced on the chance to build rapport. "The book might have been the tipping point." She softened her voice, sympathetic. "But you know Marjorie was broken long before that happened."

Shaneah dropped her gaze.

"All those years apart, all the suffering you endured." Zee willed her to make the connection.

Shaneah's head snapped up. She dashed a tear from her cheek. "What does that have to do with . . . what happened?"

"It was his motive." Although Zee's other suspects had suffered significant losses—a lover, a reputation, a life's work—none had a grievance as deeply wounding as Gregory's. "Twenty years of festering loss. And then, when he finally finds his daughter, she's ruined. You heard his indictment. Lenore murdered Marjorie's spirit."

Every muscle in Shaneah's face tightened, a barricade of flesh and determination. "Then why not kill Lenore?"

This was the trickiest part. Zee had to project confidence. Sara Jane had forced Zee to consider that the book had not been the cause of Bette's death. That triggered a cascade of deductions that led Zee inexorably to her conclusion. Hiding her own anger at her friend's death, she clothed her next statement with empathy. "Because Gregory is *not* a cold-blooded killer. He's a father who was tried beyond what he could bear." She inhaled. "The truth is: Bette was never supposed to die."

"What?" Confusion knit Shaneah's brows.

"That was never Gregory's intention. But something happened that pushed him past his breaking point."

Behind her, Gregory moaned. Shaneah whirled.

Zee craned to see. Agitation warped his gaunt features, but his eyes remained closed.

"Greejie." Folding a towel, Shaneah patted his glistening skin. His face smoothed.

For a moment, Zee was in her dad's hospice room, seeking to comfort him. How she would hate anyone who intruded into their last precious moments together. But the stakes were bigger here. She could not give up.

Resting her hand on her husband's shoulder, Shaneah glared at Zee. She spoke with barely restrained impatience. "Are you finished?"

She met Shaneah's eyes. "Gregory went to Bette's that day. He saw Marjorie flee the building. He went up to Bette's apartment, but he heard Lenore and Bette arguing. He waited, and when Lenore left—the last person to see Bette alive—he went in."

Shaneah's tone was incredulous. "So, then he killed her? Is that what you're saying?" She advanced toward Zee.

Zee wanted to help her to make the leap, but above all, they had to stay in that room until Gregory woke. Behind Shaneah, his body twitched on the recliner. "I'm saying something happened, and the pain of it was beyond bearing."

Shaneah shook her head.

In desperation, Zee spun a scenario. "Bette might have mocked him, or insulted him, or threatened Marjorie." Zee's gut twisted to paint her friend in this light, but she pressed on. "He struck her. It was a terrible thing. But then he saw a way to balance the scales of justice, to avenge all the pain Lenore had caused—stealing his daughter, hiding her, turning her against you."

Shaneah's eyes narrowed to slits.

Zee shot a glance toward Gregory, willing him to fight his way back into consciousness. She raised her voice until she was almost shouting. "The BA literature was already there, spreadsheets, testimonies, evidence of Lenore's presence. He could testify to seeing her." A rumble of thunder punctuated her argument. "Lenore had a powerful motive. Her life work would be ruined. She would be blamed. No doubt."

For the first time, Shaneah's gaze wavered. She stammered, "That's a monstrous accusation."

Zee zeroed in on her vulnerability, hating that she had to widen the wound, steeling her heart. "In Gregory's mind, perhaps weakened by his suffering and disease, this punishment was no more than Lenore deserved. It was karma."

Shaneah's face hardened. She bared her teeth. "How dare you twist my husband's words."

Zee tensed, her mind and muscles slipping into self-defense mode. "He didn't plan it, but after it happ—"

Shaneah leapt at her, clawed hands slashing. "Who do you think you are?"

Evade. Escape. Zee darted around the rocking chair.

Shaneah pursued her. "You don't know him. You don't know us." Her voice rose. "You don't know anything."

Wriggling between the furniture, Zee banged her knee against Gregory's recliner. Pain ribboned through her leg. She grunted, stumbled.

Screaming like a wild thing, Shaneah grabbed Zee's hair.

"Ow! Damn!" Zee tore free. A hot iron seared across her scalp.

Shaneah's eyes flamed.

Zee caught her foot on the rug, stumbled. Shaneah's fingers scrabbled for purchase on Zee's shoulder. She batted them off. "Stop this! You're being irrational!"

"I'm irrational?" Shaneah screeched. "You come in here—" She swung a wild fist.

Zee ducked and spun away, then dizzy, latched onto the stem of the floor lamp next to the couch. Shaneah yanked on it, trying to wrest it from Zee's grasp. Zee tugged back, an idea forming. When Shaneah jerked it again, Zee released her hold. Shaneah staggered backward.

Seizing her chance, Zee scrambled for the archway. Shaneah had lost all control. A horrifying thought penetrated the throbbing in Zee's skull. Shaneah's anger was too great to be solely in defense of Gregory. She was furious enough—to kill.

Zee would think about that later.

An object hurtled past her ear. Instinctively, Zee swerved. Her knee buckled. Shaneah's roar filled her ears. Zee threw a glance over her shoulder. Shaneah's hand, like the flat of a spade, flew toward Zee's face.

Zee grabbed a coat on the tree, thrust it in front of her like a shield. It blunted the force of Shaneah's strike. Miraculously, it propelled Zee toward the archway. She started to drop the fawn fabric clutched in her fist when another puzzle piece fell into place. AnniElla had described a man in a light brown coat. Still retreating, Zee shouted. "There's a witness who saw him."

Shaneah's attack faltered. "Not possible." Her mask reassembled. "It wasn't him."

Either a delusional denial or the truth, Zee didn't care. It didn't matter that she was no longer sure who killed Bette. One of these two had done it. Surely, she had enough on her phone to get Bern—

She stopped halfway out of the room. She'd forgotten to turn on the recorder.

As Shaneah closed the distance, a feeble moan brushed Zee's ear, so faint she couldn't be sure she heard it. Hope flickered in her chest. If Gregory was waking, she still had a chance to get to the truth.

CHAPTER 44

Zee BACKED INTO THE NARROW HALLWAY, straining to hear another sound from Gregory. A cough, a grunt, anything to let her know he was waking up.

Shaneah barreled toward her, an avenging Fury. "You meddling bitch!"

Zee hurled the fawn overcoat to slow her down, drew a breath when Shaneah tangled in it.

Now was her chance to escape, but if Gregory was regaining consciousness, she couldn't leave. A low noise at the edge of hearing feathered against her ears. It was a weak groan. Her heart jumped. Or the faint rumble of thunder.

Unsure what she'd heard, her feet refused to head for the door. Not when she might finally get the truth. She ducked to avoid the slash of Shaneah's clawlike hand, threw a glance toward the front door, then braced her heel against the baseboard and slipped in the opposite direction.

Bad move.

She found herself trapped in the Earthkins' tiny kitchen, knee throbbing from the sudden move, hip and shoulder burning from evading attacks. Shaneah blocked the door. The only other way out was through a window over the counter at Zee's back. Impossible in her abused body, even if she wasn't trying to fend off a predator.

Shaneah advanced, a huntress now, eyes like shards of jade. "What did you think you were doing, coming here today?" Every word laced with menace.

"Saving Marjorie," Zee snarled back. "She didn't kill Bette."

Stopping just out of reach, Shaneah lowered her voice to a growl. "Neither. Did. Greejie."

A wave of fiery self-recrimination swept through Zee. Early on, she had pegged Shaneah as having the passion and guts to commit murder. She should have listened to her intuition.

And yet, Gregory had wanted her here, said he needed her to be a witness. To *his* confession, she had expected. But his plan must have been to force Shaneah to admit what she'd done.

He had to wake.

Zee strained to hear a sound, any sound, from the living room. The refrigerator motor drilled in her ear, burying any chance.

Lightning flashed, illuminating manic triumph in Shaneah's face.

Despite the cold sweat on her brow, Zee refused to cringe. She mustered fury into her eyes, as if she could transform her glare into a weapon. "If your husband didn't kill Bette, then you did."

Shaneah reached beyond Zee's shoulder, hissing, "I *would* kill to save Marjorie from destroying herself."

Zee's joints turned to water, then froze when Shaneah straightened. Inches away from the tender skin at the hollow of Zee's throat, gleamed the point of a large, sharp knife.

Zee hardly dared to breathe. "There no need for this. I'll leave."

Shaneah's eyes glinted like shattered glass. "Oh, *now* you'll leave." Thunder rattled the window. Her gaze lost its focus.

Grabbing her chance, Zee darted sideways.

Shaneah's arm shot out and clamped her shoulder. Pain shot through the joint. Shoving Zee against the porcelain, she grazed her throat with the blade. "I won't let you write those unspeakable things."

Anger overrode caution. "So, are you going to kill me too?"

Shaneah jerked as though Zee slapped her. A derisive laugh escaped her lips. "You *are* insane. I didn't kill anyone."

Zee's knees buckled, even as her brain warned the denial might be a lie. She gripped slick palms against the sink.

Shaneah snorted. "You've been wrong about everything from the moment you barged in here." She leaned close. Gregory's sickly musk clung to her hair. The knife drifted lower, near Zee's breastbone. "You're not going to write one word."

Zee's heartrate ratcheted. She was alone. No help was on the way. No one even knew she was here. Her ears scoured the air, desperate for a sign from Gregory.

Nothing but the thudding of her heart and the building storm.

He might already be gone. She had to get out.

Get her to lower her guard.

Lifting her hands in surrender, she met Shaneah's eyes. "All right. You win. I only wanted justice for Marjorie, to free her from the burden of guilt that she must be carrying."

The hard lines in Shaneah's face eased a fraction.

Zee's hopes lifted a corresponding increment.

"You're wrong about us, you know." The knife didn't move.

Zee tried again. "I'm sorry I—"

"Shawny . . ." A strangled call came from the living room.

Shaneah's head snapped toward the sound.

Lunging sideways, Zee swung her arm with all the force she could muster. Her forearm slammed into Shaneah's wrist.

The knife clattered to the floor.

Ignoring the fallen weapon, Shaneah dashed toward the living room. "Greejie, I'm here."

Zee clutched her spasming shoulder and limped as fast as she could for the door. Once she was safe, she'd call Rico. They'd figure out what to tell the police.

As she speed-hobbled past the living room archway, a ragged cry burst from Gregory. "No!" He coughed, a garbled expulsion of breath. "Stop."

Zee broke her stride. Cautiously, she leaned back to look.

He slumped in his recliner, one hand floundering like a broken birdwing. "Come."

Shaneah shifted to create a barrier. "Can't you see he's dying? Leave us alone."

"Need." Gregory touched his wife's arm. "Her."

Sobbing silently, Shaneah sank to her heels by his side. "I don't understand."

One part of Zee's mind clamored for escape. Another part turned her feet toward the living room. This was her chance. She had to take it.

Her fingers found her phone. She pressed Record.

With a watchful eye on Shaneah, she pulled a footstool close to the recliner and sat at the level of Gregory's eyes. Sweat sheened his face. His chin trembled. The cords on his thin neck stood out.

She could see him gathering the remaining shreds of his life force. Hardly daring to breathe, she waited.

Air rasped in his throat. "I went there." Eyes closed, he expelled the words. "Pleaded for . . . help to reconnect."

He clung to life by the thread of his voice, a spider hurling itself across an abyss, hoping to anchor its silver skein for a few more priceless moments.

"Shh . . ." Shaneah patted his arm.

His hand crawled atop hers, stilling it. "Truth."

Shaneah swallowed hard but stayed silent.

"Gregory," said Zee, "what happened with Bette?"

He stared over Zee's shoulder. A tear swelled at the corner of his eye. "She laughed. Said she would crush what was left of . . . Marjorie." Anguish twisted his face. "Something inside . . . broke." His lids shuttered. "I hit her . . . with that big dish."

Shaneah lowered her head to his sunken chest. Her hair spread like a breastplate of flame. "Oh, Greejie."

"Never thought Marjorie . . ." His hoarse inhalation sawed the air. ". . . would confess."

The tightness in Zee's chest loosened. Shaneah had to believe now.

And the Angry Knight of the Tarot made sense. Gregory was that someone seeking forgiveness, trying to make reparation for the crime of murder. The torment in his soul had ravaged his body. He clung to life now, only to be sure the truth was known.

"You sent me the texts," Zee said. "To get me to look at Lenore and BA."

"Tried to help. Shawny . . . never . . . quote Bible."

Shaneah crumpled into a heap beside the chair. She raised tearful eyes. "Why did you let Marjorie go to jail?"

Zee hadn't had the heart to ask that question.

He reached toward Shaneah, his hand traveling a pathetic few inches before it dropped. "She . . . had to atone. Karma. But then . . . all went wrong."

A knife stuck itself in Zee's ribs. She wanted to scream, to rage at his convoluted reasoning, to curse his mangled spirituality. In a flash, she recalled his overwhelming relief when he thought she said Marjorie didn't do it. He'd cried out that she would be released.

The urge to vomit rose bitter in Zee's throat. He didn't mean from jail, but from some supposed karmic debt.

"Why didn't you tell me?" Shaneah's voice cracked.

His panting filled the room. "Keep you clean."

"We are one." Shaneah's whisper fell like cool water. She slipped her arm around Gregory and cradled his head in the hollow of her shoulder. "I would have helped you do the right thing."

Zee's doubtful fingers touched the tiny nick in her neck. But that Shaneah—the fierce defender who could not imagine what her husband had just confessed to—no longer existed. Her offer of help was a cry from across a chasm into a past that could not be changed.

A tear tracked along Gregory's desiccated cheek. Shaneah wiped it away. "Sh-h. All is well."

He withered in her arms. Zee wished she could leave them to find what peace they could. Instead, she had to rob them of time yet again. To eliminate one remaining possibility. Although it seemed unlikely, he might have confessed to protect Shaneah, so she could be there for Marjorie.

Zee steeled herself. "Gregory," she said softly, hating herself for drawing his attention from Shaneah. "The police might not believe you."

Shuddering, he roused himself. From dark caves, his burning eyes found Zee. "Dresser. Bottom. Blood on shirt. Weapon." The final word expended, he sagged against Shaneah. His bony fingers caressed a strand of her hair.

Zee could scarcely believe her good fortune. Physical evidence. Far more than she'd hoped for. She stifled the urge to run from the room to check.

"Greejie." Shaneah's voice cracked. "You can't die in jail."

His eyes shifted toward the cold fireplace. His face lifted. A trembling sigh escaped from deep inside his emaciated frame. "I won't."

Shaneah twisted to look in the direction of his gaze.

"Guru Ram," he whispered with effort.

Zee turned to look. The shock knocked her backward.

Light shimmered in the corner of the room. A soft white, pulsing with threads of gold. A figure stood in its midst, face shining like a Madonna.

Under the vision's steady gaze, Zee's breath seized. Her heart expanded, filling her chest until she feared the hammering organ would burst free of her body.

The illumination grew in brightness, until Zee raised her hand like a shield. Light and shadow rippled across the face. Her features shifted. Familiar hair, eyes, smile. Not the guru. An electric jolt shot through Zee's heart. "Mom?"

A message poured from the vision:

Hear with the ears of your heart.

The image fragmented.

No. No, stay. Zee cried silently, stretching toward the fading light. It withered until nothing remained but a dark corner.

As the ordinary room came back into focus, her heart sank. She couldn't have seen her mother. It had to be another hallucination, like Oya. A salty tear dripped onto her lip. How she wished she could have the faith of Gregory and Shaneah.

A muffled sob drew her back to the recliner. Shaneah stroked Gregory's pale face, serene in repose. She folded his hands across his heart and slowly bent her head to kiss his bloodless lips.

CHAPTER 45

Detective Bernstow slammed his fist on the table in the interview room. Sgt. Jones's laptop jumped and clattered against the metal surface. Zee cringed. Beside her, Shaneah remained stoic.

Bernstow leaned across the table. The storm that had pummeled Zee on her way to the station was nothing compared to the thunder on his face. "Are you ever going to stay out of my business?"

Zee bristled. It wasn't her fault that Bernstow had fixated on the wrong person. He should be glad the case hadn't gotten near to trial. She stifled a retort.

The scowl on his face dissipated. "At least you got her to come here right away."

Not exactly. Shaneah had wanted to remain with Gregory, to chant and pray. Zee acquiesced, grateful to have time to absorb her own experience. Afterward, they had called a doctor to make the formal pronouncement. An agony, that moment when those irrevocable words tore Shaneah's world asunder.

Finally, they had headed to the police station, where Shaneah handed the duty officer a plastic bag containing the blood-stained shirt and glass candy dish, which, after numerous questions, had landed them here with an annoyed Lieutenant Bernstow, who'd been called from his dinner into a raging tempest.

Zee would not correct him on the order of events.

Bernstow paced the room. "We'll test the shirt. If it bears out," he swiveled toward Shaneah, "it's up to the D.A. I'd guess he'll reduce the charges against your daughter, might drop them altogether." He leaned his battered hands on the table. "I suggest you get her professional help."

Shaneah's voice was raw. "If she will let me."

"It's her choice." Bernstow's tone softened. "But I'll try to exert some influence."

Zee hid a smile. The guy had a heart after all. She squashed the snarky reproach while she entertained a more hopeful idea. She touched Shaneah's shoulder. "Maybe you and Lenore could work together."

Shaneah stiffened, but she did not pull away.

Zee pressed. "Twenty years is long enough for your family to suffer this way, don't you think?"

The matted red hair dipped a fraction.

It was enough for now.

"All right, I got roast beef to get back to." Zee detected a hint of sentimentality beneath Bernstow's gruff voice. He flung a hand in Jones' direction. "Print their statements before this turns into a sappy movie."

Another hour later, Zee left the police station in a decided funk. She should have been satisfied. She'd solved the case, saved Marjorie, even gotten Lieutenant Bernstow to credit her success.

The Mini's door squeaked as she yanked it open. Maybe it was the aftermath, the ugly picture of the "spiritually awakened" Earthkins. Zee flipped on the wipers to clear the stubbornly dripping sky from her windshield.

The Earthkins were not her problem. She'd done what she could, helping Shaneah take a step toward healing some of her family's wounds.

"So why am I not celebrating?" Zee asked *Po* as she floored the accelerator and then realized she was in a 35-mile-per-hour zone.

She backed off on her speed and caught a red light. A temple bell chimed from her phone. She could not bring herself to answer it.

Her spirits sank further.

Bette de la Cornne had died tragically, but her friend's image had been tarnished. Maybe Bette could have avoided her fate if she'd been more charitable toward Marjorie or Lenore.

The traffic light bloomed, a scarlet chrysanthemum on her misting windshield. Bette's decisions diffusing outward, staining the territory of others' lives. The wiper blades swiped it away.

If only it were that easy to let go.

The BA meeting flashed before her eyes. Maybe Lenore was right to encourage people to express their rage. Gregory had repressed his until it broke him.

Zee shook her head. That organization was as addictive and manipulative as the religious indoctrination it purported to cure. Maybe that was why Bette's book was so popular. It warned—

A horn honked behind her. Zee squealed *Po*'s tires. She could run in circles forever, speculating, but the truth was, she wanted to forget the whole tragic mess.

Except for what she had felt in the Earthkins' apartment.

Her phone rang.

An icy premonition swept through her. Hands shaking, she pulled to the curb and grabbed her cell.

"Ms. Morani, it's Darla at Leehammer Pavilion."

CHAPTER 46

Z_EE HURTLED _Po_ THROUGH THE RAIN-SLICK streets, heedless of the fishtailing tires. She skidded into the nearest parking space in Leehammer Pavilion's lot. Urgency turned her feet into wings, threatening to tear her heart from her chest. She burst into her dad's room, her pulse rippling through her body.

He lay still.

Gentle light haloed his bed, limning his froth of white hair. She tiptoed near, breathing slowly to calm the roar of blood in her head. Her eyes sought desperately for a sign of life.

There. A flutter in his throat. She stifled a cry of relief. Sank against the bedrails.

There was so little of him now, resting amid the blankets, hands at his sides. She stroked his long, thin fingers. Someone had trimmed his nails, shaved him too, even washed his hair. Gratitude swelled in her heart for those simple caring tasks, valuing the dignity of a person who could never acknowledge it.

The walls of his room grayed into the darkness outside, as if to emphasize the thinness of the boundary he approached. Softened by the light, the room became a nebulous cell, swimming through time. Encased, enclosed, alone just the two of them. Their voyage propelled by his shallow, spare breaths, until the nuclei split and she was left behind.

A tiny click and a shaft of illumination told her the door opened behind her. The draft carried the scent of laundered cotton and citrus. Fontina.

Zee fell into her embrace, comforting as a warm blanket. Eyes closed, she breathed in the presence of her sister of the heart. "Thank you for coming," she whispered.

"I would be nowhere else," Fontina whispered.

A gentle hand brushed Zee's shoulder. Rico. Tears brimmed in Zee's eyes. "You're here."

He swept his arms around her, pulled her tight against his chest. "I wanted to be with you."

"The paper—"

"—be damned."

A surge of emotions welled in Zee, too many at once. Unable to speak, she simply gave herself into his shelter. The heat from his body warmed her shivering limbs. The love in his heart eased her own ache.

She rested there, until a barb of fear branched in her heart. Rico never disregarded his job, unless . . . She pulled back to see his face. "What happened? Are you leaving the paper?"

"Leaving?" He loosened his hold to meet her eyes. "What made you think that?"

"You've been distant, distracted, unhappy at work. I thought you were looking for another job."

His lips curved upward, but the ease failed to reach his shadowed gaze. "You're almost right. I'm looking *at* another job."

Zee cocked her head.

"Karl's leaving. I've been offered his position."

"That's great." Zee's smile faltered. "Isn't it?"

He ran fingers through his mist-dampened hair. "I'm not a suit-and-tie guy."

Zee grasped his hands. "It's a big step up for your career."

"If I want it." He caught her eyes. "It would affect our partnership."

A cold stone dropped into Zee's gut. She'd lose access to him behind a desk. She couldn't call him on the spur of the moment for information or to bat around an idea. He wouldn't be there to save her backside from stupid decisions. But most of all, they'd no longer share the joy of working together as peers. He'd be—oh God—her boss.

Pinned beneath his gaze, she smoothed her face, forced lightness into her voice. "We'll be partners in a different way."

Tautness drained from his shoulders. He cradled her cheeks in his palms, lowered his lips to hers. His heat dissolved the icy rock in her stomach.

"Promise me you'll think about it," she murmured into the folds of his leather jacket.

"We'll think about it together."

A soft squeak drew her attention. Zee jerked her head toward the bed. Her dad lay still beneath the blanket, eyes closed. She hurried to him, dropped her ear near his mouth, held her breath until she heard the whisper of his.

Still there. Still here.

"Would you like us to sit with you?" Fontina asked.

Zee swallowed to ease the tightness in her throat. "I'd like that very much."

Pulling three chairs near the bed, Fontina gestured for Zee to sit in the middle one. In the silence that draped itself around them, Zee's thoughts drifted back to that hallucination in the Earthkins' living room. Whether or not Zee had seen her mother, at this very moment, her dad might be crossing to her. Somehow Zee knew she would welcome him into that transcendent light-filled, love-filled space.

Fontina squeezed Zee's hand, kept her voice low. "Something has happened. Do you want to talk about it?"

Zee wasn't ready. Instead, she shared other news. "Gregory confessed."

"What?" Fontina raised her brows.

Rico turned toward Zee, leaned forward. "The spiritual guy?"

"Him." Zee told them the story. "I think he saw his guru at the end."

Fontina's hand flew to her heart. "What a blessing."

"I think so too." Zee rubbed her thumb across the opal ring—her mother's ring—on her finger. "They were sincere in their beliefs. They just went too far. In their idealism, they lost sight of their humanity." Her gaze strayed to the small figure of her dad on the bed. A strand of barbed wire around her heart pricked as it loosened.

"They are two dimensions of the same reality." Fontina played her fingers through the fringe on her shawl. "Something I've been understanding better recently."

Zee caught her eyes. "Have you decided what to do about your teacher?"

"Yes. But the decision is not actually important now. It's how I got there." Fontina stroked the old coin on her necklace. Its surface glowed in the soft light surrounding the bed. "I've lived for years, feeling immeasurable gratitude for the gifts my teacher gave me. I felt a sense of obligation to him, pained by the knowledge that I could never fully repay him. It was time for me to learn to let go of that."

"So, the answer is no," said Zee.

"The answer is yes." A smile played across Fontina's lips. "Emilio helped me think through all the factors influencing my decision. When we got to the end, we both came to the same conclusion. We will offer to lease the space for a year, while my teacher searches for a permanent home for his center."

Relief eased tension Zee hadn't realized she held. Her friend had found her equilibrium again. She felt Fontina's solidity in her own body. "Sounds like a good compromise." The next words tumbled out before Zee could stop them. "But are you sure you can keep your balance, so near to him?"

Fontina's eyes crinkled.

Chagrin warmed Zee's cheeks. "Forgive me for asking. Guess I'm afraid because recently I've been exposed to too many people going haywire over spirituality. I should know better about you."

Fontina's smile broadened. "Over and gone."

Zee met her gentle grin at their teenage code for banishing injury, real or imagined.

"Your concern is justified." Fontina tugged her shawl tighter. "I feel it too. This compromise is a way for me to confront my fear, to test my own ability to stand in my truth."

"Fear." Rico's voice was so soft Zee almost missed it. "Never a great reason to do something, or not do it."

Zee snaked a hand over to clasp his, but kept her focus on Fontina. "You're always so clear in your process," she said. "I just seem to muddle around and hope for the best."

"Or you allow yourself to be led by the spirit," said Fontina. *Hear with the ears of your heart.*

"I saw my mother." The words fell from Zee's lips. "When they saw their guru."

The reality of it cut, keen as a razor. Her mother *had* been there, with her. Zee rocked forward and back, hugging herself through waves of fire and ice. To see her, and then to lose her again. Unbearable. And then—

—beneath the agony of loss, she tasted nectar, a sweetness far beyond the tongue. It flowed like concentrated gold. It was in her body and beyond her body, in another body of hers altogether, interwoven with this one.

The gilded stream pooled in her heart until the tightness that bound her released.

From the edges of awareness, her mind lobbed protests. They disintegrated in mid-air. Perhaps she'd rationalize everything later. Perhaps not. It didn't matter.

Fontina's fingers laced into hers.

A long, low sigh came from the bed, hitching, gravelly, like the last vestiges of a barrier crumbling.

Zee jumped up, grasping for his hand. "Dad?"

His skin was cool. She raked his body with her eyes, willing them to discern the tiniest flicker of movement.

His throat was still.

She bent to listen at his mouth.

No whisper of breath brushed past.

Her head dropped to his silent chest. She clung to his lifeless hand while her world shifted on its axis.

Gone.

Gone.

Her heart beat the words like a drum.

All gone.

Everything gone.

Something tore away inside her.

Tears pricked behind her eyes. Her throat tightened, but the force unleashed would not be denied. A cry swelled upward, battering itself against her teeth. She staggered upright to let it out.

Fontina's warm arm circled Zee's waist. Rico cradled them both in his embrace. They stood next to the bed, locked, shuddering together as sobs wracked Zee's body.

For twenty-six years, she'd shed not one tear for her mother. Anger at her betrayal had dried them up before they ever formed.

And when her mother's memory faded, she'd transferred that outrage to her dad. She'd pulled away from him as much as he'd pulled away from her—she saw that now.

Foolish, arrogant, stubborn.

Hardened.

She'd detested their marriage as a sham. Never understood how much they had loved each other, how much they had loved her.

What a mess she'd made of her life.

What a prison.

And now all the walls were falling down.

Sheltered in the arms of her friends, Zee mourned the death of her father, grieved the ending of her life as a child.

And set herself free.

T ERRI MAUE HAS BEEN IN LOVE with words for as long as she can remember. Even today, she's still awed by the fact that little black marks on a sheet of paper have the power to fill her mind with images, ideas, and emotions.

Many of Terri's interests find their way into her stories. She holds a first-degree black belt in TaeKwon Do and has taught self-defense classes. She is intrigued by psychic phenomena and all forms of spirituality, believing that everyone has access to realms beyond the physical and can enter altered states of consciousness without drugs. Like her protagonist, she loves food, especially pastry. Fortunately, her husband, Eddie, is a good cook.

Terri is a member of Sisters in Crime, Mystery Writers of America, and several Las Vegas writers groups. She and Eddie are Ohio transplants who now live in Las Vegas, Nevada. Visit her on her website terrimaue.com to find out what she has in store next for Zee, Rico, and Fontina in the not-so-sleepy town of Valerian, Ohio.